Across a Jade Sea

Volume Three
Fealty's Shore

L. Shelby

Air Castle Media

Across a Jade Sea
Volume 1: Serendipity's Tide
Volume 2: Treachery's Harbor
Volume 3: Fealty's Shore

Also by this author:

Coral Palace
Cantata in Coral and Ivory
Velvet Lies: A Coral Palace Novella
Pavane in Pearl and Emerald

Lioness (forthcoming)

Ice Wolf Investigations
Eyes of Infistar
Sails of Everwind

Across a Jade Sea, vol. 3: Fealty's Shore
Text Copyright © 2012 Michelle Bottorff
Cover and Interior Art Copyright © 2013 Michelle Bottorff
Edited by Rebecca Friedman
Published by Air Castle Media   www.aircastle.org
All rights reserved
ISBN: 978-0-9921528-0-2

Chapter One

I Have a Miserable Sea Voyage

The one thing that Dachahl forgot to bring with us was a doctor. Of course, ships as small as the Volcanis didn't usually have a doctor. But it seemed he had promised not to excite me until a doctor said it was safe— or at the very least until I stopped having dizzy spells. Ten days into the voyage I still hadn't found my sea legs, and Dachahl had stopped even looking at me.

I was sure my difficulties had nothing to do with the bang on my brain-box the traitorous translator had given me. My head felt fine. But as long as I couldn't make it from my cabin door to the galley without staggering and thumping into a wall or two, there seemed to be no way to convince my husband of that. I finally decided that I was tired of meekly waiting for him to change his mind, and ignoring every order he had given me, I dressed myself in one of my Empress Katronika engineer uniforms and headed for the engine room.

The Volcanis was powered by twin four-stroke diesel motors—both less powerful than the Katronika's engines, of course, but they still looked like old friends to me. A steam ship probably would have been faster. But only if we hired on a bunch of men to shovel coal like madmen the whole time, and Dachahl doesn't trust coal heavers not to be bribable. So instead of a crew of twenty or more men, including over a dozen desperately poor unskilled workers, we had a crew of six, plus two cabin boys. Dachahl and I were the only passengers. And we weren't even passengers, really. I was listed as emergency engineer, and Dachahl as the shipowner and emergency navigator. Apparently he knows how to use a sextant and stars and a pocket watch and all that to pinpoint his location exactly. Must be something they taught him at his military academy.

Unfortunately he also had enough rye in his granary to guess that I'd end up down in the engine room eventually, and he'd given our chief engineer—a jolly roundish Xercalian named Dyophos—strict instructions. Dyophos determinedly put himself between me and the engines, and wouldn't let me anywhere near them. I had planned to be very calm and reasonable—I was on the roster as a back-up engineer, I needed to familiarize myself with the engines. I told Dyophos as much—very calmly and reasonably—but it did me no good. He didn't speak Dostrovian, and couldn't understand a word I was saying.

And when Dachahl appeared, wild-eyed and commanding, I discovered that it was very hard to remain calm. Just the sight of him seemed to put my heart into overdrive, and when he came over to me and grabbed my wrist, he was closer than he'd been in days. I was distracted by the broad shoulders, and the smell of him, and I found myself just staring into his dark, dark eyes and not even trying to reason with him. He didn't reason with me, either. He just lifted me up over his shoulder and carried me back to my cabin. I didn't struggle, but I wasn't calm.

I think I had been hoping to get a reaction out of him even more than I had been hoping to spend some time with the engines. I had been convinced that anything would be better than having him avoid me. But when he put me down on my bed he looked very angry, and I felt a sudden attack of seasickness.

"The engine room is *loud*," he said, his tilted eyes narrowed to slits and his voice growling.

"It wasn't bothering me," I assured him.

"Loud sounds are bad for you, therefore you are not to go into the engine room." And then he went over the entire list of restrictions, cowlick to heel. At least he was in the same room with me for once.

"I know you have a good reason to be cautious about this, Dachahl, and I don't want to scare you—but what's left for me to *do*?"

"You can sit on the deck."

"But what can I *do*?"

"You can read a book."

I tried not to grimace. What I wanted to read was the transcript that Ambassador Hahtung had sent of the interrogation of the traitor Foha—but it was written in Xercali, using Hadahnchi characters. Dachahl was the only person on the ship who could understand it, and all he would say about it was that Foha had named a half dozen fellow traitors, but that he was willing to bet that none of them was actually guilty. "We will have them investigated when we get to Changali," he had told me, "but we will probably discover that they are his enemies, not his friends."

I looked over at the cabin's bookshelf, which already had every book on the ship that had been written in Dostrovian on it. All three of them. "I found you listed in the Seafarers' Almanac," I told Dachahl, as cheerfully as I could manage. He winced.

"I could play cards with you," I suggested.

"No."

"I could play cards with Raourque?" I countered, and then regretted it when he agreed. Patis Raourque was our navigator and quartermaster, and the most attractive man on the ship other than my husband. At least Dachahl didn't look any happier giving me permission to spend time with him than I had been suggesting it. "I don't want to be with Raourque," I confessed. I didn't care how attractive he was, and I didn't speak his language. What I really wanted was a two-person activity that Dachahl couldn't either deny me, or shove onto someone else. And thinking of the transcript I couldn't read seemed to have helped me come up with one. "What I really should be doing is learning more Hadahnchi. You should teach me how to read it, Dachahl. You said it was easy."

His wince became more pronounced. "Batiya, I..."

"Please."

He closed his eyes and took in a deep breath. "Yes."

I was fit to be pickled. For the longest time I was sure that I couldn't have heard him right, even though of course he must have realized that me learning his language was an extremely important thing for me to be doing. But the half-amused, half-desperate look on his face eventually convinced me that I had heard him correctly. "We start this now?" he asked.

"Yes!"

He left. And he was gone for a very, very, very long time. So long that I was starting to think that I'd misunderstood, or that I'd dreamed it, or that something horrible had happened to him. But when he finally came back it was obvious that he'd just been preparing his teaching materials. He carried several sheets of paper. He pulled down the folding table, sat across from me, and placed the first sheet between us.

"These are the characters in the Hadahnchi writing system. They number one hundred."

"A hundred letters? I thought you said your writing system was easier than ours!"

"This is simple. These characters represent not just single sounds, but sound groups."

He placed a second paper on top of the first one. "You will start by learning the signs for some of the words you already know."

The second page had lines of Hadahnchi characters, and underneath them were sounds written out in southern letters. When I tried sounding some of them out, I recognized some of the phrases I knew how to say in Hadahnchi—'Thank you', 'This is nothing', and 'A pleasure to meet you'. The line at the very bottom was the numbers from one to ten.

I studied the sheet, and then compared it to the first sheet. "You have one character for every possible syllable?" I started trying to figure out how many characters would be needed to write Dostrovian that way, and almost went cross-eyed. "I think there are way more than a hundred syllables in Dostrovian."

"I don't know how many syllables Dostrovian has, but Stoi Kat has well over a thousand. Hadahnchi has more than one hundred, also. But the rest of the syllables are made up of a syllable that already exists, with the starting sound of another syllable on the end of it. These only appear at the end of the word. They are written as if the word had an extra syllable with an 'ah' sound at the end, that someone forgot to say."

"What about the words that already do have an 'ah' on the end?"

"They are written the same way. You are expected to be able to tell the difference by how they are used." He tapped the paper. "Twenty-five one-character words are on this paper for you to learn." He handed me the rest of the papers, which were blank, and a pen. "Tomorrow, I will ask you to read and write them for me, and if you can I'll teach you some more." His expression was very bland, which meant he didn't want me to know how he felt about this. "Don't try too hard. You have plenty of time." And then he got up and left.

I guess I had spent maybe ten minutes with him. I felt more dreary than a dog in a ditch, but at least I had something to do.

I wrote out each of the phrases twenty times. And then I found a blank sheet of paper, tore it up into little squares and wrote a character on one side, and how to say it and what it meant on the other. I mixed them all up and practiced until I could get every single one of them right.

It still wasn't tomorrow. And I still didn't dare sneak off to the engine room. Dachahl was probably watching my cabin door.

I trawled my room for something else to do, and while digging through my drawers discovered my marriage certificate. My marriage certificate, I remembered, had both Hadahnchi and Dostrovian writing on it. Maybe I could surprise Dachahl by learning some characters he hadn't taught me. I unfolded the paper with eager fingers, and began studying it.

It took me a long time to even identify my own name. The problem was that it started with one of the characters I knew—'pah'. If my name in Hadahnchi started with a 'pah' I wasn't going to be able to learn the character for 'bat'.

I moved on to Dachahl's name, and that was a lot less confusing. At least, it was less confusing once I realized that Chunru was actually two words. Chun Ru. Or maybe Chun-ru? Anyway, it was written as 'Chunahru' and used three characters, not two. Which was fine with me, because that gave me one character I didn't already know, and there was another new one in Dachahl and two in Pralahnru. Four characters I had sounds for, even if I didn't know what they meant as individual words. I went back to my own name then, and stared bewildered at the 'pah'. Why 'pah'? Why not something that started with a 'b' at the very least? But there weren't any 'b' sounds listed anywhere on the paper he had given me. Apparently, Hadahnchi didn't do 'b'. But I had a 'tahn' on my list, so it did do 't', and I had a 'li' too. I added my name's middle character to my list, and put a 'ti?' next to it. The last character was a 'ha'. Hadahnchi must not do 'y' either. Pahtiha. My name was Pahtiha? I said it aloud and laughed. And I laughed harder when I figured out what my family name probably sounded like. But I was now up to thirty-two characters I knew how to say.

I continued to examine the certificate, and was extremely delighted when I spotted a couple of my new characters being used as single character words in the middle of a bunch of numbers.

The section with all the numbers had to be the date I was married. I was sure of it. But when I compared the numbers of the Changali date with the numbers of the date in Dostrovian, there didn't seem to be any connection. It wasn't just the clocks that were strange, way up north, the calendars were strange too. Grumbling, because I had thought I was going to be able to awe and amaze my husband by pulling a brand new word or two that I had never even heard before out from behind my ear, I lay down on the bed and drummed my fingers against the mattress. They were words in a date. They could mean day, year, hundred or thousand, or maybe the name of a month? There had to be some way to figure it out.

After staring at the wall for a while, my gaze dropped to the Seafarers' Almanac. An extremely handy book that every sea captain was required to have on hand, and which had written out in black and white for anyone who cared to look it up the information that the heir to the Shanali Empire was formally titled 'Chunru'. Finding that out had made me feel like I was a primary-school dropout. If I had thought to borrow my Uncle Stan's copy, I would have known that Dachahl was a prince, right from the very beginning. The entry on Shanali had a lot of other information too, some of which was only of interest to merchants, some of which Dachahl had already told me, and some of which had been new and even interesting—the first six times I'd read it. There was no information about calendars in the Shanali entry. I was sure of it. But there was a section full of charts and tables at the back...

I grabbed the book and two minutes later had discovered that they didn't do months, but 'seasons'. They divided the year into six seasons of six ten-day weeks each. The extra days that appeared here and there were all official state holidays. And my one-character words weren't the words for any of them... one came between the numbers and the name of a season. Triumphant I wrote 'of' on the back of that character's slip. The other was clearly a different kind of connector... I glossed it as 'and', figuring I'd learn when to use one connector and when another later. Then I mixed up the whole pile and went through it again. But even though there were only a few new characters, I couldn't seem to remember any of them when they were mixed with the others, and I even seemed to be having trouble remembering the ones I had learned before. When Gokatos, the steward, arrived with my dinner, I was curled up in a ball sulking.

"Miss? Are you... hurting?"

"Hurting?" I uncurled and turned around, and discovered an anxious look on his long dour face as he gazed steadfastly down at his shoes. "Why would I be hurting?" Had Dachahl told the rest of the crew about his conviction that I was going to be permanently nicked in my noggin?

But from the very embarrassed way he held his string-bean body and looked anywhere other than me, as if he was afraid of seeing something he shouldn't, I figured he had a different reason for asking. "You thought maybe my husband was the sort to thump on his wife when he's angry."

"I'm sure I never did, miss... er... Highness," he replied. "It's just how he carried you back here, and we hadn't seen you since, and then I was told to bring you a dinner tray... I was thinking, you'd bumped into something."

"I haven't bumped into anything since yesterday, and I don't want a tray. I'm going to come eat with the crew." I jumped up and grabbed my uniform jacket from its hook.

"Are you sure you should do that, miss?"

"Don't worry, I'll pretend I'm a landlubber and cling to the rails all the way there."

Gokatos slipped his finger under his collar, and tugged at it. "Your husband looks…"

"Hotter than a clinker? Grumpy as a badger? Like he's been hawking coal in Hintangee?" I laughed. "He's just worried about me. If he sees I'm no clumsier today than yesterday, he'll go back to just looking glum."

I put one arm into the jacket and Gokatos coughed politely. "I'll just take this out so you can change then."

"Change?"

Poor Mister Gokatos, he couldn't seem to figure out how to tell me that an apprentice engineer's uniform was not what a lady should be wearing to dine with her foreign prince of a husband—who'd clearly tipped his wagon—and a handful of humble seamen. But I was listed as an emergency engineer, even if Dachahl wouldn't let me go near the engines—so I finished putting on my jacket and stood there smiling at Gokatos until he backed away apologetically.

The way Dachahl jumped to his feet, scowling, when I arrived in the lounge probably didn't reassure him. "No bumps at all, this time," I told him. "You can ask my escort."

His gaze moved to Gokatos, who shifted from one foot to the other. "No bumps or slips from bow to stern, sir."

I grinned at my husband. "I was a good girl. I followed all your rules." I dropped into the seat next to his, and after a moment's hesitation, he sat back down.

"How did your studying go?" he asked me.

"I am going to awe and amaze you."

He frowned.

"What's the weather report like?" I asked the room at large. This was a question that was asked so frequently by so many sailors, speaking so many languages, that they all understood it, and I understood what they said when they told me in a mixture of Xercali and Rachian that there were clear skies and calm seas all the way to the Indigo Islands.

"Why don't we go out on the foredeck and sing songs," I suggested. "Make an evening of it."

"No loud music," Dachahl said.

I put my hand on his. "I think the doctor meant brass bands and dance halls." His hand twitched, but he didn't pull it away. "Sound good?" I tried not to make it sound too much like I was begging for permission.

"Yes."

My heart thumped a little faster. "Will *you* sing me something?"

"You want *me* to sing?" His eyes were wide. "Batiya, I'm not a musician."

"I just want a chance to say, 'I find it very interesting'," I told him, picking up my fork. "Are princes not supposed to sing in Changali?"

"Not unless they're at a gathering for men, and they've drunk far too much dadung."

"Quick someone, pour him another brandy!" I ordered.

Dachahl covered his glass with his hand, but his eyes were smiling. "Batiya, you are not supposed to hear this kind of song."

"I won't know what any of the words mean, so how can it matter?" He didn't appear convinced. "Are you worried that I'll start humming the tune in the bath, and make the maids all throw their skirts about?"

"Throw their skirts?"

"I mean, scream and run around—as if there's a mouse. I suppose they wouldn't do that in Changali."

"No, I have seen this," he assured me.

"You did?"

"Yes. Once. A lady in a formal *lahnpran* did this. But it was not a mouse, it was an insect." He pondered a while. "I think the word is beetle." He held his fingers at least an inch and a half apart. "This size. With horns." He looked at me solemnly. "If such an insect crawled under your *lahnpran*, would you throw your skirts too?"

"Not if it would bring shame and dishonor to the Imperial House." I hoped. A beetle that size would be awfully hard to sit still for, if it was under my clothes. "What I want to know, is how you know exactly what kind of beetle it was, and how big it was. Did you, by any chance, find it first, and accidentally send it off in the lady's direction?"

"No." His face twitched.

"No? You're sure?"

"This was not an accident. She nearly sat on it. That would have been very unfortunate. So I rescued it, and then I handed it to her as a gift." I snickered, but Dachahl managed to stay completely serious. "To receive an gift from an imperial prince is a great honor. I do not understand why she screamed and dropped it."

I laughed, but Gokatos, the only person there besides me who understood his story, looked like he swallowed a frog. "How old were you, Highness? Six?"

"About sixteen."

"Did she come shuffling out to your academy's exercise area in her trailing hems, expecting you to scrape and bow, when you actually wanted to be sword-fighting?" I asked.

"Batiya, how do you *do* this?"

I shook my head. "It'll sound so obvious if I explain it that you'll decide it isn't worth admiring me for. But it proves I've still got my head facing forward, doesn't it?"

He did not reply, and a short time later he excused himself and walked away.

Gokatos looked over at Dachahl's mostly untouched meal, and looked even more dour and droopy than usual. "There's another plateful for the fishes."

"Don't throw it overboard yet," I told him, and got up to follow my husband. I found him at the bow of the ship looking north.

"I couldn't believe that you would turn someone's party into a slapstick routine," I explained. "You'd told me earlier that you were attending a military academy and living in uniform at that age. A formal gown is a very odd thing to wear to a military academy, particularly if there isn't some kind of party going on—unless, of course, you know you'll be able to meet a prince there and are trying to impress him. So she was chasing you. And if you had enjoyed being chased, you probably wouldn't have handed her a bug."

He didn't look at me. "I wasn't wanting to be at swords—I was supposed to go riding that day."

"And the reason you won't look at me, is because I didn't get all the details right?"

"No."

"Then it must be because you are almost, but not quite, convinced that I really am all better, and you're trying to stop up the leak before the entire dam goes downriver."

His hands tightened on the railing. "Yes."

"It won't work," I assured him. "Anywhere you try to go on this ship, I will follow you and continue to be amazing. So you might as well eat—it will give you something useful and entirely safe to be doing with yourself."

He laughed. "Batiya, I will eat."

"Good!"

"I will also sing you a song."

I think I might have looked like a fish, because he laughed again. "You're going to sing me naughty songs in Hadahnchi?" I asked, incredulous.

"No."

"Then what are you going to sing?"

"You will find out, after we finish eating."

I was so eager to get back to the galley that I forgot my resolution to always hang on to a railing and almost lost my balance, just barely catching myself before Dachahl saw. But I really wasn't dizzy. As long as I kept one hand on the railing, I had no trouble walking—I didn't even need to hang on. And then I finished eating so quickly that Dachahl laughed at me, and all the other crew stared at him in wonder.

"Would you like some more?" Gokatos asked.

"No, I'm fine. I'll just wait for the rest of you."

Dachahl smiled, and ate very, very slowly, while I kicked the legs of my chair and twiddled my thumbs. Dachahl's bites seemed to be getting smaller and smaller, and I finally jumped up and said, "I'll just wait on the foredeck for the rest of you."

And then it was my turn to lean on the bow railing and stare north.

"The sunset turns your hair mahogany, with copper threads shining in each curl." It had not taken him very long to finish, once I was no longer there to tease.

I turned, and although I couldn't think of any pretty things to say, the sight of him made my heart glow. "Are we going to sing now?"

"The crew decided that since this is your idea, you will sing the first song."

"I guess that's fair," I replied, knowing that I wouldn't get very far saying it wasn't. "Who's after me?"

"They say Raourque will spin a bottle."

"What if I get the spin?"

"Then you sing again."

"That's no fair at all!" I protested. As I expected, nobody else cared whether I thought it was fair or not.

We all sat in a circle. Dachahl was to my left, and our pilot—a Rachian named Nelois—on my right. I started by singing, 'I'll Always Roam the Waves'—skipping the verses I wasn't supposed to know. Then Dyophos, who was on the other side of Nelois, sang something in Xercali that made Dachahl scowl. I assumed it was a little bit naughty. And then Nelois got picked three times in a row. Making me suspect that Raourque, who was in charge of the bottle, was somehow picking him on purpose. He did have a wonderful voice. But he sang in Rachine—neither Dachahl nor I could understand what he was singing about.

Then it was my turn again. I sang the version of 'Pretty Polya' that was safe for mixed company. And then Dyophos was picked again. And then Nelois twice more. That made me positive that Raourque was picking him on purpose. Although, when one of our two cabin boys, Nelois's nephew Echance, finished cleaning up the galley and joined us, and I saw his reaction to his uncle's songs, I began to doubt that Nelois's voice was the only attraction.

"I think maybe we should take turns spinning the bottle," I told Dachahl.

"The last person to sing, shall also spin," he decreed, and then translated that into Xercali, which was understood by everyone but me.

Nelois laughed, and flicked the bottle with his finger. And when it stopped spinning it was pointing at me again. So I sang the ghost ballad 'Down Skartosik Hollow', because I was running out of songs that were lively and not hymns and that Dachahl wouldn't disapprove of.

My bottle spin pointed to Gokatos, who looked very uneasily at Dachahl, and then started singing one of those songs that sounded as if it was about something completely innocent—carrots and turnips, in this case—but was actually extremely naughty. Dachahl stopped him halfway through, and asked if he really didn't know any other kinds of songs.

"I'm sure I don't know Van's Knobhouse else. Except maybe some hymn tunes, but not the words."

"Besides," I added, "it isn't fair that he has to sing something proper when nobody else is."

Dachahl's eyebrows went up. "You know what Mister Nelois has been singing?"

"Not exactly. But if they were just funny songs, there would be no reason for Mister Raourque to kick Echance every time his grin got a little too big."

He turned to Nelois and questioned him in Xercali, and then he turned back to me, frowning. "Was I wrong?"

"No. This was the sort of thing you were expecting when you asked for singing?"

"I never really thought about what sorts of songs would be sung," I confessed. "I just thought singing would be an easier group activity for me to share in. They say music is supposed to cross language barriers."

"This is said?" The smile he had on was very hard to read. He reached for the bottle and turned it around to face himself. Then he began to sing in an odd breathy voice with lots and lots of nose to it. And if his voice was odd, the notes were even odder. They jumped about in the most peculiar way, first sounding too close together, and then not quite the right distance apart—as if the music was being stretched and bunched. Even stranger, there didn't seem to be any kind of beat that I could tap my toe to. I listened in astonishment until he was done, and then I drew in a deep breath. "That was very interesting."

17

"Do you still think music crosses language barriers?" he asked.

I shook my head. "I couldn't tell if the song was supposed to be happy or sad. I couldn't even tell that you were singing in Hadahnchi."

"I wasn't. That was Stoi Kat."

I made a face. "Five languages. Five. I'll never catch up." And then, because it didn't seem likely I'd ever be able to figure it out on my own, I asked, "What did it say?"

"The petals of the vlai flower float down the stream. The setting sun turns them to red and gold, and I remember fire. Warmth dwells in the lands I knew in childhood, and it sings from the hills. But the vlai flower has come through dark chasm and endless jungle, and I do not know how to find my way back to the dawn of my happiness. There, where fire burns beneath the scented shade and the winds all blow from the sea, I will return in the night, when only the shadow of warmth can be found. But even this smells sweet to my soul."

"That's beautiful," I told him. "Thank you."

He smiled. "Perhaps we should leave before the bottle points to me again."

He didn't mean that 'we' the way I wanted him to mean it, but I was going to take it any way I could get it. I jumped to my feet and told Gokatos to tell everyone to carry on without us. "You'll have more fun if I'm not here anyway." Then I grabbed my husband's arm, which was enough to keep me steady, and far more fun than holding the railing.

He stopped outside my door. "You should rest."

"I was going to. How can I awe and amaze you if I'm not well rested?"

His fingers stroked along my hand and arm. "You don't have to do anything special to amaze me."

"That's good," I told him, "because your rules make it impossible for me to attempt anything special. I'm going to have to awe and amaze you by doing something completely ordinary. That's much harder."

He stared at me for a moment, and then suddenly he pulled me into his arms. "Batiya, I love you."

"I figured that out already," I informed his chest.

He laughed and let go. "I will see you tomorrow."

"Language lesson. Right after lunch. Don't be late."

I don't think I went to sleep any faster than I had the six nights previous, but I went to sleep happier. And when I woke up in the morning, I was relieved to discover that I still knew most of the characters I had known the day before, and that learning the new ones was not a problem. So I spent the rest of the morning learning the calendar system better, and then deciphering their counting system. Doing that gave me another word to add to my collection. I was studying my marriage lines again, trying to find another word to learn, when Gokatos arrived to announce lunch.

I still have no clue what I did that made my husband stare at me suspiciously and suggest that we have our lesson on the deck. Maybe it wasn't me at all. I agreed at once, saying that we shouldn't waste the lovely day. As soon as I was done eating, I hurried off to get my slips of paper, and then I went to the foredeck to wait for Dachahl. When he finally got there I showed him my scraps and explained what they were for. "So you show them to me, and for every one I get right, you give me a reward," I told him.

"What kind of reward?" he asked warily.

"That's for you to decide. You're the teacher."

"Something small if I have to give you one for each of these."

"But I might miss some!"

"No. This I do not believe. If you thought you would miss some, you would not look so pleased with yourself."

"Then maybe it should be one reward for every ten. That way it can be something better—like singing me some more songs."

"This is a punishment for me, not a reward for you," he protested.

"An hour of your company?"

"Changali hours or southerner hours?"

"Royals are not supposed to haggle!" I told him indignantly. "A kiss on the forehead?"

"Hours," he said firmly. "Changali hours. Two of them for all the words."

"Three hours," I countered. "And there are no Changali clocks on this ship."

"Two and a half."

"Three," I insisted. "Maybe more."

"By tens, you said. That's two and a half."

"It's three." I pointed to the papers in his hand. "Try it and see."

He counted them instead, and when the count reached twenty-eight and he wasn't through the stack, his eyebrows rose, and he started over, checking to see what was written on each one.

I leaned over his arm so I could see too. "Chang. Prah. Do. Fahn." I couldn't keep up with him. "You're going too fast. How will you know if I remember what they mean?"

He kept flipping. He hesitated a bit when he got to the character for year, and then stopped completely when he reached the one for a hundred. "Tu," I recited proudly. "Hundred. Tusa—two hundred. Tusa na tahlchu na di—two hundred and thirty-four."

"I didn't teach you this!"

"Tahlprang na di lah hidahn lah tuchu na tahl na fahn lah chunfanglang. The fifty-fourth day of the late winter season of the three hundred and eighteenth year of the empire—our wedding day. *Tahl na fahn lah hudafi lah tusa na tahlnung na nung lah chunfanglang.* The eighteenth day of the late summer season of the two hundred and ninety-ninth year of the empire—my birthday. *Tahlsa ni rah lah dahpri lah tuchu na tahl na fahn lah chunfanglang.* The twenty-first day of the spring season of the three hundred and eighteenth year of the empire—today."

He looked down at the papers in his hands. "Why am I still surprised when you do this?"

"Two hours and a forehead kiss?" I suggested. "Because I awed and amazed you by doing something completely ordinary."

"I am awed and amazed," he admitted. "But the doctor told me that it might be dangerous to make your heart go faster."

"Then a forehead kiss should be perfectly safe. But no picking me up, throwing me over your shoulder, and carrying me off like a barbarian warrior," I warned him.

His eyes went wide. "When... I... you...!" I had startled him out of his sentences. "No!"

"I found it very exciting," I assured him. At least, it would have been exciting if I hadn't been so afraid that I'd made him angry with me. And it had made my heart beat faster. "But it didn't hurt, didn't make me any more wobbly than before, and I awed and amazed you afterward."

"Yes?" Now he sounded excited. "Yes!" Then he thought twice. "But why do you wobble?"

"I don't know. Maybe my sense of balance was just never that good. This ship rolls about way more than the Empress Katronika did."

"But you were very sick when you came on this ship?"

"Very."

"And you are certain there is nothing wrong with you anymore?"

That was a trick question, I was sure. "I still have a bit of a bruise. It hurts when you push on it, just like any other bruise. And it's time to take out my stitches."

"Take them out?"

"Yes. I can't do it, so you'll have to."

"Me? No! We can find a doctor at the Indigo Islands."

I thought he hadn't wanted to stop at the Indigo Islands. We weren't carrying cargo, so it had been easy enough to find room to bring fuel and supplies for the entire trip. "I don't trust islander doctors," I told him. "I'd rather you did it. Please."

"Yes." I sighed in relief. "And Batiya, when you learn all the Hadahnchi characters, I will give you a very big reward."

I blinked. "What reward?" I asked cautiously.

He grinned. "You choose."

"I'm going to learn all the rest in just one day," I declared. But I didn't. It took me two days. And then he moved into my cabin, and stopped treating me like an invalid for two glorious weeks.

After that our clear skies deserted us, the seas grew dark and choppy, and I got very, very seasick.

At first my queasiness was just a source of amusement to the crew and an embarrassment to me. But having everything I tried to eat come right back up again wasn't funny for long. Especially as the first day stretched into the second day, and I grew weaker and more and more dehydrated. Until then it hadn't really occurred to either Dachahl or me that there were no other women on board. No one he was willing to have tending me— helping me gulp down soups and jellies and then helping me change my clothes and blankets when I didn't manage to get everything in the basin when it came back up. That happened so often that he finally took the jade medallion off me and put it around his own neck, just so it would stop getting in the way.

After the third day he was so tired from looking after me that he started talking to me in Hadahnchi, and as time went by and things got worse, he started babbling, a constant stream of words, as he tried to calm and soothe me.

I don't remember much of the last few days. I think I tried to send him away—not because I wanted him to go, but because he looked so terrible that I was afraid for him. I think Gokatos came in a few times. And then it was

Raourque, and I worried that I was already dead. Or Dachahl was dead. But that wasn't it.

It was over.

We had reached the harbor at Pai Lan Chung. The Volcanis was docked, and Dachahl had asked Gokatos and Raourque to help me walk down the gangplank to dry land, because he was busy ordering people around—overriding the rules and procedures of the dock, summoning serving maids and doctors and court officials, and I never discovered what else.

I thought I felt better before I even got out of bed, but when I tried actually standing I discovered that I was wrong. I couldn't stand, and Gokatos and Raourque had to carry me ashore.

Dachahl appeared almost immediately, and directed my bearers to help me sit on a small platform on sticks. And then two local fellows picked it up, and Dachahl walked beside me while I concentrated on remaining upright. We arrived somewhere, and Gokatos and Raourque reappeared—they must have been walking behind us—and helped me up a few stairs and into a building. We went through one room and into another, and there was a mattress on the floor like the beds at the Changali Embassy. Dachahl helped me lie down, and spread a blanket over me, and I closed my eyes to please him.

I heard footsteps retreating, and in the other room the sound of Dachahl talking to Gokatos and Raourque in Xercali. But I was not alone. I opened my eyes again, and saw a Chang woman wearing a short *lahmpran* over a shirt and wide pants that came in at the ankle. "May I have a drink?" I asked her in Hadahnchi, and she started and shrieked.

Dachahl came running back. "What is it?" he asked in Hadahnchi.

"I asked for a drink," I answered in the same language.

The woman began babbling something about how she regretted and that Chunru hadn't said that the lady spoke Hadahnchi.

Dachahl ordered her to fetch something, and she jumped to her feet and ran for the door, regretting all the way. Except that there wasn't a door—I had somehow missed that on the way in—there was a curtain instead.

Dachahl came and knelt beside me, pushing me down when I tried to sit up. "Wait until she comes back," he ordered, still speaking Hadahnchi.

"She understood me!" I said proudly in Hadahnchi. I didn't think I could carry on a complicated conversation, but I wasn't doing too badly for a beginner. "Where are we?"

"At a house for travelers. You can't be taken to the palace until I am ready to present you to my father."

I actually understood all that. Although I had to figure out the 'present' part. The next thing he said I didn't understand. Something about something happening on one of the days of the Changali week. I didn't even know what day it was, so it told me nothing at all.

"What happens?"

"My father is not here. I have sent a message. He will come home, and then we will see him."

"How many days from now?"

"Two days. You will rest here until then. Do you need me to stay?"

"No. I need something to drink, and then I want to rest. You go."

He smiled at me. "I will return very soon."

He left, and the woman returned a little while later carrying a tray with far too many dishes. She asked me if I wanted something, or something else, and I had to admit to her that I didn't know those words. "Is there one good for making ill people..." I couldn't figure out how to end the sentence. "Is there one that makes me strong?"

"Yes, yes," she told me. "They are both good."

"This I cannot choose," I told her. "Would you be kind, and choose for me?"

Pouring out the tea was something she had obviously done hundreds of times. She hardly needed to look at her hands, and spent most of her time staring at me. After a great deal of looking, she asked me if I was... something.

"I am sad to have to tell you, I do not know this word."

"Are you Chunru's woman?"

I understood that question, but I had no idea how I was supposed to answer. "This you must ask Chunru," I said at last—and found myself very curious about whether or not she would. Remembering her many regrets when he had ordered her around earlier, I rather suspected she wouldn't. "Would you be kind and bring me something small to eat?" I asked her.

She bowed and left. I lay down again while I was waiting, but I looked around the room instead of closing my eyes. It seemed a very nice room, if you ignored the fact that there was a mattress lying on the floor. There were a couple low tables with tall vases filled full of even taller flower arrangements, and a little low writing desk against one wall. Behind the desk were six landscapes hung one above the other. Up and down decorating, for a room where people sat on the floor.

Opposite the desk was a long low table that looked like a useful all-around surface. It had cushions tucked underneath it. Too many cushions. Perhaps the table was usually pulled away from the wall, and the bed was kept rolled up in a cupboard, like Lady Hahtungra's bed? But there were no cupboards in this room.

When the woman came back, I tried to ask about the lack of a place to put the bed so that I would have something to say, while she set up a tray on its little legs and dished out the food onto a square plate, like the ones I had seen at the Embassy. Either she did not understand, or she was pretending not to understand.

The first thing I noticed was that there was too much food. "I am sad to say that I have been ill. I cannot eat all this." The second thing that I noticed was that there was no fork. Only a couple of sticks. From out of my hazy memory of the past week I dug the word for spoon, and asked her to bring one.

She did so. But when I began trying a few dishes that looked like they wouldn't be too difficult she said, "You do not eat like a Chang."

"This food is new to me." I only ate a few bites, and then I put down my spoon, worried that the unfamiliar tastes would disagree with my poor shuddering stomach. "I am sad that I cannot eat more. Chunru said that I must rest. Will you be kind and carry the food to that place?"

I could tell from her expression I had said something wrong, but she understood me—that was good enough. I lay down and closed my eyes, and for the first time in over a week stomach pains did not edge into my dreams.

Dachahl woke me, and I discovered that the table had been pulled from the wall and all of the cushions had been set around it. "Can you sit up?" he asked me.

I could. The few mouthfuls I had taken earlier seemed to have done me a lot of good.

"People have asked to eat with me, but I want to eat with you. Also, I promised the ship's crew a fine meal on shore. I thought we could eat all together?"

I made a face. "I'm not dressed for a formal dinner."

"I have explained that you are ill." If Chunru didn't think it mattered, then nobody else had better think it mattered.

"The woman who was here, she wanted to know if I was your woman."

He frowned. "What did you tell her?"

"I told her to ask you."

He smiled. "Clever Batiya."

"I think I am just clever enough to know that I do not need to answer any questions."

"Not even, 'Are you in good health?' Everyone will ask you that."

"Chunru has said I must rest," I informed him.

"This is not really an answer," he said, but I could tell he was pleased.

"I took lessons from you," I told him, and moved over to one of the cushions by the table.

He called something I didn't understand, and the woman I had seen before came in and rolled up my bed, and took it to another room. When she returned, Dachahl told her to bring something—his guests, I assume, for when she returned she carried nothing, but was followed by the crew of the Volcanis, and two Chang men with their hair up in a topknot like Dachahl and Lord Hahtung. Important men, I deduced. They were certainly much too grand to be eating with the crew. If they had come to this dinner, they must have been very, very eager to talk to the Chunru.

Dachahl introduced the crew very briefly, just waving in the direction of each and saying his name. He didn't introduce me at all. But, just as he predicted, when everyone had taken their seats the Chang lord who sat across from me bowed over the table and asked if I was in good health.

I answered him just as I had answered my husband, and his eyes opened wide, and his jaw went slack.

The lord sitting next to him said, "The lady knows our language?"

"This I cannot know in less than a season," I informed him, with a smile. "Please be kind, and do not speak to me. I find it difficult to answer."

They both looked over at Dachahl, who looked back with absolute calm. After a long silence, the lord across from him looked at our first mate, Thaphysis, who was seated on the other side of Chunru, and asked him if he was in good health.

Dachahl translated, and Thaphysis responded that he was in excellent health, and Dachahl translated that, and then the routine was repeated all around the table. By that time the woman had returned carrying a tray, and behind her was another younger woman with another tray, and the Chang lords were silent until the women left the room again.

"Eat slowly," Chunru commanded. And then he picked up his sticks in one hand and began picking food up by manipulating the sticks as if they were the jaws of a pair of pliers. The woman had provided forks for me and all the other southerners. I supposed that this close to the harbor the peculiarities of southerners were known. But the crew was slow to begin eating with theirs—they were too busy watching in fascination as the Chang ate with their sticks.

I didn't gawk or goggle, I just ate. And when I had all I thought I could handle, I put my fork down and waited.

Soon Dachahl noticed that I had stopped eating, and he turned to me. "Would you like to leave first?"

"If Chunru thinks this is good."

He called for the woman, and gave her instructions I couldn't figure out. They were too quick and complicated. Then he told me, "You go."

I got to my feet, and all the crew looked over at me, and Gokatos asked, "Are you leaving, Princess? Are you sure you'll be well then?"

I smiled at him. "Yes, thank you. I already feel much better. Please tell all the others that I said thank you for the safe voyage, and for helping my husband look after me."

Then I bowed a small bow to each, and a medium bow to the two lords, and a very deep bow to my husband, and turned and followed the woman through a curtain. Behind it were a set of stairs, and up at the top there was a very long room, with windows in all four walls. Here I saw chests of carved dark woods and bright-colored lacquers, and cupboards for storing blankets and rolled-up mattresses, and a great many screens. But there was only one bed laid out, right in the middle of the floor. Beside it was a small table with a lantern on it, and another slightly larger table with a bowl of water, and cloths and what looked like a cup full of sticks, and then beside that was a third table slightly larger again, with a brush and a comb and a mirror.

The woman bowed, and asked me if she should bring the *hahlu*.

"I am sad to say that I do not know this word." She sneered at me. I saw it quite clearly. "Did Chunru say to bring this thing?" I asked.

"You did not hear him?"

"Then why do you ask? Why do you not do as Chunru commands?"

It turned out that he had told her to bring me a bath. Remembering how he had Lady Hahtungra help him bathe, I decided that it would be a bad idea to turn all pimpernel, and I started taking off my clothing without waiting for her to leave. This felt rather odd. But I was too eager for the bath to be nearly as embarrassed as my mother would have wanted me to.

"You know what this is for?" she asked me.

"Naturally. In Dostrovian the word is 'bath'," I told her. "I am very glad that Chunru told you to bring this. The weather made this something I could not do on the ship, since a week. This you say, how?"

She said *hahlu* again, and I repeated it, and then said, "Please be kind and bring water."

She bowed and left, and I tried to feel sorry for her, carrying water up the stairs, but it was hard because I didn't really like her. But even if I had felt pity, it would have been wasted, because she didn't carry any water. She set up a couple screens and left, and the younger woman brought the first two pitchers, and the rest was brought up to the top of the stairs, by a man it sounded like, and then the younger woman brought it across the floor and around the screens.

"I am sad this is much work for you," I told the younger woman as she brought one of the last pitchers.

"This is nothing," she replied, but only after she had jumped and splashed water on my head and shoulders. "I regret..." and I didn't understand the rest.

"This also needs to be clean," I told her and yanked on my curls. "Will you be kind?"

She poured the next pitcher over my head, and rubbed my hair with something that smelled of spices. And she went on rubbing and rubbing, and I finally realized that she was amazed by my curls. "You are kind," I told her sternly, and she said, "I regret, I regret," and finally got around to pouring the last pitcher over me and rinsing the shampoo, or soap, or whatever it was out of my hair.

And that was when I heard footsteps and Dachahl's voice behind the screen, asking if 'she'—me, presumably —was finished.

The younger woman squealed, and dropped to her knees and pressed her face to the floor.

"I don't know that I'll be able to finish, Chunru," I answered in Dostrovian. "You seem to have terrified my back-scrubber into utter uselessness."

"I will do it myself, then," he replied in the same language, and walked around the screen. There was another squeak from my helper. My husband looked down at her, and frowned. "The hostess does not attend you?"

"Unless it's a deadly insult for her not to, I'd rather she didn't. I like this one better." I sat up a little more, so that I could look over the edge of the bath to where she knelt on the floor. "But I don't think she knows if she's supposed to be getting back to work, or crawling out of the room. Also, the only thing odder than having someone else give me a bath, is to have them do it while you're here. I'm curious–" I added, "–have you just answered the question of whether or not I'm your woman, or do you just walk in on anyone in the bath?"

"This much they knew when I ordered one bed for us two. They want to know your status."

"I wouldn't mind knowing that myself," I mumbled. When we were being chased about by assassins it had been easy to set my fears about the future of my marriage aside. But now I was here, in the very strange and uneasy situation of having a marriage that was not yet officially recognized.

"Would you like me to go away?"

"You could send her away instead," I suggested.

"Next time," he promised, and walked away.

As soon as he was gone, my helper sat up. "Much regret, much regret," she told me. I was regretting too, but not apparently for long if he had ordered only one bed, and it was nobody's business but his and mine how long it had been since we'd shared one.

Now that Chunru wasn't around to terrify anyone, I finally got my back scrubbed, and then it was two big towels for me, and a bit of anxious uncertain patting at my hair with another. I removed the towel from her hands and rubbed briskly, and she watched in utter fascination as my curls emerged from the onslaught curlier than ever, and no more obviously in disarray.

She took the towel, hung it over a screen, and then headed over to the closest clothing chest, which she opened as if it was something she did every day, and then froze as if she had no idea what to do next. I drifted over to her, and discovered that the chest was empty. She looked up at me, her expression bewildered.

We had to open every chest in the room before we found me something to wear to bed. And when I did produce a nightgown, finally, she looked at it so dubiously that I almost laughed. When Dachahl came in later, while she was brushing my hair, I told him he'd caused a terrible scandal.

"How?"

"Chunru's woman is not supposed to sleep in worn-out flannel," I explained.

"You don't usually wear anything when you sleep," he told me with a grin. "Do you want to explain that to her, or should I try?"

"We're just going to let her think it's a southerner peculiarity," I told him. "It gets very cold at night up in our southern mountains."

"You don't live in the mountains," he reminded me. "You live next to the sea."

"We get very chilly fogs."

"Fog? Fog! Yes, I remember. I have somewhere I want to take you."

"Tonight?"

"No. Later."

"That's good, because I don't want to go anywhere for a while yet."

There was a long silence from my husband, and then, "Is she ever going to stop brushing your hair?"

"Not until you tell her to do something else. That's why my bath lasted so long too."

He said something abrupt that I didn't understand, and my hair-dresser dropped the brush and bowed her face to the floor.

"That's just silly," I complained. "I don't care whether you're the emperor's son or not, she's no use to anyone if she's crouching on the floor shaking too hard to speak."

"The palace staff won't be quite so intimidated," he assured me.

"They couldn't be, could they?" I turned to the woman, who I was sure was at least ten years older than I was, and said, "Please be kind and take the bath to that room."

Dachahl waited until she had finished dumping the bath water out the window, and hauling the bath to the stairs, to tell me that I couldn't tell her to take something to 'that' room, unless I had already been talking about some other room.

"But I don't know which room it belongs in."

"So you say, 'take it to *another* room'."

"You may take yourself to another room if you want, I'm going to lie down."

"And go to sleep?"

"Probably. It seems to be the right time of day for it."

The light coming through the windows was turning everything crimson.

"Then the thing you are wearing must come off. You said so yourself."

"You take it off, if you dislike it so much."

"I don't dislike it," he told me as he started to do just that, "I just like what's underneath it more."

It was very hard to object to that, and it wasn't until much later that I remarked, "Those men at dinner. They wanted to say something to you that they didn't want me to hear."

"They wanted to ask me where I'd been."

"Coming back on a southerner ship with a southerner crew didn't tell them?"

"Not everyone is as clever as you are."

"You didn't tell them?"

"I said that my father had given me errands to run, and that I had been separated from my crew, and commented on the roughness of the seas."

I made a face. He couldn't have seen it, because it was dark—but he might have felt it, I did have my head on his chest at the time.

"Will this be very hard for you?" he asked.

"Don't be silly. I'm going to be even better at not answering questions than you are, because I can pretend not to understand anything they say—but I bet everyone already knows you speak five languages."

"But you don't like this."

"My father told me I should live my life so I never had to be afraid of telling the truth."

"I think your father is a wise man, Batiya, but–"

"He hardly ever says anything, Dachahl. I learned everything I knew about engines from watching him, not by listening to him tell me things. So I guess I can also learn that just because I'm not afraid of the truth, doesn't mean I have to tell everyone I meet everything I know, either."

His arms tightened around me.

"But they couldn't possibly have only wanted to ask you where you'd been. They had to have guessed that, wherever it was, that's where you found me, and so I would obviously already know all about it."

"Yes, you're right. That wasn't all. They were very nervous about something that my father is planning. I think they would have told me why if I had been a bit more friendly."

"You don't want to know what they were nervous about?" I asked, thinking a bit woefully about all the things we already knew were hiding behind trees waiting to jump out at us—his father's reaction to our marriage, the possibility of a scholar's revolt, and that someone at the palace had asked Tertar mercenaries to kill him, and that unless that transcription of Foha's interrogation was a lot more useful than Dachahl thought it would be, we still had no idea who was a traitor here and who wasn't.

"I would like to know, but I can't be seen being friendly with my father's political opponents, Batiya," he explained. "People talking is people talking. But as the future emperor, I'm a political power. If I seem to be positioning myself in opposition to my father, every lord in the four kingdoms will start choosing sides."

"I'm on your side," I told him, snuggling closer.

"Good," he said. "That's where I want you." But there was something other than satisfaction in the way he held on to me, and I wished I hadn't shared my observations about his guests.

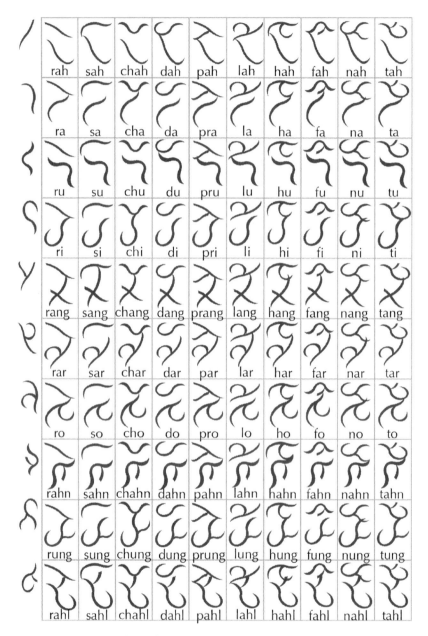

The Changali writing system

Chapter Two

I Meet the Emperor of all Changali

The next day we didn't go shopping. He asked me if I wanted to, and I admitted that I had never enjoyed it much. Mama never thought the things I liked were appropriate, and now that I was in a strange country I was just going to make even bigger mistakes, and they would matter a whole lot more. "When we get to the palace, you can just tell your staff to buy me whatever I'm supposed to be wearing."

"I could help you choose."

"Your mother died when you were small, and you don't live with your sister. I would like to be able to pretend that you have no idea what ladies are supposed to wear to bed."

"I can know what *I* want you to wear to bed," he protested.

"The same thing I wore last night?"

"Yes. But we could arrive there from a different direction."

"Then why don't you go shopping and buy me things, while I look around."

"No. I will show you places. We will see the tomb of the first emperor, and the Temple of the Singing Wind, and the spring gardens..."

I knew he was worried about what his father was going to say when he got here. I was worried too. So I told him that I wanted to see everything, and I reminded him that I should be practicing my Hadahnchi. Between playing tourist and language lessons, we almost managed to forget what was coming next. Although it would have been a little easier, for me, anyway, if we hadn't been joined by some pigtailed men with swords and rifles the moment we stepped outside.

Dachahl didn't seem to notice them, which, since he wasn't blind, meant that they were normal. He was the imperial heir—of course he had armed guards accompany him everywhere. I decided that I was glad that I was going to have so many people helping me keep him alive, and told myself that it would have been nice if they'd been with us the whole time.

We ate a lunch bought from a street vendor—one of the guards paid for it. And then we sat side by side under a tree. "You need work," I told him.

He didn't seem to understand. I wondered if I should switch into Dostrovian, for clearer expression and a little more privacy, but it seemed too much like admitting defeat. "You do much. This is something I like of you."

"Naturally."

"Today you have nothing that you are doing."

"I am showing you places!" he protested.

"I need to rest," I confessed. "You don't need to rest—you look good. I will rest. You will go do work."

"No!" He said it so fiercely that I turned to look at him. His jaw was clenched, his brows lowered. "Today I stay with you."

I decided I didn't want to argue with him.

"Come one more place with me, Batiya," he begged.

"Where?"

"I will show you."

He took me to the palace—at least, it looked like a palace to me. All towers and gold roofs. Besides, there were guards at the gate that looked exactly like the ones that had been following us around all morning. We didn't go into the palace, though. We went around it, and there were gardens and a lake, and in the center of the lake was a tiny island, and leading out to the island was a series of long bridges.

One of the guards jogged across the bridges in front of us, but once he had convinced himself that there were no assassins lurking on the island, or under the water around the island, or under the bridges, he went back to the shore.

"This is a bit like your water tower," Dachahl said. "Only we go sideways instead of up."

And instead of a metal platform, there were comfortable-looking wooden... couches? Lounges? They had no backs. They were covered with woven mats, and it looked like you were either supposed to lean sideways on the armrests, or just lie down on them. Dachahl seemed to want us to do both. He would lean on the armrest, and I would lie there in his arms and watch the dragonflies dart across the water.

"You will tire of doing nothing," I told him.

"I have something to do," he insisted.

When I woke, the sun was getting low in the sky and my husband was curled around me, almost as if he was trying to protect me from something. I wished it was mosquitoes that he was trying to shield me from—but he would never get this anxious about something so small.

"Dachahl, I have never met an emperor before."

"This can't be that much different from meeting a king."

"I don't try to touch him, never turn my back to him, and call him Your Majesty?"

The hand that had been running up and down my arm stopped moving. "I wasn't supposed to turn my back to him?"

"Did you?"

"When I heard that a messenger from the Embassy was with you, I did. Perhaps other times as well. I don't remember."

"I guess he forgave you. But the rules are different here, Dachahl." I pushed myself upright, and frowned at him. "Can't you tell me what to expect?"

"No rules exist for this." He leaned toward me, taking me by the shoulders, and stared deep into my eyes. "Batiya, I don't know what is going to happen. So I trust you to do the right thing, more than I trust myself to give you the right instructions."

Oh. That was a bit frightening. But it was also very complimentary. So I ignored the fact that he hadn't said anything hopeful like 'my father will love you' or 'everything will be fine'. Dachahl trusted me to handle this. I trusted him to protect me. "Dachahl, I would love to stay here with you forever, but I'm getting hungry again."

He helped me to my feet, and we walked back across the bridge. I wasn't entirely certain, but I thought that we now had a different set of guards. They followed us back to the house we were staying in, but they did not come inside, and Dachahl and I ate dinner alone, just the two of us. My stomach seemed to be back to normal, and he seemed to want to feed me a little bit of everything, so I let him. I asked what was in my favorites, but he wouldn't tell me. "Better not to know," he advised me.

When we went upstairs, we found a Chang man folding clothing and putting it away in the chests. Dachahl seemed to know him, but he didn't do any introductions, he just ordered a bath for tomorrow. I guessed that he must be another one of the palace staff. A valet, or something like that. He finished what he was doing with the clothing, and then bowed and left. And as soon as he was gone, my assistant from the night before appeared at the top of the stairs and bowed at us.

"Does she think I don't know how to get undressed by myself?" I asked Dachahl in Dostrovian.

"She probably wants to play with your hair again," he told me.

"There is nothing that can be done with my hair. No matter how you brush or comb it, it still goes all over everywhere."

He laughed, and told her that I didn't need her tonight. Tomorrow, however, she was to help me dress for the palace. Her eyes went very wide, and she looked a little bit dazed, and wasn't quite steady on her feet as she turned and left.

In the middle of the night I woke, feeling chilly, and discovered that Dachahl had got up, dressed himself, and was standing by the window. I went over to him, and he wrapped me in his *choliang* and held me so tight for so long that I must have fallen asleep standing up. At least, I don't remember going back to bed. All I remember is my helper's reaction when she woke me. First she snatched back the hands with which she had only moments before been shaking me, and then she reached out and very carefully and cautiously touched the *choliang* with her hand—as if making sure it was real.

It was real. And it was really silk. I looked down at the intricate pattern and for a dizzying moment was reminded of those first two days in the boat. But from the arrangement of the screens and the sound of splashing, it was clear that it wasn't Dachahl's *choliang* that I should be thinking about, but my own *lahnpran*. I got up, and clutching the *choliang* about me I started going through the chests until I found the *lahnpran* and the long linen *fiahn*. A little more digging produced the sash, pants, and slippers. But the hat appeared to be long gone. Dachahl probably threw it overboard, or contrived to leave it behind in Syrcan.

I gave everything to my helper, who hung the clothing reverently over one of the screens while I stepped into the waiting tub. This time the hair washing went quickly, and the drying even quicker, and it was getting dressed afterward that was the problem. Commoners didn't wear sashes, apparently, or if they did, they didn't wear sashes made out of ten yards of silk.

Dachahl, looking magnificent, finally set the screen between us aside and came over to see what the problem was. He took one look, and then ordered his valet to assist me. In less time than seemed possible my waist was wound about, my collar was adjusted, and all that was left was for my helper to slide my slippers on my feet and then bow her way over to the stairs.

"Are we ready to go?" I asked.

Dachahl frowned, and then fished the jade imperial seal out from under his shirt. He took it off, and then he hesitated.

"If I'm not really your wife, then I'm not supposed to be wearing it, am I?" I was pretty sure I wasn't even supposed to touch it.

"You are my wife," he said fiercely, and looped the cord over my head.

There was a thump from the direction of his valet, and when I looked over at him, I discovered that he had dropped to his knees and was pressing his forehead to the floor, shaking.

"I thought you said the palace staff wouldn't be as intimidated," I said, trying to make a joke of it.

Dachahl's jaw tensed, and he tucked the seal under my *lahnpran*. "Now we go."

We rode to the palace in an automobile. It was huge, with a separate compartment for the driver, room for at least six people to sit inside, and a platform on the back, where our guards stood, clinging to a hand rail. If the size of it didn't make it noticeable enough, it was colored bright red, and had green creatures that matched the one on the imperial seal painted on it.

I recognized the road there, from having walked it the day before. But today the distance seemed much shorter. Much too short. As we got closer and closer my stomach clenched tighter and tighter, until I was glad that we hadn't eaten breakfast, because I was sure that if I had, it would have ended up on the floor.

There was a door-guard or footman, or something like that waiting to open the automobile door. Dachahl got out first, and then he helped me, while the guards and the footmen stood by with stiff expressionless faces. I wondered if they thought I was going to trip over my hems. If they did, they were going to be disappointed. This was not my first visit to a palace. It was not the first time I had worn a formal *lahnpran*, and not something that was going to intimidate me. I swung my feet out, swirled my hems so that they fell where they should, and taking my husband's hand I gracefully rose to my feet.

"Batiya," he said, "you look beautiful."

I inclined my head. "Naturally."

For half a moment I saw him smile, and then he was serious again. "One step behind me," he said in Dostrovian.

I followed him with my chin high and my gaze on the back of his head. I tried to ignore the places we walked through, the paintings and the statues and the flower arrangements that I caught glimpses of out of the corners of my eyes. I will see it all later, I told myself. Dachahl can show it to me. He likes showing me things.

And then we stopped in front of a magnificent red and green brocade curtain. We stood there for a couple or three breaths, and then the curtain parted in front of us, and Dachahl bowed. I bowed too. And when he straightened, I straightened. Then, finally, I could see my father-in-law.

He was just as magnificent as my husband. He was kneeling on a small stand, on a large platform at the far end of a huge room, and his clothes were just like Dachahl's except that he didn't have a *tirah-fa* stuck into his sash. But he was just as proud, and he had a welcoming smile on his face. "My son," he began, and I didn't understand the rest of what he said, but he looked very, very happy to see his son returned home.

Dachahl walked forward, and I followed him. "I only–" something I didn't understand "–in Xercalis for four days," he told his father. And then he said something about something being important, "–and so I came back at once."

The emperor frowned. "You could not–" something "–the task I gave you?"

"I completed that task first."

"In four days?" The emperor was overjoyed. The emperor beamed. The emperor jumped up from his royal seat and clasped his son's shoulders. "Dachahl," he said, "I am *pleased* to have you back."

I felt that the emperor and I had a great deal in common—we both thought Dachahl was the most wonderful person in creation. Unfortunately, that didn't mean that he would also think kindly of me, and now that he was down off his dais, it didn't seem possible that he could continue to ignore me, either.

He didn't.

He asked his son with bland politeness, and a hint of subdued curiosity, who I was.

"Father, this is Batiya Dachahlra."

The emperor froze. There was a moment of very painful silence. And then the emperor said, "This, I did not hear." We'd really set the fire-alarms clanging, now.

Dachahl was tensing for a fight. I could see it in the way he held himself. I could hear it in his voice as he told me to take out the seal.

I pulled the seal from under my *lahnpran*. The emperor stared at it as it dangled from my fingers. "Chunru," he said, very slowly. "What have you done?"

"In the three-hundred and eighteenth year of the empire, on the fifty-fourth day of the late winter season–," I listened to him recite our wedding date, remembering how I had used it to work out Changali numbers, "–on the ship Majestique, which flies a Rachine flag, I took vows that made this woman my legal wife in all twenty-seven countries of the Geshik Pact. The captain, quartermaster, and ship's doctor saw this done."

I couldn't understand very much of his father's reply. But I understood that he was saying that our marriage didn't count as a marriage.

"I have made vows under heaven, Father," Dachahl replied. "These vows, I will keep."

It was easy to read emotions on a face so like my husband's. The emperor stepped forward with something like determination, only wilder and more fierce. He reached for the seal around my neck, and then there was Dachahl's shoulder blocking the way. "They were my vows and I made them freely. I cannot set them aside."

The emperor made a few incoherent noises, and then he must have calmed down a bit, for Dachahl moved back to where he was. As soon as I could see the emperor again, I took off the seal, and presented it with a bow. I felt the heat of his hand as he picked it up, but I didn't look up until the seal was gone.

The emperor was staring at me. "She doesn't even know what she's done!" he told Dachahl.

"I carried it home safely," I answered. "This Chunru asked of me, when he was hurt, and surrounded by people who wanted him dead."

"This I can kill you for," his father told me.

I looked him in the eye. "You are the emperor. You can kill me for anything you want to kill me for."

Dachahl laughed. "You won't frighten her with threats, father. She has saved my life so many times, I forget the number. Guns, knives–" he listed more words I didn't know the meanings of, "–all these things she has faced for me. She spoke to King Harluce, when his anger with Lord Hahtung made it impossible for me to arrange to see him."

"Then give her–" something, "–do not marry her," his father told him. "This can not happen."

"This already has happened."

"This did not happen if I say that this did not happen."

Dachahl was almost yelling. "In all the rest of the world, for the past two moons we have been married."

Two months? That had to be wrong. Of course, a 'moon' was a bit shorter than an actual month, but still, I couldn't believe it had been that long. But when I tried counting days, I only came a little bit short of what he had claimed, and I wasn't sure how many days I had been sick on the Volcanis.

And it soon became obvious that his father was counting days also. "You met her in the middle of the ocean?"

"Yes."

"And you married her before you reached land?"

"Yes."

His father stepped back. "Why?" He looked like he didn't know whether he should be more horrified, or more broken-hearted. "My son, why this?"

"My honor, and my liver and my heart all demanded this of me, father." And he went on to tell the story of how we met, while I wondered what one's liver had to do with anything. I could only follow bits and pieces of the story anyway. Although I followed enough to wince at the bit where he was explaining that I had sacrificed my reputation when I had refused to turn from him as he lay helpless and ill on the Majestique, and what had happened to me as a result. I hadn't married him because of my supposed ruin, and I didn't like to think that he married me for that either.

"She is a southerner," his father said simply, when he had finished. "I cannot allow her to become empress. This is not saying you cannot have her, Dachahl. But your wife must be Chang."

The two of them glared at each other, while I tried to remember why that statement bothered me. "Chunru, didn't you say that the second emperor married the daughter of the chief of some islanders?"

The emperor looked irritated. "Close ties exist between Changali and the Apiniach people."

"You told me you wanted closer ties between Changali and the southerners," Dachahl responded.

"Not this close!"

"Why not?"

"Because the Apiniach do not look like *that*!" He pointed at my nose, but he really meant my eyes and my skin and my hair.

Dachahl hissed angrily, and I put a hand on his arm. "If my hair was blonde like Katrika's, would that make things better or worse?" I asked him in Dostrovian.

He looked at me. "Batiya..."

"And she has a name that cannot be said," his father added.

"Please be kind, and call me Pahtia," I answered him.

He glared at me. "You! How can you–" I didn't understand the rest of his complaint.

"I am very sad that I must say this, but I learn Hadahnchi for less than one season. I do not know those words."

He turned to Dachahl. "This you will say to her."

"I will not," he answered. "This isn't true. She did not know who I was, father. When she married me, I was nobody and I had nothing." The emperor made a few incoherent sounds, and then Dachahl continued, "And, if you force me to marry another woman, the rest of the world will not be able to–" something "–the empress you have chosen."

"Better to have harmony at home and conflict in the market," his father answered.

"The Cholipardo people will not accept an empress that is my father's choice and not mine."

"The Cholipardo people are *hardoluno*," the emperor sneered.

"I am of Cholipardo."

"You are *hardoluno*."

"Yes."

I wanted to know what *hardoluno* meant, but it didn't seem the right moment to ask. But Cholipardo. Didn't I know that word? It was one of the Four Kingdoms, but wasn't there something else? I was so busy trying to remember that I missed what the emperor said next.

Then Dachahl yelled, "No!" and he put his arms around me as if trying to shield me from some attack. "I said I would protect her, father," he said quietly but fiercely. "If I cannot do this, then I–" the rest was something hard to follow about him not living. "If Batiya dies, there will be no Chunru. I will see this done."

If something happened to me, he was going to kill himself? I gasped. "No, Dachahl! Don't say that!"

"Yes," he insisted.

"But I could die from anything. Getting sick, an accident, bad food…"

"Poison. Sabotage."

"I could die just from having a baby. What would happen to our child if you killed yourself?"

His arms loosened a bit. "Our child? Batiya, what is–" But I was already ducking out of his grasp and throwing myself at his father's feet.

"This I cannot do," I said. "If he is to kill himself for me, I cannot do it."

"Batiya!"

"I worked so much to keep him living. I would not have done this, if… I do not want him hurt! I will go home."

"You will leave?" the emperor asked me.

"Yes."

"You will tell no one that you are married to my son."

"Yes."

I didn't understand what he said next. "I do not know those words," I said, although the tears that were dripping down my nose and onto the carpet were making it hard to speak.

"He said he would give you much money," Dachahl explained, his voice rough.

"I do not want any money," I said. "I do not need money. I... He said he... He made me happy. I thought I made him happy. I did not know this would hurt him so much. I regr–"

The sharp intake of breath from Dachahl warned me that I was saying something wrong.

"She regrets, Dachahl," his father said triumphantly. "She regrets!"

"No!" I protested. What had I said? "The word is different in Dostrovian." I tried to remember what I should have said instead. "I am sad!" That was the word that was in the polite phrases Dachahl had taught me to say. When he spoke of regret it was to tell me it wasn't allowed. "I am very, very, very, very sad. I think about Dachahl killing himself and I am so much sad I cannot stay."

I felt Dachahl's hands on my shoulders, felt the warmth of him bending over me. "Me, you do not regret?"

"You I never, never, never regret," I told him.

"Then don't go."

"Your father said he would have me assassinated, didn't he?" I said in Dostrovian, because I was afraid to say anything else in Hadahnchi. "I understand that you were trying to protect me, but I can't... Not like that, Dachahl. I can't let you protect me like that. I'd rather go home."

"I'm afraid to take you on a boat," he confessed, his voice hoarse. "What if the seas are rough? This might kill you."

That stopped me for a moment. "I..."

"I won't let you leave," he told me in Hadahnchi.

"She wants to go," his father told him.

Dachahl practically snarled at him. "She wants for me to not have the pain of knowing that my father is trying to kill my wife!"

Yes. Dachahl kept saying how clever I was, but he was no Slow Stan himself. I had never thought I would willingly leave him, but I couldn't face *that*. I couldn't face knowing I had put him in that situation—and his father had been so proud and happy when he came home! I couldn't bear it.

"But Batiya, you asked about what would happen to our child?" I couldn't see what that had to do with anything. "Is there one?"

What did he mean? Of course we didn't have a child yet. We'd been married only about two months. It took nine months to... Oh. We'd been married for two months. "I..." I had been so busy with assassins I had forgotten to count. "That's why I got so seasick?"

He stared at me. "You don't know?"

"I should have asked my mother?"

Dachahl stood up. "I want a doctor," he announced.

"A doctor?"

"I want to know if I'm a father."

"They always say that they are mother to your child, Dachahl," his father said wearily. "This is the oldest trick known to women."

"She didn't say it. She doesn't know. She was–" something I couldn't follow "–until I touched her. I am the one who thinks that this is. I want a doctor," Dachahl insisted. "And if he says my wife is with child, then what will you do, father? Will you kill your own grandchild?"

"You're saying she never kept you from her bed?"

"Yes."

"She might have been a mother when you married her."

"No."

"Or been with another man since."

"No."

"This many fools have said."

"In less than four seasons, you will know I am right."

"Who can know a child's father?" the emperor asked scornfully.

"When I tell you, that if she is with child, it is not possible for any other man to be the father, you will not believe me," Dachahl said fiercely. "But when the child is born, I am certain that even you will be able to see that the father is Chang. And no matter how much a fool I am, it is not possible that she could have found herself a Chang lover. I feared for both of our lives when we stayed at our Embassy in Xercalis; she was there for only two days, and was always either with Lady Hahtungra or myself. This was seen by everyone in the Embassy. So will you wait and see? Or will you order her death before the child makes its appearance, and hope that your son is a fool?" He growled. "Or perhaps you would rather hope that *I* am not your son?"

The emperor walked over to the dais, and sat on the little platform. "You may send for a doctor."

"Thank you, father."

I stood up a little shakily. "I am not to be killed?"

"No," Dachahl declared. "That I would never allow. If there is no child, I will take you back to your family."

The emperor said something I did not understand, and Dachahl growled back something else that I did not understand, and then he stalked over to the curtain and barked out the order for the doctor. Then he remained at the curtain glaring at his father, and his father knelt on his backless throne, looking grim and withdrawn, while I just stood in between them, wishing there was some way to make them happy to see each other again. "This marriage, my family also did not like," I said a little ruefully.

"Your family treated me as a son," Dachahl protested.

"Not when they learned you were Chunru."

"Only because they thought I had deceived you."

"This, your father thinks also."

"That I deceived you?"

"That *I* deceived *you*."

"I told him it could not be. He can trust me to go halfway around the world to deal with a matter that Lord Hahtung cannot deal with, but he can't trust me in this?"

"Perhaps he knows you are the kind of man who once you say no, will never say yes," I suggested.

There was a small sound from over by the throne, and when I looked that way, I saw the emperor looking at me. I bowed my head, and looked at the floor. "Chunru, you did not say anything to your father about Foha."

"Who is Foha?" the emperor asked.

"Lord Hahtung's translator," my husband replied. "He hit Batiya on the head, and he tried to shoot me."

A long silence followed that statement, and when I peeked at the emperor he was looking stunned. "He shot at Chunru?" he finally managed to say. "Where is he?"

"I gave him to King Harluce," Dachahl answered. And he explained how Foha had been taking advantage of his position to interfere with the emperor's plans to modernize Changali. As he did so he left the curtain and walked back over to his father, and although his father didn't look happy, at least it wasn't Dachahl that was upsetting him this time. Chunru had done everything right except marry me.

I wrapped my arms around my middle. Was I really carrying Dachahl's child? Maybe it would be better if I wasn't. Maybe the best thing was to go home, and tell Papa that I'd made a mistake. But I didn't want to leave him. And when I watched him discussing intently with his father, I didn't want to take him back with me either. He looked so right here. This was where he was supposed to be, and what he was supposed to be doing. He needed to stay... and I needed to find some way to stay with him.

When the doctor arrived, Dachahl and his father turned to look at him as if they couldn't remember what they had wanted him for. I would have been happy to leave the two of them talking, but before I could suggest that the doctor and I go off somewhere private, the emperor remembered why he had been summoned, and demanded that I be examined right there with him watching.

The doctor walked over to me and jabbered something at me.

"I am sad to say, I do not know those words," I answered.

"He's speaking Stoi Kat," Dachahl told me. He came and stood next to me. "He wants you to take your sash off."

If Dachahl wasn't upset, then there was nothing to worry about. I pulled the loose end out and passed it from hand to hand, rolling the sash up as I went.

The doctor said something else. "Now he wants you to lie down."

On the floor. At least it was covered by a very luxurious carpet. Dachahl was frowning now, but he was looking more worried than upset, so I smiled reassuringly, sank gracefully to my knees—that was one of the moves Lady Hahtungra had shown me—and then curled up, rolled over on my side, uncurled, and then rolled onto my back. Very dignified, I hoped. At the very least, I had managed to not tangle my hems too badly.

The doctor kneeled on one side of me, and Dachahl crouched on the other. And then the doctor took my pulse, and my pulse, and my pulse and my pulse again. At least I assumed he was taking my pulse. And then he slid his hand inside my *lahnpran* and pressed down on my middle, and asked my husband questions. Most of them Dachahl didn't even bother to translate, he just answered them himself. But there were a few whose answers he didn't know. "My governess did not teach me the words for this," he confessed. "Fifty three-days have passed since we were married. How much before then was your last... time of the moon?"

"It was just before I met you. Twelve more days." Sixty-five days.

He told the doctor, and he and the doctor talked some more. "Is there a baby?" I asked.

Dachahl looked grim. "Either there is a baby," he said very slowly, as if he didn't want to ever get to the second half of the sentence, "or you are very sick, and might die."

There was no way I was dying. I grinned at Dachahl. "If he told Chunru that his woman was going to have a baby, and she died instead, then Chunru would be very angry and would want to slit his throat. But if he tells you I might die, and I just have a baby instead, then you will be far too happy to get angry with him about telling you the wrong thing."

Dachahl looked a little less grim.

"Hold my feet down," I told him. "I'm going to sit up."

He looked a little bewildered, but he obediently put his hand on my knees, and I sat up and then tucked my feet underneath me like a proper Chang. "You don't feel ill?" he asked.

"The only thing wrong with me is that I haven't had breakfast."

"You're supposed to be ill. You should lose your breakfast every morning, be tired, go from happy to sad like a pendulum, have sore..." He stopped his list.

"Your governess didn't teach you the right words?" I checked where he was looking, and discovered that my *lahmpran* was hanging half-open, and revealing far too much almost-transparent *fiahn* on top. "Can you send for someone to help me with my sash?"

"Yes."

He straightened up and strode over to the curtain, barked out that order, and then came striding back to kneel next to me again. "This is not a good time for me to have taken you away from your mother. May I find you someone to... help you?"

I hesitated. "Will she hate me as much as your father does?"

Dachahl glanced over his shoulder at his father. "It is not you that he hates–"

"It's that I don't look like I belong here," I concluded. It would have been easier if it had been something I could change.

"We will at least be able to prove to him that you did not trick me," Dachahl said in cheerful tones, and then added, "I am not so easily tricked!"

"Maybe I'm really, really good at tricking people," I retorted.

"You couldn't trick a two-year-old," he told me. I snarled, and he laughed, and his father said something I couldn't understand.

"When the maid comes to help you with your sash, you must turn your back toward my father," Dachahl told me quickly, and then he stood and walked back over to his father, and they began discussing something I couldn't follow.

The maid appeared silently and unannounced, and I stood and turned away from the dais, and she stood behind me so that we both had our backs to the emperor, and then she leaned awkwardly around me to make sure the sash was smooth and tight. When she finished making me look all proper and presentable, I turned around again, but it looked like Dachahl and his father had forgotten about me completely.

I didn't want to interrupt them, but neither did I particularly want to just stand here doing nothing. Did I have to stand? No one had seemed to be in a hurry to make me get up after the doctor had left. Moving back to the floor, as Dachahl put it, would probably be allowable. But facing forward or backward?

The sight of a clock on a table at the side of the room decided me. I knelt down facing across the room, and studied the clock. As Dachahl had said, there were only ten hours marked on it. It was probably about nine o'clock, so three hours to noon, and noon had to be a significant hour, because that was when Dachahl had said all the figures in the great clock had moved at once. So that probably meant that both hands on the clock would come together at noon. And by the angle of the hands, it was obvious that they would point upward when that took place. So, in theory, even if the hours in Changali were longer, to make up the difference between ten and twelve, the hour hand should still be pointing nearly directly sideways... and it wasn't.

But hadn't Dachahl told me that his hours weren't longer? And when he had negotiated my prizes for having memorized characters, he had negotiated for Changali hours, as opposed to southern ones, which made me think that it wasn't a joke and that they really must be shorter. But if the hours were shorter, and there were less of them... it had to be a gearing problem. If there were fewer teeth, then the gear had to go around more times to compensate. Between noon and noon, the hands on a Changali clock went around not twice, but three times.

I looked back over at Dachahl and his father and wished that people were as easy to figure out as machines. I tried to imagine I was Dachahl's father. So very proud of my magnificent son—that was easy to imagine. He had sent him on an important mission, and he accomplished it in four days! Strong, clever, responsible—no son could be more pleasing. But then there was me. I am a mistake. Why am I a mistake? Because Dachahl is a prince, and I am a nobody? He hadn't even asked about my parents. Because I wasn't Chang? But princes married foreigners all the time, so why would that matter so much?

No, it was all because of what I looked like.

I supposed I should be used to that. Ever since I decided that cutting off my hair was better than continually catching it in bits of machinery, I had never managed to look how I was supposed to look ever again —and to be honest, I'd only rarely managed to look right before then. But people did seem to get used to it eventually. So maybe this wouldn't be so bad.

But nobody had ever threatened to assassinate me because of how I looked before. He had changed his mind because of the baby, though. I wrapped my arms around my middle again. The baby was half wonderful son, and half horrible mistake. Would he look half all wrong, and be hated for that? But Talalis had been such a beautiful little girl. Surely my baby would be even more beautiful with Dachahl for a father.

Even with me for a mother?

But Dachahl didn't seem to think I was a mistake. Did I have to believe that Dachahl's father was right, and he was wrong? No. It wasn't supposed to matter what people looked like. All I had to do was be a good wife to Dachahl, and a good mother to our children, and a good princess, and if I did that and anyone still had a problem with how I looked, then they were the ones making a mistake.

I squared my shoulders, and lifted my chin and gazed confidently over at my husband—and he and his father were still talking.

It was a very long morning.

Finally Dachahl came over and held out his hand, and I took it, but got up without putting any weight on it, just like Lady Hahtungra had taught me. And then Dachahl and I bowed to the emperor and walked through the curtain, which parted before us as we approached and then closed behind us.

We walked down the corridor and around a corner, and then suddenly Dachahl picked me up and swung me about in a circle. "Clever, clever Batiya!" he crowed.

"Chunru," I protested. "You'll get my hems tangled!"

"This is not a problem. I am going to carry you."

"What if I'd rather walk?" I asked, but by the time he put me down my hems were all twisted about my feet, just as I'd feared, and I couldn't take a single step. "I don't know what I did that was so clever," I said as I tried unsuccessfully to edge my feet further apart than three inches. "I did figure out your little clock riddle, but I haven't had a chance to strut that out to you yet."

"You made me a father!"

"That doesn't take clever," I told him. "Some of the stupidest people I know have managed to have babies."

"Not *my* baby."

"I suppose making myself the mother of the next Emperor of Changali would have been very clever, if I had done it on purpose, or even realized that it had happened instead of having to have you point it out to me–"

"This was not your fault. I took you away from your mother after two days."

"And you didn't let us have any private talking time," I agreed. "But that isn't where we'll find the lump in the porridge. Your father said he wouldn't kill me—he never said that he'd let us be really married. If we can't convince him to let us be married, I'm not the mother of the next emperor anyway."

Dachahl picked me up and started carrying me down the hallway. "Yes," he insisted. "We have more than half a year to do this," he added. "We will succeed. I have already convinced him to let you stay in the palace with me."

I suspected he had refused to stay in the palace himself if I wasn't allowed to, but I was still very glad to hear that he had succeeded in that much. "That was very clever of you, Chunru," I told him.

"Yes? Then why are you calling me Chunru? Nobody else is here."

"You told me I wasn't supposed to call you Dachahl when I was angry at you."

"You're angry?"

"You can't fool me, Chunru, you tangled me up in my hems on purpose, just so you would have an excuse to haul me around."

"Yes," he agreed. I couldn't see the smile on his face, but I could hear it in his voice, and knowing I wouldn't be able to get his heels down on the road any time soon, I just put my arms around his neck and held on tight.

He carried me down corridors lined with paintings and flowers, and then through another magnificent curtain into another room with paintings and flowers. The palace gardens and greenhouses must be huge. "These are my rooms," he announced. "Your rooms haven't been prepared yet."

"I don't get to share your rooms with you?"

"You want to?"

Yes. I wanted to know that however much time he spent out doing princely things—which I feared would be quite a lot—when he came to bed, I would be there waiting for him. "Will it cause problems?"

"Not for me." He seemed pleased with the idea.

"For the palace staff?" I asked.

"I don't know why it would."

I thought about it, and couldn't think why it would either. It would be fewer rooms to look after, fewer hallways to walk, and schedules no more complicated than before. There was certainly room enough for two. I would probably have to get used to having people help me bathe and dress while my husband was there watching, but he already seemed to think that was normal. "Then, please, I would like to live with you."

He set me on my feet. "When said like this, I can't think why I did not insist on it."

He strode over to the wall, and pushed on what looked like an ornament in the shape of a dragon's head. "This is Chunru, I want a noon-meal for two."

"This will be done, Chunru," the dragon's head replied.

He pushed on the head again. "Also, tell Langso to bring my wife's belongings to my rooms."

"This will be done, Chunru."

I contemplated the dragon's head for a while, and then confessed that I was completely boggled.

"It's like one of your telephones," he explained.

"I could figure out that much," I told him. "But your father is the Emperor of all Changali. Shouldn't *he* get a magic button to summon up whatever he needs too?"

Dachahl laughed. "Because he is emperor, he is too important to do his own summoning. He's supposed to be constantly surrounded by people ready to race to do his bidding. They only race as far as the curtain, and the watchers in the curtain alcoves do the actual summoning with a 'magic button', but it's the look of the thing that matters."

"But there wasn't anyone there but us."

"I am his son. I asked for the honor of a private audience."

"I'm very glad that huge empty room isn't usually quite so empty," I admitted. "But I need you to push your magic button again, and summon someone to untangle my hems."

Instead of pushing his button he picked me up again, and deposited me next to the table. I sank to my knees, but before I could slide my feet out in front of me to get my hems sorted Dachahl sat down right next to me, and put his arms around me and pulled me close.

"Is it because I said I wanted to go home?" I asked him. "I didn't mean it!"

"What?"

"Why you are trying to stop me from going anywhere. You'll start tying me to the bedpost next!"

This complaint just made him hold me tighter. "Bed post?" he asked. "I do not have a bed post. Is tying women to things a southerner custom? My governess did not tell me about it."

"Nobody told me about it either. It happened in one of Naditte's novels."

"I have nothing to tie you to, so I'll just have to hold you." And he did, hanging on and squeezing me until I could hardly breathe, for a very long time. And since I really didn't want to go anywhere else, I let him.

When I heard a sound at the curtain and saw it shudder a little, I warned Dachahl, "I think our lunch has arrived," but he just loosened his hold on me a little—he didn't let go.

"Come!" he ordered. A huge serving tray was carried in by two men, and two more men set the dishes on the table before us. They moved quickly and smoothly, and didn't even blink at the sight of the Imperial Heir with his arms around a strange southern woman. But they would be talking about it all over the kitchens, I knew. A burgie would be humiliated, but Dachahl was royal. He didn't care.

I wondered how farmstock-bred and hopefully-royal-by-marriage me was going to respond. I decided I was going to be amused, as soon as I recovered from the shocks of the day. "It... was all real," I said when they left.

Dachahl didn't answer.

"Your father really said he would have me assassinated, and he really meant it."

"I told you the curses on the other royal lines weren't so pleasant to hear about."

"And you really would have vowed to kill yourself in order to stop him."

"Yes!" he said fiercely. "And you really would have left me." His voice was rough and strained and his hold on me tightened.

"If I have to choose between both of us dead, or both of us alive, but not together, I..." Something in the way he was holding me warned me that I was saying dangerous things. "In Changali, that would be the wrong answer, wouldn't it?"

"But not for a southerner. I should have remembered."

"Dachahl, I did not know how badly my saying that would hurt you. I... regret." I held my breath, hoping that I had used the term appropriately this time. And then I felt him relax. I couldn't relax myself though. There was one more thing I needed to know. "If your father doesn't accept me, then what happens after the baby is born?"

Dachahl tensed up all over again, and did not answer.

"We're back to your father thinking assassins might be a good idea, and you threatening to kill yourself if anything happens to me, and our only other choice is me going home, aren't we?"

He still didn't answer.

"I need to make him like me somehow, but I've never actually tried to make anyone like me before. I don't know what to do." And the thought of even trying to do something like that made me uncomfortable.

"Batiya," Dachahl said very, very slowly. "Many, many people have tried to make my father like them, so that he would do something they wanted. This never works."

It was probably a good thing for Changali that his father could see through that sort of thing, but where did it leave me? "Then what do I do? We only have seven months—am I supposed to stare at my thumbs the whole time?"

"You will reveal your character," he told me. "And my father will see your true worth."

"Reveal my character how?"

He didn't know either. "You must not worry about this," he insisted.

He was probably right, worrying wouldn't do anything but make me feel worse, and I was already feeling weak and a little dizzy. Although that might be improved by doing something about my empty belly. I turned my head, and examined the dishes the servants had placed on the table before us. "Dachahl, I would rather not be tied up," I said a little shakily, "but after we eat, you can hold me for as long as you like."

"Good."

"Right now, though, could you please let go of me, and teach me how to eat with sticks?"

He laughed and let go, and showed me how the sticks were supposed to be held.

I waited until I felt a lot calmer and we both had food in us before I brought up the subject of our differing views of death. "For a Chang, both being dead, means being together?"

Dachahl's sticks hovered halfway between the plate and his mouth. "You think men and women go to different realms?" he asked, wide-eyed.

"No." Was there anyone who did think that? "But, you can't have a life together if you're dead, can you? And dead lasts for forever anyway, so no matter what happens, you can't miss out on being dead together. So why rush into it? If you choose the pain of living separately, maybe you will be rewarded by having a chance to live together later."

Dachahl put his food down. "Hoping for another chance? This does not sound very terrible."

"Always together, even if only in death, doesn't sound all that bad either," I admitted. "If neither your solution nor my solution is really so terrible, then maybe you don't need to hang on to me after all."

"Yes, I do." He tapped his sticks on his plate. "You said, for as long as I like."

"Do you have any idea how long that will be?"

"A week," he told me, completely straight-faced. "And then I will let you have a few hours to walk around, before I hold you for another week."

Somehow that schedule didn't sound nearly as horrible to me as it should have. "What about meals? Do I get to eat?"

"Yes. I feed you all the food you want."

"Let's do that then," I agreed.

But his father summoned him before we'd even finished eating, and he didn't get a chance to hold me at all.

Sitting waiting in Dachahl's rooms was more comfortable—but only slightly more interesting—than waiting in the audience chamber had been. I watched Dachahl's valet unpack his things and put them away. And then he unpacked my things and put them away.

Including my underthings. I didn't like that much, but I couldn't bring myself to complain. "You will find a woman to help you with this?" I half-asked, half-requested, instead.

"Yes, Princess. I regr–"

"This is not for regret," I told him. "When you have time, you will see it done."

"Yes, Princess."

I wondered a bit that he was calling me 'Princess'. Dachahl had called me his wife, but he had promised me that he would consider us married, no matter what, so of course that's how he called me. But the servants—would all of them call me 'Princess', or only this one man, who had seen Chunru place the jade imperial seal around my neck? "Your name is Langso?"

"Yes, Princess." I think my knowing his name surprised him.

"I do not have enough Changali clothing. You and the woman you find to help will do what needs doing for this?"

"Yes, Princess."

"This is very good," I told him. "I am happy that you are good at what you do."

I had surprised him again. "Yes, Princess." He bowed, and left me alone.

I correctly predicted the movement of the figures on Dachahl's clock, memorized every painting in his rooms, and was starting to feel hungry again when I received my first visitor. There was a silvery rattle of chimes outside the outer doorway, and when I entered the first chamber, saying, "What is this?" a woman's voice responded in

Dostrovian, "Chloys Phabilos to speak with you, Highness."

It was a Xercali name, so I said "Come in," expecting to see a southerner. But it was a Chang about my own age who entered. Her long dark hair fell straight down her back, and she wore a knee-length *lahnpran* over her shirt and puffy pants.

"Chunru asked me to tell you that he will not be dining with you this evening," she said. She seemed a little nervous. "He said I was to offer you my own company instead."

"I would love to have your company," I answered. Although I couldn't say I wanted it instead of Dachahl's.

She came further into the room, and stared at me as if I was the barn tom, and she was a mouse. Why would she find me so frightening? She spoke Dostrovian, so it couldn't possibly be because I was a southerner, could it? What else was there? Because I was almost sort-of a princess? But we were in the Imperial Palace, that ought to be common and expected. Because I was married to Chunru?

"They must be talking about me everywhere by now," I attempted.

She jerked a bit. Almost a cower. Clearly I was being talked about. I wondered what was being said. "I met Chunru when his ship sank, and the ship I was on tried to rescue him," I told her, figuring that covered the most relevant parts of my story. "I did not know that he was a prince until after we were married."

Her eyes went wide. "If you did not know that he was a prince, then why did... that is... if it is permitted to ask...?"

"Why did I marry him? Because I thought he was the most wonderfully splendid man in the whole wide world," I said, somewhat wryly. I still thought that—but oh, the trouble it was going to cause us.

"You... must be very... brave."

What? That comment fit very precisely with what I had been thinking, but not at all with what I had been saying. How much courage did it take to marry the most wonderfully splendid man in the world, when you didn't even know that he was a prince?

Although, if that man was Dachahl—autocratic, ruthless... "Do you know Chunru well?" I asked.

"My mother, Mrs. Phabilos, came here from Xercalis to teach Chunru. She adopted me when I was five, so that she would have a child, and Chunru would have someone else to speak Xercali and Dostrovian with."

So she knew him very well indeed, and found him intimidating. She really was a mouse. "If you promise to help me learn how to be a Chang, I promise to protect you from Chunru," I offered.

She looked at me even more amazed than before, and no less nervous.

"I'm not at all afraid of Chunru," I assured her. "You shouldn't be afraid of him either."

Chloys shivered. "He's Chunru. I must do what he demands of me."

I frowned. It just didn't seem to be possible that Chunru would use his position to force this mouse to do anything terrible. "If he tells you to do something you don't like, let me know that you don't like it, and I'll get him to change his mind," I advised her.

She looked at the floor. "Yes, ...Princess."

I tried to imagine what Dachahl had done to the poor girl to make her so scared of him. She had been five when she'd met him... so what would that have been like? I imagined what Vanitri would have done to a little mouse of a girl who suddenly became his classmate when he was no more than ten, and she was only five, and nearly burst out laughing. "I suppose it must have been very difficult growing up with Dachahl," I said, doing my best to commiserate with a fate that didn't seem at all terrible to me. "I bet he kept wanting you to admire his bugs, help him catch frogs, be his prisoner when he played pirate..."

"Fight with swords," she added in a whisper.

"You should have said, 'No, you big bully, I'm telling Mama!'," I concluded. "It would have been very good for him."

"Did he tell you about me?" she asked, sounding amazed.

It really would have been amazing if he had. "I have older brothers," I explained.

She gasped. "I am not the sister of Chunru!" She sounded horrified and confused. "I said to you I was... did I say something wrong?"

"I understood what you said," I assured her. "You are the daughter of his governess. And today he sent you a message saying, 'tell my wife I can't eat with her,' and you were afraid you had been handed another frog. But here you are anyway."

She looked down at the floor. "Of course you are not a frog, Highness."

"I am very glad you came," I told her, "because with Chunru gone I am very lonely." And also because I needed her help. "Will you please order dinner for us?"

"I... don't know what you like, Highness."

"I don't know what I like either," I told her cheerfully. "Order what you like, and that way we know at least one of us will enjoy the food."

I ate with sticks again. Awkwardly. Chloys offered to order me a fork. "I need to learn how to eat this way," I explained. "I also need to practice my Hadahnchi. So although it is delightful to be able to speak with you in Dostrovian, I think we shouldn't unless I get stuck." I asked her to explain the dishes to me, and Dachahl was right—dishes that had tasted just fine when they were mystery substances suddenly seemed a lot less appetizing when I learned what was in them. I ate them anyway, figuring I'd get used to the idea of eating fish bladders and squid and so forth.

Just as we were finishing, Langso returned with a woman who he introduced as Falahni. "You will allow her to take care of your clothes?" he asked.

"Yes," I answered.

"Will Chloys be your *harlalang*?"

I looked over at Chloys for clarification.

"He wants to know if I will be your secretary," Chloys explained.

"If you want to, I'll be up on the wall," I told her. She looked horrified. "I'll be very happy," I clarified. She bowed, and just that suddenly, I had a secretary and a maid.

But no husband.

The clock was halfway around its third revolution when Dachahl finally came in, looking bleary-eyed. He scowled at Chloys and the maid, most unfairly, since they had only stayed so late because I'd asked them to—not wanting to be left alone with nothing to do.

"Out," he ordered. They bowed, and fled.

I got to my feet. "Is this command for me also?"

"No," he answered, surveying the silk gown that was apparently what Chunru's woman was supposed to wear to bed. Like most Changali clothing, it fastened at the side, and Falahni had brought me two of each of the ones she had presented for my approval, one fastened on the right, and one on the left. That way I could pick one that wouldn't have me lying on my buttons all night.

A curious feature that I had never noticed in other Changali clothing was that the bed-gown only covered one shoulder and only had one sleeve, which didn't make me feel as lop-sided as I was expecting because the sleeve was of silk gauze so fine that it was hardly there anyway. And, because the buttons only went down to my hip, my left leg showed from nearly top to bottom every time I moved.

I hoped Dachahl approved because I was sure my mother wouldn't. "Do you like it? If not I can take it off."

"Yes."

"Yes, you like it, or yes, take it off?"

"Yes."

The next day was a lot like that one. Chunru was gone from shortly after breakfast until very late at night, and when he came in he was very glad to see me, but in no mood to say a word more than he had to. I spent the morning with Chloys writing a letter home, practicing my Hadahnchi, and learning my way around the palace. I asked her to introduce me to more people, but it seemed that there was nobody in the palace she felt was suitable for me to meet. And she was still almost as nervous of me as she was of Dachahl. I think I would still have felt entirely lost and abandoned if the message that said Dachahl couldn't join me for lunch hadn't come with a gift.

It was a box, made out of wood, with a flower inlay in three colors of jade. I hadn't realized that jade came in colors other than green. When I opened it up, tiny metal figures dressed in real cloth clothing sprung up from inside, jerked a little, and there were two notes and then a grating sound, and then stillness.

"This is a Tilardu treasure box," Chloys told me. "A masterwork of the great Tilardu Doduchru, and an heirloom of the imperial house, but..."

"It's broken," I noted.

"Chunru threw it on the floor once when he was a boy, and it hasn't worked since. He got in a lot of trouble with the emperor." I had already figured out that she was even more terrified of the emperor than she was of Dachahl. "Tilardu died without ever having taken on an apprentice, and none of the other clockworkers are worthy to touch the great master's creations, so it can't be repaired." She looked troubled. "I don't know why Chunru would give you a broken treasure box."

Underneath the frozen figures was a compartment lined in silk, and inside that compartment was a leather roll-case. I undid the clasp, and unrolled it to reveal neat little pockets filled with a gleaming row of the smallest screwdrivers, wrenches and other tools that I had ever seen. "Dachahl, I love you!" I muttered gleefully under my breath. It might not help my situation much, but at least it was something that I could do, and that I liked doing. So to Chloys's horrified amazement I began disassembling the box.

To distract her from the apparent terror with which she observed my actions, I had her order me a tray lined with cotton cloth, with extra cotton cloths on the side. And then I had her write a letter to the most famous clockmaker she knew about, asking what sort of oil was best for use on a Tilardu mechanism, and could a sample please be provided.

While she was doing that, I dug the magnifying spectacles Mister Korbosk had given me as a wedding gift out of the chest Langso had stashed them in, because I had never seen such delicate machinery before.

"You said this is an heirloom?" I asked. "How old is it?"

"I... I think two hundred years?"

"That's amazing. Do you have any books about this Tilardu, who made it?"

"Ah... in the imperial library?"

"Please be kind and find one about him, or just about clock working, if this is as good as you can do, and then read it to me."

I was occupied, and almost happy—except for my unease about the future and my not seeing my husband much—but Dachahl came back that day just as late, and once again not in a mood to say one word more than he had to.

The next morning I ordered Chloys to find out what my husband had been doing with himself. It turned out that she already knew, and just hadn't said anything because it was a subject that made her more than usually nervous. Dachahl's father might not have liked anything about me, but he had taken what Dachahl had said about Foha and the likelihood of another conspirator somewhere in the palace very seriously indeed. And Dachahl and some general who was in charge of palace security had been putting every scholar in the place under a microscope and discovering which ones seemed most dubious, and firing them. Not a pleasant job at all. And when I gave her a break from reading to me later that day, she came back only a few minutes later, looking a bit shaken, and informed me that one of the palace secretaries had been arrested and that everyone thought he was going to get executed. That didn't sound pleasant either, but I hoped that it meant that Dachahl would feel safer, and wouldn't be as busy, and could relax a little and have more time to spend with me.

It didn't turn out that way. And when the third and fourth day went by just the same as the previous two, I decided that something needed to be done.

"Is he still hunting for traitors?" I demanded of Chloys.

"I... don't think so," she answered very hesitantly. "I've heard talk about an education committee. You... didn't know about it? They... they say it's your idea."

"My idea? If it was my idea, how would anyone but you know about it? I've hardly said as much as three words to my husband in the past three days, and I haven't spoken to anyone else at all."

Chloys ducked her head. "I thought you'd discussed it with him before you came."

I supposed we had, briefly, discussed the schools—but they were Dachahl's idea, not mine. Still, rumors always did get twisted about in funny ways. I was more concerned about the word 'committee'. Engineers tend to be very wary of the word—we think it means a whole lot of discussing and not very much doing. Which didn't sound like my husband at all. "Are they forcing him to talk all the time he's not here?" I demanded.

"Yeeessss, I think so," Chloys replied.

"Then it's no wonder he comes back every night looking like he wants to kill something," I ranted. "At this rate, he'll shoot his horse and jump the river!"

"I don't think he'd do *that*, Highness. He really likes his horses."

And he probably hadn't had a chance to even go visit them since he got here, let alone go riding. It wasn't right. Dachahl's father had to know how much Dachahl hated being made to talk. Was he loading him down with that kind of duty because he really needed him that badly, or was it a punishment for having caused so much trouble, or was it just a means of keeping him away from me? Maybe all three?

But if he really needed him that much, then he ought to be taking better care of him, and if he was punishing him, he was cutting his toes off to make his shoes fit better, and if he was trying to keep my husband away from me, he'd better be ready to collar the bear, because I wouldn't roll over!

I looked over at Chloys and discovered that she was looking back with a mixture of awe, and terror, and guilt. "Would you like me to stay with you at night?"

What? No! Definitely not! Have the only time I did get with him interfered with? "Why would I want you to do that?"

She turned away, and blushed, and told me it was nothing. But, of course, I had to keep puzzling at it, until I realized that she was worried that I might get hurt. "I'm fine," I assured her. I couldn't say that my husband had been being particularly gentle with me, these past nights, but I couldn't say that I minded, either. "He's the one who needs your help," I told her. "We're going to have to rescue him."

Chapter Three

I Wear a Bonnet My Husband Doesn't Like

"Us... rescue Chunru?" Chloys squeaked.

"Naturally." He wasn't likely to be able to rescue himself. Doing the right and proper thing was too important to him. As long as the work his father had assigned him was important to the empire—and if he was discussing schools that was very important indeed—he'd never tell his father to jump off. I needed to create a reason for him to get the breaks he so desperately needed. I looked around the room for inspiration, and my eye fell on the sword rack, currently holding two swords. Neither of the matching *tirah-fa* were there. Dachahl was wearing one, and the other had probably gone back to the swordsmith to see if the damage I had done to it was repairable.

"Chloys, where does Chunru go to practice sword-fighting?"

"He takes private instruction in his chambers."

In here? That was no good.

"And... I think he sometimes goes to the practice yards where the young officers train."

Perfect. "Would you show me where that is?"

She looked very uncertain. "You want to go to the practice yards? I thought you were rescuing Chunru."

"This is correct."

"But... I don't think Chunru would *want* you to go there," she protested, even more uncertain than before.

"Why not?"

"There are... young officers... and they are... training."

I had grabbed that much already, and thought it sounded very promising. In a good mood, Chunru might not mind taking me such a place himself. But when he was already in a bad mood, discovering I'd gone and got myself entirely surrounded by young men was sure to make him blow smoke and bellow. "This is not forbidden? I will not be shamed if I go there? Is this the sort of place Dachahl's sister would never go?"

"I think the Princess Lulahn might sometimes go there," Chloys admitted. She looked terrified.

As long as it was just Dachahl who would be upset, my plan should work. "Don't worry," I reassured Chloys. "Chunru won't be angry with you, because you are going to write him a message that says that I went out to the practice yards, and you went with me because you didn't know what else to do. But you weren't quite sure that was the right thing, and so could he please tell you what you should have done instead?"

"I can do that," Chloys admitted.

"Naturally. You are very good at writing messages. So hurry and write this, so we can go."

"Should I call Falahni?" she asked in an agonized whisper.

"What do we want Falahni for?"

"You... do not wish to change your clothes?"

I looked down at my calf-length *lahnpran*—the shortest one that Falahni was willing to provide me with. "What is wrong with what I have on now?"

"There isn't anything.... this is much better... Chunru won't be so..." Whatever her reason for assuming I would want to change clothing, she had trouble expressing it.

"I want to wear something that I will be able to move in," I explained. "If this is not good, I will wear southerner clothing."

"No, no. This that you have already is good," she assured me. But she looked more puzzled than ever. It took me a bit to figure out why. Apparently the only possible reason she could think of for going to the practice yards was to collect admiring glances from the men there. I was probably going to shock the poor girl right down to her embroidered slippers.

We sent the note off with Langso, and walked down a couple of corridors, and then suddenly we were outside. The practice yards were dusty and warm, even in the early spring, and in spite of a pleasant breeze, full of sweaty males with their shirts off. They were doing all sorts of athletic-looking things—Chloys tried to pretend she wasn't interested in watching. I tried to find someone who appeared to be learning swordplay, instead of archery, running, marching in formation, climbing ropes, or something that looked like a very, very odd sort of dancing. I finally spotted a couple of men in masks and pads, wielding sticks, over on a patch of grass just past the main square.

I headed in that direction, Chloys trailing behind me. I was also trailed by a growing silence, and an entire stadium worth of stares. At first I thought it was just because I was odd, and important, and because Chloys was very pretty, and I wasn't much worried, just a little surprised. These were supposed to be soldiers, weren't they? It didn't say much for their military discipline, if they were all stopping what they were doing so that they could gawk at us.

As they moved closer to me I realized that their gazes were unfriendly and maybe a little threatening. But I was too glad to be out in the open air, and too sure that Chunru would be just as glad, to change my plan.

Fortunately the two with the stick swords were concentrating hard enough that I got quite close before they stopped. I went up to them, and smiled, and told one of them, "You are very good, like Chunru."

I didn't actually have a clue how good he was, just that he was better than his opponent. "This I want to learn," I told him. "This you teach me."

Chloys choked. The man I was talking to, and every other man in eye-range, just looked bewildered.

So I walked over to the extra equipment lying nearby. Extracted a practice sword like theirs, and facing off against the less skilled of the two, I attempted to duplicate how the men had been standing. And when that only got me yet more baffled looks, I attacked.

I landed a blow on the man's padding, too, but only because he was so startled. He easily fended me off once he realized what was happening.

I turned to the other man. "I do not do this right. You must teach me. Show me the feet."

He was frowning at me so hard I was a little surprised—but very delighted—when he demonstrated the stance. I think everyone there was even more surprised when I very nearly duplicated it. But when I tried to move, it was clear I hadn't got it right. "This is not right to move," I announced.

The frown did not lessen, but after a long pause he actually answered. Although I didn't understand what he said.

"You should bend your knees more," Chloys explained in a voice that was breathy and faint.

I followed the advice, and found it a distinct improvement. I smiled at my instructor. "Thank you! This is good?"

I could tell it was, by the way he looked at me—as if he was suddenly having to re-evaluate where I fit in his universe. "Yes... Princess." He seemed almost more wary of me than he had been before, but also a little more respectful.

"Now you show me the hands."

He demonstrated the proper grip, and after taking a good look I managed to duplicate that too. He was showing me how to adjust my strike when Chunru arrived, striding across the field, his *choliang* swirling about his knees and his pitch-black hair whipping about behind him.

"Chunru!" I didn't throw myself into his arms, mostly because we were in public, but partly because I wasn't all the way sure he'd catch me. But I don't think anyone could have doubted that I was happy to see him.

Nor could anyone doubt that he wasn't happy to see me surrounded by a great many shirtless warriors. My helpful instructor backed up a step, and my husband's glare adjusted to follow.

"I am learning sword-fighting," I announced proudly. "You will show me how this is done?"

His eyes narrowed. "Yes." He removed his *choliang*, and then glared at the wide bell-like sleeves of his shirt. I stepped forward, removed his *tirah-fa* from his sash, tucking it into my own, and then I started unwinding his sash. I was actually better at taking his off than my own— more practice. Once the sash was gone, he could pull off the tunic and shirt.

There was a murmur. I had got used to the scars, but I supposed that most of the men here would know that he didn't have a single one of them when he left here, just over a season ago. Dachahl just held out an imperious hand for his padding.

I could tell that the officers were a lot happier to see him than they were to see me, so I let them strap him into the padding, while I just collected his clothing. Then I stepped back out of range. I wanted to watch the fight, not get chased all around the field by it. And although everyone on my side stayed behind me, I was startled to see how close some of the other men were standing. They soon learned their mistake. Dachahl dove in like a hawk, and my fighting instructor stumbled back out of the way, and the viewers had to fall back.

Dachahl's opponent got his feet under him, and they exchanged a few strikes and blocks, and then Dachahl's stick slammed through the other's defense, and he had to back up again while he tried to recover. Only Dachahl never gave him the chance—he stepped up the onslaught, and his opponent eventually figured out that he wasn't even going to have a chance to retreat. For a while he fended off the blows as best he could while Dachahl pounded a bushel of dust out of his padding, and then he surrendered.

Dachahl bowed, and they both said, "you have no back," which I guessed was the Changali equivalent of shaking hands and saying 'good fight'. Dachahl started taking off his pads, and nearly half-a-dozen men jumped forward to help him. But they all moved out of the way when I stepped forward with his clothes.

"Batiya," Dachahl told me in Dostrovian, "I'm supposed to be discussing the new education program with some committee right now, and now I need to clean myself before I can even make an appearance."

"I think you should go as you are," I told him in the same language, as I pulled his shirt over his topknot. "You look very..."

His face emerged from the fabric. "Very?"

I shook my head.

"When I see you tonight, I'm going to make you finish that sentence," he warned.

I thought maybe I was blushing, so I ducked my head.

"Batiya, how did I end up out here, instead of where I'm supposed to be?"

"You are supposed to be here," I told him.

"I am?"

"Because you are teaching your wife to defend herself."

"*I* will defend you!"

"While you are off discussing schools with committees, and I am somewhere else?" He frowned. "But you don't have to worry," I told him. "I was doing very well, I'm sure I won't have trouble finding someone else to teach me when I come back tomorrow."

Dachahl looked around at the gathered men, and growled. Then he looked at me, and his expression turned suspicious. "Batiya, what is this really about?"

"I am arranging to get you outside, and moving around, so that you don't turn into a mushroom," I explained, delighted at the success of my scheme. "Tomorrow I will be staying here with all these strong young men even longer, so make sure you have space in your schedule."

"You're really going to force me to teach you sword-fighting?"

"Would you rather teach me to ride a horse?" I asked.

"No!" he barked. "No horses. Not until after the baby. Promise me."

I eyed him thoughtfully. This was like the head injury, I thought. Only somehow having a baby was involved too, so it couldn't be his cousin this time. "Your mother?" I guessed.

"Yes, my mother," he snapped. "Promise."

"I promise not to try riding any horses until you say that I can," I said, and meant it. "But I'd like to *meet* your horses, when you have time?"

"Yes." He turned to one of the men standing nearby. "I will be giving my wife lessons in swordplay starting tomorrow. Can you arrange for her equipment?"

The man bowed. "Will the princess want a lighter practice sword?"

Dachahl laughed. "No." Then he turned to me. "You will go rest now," he ordered in Hadahnchi so that everyone knew what he'd said, and so I couldn't stay without making both of us look bad.

"Yes, Chunru." I finished wrapping his sash around him, and he took his *tirah-fa* and *choliang* back, kissed my forehead, and then strode back across the yard to the palace.

When he was gone, Chloys edged toward me and asked in Dostrovian, "Was this what you planned, when you said we would rescue him?"

"Of course. We did a good job, don't you think? He looked much less like an eight-year-boar afterward."

"But... Highness... He said... Are you... going to have a baby?"

"I don't think the emperor wants people to know yet," I warned her.

Her jaw went slack, her eyes widened... she squeaked. Several heads turned to look in her direction, and she blushed. "I regret my loss of composure," she babbled in a hurried whisper. "I just, I... Chunru a *father*?"

"I think he'll make a good one," I told her, and then I bowed to the two sword-fighters and thanked them for their 'good' teaching, and, feeling very pleased to have accomplished something, headed back to my rooms and the treasure box.

I only had it halfway disassembled but I was pretty sure I'd discovered all the problems. One of the anchors that held the mechanism to the box had pulled loose, and as a result one of the shafts of the mechanism had got bent. The screw that had held the anchor in place had been dislodged and fallen into another part of the mechanism, jamming it. I had finally got to the point where I could work the screw back out—then I would need to straighten the shaft, drill a new hole through the anchor so I wasn't trying to return the screw to the same damaged hole, and reassemble everything.

But it was tempting, very tempting, to finish taking it all apart, just because it was so amazingly intricate.

Also, I had no idea where to find a good drill. Maybe it would be better to get a newer, longer anchor, carve out a bit more of the wood so it would fit just as snugly into place as this one did, and nobody would even be able to tell that it had needed fixing.

Chloys interrupted my musings. "You really did rescue Chunru."

"We rescued Chunru," I corrected. "I'm very lucky to have your help."

She blushed, and looked pleased for what was possibly the first time since I'd met her. "When are you expecting the baby?" she asked.

"About the end of the fall season." I was in no hurry to see it happen. The longer away it was, the more time we would have to convince Dachahl's father to accept our marriage. Something that I still hadn't managed to even get started on. Somehow I didn't think he would be pleased that I had pried Chunru out of the grip of the committee, got him outside, and made him smile. He should be pleased about that, but he wouldn't be.

And while I was thinking about that I remembered the officers who were not just gawking at the strange foreign princess, but glaring at her. What did they have against me?

"What is said about me, around the palace?" I asked. "How much do people know about how Chunru and I met, and that sort of thing?"

"They know that you were in some accident together at sea, and that he married you after the southern custom, and has petitioned his father to acknowledge the marriage," Chloys told me carefully.

That must be the official version. It was remarkably accurate. "That's all they're saying?"

She hesitated. "I have heard that you are a southerner sorceress and that you have cast a spell on him that makes it so that he can see no other."

I rather liked the sound of him seeing no other, but I suspected that the average Chang wouldn't be quite so delighted. "Is there more?"

"That you saved his life, and marrying you was the price you forced him to pay."

"Do they think it was a fair price?" I asked.

She stared at me. "This is just... something that can be heard. I didn't believe it."

"Of course you don't believe I could force him to do anything," I told her. "You know him. But that isn't what I asked."

"They... think that as a Cholipardo prince, he will never be convinced that it wasn't fair."

That was nice to hear, also—but it wasn't an answer to the question I had asked. If she wouldn't answer the question, then the answer was probably no. "Anything else?"

She looked even more hesitant than before. "That the purge of the scholars was your fault, because you have convinced Chunru and the emperor to turn their backs on Changali custom and culture, and do everything the southern way," she said in a very small voice.

"I think that a culture that produces someone like Chunru must have much greatness in it," I told her. "Bringing some good parts of southern culture to Changali is what the emperor sent Chunru to do, before I even met him. So why am I supposed to be the one driving the horse?"

"I... don't know," Chloys admitted.

Not sure I wanted to hear any more rumors, I went back to contemplating the box. I would need a chisel, and I probably needed to send the damaged anchor out to a metal shop, so that a new one could be made. I would ask them to make me a new shaft at the same time. Langso would either know where to find one or who to ask. I got up and pushed on the dragon head, and Chloys went back to reading the biography of Tilardu, Master Clockmaker.

Dachahl returned to his chambers much earlier than usual—in time to eat dinner with me—but I had hoped to see some positive effect from having got him outside, and instead he was scowling just as fiercely as he had the three nights previous. He sent Chloys away just as curtly, too, but I was too happy to see him to care. This time I really did throw myself into his arms, and he did catch me, and that must have made the scowl disappear, because he laughed.

And, after he had eaten, he finally spent some time talking to me. "My imperial father desires that the plans to educate the peasants be put into effect as quickly as possible, so I have been arranging to have this done," he explained apologetically. "We have to find places for the schools, arrange for builders and materials, find teachers and supplies, decide what will be studied... and he wants it all planned out and ready to announce by the end of next season."

"What about the conspiracy, and the panicky scholars?"

"I delivered the transcript of Foha's questioning to General Duprang—he is my father's head of security—and told him everything I knew about the conspiracy. I did that the first day we were here. I feel that a year has passed since then. General Duprang and I then investigated the people named and discovered, as I had feared, that they were people Foha wanted to see hurt, not his friends. So we investigated every other scholar in the palace, and finally found evidence that one of them had been in communication with Tertan. My father examined the evidence and ordered his death. Eleven other scholars were asked to remove themselves from the palace." Dachahl scowled. "I can see that this was necessary, but now every scholar that remains is even more nervous than before. Many think their friends were unfairly dealt with, and some of them probably were." There was a long pause and then he added, "My father seems to think that starting on the schools as quickly as possible will be the best way to deal with all this."

"So that before they can get fired up enough to blow a full head of steam off, it will have already happened?" I asked, startled and a little incredulous.

"I do not know exactly what he thinks," Dachahl admitted. "He trusts me a little less than he did before." Because of me. But Dachahl didn't like me apologizing for things that weren't really my fault—so I just waited for him to say something else. "I don't see how all this rushing will help, Batiya. The secretaries that are working with us seem to be getting more and more frightened as each hour passes. It isn't just that they fear they will be suspected of joining conspiracies, either. As far as they can tell, the southerners don't have a scholar class. They think that if father's southern-inspired plans are put into action, they are all going to be demoted to craftsmen."

"That's not being demoted!" I protested. "Someday craftsmen will rule the world."

"This will not happen," Dachahl told me. "The craftsmen will be too busy bending over their workbenches to do any ruling, and the world will revolt."

I wasn't sure I could argue with that. I would certainly rather be bending over my workbench than ruling the world. "If you are going to open hundreds of schools, then you will need hundreds of teachers. They can't be demoted—you're going to need them all."

"For one generation."

I sighed. "So, you can't water the whole farm today—tomorrow it might rain."

"If you are saying that we've got plenty of time to come up with an answer, I know that. But I can't announce to the committee that I intend to have a plan later. That won't make them any less anxious. I have to say that I have a plan now."

I leaned my head on his shoulder and tried not to get too distracted over my delight that he had time to just sit and hold me. "Does the plan have to work?"

"Does it have to work?" Dachahl repeated. "What good is a plan that doesn't work?"

"Maybe it does something different than it says it does."

"This is an idea so clever that it fills me with a fog of admiration."

"This means you don't understand it?"

He laughed. "Yes, that is what this means."

"You're trying to find a way to preserve your scholar class after introducing universal public education, so that your scholars won't panic and revolt."

"Yes?"

"But I don't think it's possible to preserve the scholar class. So what you really need is a plan that keeps your scholars from panicking by pretending to preserve the scholar class."

"But we must preserve them!"

"Why?"

"These are our people, Batiya, we can't let them be destroyed!"

"They aren't going to be destroyed, they're going to be transformed into something new. They're going to adapt to a new way of doing things. It might not even hurt much. You saw how quickly my mother adapted to having a telephone in her house."

"What will they turn into?"

"How would I know?" I tried to think of something that would be considered not as 'low' as being a craftsman. "Managers? Financiers?"

"Financiers?"

"They buy and sell things—and lend money."

"Shopkeepers, merchants and money-lenders? But these are lower than craftsmen!"

I sat up and turned around so I could look at him. "Merchants are lower than craftsmen?"

"Naturally. They don't make anything. They just move things that other people made around."

"Dachahl, who do you think the burgies are?"

"Landowners," he replied promptly.

I shook my head. "Most of them do own some land, but as a class, it's our royals who were the landowners."

"Not the warriors?"

"We threw warriors and landowners in the beater, and mixed them together. Landowners were expected to fight, and if you were good at fighting, you were given land. That was where our ruling class came from for centuries. But about a hundred years ago, the burgies kicked them out of their seats of power."

"And these conquerors were merchants?" He'd figured it out. "But they contribute nothing to society!"

I wasn't convinced that was true, but I didn't like the burgies enough to attend their harvestfest—I wasn't going to defend them. "They may be leeches, but they live like lords." Became lords, once the royals figured out how profitable selling titles could be. "If your scholars don't know where they came from, they might not mind joining their party. Don't say buyers and sellers, if those are bad words. Say mathematicians, and information specialists."

Dachahl thought about that for a long time. "I think you have given me something."

"I may have given you the means of doing our great-grandchildren out of a job," I warned him.

He didn't believe me. "Your lords may no longer have much power, but you still have kings."

He had dealt with the Xercali king, whose power hadn't eroded as fast as that of the Dostrovian monarchy, so it made sense he would think that. Especially if he didn't know that the Rachinians had thrown out their monarchy twice in the past two hundred years. Of course, they always seemed to accept them back again eventually, but still—there was no guarantee of labor in being royalty. But it wouldn't hurt my feelings if all my great-grandchildren went back to engineering, so I didn't argue, I just settled back against his chest. And tried to think how I should introduce the thing I had been wanting to discuss with him.

"I don't know how I'm going to show my true character to your father, Dachahl, when I stay here in my rooms all the time, and he's somewhere else pretending I don't exist."

"He doesn't pretend you don't exist," Dachahl protested. "He knew that you were at the exercise yards today. He told me so."

"Did he not like it?" I asked, a bit ashamed at how anxious I felt.

"I don't know why he would have any reaction at all. But he seemed pleased." Pleased? "And he has been telling everyone that you are the example of what his education program is supposed to accomplish."

What? I turned to Dachahl, wide-eyed. "He's been telling people I'm... an example?"

"This is what he has been saying," Dachahl confirmed.

"Because I'm an engineer?" I asked, bewildered.

Dachahl hesitated. "I... I think he does not know this. He asked me if you could write, and I told him you could even write Hadahnchi, and this was all he allowed me to say before he made his announcement."

"You would think he would want to know a little more about how educated I was, before he went around claiming me as an example," I told Dachahl.

Dachahl's arms tightened around me, and I could tell that he too found something not quite right about his father's behavior. "I think this is a political maneuver," he admitted. "It doesn't matter to him if you are really an example of anything. He chooses you to be seen as an example. He feels this is to his benefit somehow."

I couldn't see how making the southerner woman that everyone distrusted an example of the good that would come of your new education program helped anyone. But maybe I was wrong, and it would turn out well and Dachahl's father would be better pleased with me than he was now. And maybe he would be grateful for the advice I had given Dachahl about the education program too. That would be wonderful! Supporting the new schools didn't make me feel at all like I was trying to sell rigged tickets, because I really did think they were a good idea.

I sent Dachahl off the next day feeling much more hopeful, and he came back and spent a couple hours out in the exercise fields with me, right on schedule, and clearly happy to be there, and came back to me in the evening in a better mood than I'd seen him in for some time. But the following day he arrived at our rooms that evening late for dinner, and looking like he'd lost his whole harvest. Something had gone wrong, and whatever it was, he clearly didn't want to talk about it. So I talked of other things, and tried to make him laugh, and then finally just let him hang on to me.

The next day he left early in the morning, and didn't show up for my sword-fighting lesson. Telling myself that if something bad happened to Chunru the entire palace would know about it, I asked one of the officers there to watch me as I did my strike exercises, and correct me when I made mistakes.

He seemed only slightly less shocked than Chloys was.

"But, Princess, I thought you only came out here so Chunru would have an excuse to come out here too?" Chloys protested.

"And if I just turn around and go back when he doesn't show up, he will lose that excuse," I explained.

"But you don't need to... Shouldn't you be being more careful in your condition, when you can?"

She was speaking Hadahnchi and I hastily looked over at the man I had asked to tutor me to see if he had noticed what she had let slip, but he seemed more interested in what she had said about Chunru.

"You come here to get Chunru to come here?" he asked me.

"Because he places his father's wants and the good of the empire before his own health," I explained. "You will watch my strike exercises?"

"Yes, Princess."

Concentrating on the exercises was probably good for me, too. It kept me from worrying about what had prevented Dachahl from joining me. When I finally allowed my tutor to return to his own exercises and returned to my rooms, I discovered that having Chloys read to me was not nearly as effective. My mind wandered frequently. And when Chloys stopped reading in the middle of a sentence, it took me quite a long time to even notice, and even longer to wonder why. Then I turned around and saw Dachahl standing in the doorway, staring at me. He looked... strange. Almost as if he was in shock.

"Chunru?"

"My imperial father has informed me that I am to prepare a wedding celebration."

My heart stopped beating. "He's making you marry someone else?"

"For you and me."

There was a thrilled squeal. It was from Chloys. I couldn't even make a sound. I was much too stunned. Finally I heard my voice, sounding like it was from a far distant place. "He's going to legalize our marriage?"

"After the celebration."

"That's wonderful!" Chloys said.

Dachahl looked at her, frowned, and then looked back at me. "He said that I am responsible for all the wedding preparations, and so he is removing me from the education committee so that I will have time."

I should be as excited as Chloys, I thought, but somehow I couldn't be. I was too certain that something must be wrong. "How much does this change my situation? Will your father's first solution to my presence still be possible, afterward?" Would it be possible for Dachahl's father to order my assassination, even after he'd legalized our marriage?

Dachahl's grim look gave me the answer to that. "But this is an important first step," he assured me.

"And does the husband-to-be usually do all the wedding preparations, in Changali?"

"No."

What was Dachahl's father doing? Did he hope Dachahl would do everything wrong? No, that was just petty. And what was the point of being petty, when you were granting your beloved son the favor he desired above all else, but you thought might destroy him? This had to be about something else. "He wanted you off the education committee this badly?"

"This doesn't seem possible," he agreed. "But yesterday... Yesterday he looked at my plans to find a new role for the scholar class, and he said they were very well thought out. But although he left them inside the full report, he has been crossing out all mention of them in the announcements, summaries, and official declarations."

"So he means to follow your suggestions, but he doesn't want anyone to know about them?" That made no sense. "How can your plans for the scholar class help stop the panic, if nobody knows you have any?"

"This I do not know," Dachahl confessed. He looked bewildered and hurt. "But this is still my father's empire. You are my first duty now." Whatever underhanded sneaky thing his father was planning, he had chosen the one distraction that Dachahl could not possibly ignore.

"Do you even know how to plan a wedding?" What would happen to our 'important first step' if we did everything all wrong, and became the latest laugh at the pub?

"This cannot be more difficult than planning a military campaign or an education system?" he asked hopefully. But I could tell he had been worrying about that also.

"This will be the first imperial wedding in twenty years," Chloys said excitedly. Not only did I not share her enthusiasm, she'd also reminded me of something I didn't want to think about. If the 'Shan husband wearing a sword' would be talked about for fifty years in West Borstev, then the 'imperial heir marries southerner peasant' wouldn't just make history books, there would be entire books written about that alone. "Although Lady Rahi's wedding just a couple years ago was very splendid," Chloys added, smiling wistfully.

Dachahl looked like he'd just been handed an answer. "I know how to find someone who knows how to plan a wedding," he told me, grinning. And then he picked me up and twirled me around, while Chloys looked away, blushing.

And then Chunru went back to his father to demand that his sister be summoned, so that she could play official hostess to his now official wife-to-be. It wasn't really his sister he wanted, though. It was his aunt. The one who had married off her daughter Rahi so very beautifully a year and a half earlier.

The aunt hauled all four of her unmarried offspring to the imperial palace along with her niece. Two daughters about the same age as the Imperial Princess and myself, and two sons that were considerably younger. Dachahl wanted us to be introduced informally, so he had the staff send for us when their automobiles were first spotted, and then he and I met them as they stepped out.

The Princess Lulahn emerged from the vehicle first. She saw Dachahl waiting, and bowed, and said, "Chunru," and he bowed back, and said, "Sister." The emperor had been about ten times as enthusiastic to see his son. But if I thought Lulahn's response to her brother was flat, then her reaction to me was even more of a disappointment. She saw me, she froze, and then she turned away, as if just looking at me was too unpleasant to be tolerated. Dachahl frowned for a moment, and then was distracted by the enthusiasm of her cousins. They still acted like they were in a reception line: all getting out of the automobile in order of importance, and all making formal bows, but unlike his sister, they looked like they were glad to see him.

And when they bowed to me, they looked curious, not disgusted. The two girls cast slightly uncertain glances over at the imperial princess, but they did not turn away from me, they smiled, and they said all the proper polite things, and I felt my first trickling of hope that maybe someone in his family wouldn't hate me.

Dachahl showed his sister to her rooms first—they were the ones that were usually reserved for the Empress —and when she saw which rooms she would be in, she looked pleased for the first time. "Would you dine with my wife and myself this evening?" Dachahl asked her.

"I am weary from the long journey," she answered.

Dachahl bowed, and let the curtain fall over the doorway, and then continued to the suite that had been prepared for his aunt.

His aunt invited Dachahl and me in, and it was Dachahl who refused. "I am sad to say I have duties to attend to. But my wife and I would be delighted to dine with you and my cousins, if you are not too weary?"

"I'm sure none of us are so weary as that!" she said, looking over at her children, who chorused, "Our pleasure, Chunru."

"And after you have planted yourself comfortably, perhaps you would be kind enough to visit with my wife?"

"We will be there in an hour," she responded, smiling at me. "Is this to your liking?"

"Very much," I assured her.

So a short while later I was invaded by her family.

"Did Cousin Dachahl really get in a fight with Tartar pirates?" one of the two boys asked eagerly. Tartar was how most Hadahnchi speakers said Tertar.

"That, I'm sure, is just a wild–" their mother began.

"Yes," I said, wondering where they had got their information. I was sure that was a story that Dachahl wouldn't have been telling anyone but his father and the head of security, and I was certain I hadn't told anyone.

Everyone was looking at me wide-eyed.

"I think maybe she is unclear," one of the girls said in a half-whisper.

"My sons built this story out of clouds and dreams while they were traveling," their mother told me anxiously. "This is clear to you? Nobody really thinks this happened."

"This is clear. You heard that Dachahl and I were in an accident at sea, and your sons thought the only sea accident worthy of their magnificent cousin must involve pirates."

"But... you said 'Yes'!" the girl who thought I must be unclear protested.

"Yes," I repeated again, smiling.

While the women were trying to figure out if I really had meant that Dachahl had fought with pirates, the boys —who were already convinced of it—dove in with the next question. "Does Cousin Dachahl really have horrible scars?"

"This cannot be true," their mother declared. "You saw him yourself, and–"

"Yes," I said.

"If you must insist that the sky isn't blue, could you at least say it's green, and not orange?" their mother begged.

"But, Princess Prahnani, Chunru really does have scars," Chloys said in a hesitant little voice.

"Princess Pahtia, is Cousin Dachahl really teaching you to fight with swords?" Clearly the boys had insider information straight from the palace practice yards that their mother did not know about.

"My sons!" she exclaimed. "Wherever did you hear such foolish—"

"Yes."

All the ladies looked at me, and then they swiveled about to look at Chloys for confirmation. She ducked her head. "Chunru gives the Princess Pahtia sword-fighting lessons every day... out in the practice fields... where all the young officers are."

"Can we watch?"

For once Dachahl's girl cousins looked almost as eager as the boys. "This, you must ask Chunru," I told them. "I am the student, not the teacher. I must follow orders."

"Everyone always does what Chunru orders," one of the girls said sympathetically.

Chloys choked. Aunt Prahnani studied her very carefully, and then she turned and studied me. "Do you always do what my nephew tells you to do, Princess Pahtia?" she asked.

"No." The cousins all looked like they had swallowed frogs. "But I do everything he says when he's teaching me about swords," I assured them all.

Aunt Prahnani frowned. "And if he told you that the moon was shining with a silver bright light, would you tell him it was actually a teapot?"

"Why argue with him, if he's right?"

His aunt tilted her head to one side. "But don't you find that he's right a little too often?"

I laughed. "I'm right very often also."

Her eyebrows lifted. "This is so? Then when do you say the celebration of your wedding is to start?"

"I say that the entire wedding celebration will happen exactly the way you say," I told her.

She blinked. "As I say?"

"Naturally. When it is about swords, I do what Dachahl says, and when it is about wedding celebrations, I do what you say."

"Are you saying the entire celebration is mine to do?"

"Oh, no! The emperor said that it was for Dachahl to do. But Dachahl has never done a wedding, only military exercises, and I don't know what a Changali wedding is supposed to look like. You will tell us how to do this right?"

"I couldn't possibly leave an imperial wedding to just the two of you, could I?" she answered.

"We also will help with this," one of her daughters said eagerly. "Cousin Dachahl must know that we support him."

I think that they expected a little more eagerness from me. Not that I didn't do everything they asked—and even some things they didn't, I knew that this celebration was very important and I wanted to do it right—but it was pretty obvious I wasn't excited and thrilled to be the center of a huge carnival and sideshow. "This is the deepest moment of your life!" Nachi, the younger of the two girls, finally burst out. "Do you not think so?"

"The deepest moment in my life was when Dachahl said he wanted to marry me," I told her. "Now I am already married. This celebration isn't for me. This is for the lords and the ladies, and the people in Pai Lan Chung. And most of them aren't even happy about it." I would have liked to have thought that it was also for his father, and that his father was happy about it, but Dachahl and I had been becoming more and more convinced that this really was happening just because his father wanted to keep him away from the new education program. Whenever we weren't actually planning something, I could see the pain and frustration in my husband's eyes.

"You know this, that the city lords aren't celebrating?" her mother asked, sounding surprised.

I looked over at her and just barely managed to remember that a nod didn't mean yes around here. "How could I not know? Do you think Dachahl isn't paying attention to this?"

"And he tells you?" Everyone in the room was astonished to hear that, even Chloys.

"Only when he wants to ask my advice about it," I admitted.

That, apparently, was even more astonishing than that he talked to me. "Chunru asks you for advice?"

Their astonishment would have amused me more if I had actually been able to give him any advice. But the first set of decrees had already gone out, and not only did they not have anything hopeful to say for the scholars, they specifically stated that the goal of the education program was to make the farmers eligible for jobs as teachers, administrators, and architects. This bewildered me. If I had ever started to believe Dachahl when he told me how clever I was, his father had completely knocked it out of me. He had announced at a state dinner of some kind how pleased he was that Dachahl had followed his instructions to create stronger ties with the southern nations with such selflessness—implying that his son's marriage to me had been *his* idea. Dachahl had responded that fortunately his liver had been in perfect alignment with his father's desires. That meant that he had fallen in love with me—Changali people fall in love with their livers, it seems—hearts are for different emotions. And his father had responded by saying how honored he was to have a son whose allegiance to him could never be doubted.

But if he was so pleased about this marriage, and the supposed benefit it would have on north-south ties, why did he still make no effort to seek out his son's southern wife? He did seem quite pleased—the one time we had ended up in the same room together—to hear that I had spent the day visiting the practice yards with Dachahl's boy cousins, and choosing the material for my ceremonial *lahnpran* with his girl cousins. What there was in that to please him I had no idea. Was he happy that I had hardly seen Dachahl at all that day? If so his joy was misplaced. The day before Dachahl and I had spent the whole day together. He was supposed to be picking routes for the various processions—in the twenty-three years that had passed since the previous imperial wedding, the city had changed a little. He had a map with the routes from his uncle and aunt's wedding, and we were double-checking to make sure they would still work, and that there weren't better possibilities now. And while we were doing that, we had to stop and visit every temple along the most likely routes and evaluate the special traditions each had for invoking blessings that would ensure a long, happy, and fruitful marriage, to see which ones would be best suited to the official ceremony. So we chased each other around sacred trees, and splashed each other with water from sacred wells and springs, climbed hills, and rang gongs, and had the most fun we'd had since we were crossing the Osmark mountains alone on the way to Xercalis.

The actual celebration wasn't nearly as fun. I was dressed in clothing I could hardly walk in—six layers of fabric, and four or five feet of trailing hems, and instead of getting to go anywhere with Dachahl, I was carried around on a platform by a bunch of uniformed men. Even when the ceremonies involved Dachahl and I doing things together, I couldn't get anywhere near him, because his outfit had these huge metallic shoulder pieces that ended in four-inch spikes. His hems trailed nearly ten feet, and they'd taken away his boots and given him curly-toed slippers instead. On the plus side, he wasn't wearing a *tirah-fa*, but an actual sword; maybe that made up a little for the missing boots. I would have asked him, but anything I wanted to say to Dachahl was going to have to wait, because I wasn't going to be allowed to be alone with him again until the whole thing was over.

So we did the stair climbing, and the water flicking, and the tree circling all over again, only slow and dignified. And we stood on mounds and stages and monks with shaved heads prayed over us and burned candles. They hung prayer tokens made of precious woods, or metals, or jade, around my neck. I spent one night surrounded by laughing girls, two in 'baths' that were more like pools, three nights being prayed over, and one locked in a room full of flowers.

And then, finally, it was time for the Grand Procession, and Dachahl and I paraded down the biggest avenues in the city, with old men and women throwing flowers in front of us and what seemed like half the city following behind. I was riding on a horse. Which was exactly what Dachahl had made me promise not to do, but Aunt Prahnani had insisted. Apparently it was a tradition, and Dachahl couldn't explain why he didn't want me on a horse unless he told everyone about the baby, and the one thing Dachahl and his father seemed to agree on was that it wasn't a good time to announce that I was pregnant. He had done the best he could by making it a very small horse. Actually a tiny little pony—which had pleased Aunt Prahnani a lot, because that kind of pony was native to the part of Cholipardo that she was from. So the man holding the horse's lead probably weighed more than the horse did, but Dachahl still didn't like it. I could tell. The other thing that he didn't like was that I was wearing another one of those silly Ghaz Mien hats, covering all my hair and more than half my face.

We had just finished going around the Pek Char—
which is a statue of a crab, twenty feet high, which
somebody for some reason decided to build right in the
middle of the road—when I heard the familiar crack of a
gun going off. The next thing I knew I was lying on the
ground, and my chest hurt, and my back end hurt. And
every other one of my working parts was vibrating. And I
couldn't breathe.

I heard Dachahl bellow, and the pony must have very
wisely got out of his way, for the next thing I knew he was
kneeling beside me and checking me over for bullet holes.

And I still couldn't breathe.

Dachahl kept calling my name, but I couldn't answer
because I couldn't breathe. He was starting to get all dark
and fuzzy at the edges, when I felt the blade of his sword
slip along my side, and then my sash fell away and
suddenly I was gasping for air, which hurt. It hurt like
nails being driven into my chest. But it was wonderful all
the same, and Dachahl put his arms around me, and
helped me sit up, which was even more pain while he
was doing it, but afterward it seemed to help.

But the excitement wasn't over. There was another
gunshot, and a line of red appeared on Dachahl's cheek,
and the side of my face was peppered with tiny stings.
Dachahl grabbed me and ran. Another bullet caught at
one of my long sleeves, and then we were in the shelter of
the crab's claws, and Dachahl was checking me for bullet
holes, yet again.

"I'm fine," I gasped.

At first he didn't seem to believe me, but when he
could find no blood, his attention turned to the sniper. He
sprinted back into the street, yelling for the guards.

Why couldn't he stay under cover with me?

I sat up a little, ignoring the pain that slammed through my chest, and another bullet ripped past me. "Batiya, stay down!"

I guess that explained why he couldn't stay with me. The metal claws only provided enough protection for one. And the sniper seemed to be aiming for me, anyway.

I ducked down, and then concentrated on breathing. Why did such a simple thing hurt so much? I put my hands over the center of the pain, and my fingers encountered the tangle of prayer tokens. The bullet intended for me had hit the tokens, and got no further? So prayers really do protect you from evil—my mother would be delighted. But I knew I must have an amazing bruise.

There were shouts and the pounding of feet, and a shot and more shouts. And then there was silence, except for the sound of someone crying.

I began collecting my hems—gathering them into my hands, so I could move if I needed to. Dachahl returned first, lifting me to my feet. He had guards with him, but they kept at a wary distance, mindful of his deadly shoulder pieces.

"Was anyone hurt?" I asked him.

"He killed himself before we could get to him."

There were more guards approaching from back down the parade route. The emperor's guards. And walking in the midst of them, the emperor himself. He must have abandoned his gold-roofed palanquin as being insufficiently safe. Dachahl held me to his chest and turned both of us around, so that he could face his father without skewering me with his shoulder spikes. He did not bow.

"Lord of the Four Kingdoms," he greeted his father.

"Chunru, report," the emperor replied.

"A single rifleman awaited the parade. His target was the Princess Pahtia Dachahlra. His first bullet was aimed at the heart, and was accurate."

"And accurate?" The emperor's eyes widened as he looked at me.

"I'm hard to kill," I murmured.

"The shots that followed were less accurate." At least the friction of the bullet had seared the line across his cheek, so he wasn't bleeding all over, but he was going to have yet another scar, and this one he wouldn't be able to hide simply by keeping his shirt on.

"The assassin was isolated and cut off by the palace guards assigned to me and the princess," my husband continued. "But he shot himself in the head before we could reach him."

Shot himself in the head with a rifle? That must have been messy. I couldn't resist taking a peek at Dachahl's trailing hems, but all I could see was a little dirt. But how had he managed to move so fast with all that material trailing behind him? I discovered the answer when he leaned over sideways, holding me carefully close, and grabbed his *choliang* and then swept his arm around in a couple circles, collecting the excess material about his arm. The expertise of experience, I thought, wishing I could manage my own clothing half as well.

"Do I have the emperor's permission to depart?" Dachahl asked.

That was when I realized that he was absolutely furiously angry with his father. He thought his father had arranged for the assassin.

I looked at the emperor, and realized that he was angry too. I wasn't quite certain what he was angry about, though. Because Dachahl suspected him?

"Will someone be kind and bring my horse?" I said as calmly and clearly as I could. "I wish to continue, but I cannot walk so far."

"No," Dachahl said immediately. "No horse."

The emperor was staring at me again. "You wish to continue the celebration?"

"Naturally. I have much to celebrate."

Dachahl and his father locked gazes. "You will not wish to put her at such risk," the emperor told him.

That was true, and his words made Dachahl freeze. But I wanted everything over and done with. "If you don't trust me to stay on my horse, Chunru, perhaps a litter could be summoned."

"Your palanquin," Dachahl suggested to his father, his eyes narrowed.

"Perhaps you do not understand that there may be more assassins waiting for you," the emperor said to me.

"If there are men brave enough to carry me, I will continue forward," I told him.

Dachahl smiled. "Are your bearers too frightened to continue? Because if they are, I think perhaps some of the palace guards might be willing–"

"Naturally, my bearers are willing to carry the princess."

"Thank you, you are kind," I told him. "Now I only need my hat..."

"Your... hat?"

I looked around, and seeing it lying in the road over by where I had fallen from the pony, I turned to my guards' commander, and said, "Will you be kind and get me my hat?"

He looked over at Dachahl.

"It's damaged," Dachahl told me.

"It prevents anyone from getting a clear shot at my head," I replied in Dostrovian.

"Get it!" he ordered. The guard dashed over and scooped it up, and presented it to Dachahl who settled it on my head. "This, I never thought I would be glad to see you wearing," he muttered in Dostrovian.

The palanquin was brought forward, and Dachahl helped me into it, and then he stepped away, ordering the bearers to carry it low. Then the emperor walked ahead with his guards, and Dachahl followed with his guards, and then there was me with my carriers holding the palanquin's handles down by their thighs, so that I couldn't see anything much, and nobody could see me very well either. That took care of the rest of the parade.

The parade ended at one of the many permanent outdoor stages that I had been told could be found all over Changali. They had two layers, each about two feet high, which meant that when the emperor did his official blessing of the happy couple, all three of us would be four feet off the ground, and fairly easy targets if there was another sniper somewhere. So there was another delay while workmen hastily assembled a screen around three sides, greatly reducing the number of people who could see the event, but the crowd wasn't nearly as large as had been expected either, by this point. The guards combed the crowd, and the rest of the ceremony went off without any further incident. The emperor pronounced his blessing on the happy couple without any sign that he had been hoping the happy couple wouldn't make it that far, and Dachahl responded with the traditional replies without any sign that he considered his father a would-be kin-slayer.

There was now only one more event to get through, a feast at the palace—where Dachahl's sister would welcome me into the household, and everyone would eat, drink, and be merry. Dachahl and I were late. We had to make an unscheduled clothing change. I couldn't be sad, though, because Dachahl lost his shoulder pieces and got his boots back. Besides, it gave me no time to worry about how the Imperial Princess Lulahn would manage to welcome me into the household when she refused to admit that I existed. She did it by saying all the right words, but never looking in my direction. I don't think anyone noticed. Everyone had heard about the shooting by then, and were too busy discussing it, and exclaiming over the bullet score across Dachahl's cheek, to have any attention whatsoever to spare for his sister.

I rather suspected that she would be willing to assassinate me herself because of that.

I had a collection of tiny cuts and bruises on my cheek, but Chloys had covered them up with makeup while my maid Falahni was wrapping my chest up tightly according to my directions. When they had finished re-dressing me, it was impossible to tell that anything had happened to me at all unless you looked very closely, and no Chang ever looked that closely at my cheeks anyway.

If they weren't staring at my eyes, they were staring at my hair.

But Dachahl knew that my serene and unblemished appearance was an illusion, and that I was actually badly damaged and in severe pain. He did everything in his power to hurry the feast along, refusing to linger over introductions, and insisting that the courses were run together instead of leaving time between for chatting. A number of people made joking comments that you'd expect that kind of haste from a bridegroom, not a husband. I wished that was why Dachahl was rushing. He just smiled, and admitted that husband or no, he was as eager as a bridegroom and intended to act like one. Which meant, apparently, that he was planning on us leaving the feast early, letting everyone else linger on and chat without us.

As soon as we got into the hallway, he said, "I'll carry you."

"It hurts less to walk," I assured him. But now that nobody was watching I hung on to his arm, and winced at every breath. Chloys had a doctor waiting for us in our rooms. It was the same one as before, so she had to translate—I still hadn't managed to learn more than a few words of Stoi Kat.

The doctor checked the baby first, and seemed quite satisfied that it had not been harmed. He couldn't say as much for me. As I had deduced, a bullet had been found embedded in one of the prayer tokens I had been wearing around my neck. And I had the oddest-shaped bruise I'd ever seen, right in the middle of my chest, and the ribs beneath had been cracked. He took off the chest wrappings that Falahni had put on me, and ordered me not to have them replaced. I wasn't to wear any tight sashes either, he told me. I needed to breathe as deeply as I could as often as I could, even if it hurt. Otherwise, my lungs would become sick, and that would be a very bad situation for a woman who was with child.

Aunt Prahnani arrived in the middle of my examination, and didn't blink at either the sight of my bruises, or the information that I was expecting a baby in about four and a half months.

"Are you going to have an official announcement, once the marriage has been legalized?" she asked.

"The emperor and I have not yet decided when the announcement will be made," Dachahl replied. I noticed that he did not call him father, or even 'my imperial father', and I think his aunt noticed too. But she didn't say anything, she just helped Chloys and Falahni get me dressed again.

The doctor said that he would bring me medicine I could take for the pain, but that I needed to be careful, because too much of the medicine would be bad for the baby. Dachahl looked horrified, and the two of them had a conversation that nobody bothered to translate for me, but which I was sure involved Dachahl trying to find out just how much medicine would be a safe amount, and the doctor refusing to commit to an answer. When the doctor left, Dachahl came over and sat down next to me, and was clearly about to say something when a voice on the other side of the door curtain announced the emperor.

City of
Pai Lan Chung

1) 1st night - prayers at Holy Waters Temple
2) Tour of the Five Holy Springs
3) Through High Gate and down 100 steps
4) 2nd night - Maiden's Watch
5) Shrine on hill
6) Avenue of ancient pines
7) 3rd night - bathing pool
8) Shrine of fifteen gongs
9) Well of the swallow
10) Sacred chesnut tree
11) Hill haunted by suicide lover
12) Shrine of the spirit duck
13) Sacred pool and 3 Plum Sisters
14) Appeasing the spirit dragons
15) 4th night - prayers at
        Path of Heaven Temple
16) Gathering wildflowers
17) Requesting the sea cows
        blessing
18) Climbing sacred henon rock
19) 5th night - houses of the dead
20) Shrine of twisted thorns
21) Shrine of mouse mother
22) 6th night - Flower
        Pavilion

23) Launching toy flower boats
24) Shrine of Fire hills
25) Walking path of posts
26) 7th night - bathing pool
27) Peh Chan - Crab statue
28) Stage
29) Feast at Imperial Palace

Map of Pai Lan Chung

Chapter Four

I Begin Going to Festivals

Dachahl barely had time to jump to his feet before the curtain was pulled to the side, and his father walked in. As soon as he entered, he dismissed everyone except for Dachahl and me. We were going to have the honor of another private audience. When everyone had left, he announced, "We will be seated."

I was already sitting—it seemed to be the position that made breathing the easiest—and I had no intention of moving at all for as long as I could manage it. Dachahl rather pointedly set two cushion seats facing each other, and then waited for his father to take the first before kneeling on the other.

There was a long silence.

Then the emperor spoke. "Her injuries, how are they?"

"She has severe bruising and cracked ribs," my husband replied.

"She completed the blessing ceremony and sat at the feast with cracked ribs?"

"Yes."

"But I didn't manage to actually eat anything," I confessed. Neither of them was listening.

There was another long tense silence, and then the emperor said, "Her child?"

"Your grandchild remains unharmed." The words, bit out from behind clenched teeth, were an accusation. "This disappoints you?"

"What kind of a man do you think I am?" his father demanded.

"The kind who, when I brought home the greatest treasure I could find, threatened to destroy it," Dachahl answered. "How can I ever trust you again?"

"She said she would leave you, Dachahl!"

"The Dostrovians believe that living with pain is more courageous than dying," I explained. "And I didn't say I would leave him, I said I'd leave here."

"Stop talking, Batiya," Dachahl ordered.

About then the doctor returned, and announced himself outside the curtain.

"I thought he had already seen her," the emperor said.

Dachahl explained about the painkillers.

"She has had nothing for her pain, yet?"

"This I will not be drinking now, either," I announced. "You may send him away."

Instead Dachahl called for him to come in, and he and his father waited silently while the doctor left his packages on the table, and then retreated.

"Why will you not take this?" the emperor demanded of me, once the doctor had left.

"Because it might hurt Dachahl's child," I replied.

He stared at me for a while and then asked, "Are you from a warrior family?"

"Craftsmen."

"Warriors and scholars," Dachahl corrected. I thought it would be useless to claim that my brothers were not warriors, and knew that engineering was taught in the Changali schools as part of the same program that turned out their architects, so I let the correction stand. "Here," Dachahl told his father, rising to his feet and taking the Tilardu treasure box from a side table. "A gift from my wife. I trust it will bring you joy." He did not sit down again. He just stood there holding out the box, until finally the emperor stood also.

"I know where you have aimed your thoughts," he told his son, "but I did not order this thing done. I did not need to. No man wants to be ruled by a stranger. If this woman you treasure is suffering, it is because of what you did when you claimed her as wife."

Dachahl looked like he had been kicked by a horse, but he continued to hold out the treasure box, insistently, and after a moment of slit-eyed glaring, his father took the box without actually looking at it, and swept out of the room.

"Do you really think he ordered me killed after he said he wouldn't?" I asked as soon as he was gone.

"No," Dachahl replied, sinking down next to me. He looked miserable. "You heard what he said. He didn't need to order your death. I am the one who has put your life in danger."

That was a very silly way of looking at it. He had made sure there were guards all around me, had carried me to cover when I was hurt, and had moved against the threat as soon as he could. Someone else had chosen to aim a gun at my heart and pull the trigger. "I thought I just needed your father's approval and that would be good enough, but it isn't, is it? Somehow I have to convince your whole empire to like me."

Dachahl looked, if possible, even more miserable. And possibly a little bit guilty. He must have known that convincing his father was barely half of what we faced, if that—and probably the easy half too. He just hadn't mentioned it to me, because he didn't want me to worry. And maybe he'd been right. If there was nothing I could do about it anyway, maybe I was better off not knowing that it needed to happen.

"Would you... like to go home?" he asked.

"Don't be foolish," I told him. "I wasn't expecting your people to be delighted with me. And naturally it will be many years before they realize that I am not leading you toward some horrible future, and we'll have to be extra careful about my safety until then. But as long as you aren't making any oaths to kill yourself in order to stop your father from–"

"*Something* needs to be done to stop him."

"Stop him from what? You said he didn't order–"

"But he is doing everything he can to make you less popular, Batiya. Remember I told you that he was making it sound as if my marriage to you was a part of his plans to bring southern 'progress' to Changali? This seems as if he is supporting us, but it actually makes our marriage hated by both the future-fearing scholars, and those who believe in the Cholipardo curse."

The curse, of course! That was the Cholipardo connection that I had missed earlier. Dachahl belonged to the royal line that wasn't supposed to marry for political advantage. No wonder it had taken this long for anyone to ask about my family. My family didn't matter.

Everyone had been expecting Dachahl to marry a nobody from the moment he was born.

"And he has been deliberately provoking the scholars," Dachahl went on, heedless of my musings. "Why would he do that, if he wasn't trying to get rid of you?"

That didn't sound right. "Dachahl, deliberately provoking the scholar class—that's a very dangerous thing to do. This *might* get me killed, but more likely this will cause other sorts of problems. I don't think he'd do that just to get rid of me."

"But this is what he is doing, Batiya. This cannot be read otherwise. He took me off the education committee, and he changed all the decrees. Then there was our marriage celebration. This was not needed. All that it takes to make our marriage legal is—"

"But it's better for us to have had the celebration," I protested.

"Your every breath is agony! This is better for us?"

"Yes. My ribs will heal, and now your people have seen the celebration, and have seen your father acknowledge our marriage. You knew this was important to us, that's why you agreed to do it. And it is also important for us, and for the entire empire, that you do not fight with your father. So tomorrow you will find something you can regret—being disrespectful, perhaps—and you will go to him, and–"

"No, Batiya, I wo–"

"This will make me feel safer," I insisted. "This may be the only thing you can do that will make me feel safer."

I watched as he fought with his emotions for a bit, but he finally bowed his head. "Then this I will do."

"Thank you. And then once you have fixed that bridge, maybe you can talk to your father about what is happening with the education program also?"

"Yes, I will do this." He watched me for a while, and then burst out with, "Is there nothing I can do for you now?"

"I hurt more when I lie down," I admitted. "Can you hold me so I can sleep while sitting up?"

He wrapped his arms around me, and with the sound of his heartbeat to comfort me, I managed to sleep for much of the night. In the very, very early hours of the morning, I unwound Dachahl's arms, lowered him carefully to the mattress, pulled a blanket over him, and wished that our rooms had windows.

Langso and Falahni slid silently into the room a couple of hours later, and while Langso adjusted Dachahl into a less awkward position, Falahni did her best to make me comfortable. I asked her for something to eat, but what I really wanted was something to do. I ended up writing my first really long letter home. I described the palace, and Aunt Prahnani, and the wedding celebration. But all I said about the attempted assassination was that there had been a little accident, and that I hadn't been seriously hurt, but that Chunru would probably make me 'lay up' for forever anyway, because I was collecting baby booties, and he'd turned all hen over it.

"Put that pen down." Dachahl was awake.

I put the pen down, but only because I'd finished.

"I can write for you," he said.

"So can Chloys," I told him. "But what am *I* supposed to do? Stare at the wall until my eyes cross?"

"Ah..."

Exactly. "Eat your dawn-meal, talk to your father, and then go ride a horse or something. By the time you get back, I promise I will have thought of something that you can do for me."

"Batiya!" he protested.

I guess I was being cross. I hurt. "I regret," I said penitently.

"No. Don't... You... I..." The poor man, he was completely baffled.

"Your problem is that you spent most of the night being a chair," I told him. "Eat something. This will help you feel like a person again."

"Did you eat?" he asked as he sat at the table and picked up his sticks.

"I probably had more than I should." I waited until he had food in his mouth, and then I said, "I like having you hold me, but I don't like the idea of us taking turns sleeping. And I'm worried about how your people will react to me being sick for six weeks."

He started. "This I did not tell you."

"I know how long it takes to heal cracked ribs," I told him. "What I don't know is what people will say."

He frowned. "I don't know either."

"Ask your father when you talk to him."

Dachahl didn't look at all happy with that idea, but before he could tell me he wouldn't do it, his Aunt Prahnani arrived with her daughters and Princess Lulahn.

As usual, Dachahl's sister ignored me. "Uncle Dolang says that sleeping late is a sign of a weak and decadent ruler," she told Dachahl.

Dachahl stood up. "Our imperial father agrees," he said. "Batiya, I'll return soon."

"He's going to talk to his father?" Aunt Prahnani asked. "But he visited the two of you just last night?"

"Dachahl didn't feel like talking last night."

"We brought you some gifts," Cousin Sahni announced.

Princess Lulahn turned toward the door. "I think I will visit the gardens now."

"Yes, you do that," her aunt told her, with a bit of an edge to her voice.

"Would you like to accompany me?" the princess asked her cousins. They looked nervously over at their mother.

"Would that be acceptable, Mama?"

"You're asking me? A horse-breeder's daughter?" their mother replied. "What would I know about what's acceptable and what isn't? You two are ladies. Do you think it's acceptable?"

Her daughters looked at the floor. Princess Lulahn walked away.

"We brought all our favorite books," Cousin Nachi said, as soon as the princess was gone. "We can read them aloud to you, if you'd like. Mother says that will help you with your..." She broke off, as if realizing that she was about to say something impolite.

"This will help me learn to speak better," I finished for her, seeing no reason to call a crow a rooster. "Thank you. What are they about?"

"Sahni brought books with tragic lovers and everybody dying, but I like our own Cholipardo stories better, where all the nice people live, get married, and have five sons and twenty-five grandsons, plus daughters. And I brought some poetry too, but Mama says you don't know any Stoi Kat, yet, so I guess I'll have to take those back."

"Dachahl sang me a song in Stoi Kat, once," I remembered.

"He did?" Both of the girls looked at me with slack-jawed astonishment. "He sings?"

"Why wouldn't he sing if he felt like it?" their mother asked.

"He isn't a poet," Sahni answered at the same time as Nachi said, "But he likes swords and guns and things."

He did like swords and guns, but he had also told me that my eyes were like rain.

"Young people want everything under heaven to arrive in a nicely packed basket," Aunt Prahnani said. "Wisdom is learning that nothing grows in a basket. It is in a basket only because someone put it there."

Sahni frowned. "You mustn't speak in proverbs, mother. Pahtia won't understand you."

"She's saying that Dachahl can love swords and be a poet both at the same time," I interpreted.

"I thought that was a proverb about having to work for what you get," Nachi objected.

"Wisdom isn't knowing what a thing means, it is knowing how to find meaning in it," her mother scolded. "Dachahl can't afford to only like guns and swords—he has to rule an empire one day. He must be like a flower with many petals."

Dachahl was supposed to be like a flower? I laughed, and then regretted it, and the girls crowded around me in concern as I groaned.

"Are you hurt very much, Pahtia?"

"I'm fine," I told them. "I just shouldn't laugh." Or cough. Or cry, get the hiccups, lie down, or move very much.

"Why did you laugh?"

"In Dostrovia, men are only compared to flowers after they're dead."

They all looked at me as if I had said something truly strange.

"Why don't you read me something," I suggested.

Sahni started one of her stories where everyone dies, because Nachi thought it wouldn't make me laugh. I wasn't so sure. Everything was compared to everything. Comparing warrior princes to flowers was nothing to it. Men were like letters, shoes, cattle, and geographic features, and women were like pigs—it was a compliment!—types of wood, cooking implements... I did learn, finally, what the word *hardoluno*, which the emperor had used to describe Dachahl that first day, meant. It meant having high ideals, like honor and courage and honesty and all that, and doing your best to live up to them. That sounded a lot like Dachahl, but it also sounded like a good thing, and I hadn't thought that the emperor had meant it as a compliment.

Dachahl returned looking even more strained than when he left. He bowed to his Aunt Prahnani. "My imperial father has asked me to discuss certain matters with my wife," he told her. "Have you said anything to your daughters about what you learned here last night?"

"I don't tell my secrets to the willows," Aunt Prahnani replied, "I wouldn't tell yours to the carter's boy." She looked over at her daughters. "Why don't you go find your cousin Lulahn?" she suggested.

I was a bit surprised at how little they seemed to mind being sent away.

Dachahl was quiet for a little while after they left, and then he took a deep breath and said, "Batiya, he said he planned to make an announcement about the baby in a few weeks, but admits that if people know you carry my child, there will probably be even more attempts to assassinate you."

"You shouldn't wait too much before you make the announcement," his aunt told us. "If you have the baby without warning, that would be... unfortunate."

"But we can wait for a moon or two? Give her ribs time to heal?" Dachahl asked anxiously.

"This is probably best," she agreed.

"He also said that if people know that she was hurt, it will be more likely that people will attack her, but if she appears to be unharmed, they will be less likely to try to attack her."

"And if you hide her away, people will say there is something wrong with her," Aunt Prahnani warned.

I couldn't be hurt, I couldn't be hid, I couldn't be pregnant, and I couldn't produce a child without warning. No wonder Dachahl looked like he'd sat down on an anthill.

"You can't hide me away in the palace, but could I go somewhere else for a while?"

"I want to take you to Cholipardo," Dachahl told me. "But this is not a journey you can make right now."

"You can take her to visit the Sea House," his aunt suggested. "Say that you need a rest after all the celebrations. Everyone knows that you aren't a prince who delights in ceremony. They would believe this of you."

I looked over at my husband. "Aren't you supposed to be working on the education program?"

"You are more important."

More important to him, I could believe. But he was a prince, he had an empire to worry about. "Chunru–" I began, but he interrupted me.

"This is truth. Not just for me, but for the good of the empire. Seeing that you are accepted by my people has now become my most important duty. My father may not have meant for this to happen, but he has seen it done." I couldn't grab how the emperor had done any such thing. "When he insisted on making you the symbol of his new education program," Dachahl explained. "This makes it very difficult for anyone to accept the program without accepting you. But the reverse is also true. Once they have accepted you, it will become much easier for them to accept the program. So I must do what is best for you now."

I wasn't quite certain his reasoning was sound, but I really didn't like the thought of being sent away to recover without him. "Then this is what we will do," I agreed. "I will go visit this Sea House alone with my husband, after spending a few more days here showing everyone that I am not hurt."

"But you are hurt," Dachahl protested.

"Yes, I was hurt a little when I fell off my horse," I agreed. "This is very sad. I will have to miss my sword-fighting lessons. Perhaps the officers would be kind, and fight each other to entertain me? And my husband also?"

Dachahl smiled. "Yes."

"And tomorrow I should go outside the palace somewhere."

Dachahl frowned. "No."

"Yes," I insisted. "A place I can go, where it will be difficult to shoot at me, must exist." I turned to Aunt Prahnani. "If I had not been attacked, where might you have taken me outside the palace, during the next few days?"

"The chrysanthemum festival will start in the West Gate Market the day after tomorrow."

"Absolutely not," Dachahl said.

"The empress's tomb?"

Dachahl considered that one for a much longer time. "No."

"She probably should visit the Holy Grove and pray for a son."

"Yes," Dachahl agreed at last. "This can be done. The trees will make it hard to shoot you from a distance, and the priests will not mind clearing the grove for an hour."

"Good. And then I can pretend to spend the day after that packing," I told him. "Then hopefully we can stay away at least until I can sleep lying down again, without anyone thinking anything except that we want to be alone together. This will work?"

Aunt Prahnani sighed. "I think this is the best we can do."

Dachahl got to his feet. "I'll arrange for your afternoon entertainment, and then I have some people to talk to. You don't need me?"

"I need you to do what needs doing," I told him. "Your aunt and cousins were kind and brought me things to read."

But I didn't end up reading anything because the emperor arrived at the door so soon after Dachahl left that it was obvious that he had been waiting for him to go. Aunt Prahnani bowed down over her knees when she saw who entered, but I didn't dare try.

"You sent him to me," the emperor said.

I was so startled that it took me a moment to grab his meaning. Dachahl. I had sent him. I didn't answer.

"He would not have come of his own will. Not to express regret or to ask advice of the man that he said such words to last night."

"He is not a man who says that his mistakes are not mistakes," I protested.

"He is still not certain that it is a mistake," the emperor retorted.

"Can we be glad that he is no longer certain that it wasn't one?" I asked.

"Should I leave?" Aunt Prahnani asked plaintively.

"This is not necessary," I told her. "Dachahl thinks that his father is deliberately trying to put me in danger's path. I think that the emperor is aiming at some political goal of his own, and putting me in danger's path is just something that also happens. But even if someone could convince Dachahl that my guess is the right one, I do not think Dachahl will feel the political goal is worth this much danger to me."

The emperor's eyes narrowed. "Do you know what this goal is?"

"I know that you did not try to explain it to your son."

The emperor did not seem to have a reply to that. "This is not what I wished to speak to you about. Last night my son gave me a gift saying that it was from his wife. I wish to know how an heirloom of my own house could be a gift to me from my son's foreign wife."

I realized that he must be talking about the Tilardu treasure box. "Did you open it?"

"Yes. I wondered if the gift he spoke of was inside the box."

"If you opened it, how could you not know the nature of the gift?" I asked him. "Did you think that a mechanism that has been broken for years, suddenly fixes itself?"

"You are saying you fixed it?"

"Naturally. My family works with machinery. Although, until Dachahl gave me the treasure box, I had never worked on something so small before."

"He should not have let you touch it," the emperor cried. "You might have damaged it."

"It already did not move. What further harm could I have done? Any change would have to be an improvement."

"It is a masterwork, an imperial treasure!"

"You don't have to tell me how wonderful it is," I assured him. "I probably am much better aware of that than you are. I understand exactly what it is—I'm the one who took it apart and put it back together."

His face turned a very odd color. "You say... how dare you say you understand the works of Tilardu!" He was shaking with anger. "Do you claim to be able to make such wo–"

"Naturally not!"

That made him stop mid-word, with his mouth hanging open.

"To make something like this out of nothing, is a thing I could never do. I have worked all my life with machines but I am a fixer, not a maker, and even if I was... I have never seen anything so amazingly intricate and yet so tiny. But I can see what is there, reason out what it does, fix the parts that are damaged, and make it work again. This is a simple thing to do. You probably have many clockmakers who can do the same."

"But a Tilardu mechanism has over a thousand parts!"

"Less than two hundred," I corrected. That seemed to make him even angrier. "How could I take it apart and put it back together and not know this?" I asked him. "I think the thousand pieces number must be for the great clock Dachahl told me about." I'd like to see that. "But it doesn't matter how many pieces there are."

"No?"

"No." At least, it didn't matter as long as you were very, very careful about noting down where each piece came from as you took it off, and your younger brothers didn't come in and move the pieces around when you weren't looking.

"This can be tested," he told me, and then he turned and walked out.

Aunt Prahnani turned her wide-eyed gaze toward me, and raised one eyebrow. "Are you making him angry on purpose?"

"I think," I said wearily, "that the only thing I could do that would make him happy would be to quietly die of something that Dachahl can't possibly blame him for. His daughter seems to feel the same way."

"You just have to convince him that you are doing Dachahl more good than harm," she told me. I knew that, the question was how. At this point, I wasn't even sure I was doing Dachahl more good than harm. Dachahl seemed to think so, though, and I wanted it to be true too badly to not take his word for it.

"I don't think there is anything you can do about Lulahn," Aunt Prahnani added sadly. "But, can you really fix Tilardu clockwork?"

"Anyone could!" I told her impatiently. And then I corrected myself. "Anyone who fixes clockwork, can fix Tilardu clockwork."

Langso came in about then with a message from Dachahl saying that the officers would expect me after lunch, and Falahni came in with him and asked if I was ready to bathe, and Aunt Prahnani excused herself to go 'see what her girls were doing'.

Chloys arrived about the same time as lunch, and I was about to ask her to arrange delivery of my letter when I realized that it had disappeared. For a moment I panicked that someone might read it and find out I was pregnant—and then I realized how silly that was. Dachahl must have taken it. He was the only one besides Chloys who would see more than strange squiggles.

So instead of having Chloys run errands, I asked her to accompany me to the practice yards after lunch.

We arrived, Chloys placed a bit of carpet on the grass for me, and I gritted my teeth and knelt, hoping that it would be a very long time before I had to move again. Dachahl arrived a little bit later and I asked him about my letter. "I had it sent to the docks for you," he told me.

"This was not what you wanted? It can be brought back. I do not think the ship has left yet."

"That was what I wanted," I told him. "Thank you."

"Now you give me the kiss of courage, to inspire me," he told me.

"I've seen you fight. You don't need to be inspired, you need to be reminded not to hurt people by accident."

He laughed, but he still demanded the salute. Fortunately, he did all the bending necessary to get his forehead to my lips. And it was also lucky that he was with me, for the next thing I knew his cousins and sister had arrived, and only Dachahl's quick grab kept the youngest from slamming into me.

Dachahl glared at the poor boy, who went from excited to cowering in half a heartbeat. "Pahtia is my wife," he said from between clenched teeth. "No other man is allowed to touch her. Not even my cousin. Do you understand?"

"Yes, Chunru!" he replied, totally terrorized. But when Dachahl handed me a large handful of green ribbons to be given to the winners and went to join the officers, he recovered enough to turn proudly to his brother and say, "Chunru says I can't touch Pahtia, because I am a *man*."

"If you're a man, then I'm really a man," his older brother told him. "I can't even get *close* to Pahtia."

I don't know why Naditte's friend Stolya keeps complaining about how jealous her husband is. I found it useful. And even when it wasn't useful it was still flattering. But maybe when Stolya said 'jealous', she meant 'He doesn't like it when I flirt with Vanitri'. No man who wasn't completely witless would consider flirting with my brother Vanitri a harmless pastime. Vanitri didn't flirt—he only hunted.

In my honor, they had put together an entire tournament with less than three hours' notice. I really did feel honored. I know that if Chunru said 'you will put on a tournament for my wife' they had no choice, but it seemed to me that they weren't unwilling subordinates, but enthusiastic participants. And when they came to collect their ribbons after the individual matches, there didn't seem to be a single one of them who was glaring a hostile glare, or was reluctant to take a prize from the hand of a southerner.

Nobody told me what the rules were, and nobody explained what I was supposed to do when I handed out the ribbons, so I didn't do anything much. I just said a few admiring words about their swordplay—easy enough when they had each just won a match—and held out the ribbon. Each winner dropped to one knee, and took the ribbon with both hands, and then carried it over to a friend who would tie it around his arm.

I worried that I was supposed to be tying the ribbons myself, right up until Dachahl's first match. He approached me like all the others, and then requested the honor of having me tie it on, and then almost sat in my lap getting close enough that I could reach without bending forward. If there was anyone there who thought that I ought to do the ribbon tying on everyone, they wouldn't have dared to suggested it after that display. But I thought that it might have shown our hidden numbers as far as concealing my injuries was concerned.

It wasn't until I recognized one of the ribbon recipients as the guard commander who had fetched me my hat during the Grand Procession that I realized that the participants in the tournament already knew I was hurt—that I had actually been hit by a bullet, and that I hadn't just slid off the back of a startled pony. This wasn't a show I was putting on for them. This was a show we were putting on together for the growing crowd of watchers.

And the crowd really was growing. Almost half was made up of the palace staff, but we were collecting more and more viewers who were dressed like important visitors. Especially girls. Clearly the officers had asked their sisters and girlfriends to come cheer them on. Girls who would then tell their friends and maidservants all about how many ribbons their brother or friend had received at the hands of Chunru's foreign wife, and wasn't it exciting? Pretty soon everyone in the capital would know where I had been today, and what I had been doing, without a single mention of any injuries. The officers might have known how unusual it was for me to be just sitting and watching, but their visitors were unlikely to think anything of it at all. Dachahl had taken my hasty plan and turned it into a masterpiece.

He also asked his sister to tie his second ribbon on instead of asking me again. By that time I was running out of ribbons, but that was because the first round was almost over. Each contestant fought twice for the green ribbons, it seemed. Then the contestants who had collected no green ribbons in the first round joined the crowd of watchers, and I was given a much smaller pile of blue ribbons to hand out.

Dachahl lost one of his matches in the second round, and another one in the third. I think maybe he was at a disadvantage, because the rules awarded points, rather than kills. More experienced fighters, who weren't flustered by the fact that if this was a real fight with real swords they'd be dead already, could sometimes get their points from what in reality would have been minor cuts that would have hardly slowed him down. Dachahl always went for the kills.

By then there wasn't anyone with a complete set of ribbons, but there were also more of the cool-headed ones. Dachahl collected only one ribbon again in the next round, and in the final round he lost again, and had to stand aside as someone else came to collect my last ribbon. There wasn't much I could say about the victor's swordplay by then that I hadn't said before, so I said I was happy that Changali was defended by so good a warrior, and held out the ribbon. He bowed, but he didn't take it.

"Princess Dachahlra, this honor belongs to another."

"The judges said you won." I felt a little awkward, sitting there with my hand out, but I certainly wasn't going to force the ribbon on him. "Is Chunru supposed to win because he is Chunru?"

"He outfought me."

"He killed you twice," I agreed. "For Chunru this is not a game." But the ribbons were part of a game. So I couldn't give the last one to Chunru—by the rules of the game, he hadn't earned it. "Would you give me your sword?" I asked the winner.

He looked puzzled, putting his hand on the practice sword that had been stuck through his sash. "This?"

"Yes, if you would be so kind."

He pulled out the practice sword and then, going down on one knee, he presented it to me. I took it with what I hoped was sufficient grace, and I looked over at Aunt Prahnani and her daughters for help. Sahni laughed a little uncertainly, as if not understanding, but Nachi's eyes were excited, not confused, and she ducked her head in a little bow. So I passed the practice sword to her.

Then I turned back to the victorious officer. Out of the corner of my eye, I saw Dachahl staring at me with a blank look that I interpreted as 'I hope you know what you are doing'—I hoped I knew what I was doing too. "I need your hand, so that I can stand," I told the officer. He offered it, and I leaned on it very heavily. Fortunately he was expecting me to have trouble getting up, and with his support I managed to get to my feet without looking too awkward, and before Dachahl could try to stop me. It hurt. I had to bite down hard to prevent myself from hissing in pain. He stood also, and bowed again, and before he could protest again that he didn't deserve it, I stepped forward and tied the final ribbon around his arm.

Dachahl froze, a stunned look on his face—but I knew from the comments I had been hearing all afternoon that this was the right thing to do. The ribbon tying was a politeness—a gesture of respect—not an indication of anything intimate. The tournament had been held for my entertainment, it was right that I tie the final ribbon. I saw approval everywhere except in the face of my husband.

I intended to fix that.

As soon as the ribbon was tied, I caught Nachi's gaze, and then began walking toward my husband. Nachi followed me, still holding the practice sword. And when we reached Dachahl, she returned the sword to me with a little bow. "Chunru Dachahl Pralahnru," I said, "you are my chosen defender." I leaned forward in a bow, very carefully, and held the practice sword out to him.

He didn't move. But I was sure I hadn't done the wrong thing. All the officers were cheering, and most of the crowd, too. I must have just surprised him. "Take it before I fall over," I told him very quietly between clenched teeth.

The sword was lifted from my hand, and I straightened as carefully as I had bent and blinked a few times to hold back the tears of pain, and then managed a smile.

"Serving you is a very great honor, my princess," he told me. He meant it. Aunt Prahnani seemed pleased when she caught up with us, also. "This was well done."

"Now that the fighting is over, maybe we can wander in the gardens?" I asked.

"You should rest," Dachahl responded. It was almost a clockwork reaction for him by then, I thought.

"Rest how?" I asked him in Dostrovian.

"And I should clean myself."

"You don't have to do that," I said, still in Dostrovian. "You look very..."

His cousin Sahni looked at me, horrified. "Did you just tell Chunru not to wash?"

"Yes," I admitted, watching Dachahl remove his padding and hand it to Langso. "I'm afraid that if I let him go back to the palace, someone will discover something urgent that he needs to be doing, and then I won't see him again until the evening meal."

I wouldn't have minded if the smell of sweaty cousin had sent the lot of them fleeing. But the girls decided to come with us after all, even Lulahn, and of course the boys didn't care. First they asked to be allowed to bring the two practice swords with us, and when Dachahl refused, they tried to re-enact all his fights of the afternoon using 'shadow' blades—I doubt they would have succeeded even if they didn't have to keep breaking off the imaginary fights to catch up to the rest of us, but at least they were having fun.

But the discussion of how wonderful Dachahl had been and how unfair it was that the judges had picked someone else as a winner eventually drifted to me.

"Wasn't Pahtia wonderful at the end, when she demanded the victor's sword and handed it to cousin Dachahl?" Nachi asked.

"She was like the heroine in a Cholipardo historical epic," Chloys agreed.

"Yes, I'm the perfect wife for a Cholipardo warrior," I admitted, watching Dachahl out of the corner of my eye as I added in Dostrovian, "Here's your sword—freshly sharpened, your shield—I tightened all the rivets for you, and your helmet—mind you fasten it properly. I'll have some hot pork pierogi waiting for you when you get back, so make sure you do get back—I can't possibly eat that much myself." Dachahl's lips twitched.

"You're supposed to have ankle-long hair blowing in the wind, scented with the smoke of a hundred battles," Sahni protested.

"No," Dachahl told her. "She looks right just how she is."

That was when his sister made a little noise, and then turned and walked away from the rest of us. Dachahl frowned, and after exchanging glances with Aunt Prahnani he excused himself and went off after her.

"Is there anything I can do to make Dachahl and Lulahn less like strangers?" I asked.

"They were strangers before you came," Aunt Prahnani told me.

"Lulahn always calls him Chunru," Nachi agreed. "But she used to talk about him with us. We'd wonder what sort of bride he'd choose, and we'd tell each other all the rumors we'd heard, and we'd help her pick out feast-day gifts for him. Now she won't speak of him at all."

"We were always excited when he came to visit us," Sahni admitted.

"Excited? Why?" I asked. "Did he get in trouble a lot?"

"Naturally not!" Sahni protested. "He was always very polite. He made us feel like grown-up ladies."

"But we didn't get to spend much time with him," Nachi complained. "Father was always taking him off on a hunting trip, or to watch some horse race."

"That's why you found him exciting," her mother told her. "If he lived with us, you would be no more in awe of him than you are of your brothers."

I wasn't so sure of that. Chloys could almost be said to have lived with him, and she was very much in awe of him. "Older brothers are different from younger brothers."

"Are you in awe of your older brothers?" Nachi asked.

"Batiya is in awe of no one," Dachahl said. He had walked up behind us. "Not even my imperial father can intimidate her." There was so much significance in his tone that I turned around to look at him far too quickly, and stifled a groan. "Batiya?" he asked anxiously.

"You found out about your father's visit with Pahtia this morning?" his aunt asked him.

"The emperor came to see you?" Nachi asked. "What did he say?"

"Yes, Batiya," Dachahl's eyes narrowed, "what did he say?"

I went over the conversation in my head, trying to figure out what, if any of it, was repeatable. "He just had trouble believing I had really fixed your Tilardu treasure box," I explained. "I tried to tell him that fixing them is much easier than making them, so it doesn't take a mystical master—but I don't think he believed me."

"Langso says that a gift for you, from my imperial father, has just been delivered to our rooms," Dachahl explained.

"The emperor gave you a gift?" Nachi squealed.

"This is a very frightening thing," I told her.

"Can we see it?"

"I'm sure it will be of no interest to you," Dachahl told her, but of course everyone wanted to see it anyway.

It was a clock. But the wooden frame was cracked all over, and the metal parts were rusted, and the clothing that should have clothed the figures was missing altogether, as were small bits and pieces of the figures themselves.

Aunt Prahnani and her daughters stared at it in absolute silence, but the boys were less well trained. "Why would the emperor give you junk, Pahtia?"

"This isn't junk," I told them. "This is one of the greatest treasures of the imperial house of Changali."

"This you are certain of?" Aunt Prahnani asked. "It doesn't look like a treasure."

"Something must have happened to it," I admitted.

Dachahl reached out and touched one of the rusted figures. "It sunk." When everyone turned to look at him, he explained, "It was a part of the bride price sent from Changali to Abiniach for the Princess Lianiani. Only a Tertar fleet attacked unexpectedly from the north, and the treasure ship was so badly damaged that not everything could be removed in time. The princess never did marry into the Imperial House, and the clock spent two years underwater before it was rescued by divers."

When he saw the astonished look on everyone's face he smiled. "This was my favorite of the Tilardu stories. It spoke of sea battles, and lost treasure. Most of the Tilardu works weren't so exciting for a young prince to learn about."

"But why would the emperor give it to Pahtia?" Sahni demanded.

I laughed, and the laugh turned into a groan, and Dachahl leaped over to lend me an arm to cling to as I fought the agony. "He thinks it's a test," I told them when I could speak again. "But what he's really done, is given me the best present ever. Just taking it apart and cleaning all the pieces will take me a least a season!"

"This is a good thing?" Nachi sounded very dubious.

But Dachahl knew. "This is a very wonderful thing," he declared.

"It may be even better than that," I told him. "If the tiny little treasure box could be a gift from me to the emperor, then couldn't this be a gift from me to your entire empire?"

He stared at me wide-eyed for a moment and then broke into a huge grin. "Clever Batiya!" I'm sure he would have picked me up and twirled me about if I hadn't been injured. "I will tell them to pack it up and take it to the Sea House?"

"Yes! Thank you!"

The trip to the holy grove at Chazd Ngar passed without incident, although the idea that prayers could be tied to trees was a new one for me. I liked it better than having them around my neck. I was led to a tree that was considered to be particularly beneficial for prayers involving conceptions and births, and was presented with a writing desk and a small wooden tablet. I wrote my prayer on the tablet, strung it on a pink ribbon—because pink was the color for births—and then Dachahl tied the ribbon to one of the branches. There were already hundreds of pink-ribboned prayers hanging on the tree. And hundreds of prayers with blue, yellow, green, and other colored ribbons on each of the other trees in the grove. When the wind blew, instead of hearing the hiss of leaves rubbing, there was a great clatter of wooden prayer tablets.

"Don't tell my mother I did this," I advised Dachahl. "She's First Revisionist—she'll be terribly shocked."

"But not your father?"

"Father is a Realist. Doing what keeps the people you are going to be living with happy is just what a Realist believes in."

"What about you?"

"I think that if I have lots and lots of babies, it won't really matter if the first one is a boy or a girl."

"I like the way you think," Dachahl told me.

I liked the thought of getting away from the palace and out to this Sea House, whatever it was, so that I could go all soggy whenever I felt like it. But there was still one more thing that we needed to do before we could leave— make sure our marriage certificates got signed and sealed. Dachahl's father had said he would do this after the celebration, but he hadn't done it yet. So Dachahl requested an audience with the emperor for the following day.

The first thing that I noticed when we entered was that there were only three other people in the room besides the emperor—a scholar, and two guards. "Did you ask for a private audience again?" I whispered, but Dachahl was already tensing. Of course he hadn't asked for privacy—the more people were here, the harder it would be for someone to make the claim later that it had never really happened... With no witnesses, someone could just lose the stamped and sealed document and oops! We wouldn't be married after all. Again. "He does know what this is about?" I asked.

"Yes." Dachahl was talking through his teeth again. "That's the senior imperial archivist standing next to him." If I had ever believed that his father had come to accept our marriage, this would have convinced me I was wrong. Dachahl was angry again, but he managed to speak his formal petition for the emperor's approval clearly and calmly. I managed to bow without making any pained noises or bursting into tears. I was rather proud of myself for that.

"Before I give my approval to this marriage, I must be sure that the stranger you have brought before me understands what this marriage will mean."

"My wife is hardly a stranger, father," Dachahl replied. "She has lived in your home for an entire season."

His father ignored him, his attention entirely on me. I wondered if he had heard the rumor that I was a southern sorceress who had put his son under a spell—no point in listening to anything Dachahl said, because he could see nothing but me.

"Has my son informed you, that should Chunru be dishonored by his wife, before the next turn of the moon, Chunru must escort her to the nearest public stage and ritually behead her? This is our law, and this is the rule you will live under, if I allow your marriage to be stamped and registered."

If I had thought about it, I would have guessed the punishment for adultery was death, but discovering Dachahl would have to execute me *himself* seemed extra horrible somehow. "Chunru knew this would make no difference to me," I replied, trying not to show how I felt —everyone would be sure to misunderstand the reason. "Is there anything else you think I should know?"

"If you remain barren for five years, he may set you aside, and take another wife," his father said with the air of someone who had already crowed his loudest and failed to get any cheers. "Should you be dishonored by an assailant, you must spend a year at a temple of the throne's choosing, undergoing cleansing rituals. Any child born of you within that time will be drowned."

Drowned? They'd drown my child? I must have made some kind of sound, because Dachahl spun about and grabbed me before I could wobble. "Batiya?"

"This is why you turn red and blow steam every time another man even looks at me?" I asked him.

He was startled. "Naturally."

"Is this for every Changali wife, or just Chunru's?"

150

"Also the empress." He seemed a bit puzzled. "This is not how it is done in Dostrovia?"

No, it wasn't how it was done in Dostrovia! I was carrying Chunru's child—but if I was raped by another man, they'd kill it? But Dachahl's father was looking suddenly hopeful. I hadn't reacted when he thought I would, but I was reacting. I needed to stop doing so. It wasn't as if I had been planning to let anyone rape me anyway. Everyone kept saying it was a fate worse than death—well, that wasn't stretching the yarn to make the distance anymore. "This is a very frightening possibility," I told the emperor, "but I trust Chunru to protect me."

"And knowing this now, you are sure that you wish to become Chunru's wife? You could live more comfortably as his courtesan. I would be willing to grant you an imperial charter, ensuring you the support of the imperial house under any circumstance."

"I am already the wife of Chunru," I said. "I have been his wife for two seasons. And if I were the kind of woman who could live more comfortably as someone's courtesan, he would never have married me."

The emperor stared at me for a while longer, and then finally he looked at Dachahl.

"This is settled then?" Dachahl asked. "The time has arrived for me to summon the witnesses to this significant occasion?"

"This will not be necessary," his father answered. "Present the document—this will be done immediately."

I thought I heard Dachahl's teeth grind as he removed his copy of our marriage decree from his sash and handed it to his father. His father opened it, and read it with a blank expression, and then held it out to the archivist who examined it carefully, then carried it over to his writing desk, refolded it, dripped wax into the center of the folds, and stamped it. Dachahl walked over to him and held out his hand, and looking up at him, a little surprised, the archivist placed the sealed document into it. Dachahl examined it carefully, and then he tucked it back into his sash.

His father's eyes went wide. "This needs to be placed in the archives, Dachahl."

"Do not be dismayed, father," I replied. "You may place my copy in the archives instead." I carried it to him, and placed it in his hand. He unfolded it, and frowned at what was inside. Then he looked up past me at his son. "You... made two copies on that same day?"

"Three copies. One remained with the southerners' Seafarers' Guild."

The emperor sighed. "I must have trained you very well."

"My imperial father does me great honor in saying I am well trained," Dachahl replied, pressing his palms together and bowing.

His father shoved the paper back at me, and I carried it over to the archivist. He looked over at the emperor, who closed his eyes. "My son chooses his own fate."

"And I will need two additional copies, to send home to Dostrovia," I told the archivist, just as he was about to fold it up. I said it as if what I asked was easy and obvious, and that I was merely reminding him of what he already knew. "One for the government archives, and one for my family."

"But... some of this is written in the southern..."

"Ah! Naturally you will need assistance in this task. I will summon my secretary," and before he or the emperor could say anything, I was heading back toward the curtains, where I demanded that Chloys be summoned at once. Afterward, I remained there at the curtain, trying not to breathe. By the time Chloys appeared, I was ready to face an audience again, and I smiled brightly as I led her back to the archivist and explained that she was to prepare two additional copies of my marriage decree. She bowed and knelt down next to the archivist and he moved his writing desk in front of her, and then watched over her shoulder as she made the copies.

I went back over to Dachahl, because just standing near him made me feel better somehow, and we stood in silence while Chloys made her copies. When she had finished with them she held them out to Dachahl, who looked them over, and then walked over to his father, and bowed. "Chunru requests to make use of the imperial seal."

His father frowned again, but he reached inside his clothing and pulled out the jade creature. Dachahl repeated the rubbing and signing he had done on our wedding day, and then he had me re-sign my name, and then he handed the copies back to Chloys, who turned them over and wrote that it was an exact duplicate in content and signed her name, and then she handed them to the archivist who signed his name. Finally he folded them up and stamped them, and handed them back to me. And then he refolded my copy, and stamped it, and then he wrote on a separate piece of paper, signed that, and finally bowed to the emperor, then to Dachahl and myself, and went to place the marriage decree in the imperial archives. Now Dachahl and I had finally been married in Changali just as long as we'd been married everywhere else, and there would be far too many copies of the evidence in places that the emperor couldn't easily get at, for him to be able to deny that it had happened. Now all that was left was to convince everyone that this was a good thing.

Dachahl returned the imperial seal to his father, and bowed. And I started to bow also, but Dachahl stopped me. "This courtesy is not worth your pain," he told me.

I wasn't so sure. I had never been as angry with his father as he was. When Dachahl turned to leave, I lingered a little. "Magnificence, I think you trained a very fine son." And I bowed. And Dachahl came racing back to support me as pain radiated through my chest.

"She shouldn't be moving like that!" he cried angrily at his father.

His father's expression was exasperated. "This I never demanded of her!" Which was completely reasonable, but Dachahl wasn't in the mood to be reasonable. He growled and then would have pushed me out of his father's presence if he dared. I think I enjoyed that. It made me feel a little more secure. But what I really wanted to do was wrap myself around him and let him hold me tight, and that would have been agony.

The Sea House was a small building perched up on a cliff above the ocean. It had a twisty trail carved into the rock that led from the house to the surf, which I attempted only once, but I sent Dachahl running up and down it as often as I could come up with an excuse—he needed something to do with all his frustrations besides hide them under the rug. I stayed at the top of the cliff, and between the sea birds, the view of the crashing surf, the clock project, and the books donated by Dachahl's cousins, I managed to remain sane. The nights were by far the worst, and I got tireder and tireder, until I didn't trust myself to work on the delicate Tilardu mechanism anymore. I told Langso to take it away and put it somewhere safe before I mislabeled any of the pieces.

And then I cried for two days.

Dachahl was frantic. He sent an urgent message to Aunt Prahnani, and she told him that it was perfectly normal—I was injured, and with child, and if this was the first time I had cried, he was luckier than any man deserved. I don't think Dachahl believed her. He hovered over me, looking distraught, and I finally sent him away, telling him to go ride a horse, or kill something—and not to come back until he could look at me without feeling guilty. I learned later he was only gone for two hours, and when he came back he found me lying down on my side, asleep. It was the first time I had managed to sleep lying down. From there on things got better, and a few days later I snuck up behind Dachahl as he leaned on the railing watching the surf, and wrapped my arms around him.

"Batiya, don't..." I began to tug at his sash, and he grabbed at my hands. "Batiya, I'll hurt you."

"Just living hurts," I admitted. "This is why I need you. To make everything worth the pain."

We returned to the palace the next day. It seemed a lot emptier—Aunt Prahnani had taken her children back to Cholipardo. Princess Lulahn was visiting the Prince and Princess of Nash Vaur, who had a daughter about her age, but I didn't miss her.

The first thing Dachahl did was summon the doctor, who checked my progress and declared that me and the baby were doing well. So Dachahl wrote a message to his father, asking if he would be willing to announce that his daughter-in-law was expecting his grandchild. The next morning a message from the emperor was delivered stating that he would prepare a state dinner suitable for such an occasion, and in the meantime he trusted that Dachahl and I would do our duty, and that in addition to Dachahl being put back on the education committee, we would be expected to attend the following events. It was a long list. Two long lists, actually, one for Dachahl and a different one for me. Mine seemed to mostly involve appearances at festivals. It seemed that there was a festival going on somewhere within driving distance of the palace two days out of four, and the emperor wanted me to attend them all—flower festivals, kite flying festivals, temple festivals. But there were also military reviews and athletic events on my list. Dachahl scanned down it, his scowl growing. "He's trying to get you killed."

Dachahl's list was almost all visiting with the nobility —garden parties, dinner parties, and a couple weddings. "I don't think he's trying to get me killed, so much as he's not worrying that I might be killed," I told Dachahl. That didn't seem to make him less angry. "I'm sure he's trying to keep us away from each other. But I doubt this is all he plans. In fact, he is helping us achieve our goal, as well as working toward his own. Look at this." I handed him his own list. "He's keeping me away from places where I am most likely to make unforgivable mistakes, and showing me off among the people who have the most reasons to be glad I am here. And he has you speaking with the people that need to be impressed, convinced or intimidated into agreeing with his plans, and helping carry them out. You may not like that I will be exposed to attack, but you must admit that if he wants to push his plans forward, this is the way to do it."

"Why push? The faster he goes, the more frightened the scholars will be. They will feel like they are being forced toward a cliff."

"Perhaps... that's what he wants?"

Dachahl's eyes narrowed and he looked thoughtful. "Perhaps."

"But there is one thing about these lists that I think he didn't notice, when deciding where I should go and where you should go," I added. "Most of my events are in the morning and early afternoon. Most of your events are in the late afternoon and evening."

Dachahl looked back at the lists, and then he looked at me and smiled. "Batiya, you're wonderful!"

"Naturally."

Because nobody had been told of my condition yet, I wore one of the cape-like *parsahi* jackets over my *lahmpran*. But that meant that I could only go to outside events. So although Dachahl came with me to all of my events during the first week, I only went to two of his. Still, he got to oversee and direct the guards who were charged with keeping me safe, and I got to watch him telling people how even though the southerners couldn't match northern wit and wisdom, and their workmanship lacked true beauty, they could do almost anything Changali could do, and do it bigger, quicker and for more people, because they taught their peasants how to work with machines—harnessing their power to the intelligence of the scholars, instead of leaving them to scratch in the dirt with sticks. Each southerner peasant could do the same amount of work as ten Changali peasants, he explained, and this was why the southern nations were the richest in the world.

"We're not strong-witted and we have shoddy workmanship?" I asked him afterward.

"A wise warrior knows how to pick his fights," Dachahl told me wearily. I laughed, and didn't try to talk to him anymore that night—I knew he'd had more than enough talking. It wasn't just all the parties and festivals, his work on the education committee wasn't going very well either. Apparently everything had got behind schedule while he was doing other things, because all the scholars involved were fighting back in what was apparently the traditional scholarly way of expressing disapproval—they became sloppy, forgetful, and disorganized, and were off visiting sick parents just when they were most needed. He had to pick his fights there, too, I knew. As a result, he was adhering to his father's plans exactly—all his own ideas and concerns set aside for later. I knew it irked him, but at least he seemed to be accomplishing things. One of the lords on his committee even stopped by our rooms and thanked me for allowing him to return.

"Chunru was assigned to other tasks because the emperor willed it, and not because I asked for it to be done," I explained to him. He seemed surprised. "Did you hear otherwise?" I inquired.

"I may have misunderstood something one of the imperial staff said," he told me. "If this is so, I..." He didn't seem to want to finish the sentence.

One of the staff, and not the emperor himself? But it didn't make much of a difference either way. And since Dachahl was never in a mood to talk about what he was doing, I took advantage of having someone who worked with him visit me, and eagerly asked how my husband was doing.

"Chunru is a most capable planner," he explained. "He takes the emperor's orders, and he divides what must be done into tasks and assigns them, and then he makes a chart showing which other tasks will be delayed if the assigned tasks are not completed on time, and how much that will cost the Empire. For any task that is not completed in its proper time he holds us responsible for the cost increases of all the tasks delayed. We haven't had a single lost report or letter gone astray since he returned."

That sounded like my husband. The man who discovered the identity of a traitor by charting the timing and frequency of Lord Hahtung's correspondence, and who thought that a train timetable was the most marvelous invention ever. "They taught him this at his military school," I explained, proudly. Someday it would help make him a very fine emperor, if only he didn't get himself killed trying to protect me, first.

A week later Dachahl and I were heading toward a wine festival along a winding road that worked its way around the hills, when huge boulders plunged toward us, crashing and bouncing their way down the steep slope. The automobile we were in swerved, sending me crashing into Dachahl. I think I must have screamed a little, when my ribs slammed into his elbow. And then he wrapped himself around me, protecting me from the jolts as the automobile tossed wildly from side to side. Finally it thudded to a halt that sent Dachahl and me rolling to the floor.

He was up and out the door in seconds, but I couldn't move. I heard shouts and then quieter voices, and then Dachahl was back, helping me out of the car. "Are you going after them?"

"I can't," he told me—clearly frustrated. "They'll be gone before we get there."

"What you need is one of Katrika's flying machines," I suggested.

"Hot air balloon?" he countered.

"Would you tether it to one of the cars and pull it?" I asked.

By the time the imperial automobiles were back on the road we had decided that experiments into aerial surveillance would have to wait. For now, Dachahl would inform his father that my appearances would be restricted to places where he could guard me adequately. Apparently his father had not yet heard that Dachahl had been guarding me at all. He summoned us both. "If your wife is never seen anywhere without you, people will think you do not trust her," he told Dachahl.

"When I am sure that her guards are adequately prepared for every eventuality, this can be done, not before," Dachahl replied. We had a schedule overlap coming up in just a couple of days and had planned to just go separately—I to a national sword-fighting competition, and Dachahl to a garden party—but now

Dachahl wasn't sure I should go at all. I thought giving him time to double-check all the arrangements would be a better way of calming him down than telling him he was silly.

His father must have agreed with me. "Naturally you will do what you feel you must to keep her safe."

Dachahl assessed the situation, decided I would be as safe without him as I was with, that my guards should be able to defend me from any potential attacks, and finally agreed to having me go off alone. It seemed a horrible pity to me—not just because I liked having him with me, but also because it was the only event on either list I could imagine him attending because he actually wanted to be there. I hoped his father was pleased with his dutiful son.

I enjoyed myself, right up until one of the people in the audience pulled out a sword and tried to attack me with it. I wasn't hurt—my guards had no difficulty getting between him and me, and once they'd stabbed him a couple times, disarming and subduing him wasn't difficult. Chloys screamed a lot, but I never once thought there was any need to bring out the small gun Dachahl insisted I carry with me whenever I left the palace. I would have liked to have asked my attacker why he thought killing me would be worth what Dachahl would do to him afterward, but apparently he spoke only Stoi Kat.

Dachahl got back from the garden party, and discovered that he couldn't find a single thing to complain about in the way my guards handled the situation. He also didn't seem to have discovered the reason the poor man had decided to attack me in the first place. "Did anyone find out anything about the attacker at the wedding procession?" I asked.

"He was never even identified," Dachahl admitted.

"But you know who this one was?"

"Some farmer. From way out in the country. From what little we have got him to say, he seems to have come all this way just to try to kill you." He frowned. "His weapon was stolen—spare equipment of one of the contestants. We have sent someone to his home village to ask questions, but I doubt this will prove helpful."

"He came all the way here from way out in the country?"

"This is not very strange," he informed me. "When a Chang comes to a time when all that he has known is ended—he loses his lands, or his family, for example—he often chooses to come to Pai Lan Chung. It is said to be the city of dreams. Sometimes I feel that there are more farmers starving in the streets of the Laochar district than there are farmers growing crops in all of Holahchi."

"But his dream was to kill me?" That was more than strange, that was extremely uncomfortable. "What could he even know about me?"

Dachahl looked a bit uncomfortable himself. "Anything that any farmer knows about you is likely to have been painted in ugly colors," he confessed. "Almost everything they hear comes to them from the village magistrates."

"Why would the village magistrates dislike me?"

"They're all scholars."

He sounded at that moment like he was more interested in chopping the entirety of the scholar class into little tiny bits with his sword than he was in 'preserving' them. I didn't think he would actually do anything to any scholar he didn't already know was guilty of something, but I was a little afraid he might decide to vent his frustrations on my poor duped attacker instead. "What, exactly, is the punishment for having tried to kill the wife of Chunru?" I asked warily.

"Traditionally, they are cooked."

"Cooked?"

"Lowered into hot oil. Very slowly."

I shuddered. "Are... you supposed to... do it yourself?"

"You do not want me to do this," he concluded.

"No," I admitted.

"Then you will be happy to hear that nobody has been cooked in Changali for a great many years."

I was. Very, very happy. "What happens to them instead?"

"They are told that if they answer questions, they will not be cooked. Their head will be cut off instead."

"And they always answer questions?" I thought part of his frustration was because the man hadn't been answering questions.

"Yes. They always answer. Their answers are not always correct or useful. But it is possible to get answers even from a dead man."

"Chunru! This can't be done!"

"This is done all the time in Changali," he told me. "The questioner says 'If you were attempting to kill the princess remain silent, otherwise explain your intention!' The dead man remains silent. 'Ah! Just as I thought!', the questioner says. 'If you were not acting alone, then name all your accomplices'. Our questioners have learned that answers got from dead men in this manner are usually as useful as those got from the living."

I laughed. I couldn't help it. Laughing still hurt, so then I groaned. But Dachahl refused to regret making me laugh. "But Batiya," he warned, "my father has the right to choose the traditional punishment."

My attacker was executed by a professional headsman a couple days later, right before the dinner party where my pregnancy was to be announced. I hadn't expected to have much of an appetite at that party anyway, so I guess the timing didn't matter. But I don't think it helped me feel any more comfortable, or any less odd having people who hated me come up to me and smile and congratulate me. I remembered Dachahl telling me how clever I was when he had found out I was going to have his baby, and I could see that same thought—but with a very different emotion behind it—in the eyes of nearly everyone there. How very clever you must be, to have arranged to be the mother of the next emperor. I didn't feel clever. I wanted to be home, and to have Naditte asking me what in the world I thought I was doing, because I was sure to be an absolute disaster as a mother. Or maybe even Vanitri telling me that it had better be a boy, because any daughter of mine was sure to be warped.

And Dachahl could have argued back, and been comfortable, instead of being perfectly and coolly polite while underneath he was all burning rage. "The guard officers are happy for us, most of them," I told him encouragingly. At least I had convinced one small portion of his empire that I was worthy to be his wife.

"Has anyone wished that you would have a boy?" he demanded.

"A few. Is this traditional?"

"They should all have said it."

"I'm just as glad they didn't," I answered. "Think how horrible it would be for our daughter, if we have one, to know that everyone was wishing she had been a boy."

"Think of why they wouldn't wish for a boy, and how horrible that is," Dachahl advised me.

"This must be happening because they're all surprised," I told him with determined cheerfulness. "When they get used to the idea, they won't look so..." I couldn't even finish.

Some lord approached us about then, and after expressing the usual formal congratulations, asked when the new heir was expected.

"Ten moons from my wedding date," Dachahl replied.

"A full ten moons?"

Dachahl smiled. "If not, it will be because the child takes after me and doesn't like being kept inside."

"Your confidence is... reassuring. But..." He looked toward my belly, which was clearly pushing out my *lahnpran*.

"I was married in the late winter."

I could tell that the lord was trying to count out the time-span, and estimate the length of time, and if my belly was the right size. But Dachahl, for once, was not angry. "Shall I have my secretaries draw out a calendar and send it to you?"

"Naturally not, Chunru."

"You like questions about how soon the baby will be born, Dachahl?" I asked, once the lord had left.

"Yes. I cannot show them now that their fears are misplaced. But if they can be convinced to wait, then this will become clear."

I didn't want to think about the reasons why people didn't want me to have a boy, or what it was that Dachahl thought they were afraid of, and so I didn't pay as much attention to what he had said as I should have. Two days later he came home from one of his 'gentleman' parties early, and absolutely furious. He wouldn't tell me what happened, but the next morning we were both summoned by his father, and I learned that a Lord Rodahn had been saying pointed things about how wives could not be trusted, and what a disaster it would be for the empire if one of its future rulers turned out to be half stranger, and half unknown. Apparently Dachahl had retaliated by telling this Lord Rodahn that just because his wife found his person so distasteful that she wouldn't allow him in her house didn't mean that all husbands had the same problem.

"We have been hoping to set up three of our trial schools on Lord Rodahn's land," Dachahl's father scolded. "Further, he will be a powerful enemy if he decides to oppose the establishment of schools on any of his neighbors' lands. You were supposed to be gaining his support, not offering him unforgivable insults! What do you think is more important, your pride, or the future of your people?"

"This was more than my pride, father. This touched on the honor of my wife. If we allow people to speak so without requiring that they present some proof, then doubt will fall over the imperial line—and where will the future of our people be then?"

"He didn't name any names."

"He painted so clear a portrait no names were needed. How many 'stranger' wives are married to the direct heirs of the imperial line? This cannot be read any other possible way."

"But Dachahl, you have left him no place to stand. He must insist on an apology, or claim the right of arms. The humiliation of Chunru apologizing is second only to the injustice of forcing him to choose between losing his honor or committing treason."

Dachahl frowned. "You think I should declare my regret for words spoken in drunken anger?"

"Yes. I think that you must do this." The emperor looked like he was getting ready for a long and painful argument on the subject.

"Then this I will do," Dachahl replied. His father looked like he'd swallowed a frog. "I will speak of any regrets you desire of me, if first he stands before my wife, in a public place, and states that his own drunken words meant nothing at all, and that he will always stand ready to defend the honor of the wife of Chunru."

First the emperor glared, and then he frowned. "This... has potential. He is already sworn to uphold the imperial line. This is something he ought to be willing to do. The only excuse he could give would be to show strong evidence that your wife has been unfaithful."

"No such evidence exists," Dachahl said, smugly.

"Maybe he heard that I spent the one night in the house of the Dostrovian ambassador?" I suggested. "Or he could have bribed one of the crew of the Volcanis to say someone crept into my room while you were sleeping elsewhere?"

The emperor froze. "I thought you said she never refused you her bed."

"She did not *refuse* me, I was just not always there. But what she says is not possible," Dachahl told him. "No man on that ship could have entered her room without my knowledge. I had an alarm installed that rang in my room any time her door was opened." I stared at him in bewilderment and wondered for a moment if he was inventing this for the sake of his father. It was certainly the first time I had heard of it. But Dachahl wouldn't lie about something like this. "My cousin's injury caused him to wander at night," Dachahl explained, when he saw my expression. "If you did this on a ship..."

"I might have fallen overboard," I concluded. He could have told me, but of course he wouldn't have—at least I now knew how he had always seemed to know where I was.

"What of this ambassador?" the emperor asked.

"Circumstances forced me to leave her under his protection for one night," Dachahl admitted.

"But he is a man of unassailable virtue?"

I shook my head. "No. Very much not. That's why Dachahl sent the chauffeur's wife to stay with me—and her daughter."

"Her daughter?" He looked over at Dachahl. "To distract him from your wife?"

Dachahl frowned. "Talalis Fochalri is five years old. She spent that entire night in my wife's rooms, and slept with her in her bed. I have written an imperial charter for her, in repayment for her parents' services to Chunru."

"This will look like a bribe," the emperor told him.

"I wrote the charter a full day before I knew my wife would be spending the night at the Dostrovian Embassy." Dachahl was getting angry again. "Her parents agreed to stand by my side, in spite of the risk of assassins. Her father *saved my life*."

"But you cannot prove that your wife was never with this ambassador?" the emperor persisted.

"I do not need this proved, I can know this is so. You would know also, if you ever looked past her eyes and hair, and saw her soul." He turned to me. "Batiya, I would not believe you had betrayed me, if you had spent a hundred nights away from me, and a thousand days in the company of other men, but why must you mention the few nights and days that we've been apart *now*?"

"Your father should know what could be said, and what can and can't be proved, so that he can help protect me," I explained.

"And you are so sure that he will protect you and not try to destroy you?" Dachahl sent a suspicious glare in the direction of his father.

"He needs to find a way to destroy me that will not destroy you also." I turned to the emperor. "Is this not truth?"

The emperor's black eyes glittered. "Naturally, the well-being of my son is the greatest desire of my liver."

I grinned at him. "My liver agrees with yours. This is how I know we are allies, and why I tell you everything."

The emperor swallowed his second frog of the day, and Dachahl laughed. "You should have tried to know her, father."

"I think your wife would rather spend her time watching young athletic men than chatting with a grey-hair like me," the emperor told him coldly.

Dachahl studied him for a moment, and then he said, "People have told you that she still spends time at the officer's exercise yards?"

"Will you tell me they lied?"

"I will tell you that you should have asked them what she was doing while she was there."

The emperor sneered. "What is there for a woman to be doing in such a place?"

"This is what Chloys thought also," I told Dachahl. "She was very surprised when I did not paint my face, or wear my prettiest *lahnpran*. I should have seen that this was why your father was pleased that evening, when he heard I had been there—he thought I was showing my true self at last, and you would see this, and be willing to listen to reason."

The emperor was glaring at me. "Will you say you find no enjoyment in watching the men there?"

"Nooo..." I replied, peeking sideways at Dachahl. "...I cannot in honor deny that I enjoy this."

Dachahl laughed again. And his father hissed. "She is not there to enjoy what she sees, father," Dachahl explained. "She was learning sword-fighting at first, but because of her injuries she now learns the proper use of firearms."

"And I never turn my gaze away from my teacher," I added virtuously.

"Still?" Dachahl asked. "No wonder your aim is so bad!"

"Chunru!" I protested.

"*You* are teaching her?" the emperor demanded.

"Yes, father, I am teaching her."

The emperor frowned, and I frowned too. It seemed very odd that he had known I was there but not that Dachahl was with me. Suspicious, even. As if someone had carefully crafted their report to the emperor in order to make the situation look like something it wasn't.

"I will send for Lord Rodahn and explain your conditions," the emperor said abruptly. "I am certain he will agree to your proposal. But it will be very difficult to gain his support for our other projects after this."

"If you thought getting his support by any means other than bribery or coercion was even possible, you see the man very differently than I do," Dachahl responded.

Lord Rodahn did agree to the public declaration, and I got Chloys to explain to me why everyone was so sure that he would. To ignore Dachahl's insult would turn his life into a living hell. Everyone could parade the same insult in front of him, and he wouldn't be able to retaliate, because he hadn't retaliated when Dachahl had done it. But fighting a duel with Chunru was treason—the best result he could hope for was having Dachahl kill him quickly and cleanly.

So I got all dressed up in my long trailing ceremonial *lahnpran* again, and I stood out in the middle of a stage—it looked familiar, I think it was the same one used for the emperor's blessing on my marriage. Dachahl was also there—down one layer and to the side—waiting for his turn to publicly apologize. He was wearing ceremonial finery also, but his *choliang* was only a couple feet too long for him this time, he got to wear boots, and there were no shoulder spikes—thanks be to Saint Belkov and his bloody toes!

I couldn't have picked Lord Rodahn out of a crowd. Although it seemed likely we'd been introduced. He walked toward me with a steady gait, and bowed with proper deference. But when he straightened, something seemed to be wrong. He stared at me with an expression I could not describe. His mouth opened, closed, and opened again. And just as I thought he would finally make his speech there was a flash of metal instead, as he drew his sword and stabbed at the bulge of baby that showed beneath my sash.

"I grabbed his sword hand before he could strike again."

Chapter Five

I Get My Own Personal Guard

I wasn't expecting swordplay. I didn't manage to remain balanced in a fighting stance I never had time to assume, and I certainly never managed to take the gun from its holster strapped to my calf—but I did sidestep the stab, and then grabbed his sword hand before he could strike again. Unfortunately, after so many weeks of trying not to move my arms and upper body much, I was wetter than a baby duck and almost as limp as wet straw. I just couldn't hold the sword back. The blade pressed against me, I felt a stinging in my belly, and in desperation I dropped down into a crouch and bit his sword hand—grinding my teeth together as hard as I could.

He screamed, and his other hand slammed into the side of my head. I tasted blood.

And then Dachahl was there, his sword slashing, and I collapsed and curled around my belly, while a warm wetness rained on me from above. Something head-sized and roundish bounced over the edge of the stage as Lord Rodahn's body slowly toppled sideways.

There was a lot of screaming. But none of it was me—I knew better than to scream when I was already hurting so much. I'm pretty sure I whimpered a bit, though.

"Batiya." Dachahl's voice was too close, too loud, and too urgent. I wanted it to go away and leave me alone to deal with the hurt. "Batiya, you've been cut." I knew that. "You have to let me stop the bleeding."

No. He couldn't touch me. Nobody could touch me. I had to protect the baby.

"Batiya, stop this!" The words were in Dostrovian, and they found their way through my panic. I stopped trying to knock his hands away.

"Sorry!" I managed to say.

"This is not yours to regret."

"Lord Rodahn?"

"He was more fortunate than he deserved. He did not regret for long."

We were both covered in blood, but most of it was Lord Rodahn's. Dachahl pressed his *choliang* to my bleeding belly, and I just clung to him and held on for a while. There was no way I would be able to pretend that nothing much had happened this time—not when all those people had been looking right at me when Lord Rodahn had cut me... and when Dachahl had sliced his head off. One of the imperial guards approached us close enough to drag the body away, and all around us was the disjointed and occasionally hysterical babble of the watchers, and sharply snapped orders from the few people who had kept their heads and were trying to clean up the mess.

A man approached Dachahl and me, accompanied by one of our guards, and bowing all the way down until his head practically touched his knees, announced that he was a doctor, and that it would be his honor to examine the princess, if Chunru allowed.

Chunru allowed. Some guards were summoned to form a protective screen, for the sake of my modesty, and the doctor examined my injury. It was a long slice down the left side of my belly, deeper in the middle and fading away into insignificance on either end. "Our baby—is our baby hurt?" I asked him anxiously.

"This goes into the strong top muscle of the womb," he told us. "The cut does not look as if it goes through. How long until the child is expected?"

"One and a half seasons."

"Take good care of the cut. If it doesn't become inflamed, it should heal in plenty of time."

Dachahl was helping him bandage the cut when the emperor arrived.

I heard about six different people explaining what had happened, but Dachahl stayed with me. Only when his father climbed up on the stage and stood before us did he even look at him.

"The child?" the emperor asked.

"The doctor believes it is unharmed," Dachahl responded.

"I have already heard as much as is worth listening to," his father announced. "All his lands and possessions are yours to hold, and I give his heirs to your judgement."

Dachahl bowed his head over his knees. "Thank you, father."

The emperor turned to what little audience remained, and said the same thing again, only more formally. "I, Lord of the Four Kingdoms, grant all the lands and possessions of the traitor Rodahn to Chunru, in recompense for the crime of having attacked his wife..."

and all of that sort of thing. And then he said it again in Stoi Kat.

When the formalities were over, he ordered his guards to help Dachahl and I into his automobile, even though we were covered in blood and a horrible mess, and could just as easily have gone home in the same automobile we had arrived in. But he was making some kind of statement to those who were watching. I could tell that by the way Dachahl behaved—less angry with his father than he'd been for a long time, almost grateful even. But whatever statement the emperor might have been making to his people, he didn't seem to want to make any more statements to us. He kept his lips stuck together until we arrived, and then he told Dachahl, "When you have decided what to do with Rodahn's properties and heirs, let me know."

"Yes, father."

And then he was gone.

I turned to Dachahl and asked, "Am I wrong, or is he starting to approve of me a little?"

"How can he approve of a savage who bites her opponent's hand during a sword fight? Is this how I taught you?" Dachahl demanded. He was smiling. "But I think he is starting to understand why I called you a treasure."

"I don't know why he would change just because I saved his grandchild once. I've saved *your* life a dozen times," I told him.

"And now that there are five hundred witnesses to what you are capable of, he is finally starting to believe this."

"At this moment, I don't feel capable of anything much," I admitted. When Falahni appeared with Langso I was delighted to see her, and it wasn't until after I'd had my bath, had been dressed in a clean bed-gown, and was lying in Dachahl's arms that I felt up to being glad that at last I had made some progress with the emperor, and remembered to ask Dachahl what his father had meant about giving Lord Rodahn's heirs over to his judgement.

"This has not happened for a long time, but when a lord turns against the imperial line, he is supposed to be cooked, and all his brothers and sons and nephews and grandsons are beheaded, and his lands are taken away from him. My imperial father has granted me the right to apply this penalty if I desire, because Lord Rodahn's attack was directed at my possible heir."

"You... wouldn't actually do that, would you?" I asked. "Kill all his brothers and sons and everything?"

"He has no brothers, and only one son. So it would be only one person, and it would show everyone that my father and I consider your child a true member of the Imperial House, and it may make them less likely to attack you."

"But I don't think Lord Rodahn actually even planned to attack me. I was watching him the whole time. I think he meant to take that vow right up until he was there in front of me, and he just couldn't eat his..." I trailed off as I realized that I was trying to say an untranslatable Dostrovian phrase in Hadahnchi. "He couldn't force himself to do this at that very moment. I'm sure he didn't plot this out with his son beforehand."

"Especially since he hasn't seen his son since he was a few years old," Dachahl admitted.

"He hasn't *seen* him? So what you said about his wife not allowing him in her house—that was true?"

"Naturally. If I had lied, I would be no better than he was."

"But this sounds like she is a most sensible lady. And if you know his son isn't involved, how can you punish him?"

"Punishment isn't the whole issue. Besides the message it sends, it is traditional for a lord's heirs to kill themselves if his lands are taken. This forces the ruler to provide some kind of support for the females of the family."

"But what if his son takes after his wife, and not him?" I protested. "Think what a waste that would be! You have far too many traditions that involve people killing themselves," I added darkly.

"You would call this a waste, Batiya?"

"Naturally. Do you think having the sense and strength of will to throw out a worthless husband is something that is easily come by?"

"You would do it."

"I didn't marry a worthless husband," I informed him. "I married the finest prince in the world. Isn't there anything you can do to stop him from killing himself?"

Dachahl considered that. "I could offer to give him vassalage of the lands that were his father's, if he agreed to do what his father would not."

"You mean, if he will vow, in public, to support my honor? That seems very fair."

"He might *prefer* to commit suicide, Batiya. He may find an honorable death easier to face than a life of shame, as the son of a dishonored lord."

"If all we can do is offer him a chance, then I still think we should offer him that chance," I insisted. "Write to him now, before it's too late."

Dachahl seemed a bit reluctant to write the letter, but it had been a long hard day—maybe he just didn't want to move. The answer came back to us four days later. Forang Dungharu greatly appreciated the kindness shown by Chunru's generous offer, and wished to do whatever he could to pay in any way for the crimes of his father.

"*Dungha*-ru? Son of a traitor?" I translated. "Must he call himself that?"

"Yes. To honor his father by allowing him to have family still carrying his name would be to dishonor the Imperial House."

I started to understand how difficult the choice I had offered him was then, but I didn't really understand until I stood with my husband on that very same stage, and saw Rodahn's son—who couldn't have been much older than I was, if he was even that old—with his hair cut unevenly short, as if he had hacked it off with his own sword.

He walked steadily toward us, bowed a deep bow, and then knelt and spoke his oath with conviction and only a slight tremor in his voice.

I just couldn't stop staring at the pale patch of skin on the back of his neck. "I hope," I told him quietly, "that I have a son as brave as you."

His head jerked up, and he stared at me wide-eyed. Then he gulped, and said, "Lady, my arm is your guard and my body your shield. Pl–" He stopped very abruptly, and there was an agonizing silence as he knelt there gazing up at me, his expression horrified.

"What's wrong?" I whispered to Dachahl.

"He's trying to swear his life to your service, but he's supposed to present his sword next," Dachahl whispered back. Of course nobody would have let the son of the man who tried to skewer me get within twenty feet of me while wearing a sword.

"Give him your sword so he can finish."

"I can't give him a sword," Dachahl protested, barely loud enough for me to hear him, but very, very firmly.

"Can *I* give it to him?"

Dachahl had to think about that, but finally he whispered back, "This might actually work. But Batiya, I'm wearing the sword that killed his father."

I didn't care. Dachahl could tell that I didn't care. He removed the sword from his sash and handed it to me, and I turned and held it out to Forang. He took it, his hands shaking slightly. Then he began again. "Lady, my arm is your guard, and my body your shield. Please accept the services of this sword, to protect you and your family for as long as I have breath."

"Say 'This service I accept'," Dachahl advised me in a whisper. I said it as loudly and clearly as I could.

Forang drew the sword a couple inches out of its scabbard, cut his thumb on it, and smeared the blood across the base of the blade, then he tucked it away in his sash, his hands shaking worse than before. Finally he stood and bowed again.

"Stay close," Dachahl ordered Forang, as he guided me past him and toward the edge of the stage. "I've got a revolver in my boot, but that was my only blade."

"Yes, Chunru," he said, and followed us.

We made it back to our automobile without incident. "You'd better explain exactly what I just did," I told Dachahl once we were safe inside.

"You've just got yourself a personal guard," he told me. "A young, male, nobly-born..."

He was scowling fiercely and Forang looked over at him and swallowed. "Chunru, I swear I would never–"

"He's not worried about what will happen," I explained. "He's worried about what people will say. But no one can claim that I don't need a guard. That's usually going to mean male, and young enough to be a problem— and I'm a craftsman's daughter, so a peasant lover is as easily spoken of as a noble."

"This is why I allowed you to accept," Dachahl told me, still scowling. "But he must never be alone with you. You'll have to take Chloys with you whenever I can't be there."

"I do that anyway," I told him.

When we arrived at the palace, Chloys came hurrying to greet us, and then stopped short, her eyes wide, when she saw Forang.

"This is Forang," I told her. "He has joined my staff. Please be kind and help him find everything he needs."

Chloys looked over at him, and then dropped her gaze and looked at the ground. "I... yes... naturally... that is... this I will do, Princess."

Forang looked at her, and then took advantage of the fact that she was looking downward to continue looking at her. "I do not need assistance," he said.

"You do," Dachahl corrected him. "The palace is unfamiliar to you, and you need to learn your way about quickly if you are to carry out your duties." He turned to

Chloys. "Make certain you take him to the practice yards. Tell Commander Tzir that I want a full assessment of his abilities." He turned back to Forang. "Do you shoot?"

"I've hunted on my grandfather's estate."

"Tomorrow you will go to Hunang's and tell them I sent you. You will purchase the best pistol you can afford."

"Yes, Chunru."

Dachahl walked away in the middle of Forang's bow, and I hurried to follow him. "Now I no longer have a *tirah-fa* and sword that match," Dachahl told me.

"Will you have to buy another one?"

"No, it is traditional to have a sword and *tirah-fa* that match, but they are never worn together, so what does it matter? Besides, my other *tirah-fa* should be back from the swordsmith soon."

"They have been making a whole new blade for it," I concluded.

"Yes."

"I'm being a very expensive wife," I mourned.

Dachahl laughed. "Batiya, I have been getting complaints that you do not spend enough."

"Oh." Now that he was pointing it out for me, I realized I didn't actually spend any money at all. I just expected that everything I needed would be provided. "Do I need to go out and spend money?"

"No. This way no one can claim that you married me for that reason."

"But I live in a palace, and am fed delicious food, and am dressed in expensive clothing–"

"Which you take off as soon as you get back to your rooms, so that you don't get oil from your clockwork project on it. And Chloys lives in the same palace, and eats the same food. But I should buy you more things. Jewels, and so on."

"What I really need is my own *tirah-fa* to carry around with me, so that when I feel the need to give someone a weapon, I don't need to use yours."

"Ah! Clever Batiya! This is exactly what you need. This I will get you."

I wasn't going to sit anywhere uncomfortable waiting for that to happen. Trying to get to everything on both our lists was keeping us very busy, and when Dachahl wasn't doing that, or trying to teach me to hit what I aimed at, he still had the school project to work on.

I spent whatever time I could find working on the clock, and so had my hands covered in grease when the emperor arrived at my rooms later that day.

"The Dungharu boy is not here?" he asked.

"Dachahl sent him to Commander Tzir for assessment, and then off to get whatever else he needs."

"You handed a sword belonging to the Imperial House to a shame-shorn," he told me.

"I don't like to see anything wasted. Especially people."

The emperor did not respond to that. Instead he looked at the trays where I had laid out and labeled the pieces of clock I was working on. "Have you discovered what is wrong with it?" he asked.

"Nothing's wrong with it," I responded, surprised. "It just needs cleaning."

"This is all? Just cleaning?"

"The bearings in the main shaft should probably also be replaced," I admitted, using the Dostrovian word for bearings, because I couldn't remember the Hadahnchi. "And, naturally, the case and figures will need to be made beautiful again. Do you have any craftsmen you would like hired to repair the wood, fix the paint, and sew clothing?"

"You do not do this?"

If this was a small private project for me, I probably would have tried. But for a state treasure it sounded like a very bad idea. "No. These are not my craft."

"I will think about this."

And that was all he said to me. It really didn't seem worth taking time out of his busy day to visit me for just that. I wondered what he had really come for.

Forang arrived with Chloys before Dachahl got back from what he had been doing. "I will not stay," he told me. "I only wished to report that I have done as Chunru ordered."

"I'll be attending another kite festival tomorrow," I told him. "You will come to protect me?"

"Yes, Princess. I..."

I looked up from the gear I was buffing with some metal shavings. "Speak!" I encouraged him.

"I do not understand why I should have the honor of serving you, when all of the imperial guards are so eager to..."

"They like me." Most of them, anyway. But I'd always been more at home with fighters than I had with civilized people. If I couldn't get the warrior class to support me, I would clearly have been doomed from the start.

"They would *die* for you!"

That was not a thought I appreciated much. "None of them ever offered me their sword."

"You... Chunru... I was presumptuous," he said apologetically.

"You were trying to pay for how your father had hurt me."

"They told me my father tried to cut Chunru's child from... But you smiled at me! And you said..."

"Why shouldn't I smile? *You* never hurt me. And your father didn't hurt me much either. But now that you protect me, you must do well." Failing to protect me would be one too many disasters for him to overcome, I suspected. "This is not easy work."

"Yes, Princess. The imperial guards are teaching me. I won't fail you."

The Changali kite festivals were amazing events. Every kite had a new and even more incredible shape than the one before, it seemed like. Squares and diamonds quickly gave way to birds, fish, butterflies, and imaginary beasts like the one on the imperial insignia. I was as bright as a bean in a bucket, and nobody attacked me.

But when I went to a blessing of the harvest ceremony without Dachahl four days later, a group of people suddenly pulled weapons out from under their peasant smocks and charged toward me.

Forang stepped in front of me, drawing his sword, mostly to prevent anyone else from deciding to join in. Chloys dived beneath the table holding the incense, bowls of flower petals and dried leaves, and prayer tablets.

The other guards surrounded the attackers. They were outnumbered, but they picked on the leaders, and kept moving so that they were poor targets. And the attackers, clearly more undisciplined mob than organized force, were defeated with minimal injuries.

After the excitement was over, I thanked Forang and asked him to check on Chloys. He put the sword away, and then helped Chloys to her feet, which set her to stuttering and looking at the ground. He drew away from her, but didn't take his eyes off her until she finally looked up and caught him staring. After that he wouldn't look in her direction for the rest of the day.

I found the two of them amusing, but Dachahl—when he noticed—seemed irritated. "Are we going to have to watch the two of them circle around each other long?" he asked one evening just after the two of them had been sent away.

"He is living in shame, and is worthy of no one. She is the adopted daughter of a foreign scholar and is not worthy of a man of noble blood," I explained. "They could be dancing that dance forever—anything that makes him feel more worthy of her will make her feel less worthy of him."

Dachahl groaned. "Perhaps I'll order them to marry. This would make your situation better."

"But this is not a kindness to them. At least give them a chance to see that they are who the other likes."

"This is something that can be seen by a stone, and smelled by a tree," Dachahl told me.

"Could you tell I liked you so soon?"

"Yes."

I wasn't sure I believed him. "This is not the only problem. Whenever there is trouble, he has to jump to my side, not to hers. This is not good for a husband."

"Nobody is trying to kill Chloys," Dachahl barked. But he didn't mention ordering them to get married again. Instead he frowned over the fact that I was still being attacked so often by people who didn't really have any reason to attack me, but seemed to think that they did. "Someone's behind it?" I suggested.

"Naturally," he growled. "But how can I learn the face of my enemy, if my enemy has a million faces?"

"Maybe he doesn't. Or at least, maybe the million faces are being led by just a few?"

Dachahl turned to look at me, suddenly interested. "Have you seen anything that leads you to this thought?"

"I can't help wondering how all these farmers from out in the country don't seem to have much trouble finding out where I will be."

"This is something that should be examined more closely," Dachahl admitted, and went off to talk to General Duprang.

The next day a report arrived from General Duprang, and the more my husband read, the more uneasy he looked. "He says that the farmers seemed to think everyone knew you'd be there," he told me. "He would not have thought that information would be so widely spread. We do not announce your coming to anyone but the people in charge of the events. Perhaps they tell their guests, but... farmers? New to the city? They should have trouble finding their next meal."

"So someone must have told them?"

"If this is what happened, he could not discover any sign of it. He traced them back to a tea house where they were drinking and complaining last night—but if someone deliberately turned their drunken anger toward you, he did so without being remembered afterward."

"This is possible?"

"Yes. Who remembers who said what when everyone has been drinking?" He pounded his thigh with a fist. "Whispers and rumors! This is like looking for a breeze. You cannot see if it has touched your path or not."

"If this was done, it must have been done by someone who knows where to send them. Your father's secretaries must know, and so do ours."

He didn't seem to like where that suggestion was taking him. "I examined every member of the scholar class in the entire palace. Except Chloys. Do you suspect Chloys of having betrayed us?"

Of course I didn't suspect Chloys, and I told him so. He still informed his father the following day that I would no longer be following his schedule.

"My son, it is of vital importance that your wife be seen—and that it not seem that you are afraid to let her out of your sight."

"She will be seen," Dachahl vowed. "But *I* will arrange her schedule. Her enemies must not know where she will be so that they may ambush her. I will see this done."

He did this by making a list of every event of any note being held within several miles of Pai Lan Chung and then picking my next appearance at random the day before, and letting only me, Chloys, Forang, and the commander of my guards know where I was headed. Nobody at the event knew I was coming. They would be celebrating in their usual fashion, and then an imperial guard would turn up at the gate, or the doorstep or whatever, and announce that the Imperial Princess Pahtia had been passing by, and was curious to see what they were doing, and would they welcome her. Of course—no matter how panicked they might be—nobody said no.

I rather enjoyed that. Watching the hostess or the organizers scramble to try and accommodate me, and then relax when they discovered how reasonable I was going to be, made me feel like I was actually accomplishing something beneficial. And some of the events I attended were rather fun. Like the time I went to a 'Children's Festival' and got to hand out prizes for a cooking contest and an athletic competition to a bunch of 'Champions' no taller than my waist. And the time my caravan of guards and escorts went astray and we ended up attending the wedding ceremony of some completely unremarkable members of the scholar class, instead of the remembrance party for some long-dead nobleman that had actually been on our schedule. The attacks on me also dwindled away to almost nothing, as Dachahl pointed out to his father. "And has it interfered with your purposes any?"

The emperor scowled back. "My reports say that the princess's popularity has increased with both the peasant class, and among the nobility, as has the acceptance of the new program. But this should not be working," he informed us. "To have an imperial princess wander about arriving unexpectedly wherever she pleases should not be making the people happy." I tried to imagine how happy anyone would be to have Lulahn deposited on their doorstep, and saw his point. But I wasn't Lulahn.

"People like Batiya," Dachahl explained.

That was probably a vast oversimplification. I didn't think any of the people I had visited really liked me, as such. But they liked that they had successfully entertained an imperial princess, without having gone to any extra expense, and without suffering any headaches. "They are delighted to have a chance to see your dancing fish," I corrected.

"That must be diminishing the value of the Imperial House in the eyes of the people!" his father protested.

"No it shouldn't," I corrected him. "If anyone could arrange for me to appear at their event, then I would be nearly worthless as a guest—but I'm actually a little harder to get a chance to see than before. Also, if I were being seen as a less valuable addition to an event, then that would be bad for the Imperial House—but I'm a very good dancing fish. I provide more to stare at than Dachahl's sister. I dress just as richly, and Chloys is just as beautiful, plus I am an exotic southerner, and I come with what is probably the most noteworthy guard ever to have attended an imperial princess. Any event I arrive at will be talked about for the next fifty years."

"But what will be said?" the emperor asked.

"That the poor princess still speaks Hadahnchi like a toad?" I suggested. "That she looks like a baboon? Or maybe a ghost? I keep thinking I hear something about ghosts."

"They say this because of your pale eyes," Dachahl told me. "Ghosts are supposed to have pale eyes."

"So they say I have ghost eyes, and hair like a sheep, and that they can't imagine what Chunru sees in me, but clearly he sees something, and then they try and figure out when the baby is supposed to be born. And then maybe they will mention that I seemed to enjoy myself before spending the rest of their time discussing Forang. Did his father really try to cut Chunru's baby out of my belly? Isn't it tragic that such a handsome boy should be the son of a traitor? Is that really the sword that killed his father that he's carrying? And then, naturally, someone will say this is all true, and that their wife's aunt's brother-in-law was actually there when it happened, and–"

"Will they say there is something between you and the shame-shorn?" the emperor demanded.

"Someone will probably try," I admitted, "because some people are that sort. But nobody who was there and had eyes will believe them. Forang spends every moment he dares staring at Chloys. Besides, it's hard enough for them to figure out why Chunru is interested in me. Once anyone has met me, your story that he married me to strengthen ties to the south is far more believable than that I'm a sorceress who captures the hearts of unwary young princes."

"This is not true," the emperor told me. "Everyone who dares speak to me of this matter, asks me what your magic is."

"What? Why?"

"Because when my son is with you, he smiles."

I looked over at Dachahl, who was smiling. "What my sister Naditte said, about you not smiling. This is not just at my home, but here too?" I asked him.

"Everywhere," he assured me.

"You've got to stop trying so hard to be perfect," I told him. "You're already wonderful, this is enough."

He laughed. "Should you not tell me that if I smiled more, I would be more perfect?"

"And have you decide that it's your duty to smile even if you don't feel like it?"

Dachahl laughed again, and to my astonishment the emperor also smiled. His smile didn't last for very long though. "Your plan seems to be working, Dachahl. But eventually she is going to have to go to events where she is expected, also."

"At these times, I will go with her."

"Not always, Dachahl."

"I don't think you should worry so much," I told my husband. "Forang is nearly as fearsome as you are."

"I thought you were a better judge of swordplay than that," Dachahl told me.

"He doesn't have to be able to fight well. People look at him with his cut hair, carrying the sword that killed his father and they... think a second time about how eager they are to anger you or me. "

"This isn't enough," Dachahl told me. "We've had problems at more than half of the school building sites, and there were riots in the Fungfahni district last night. My father's policies are having precisely the effect I predicted."

"If we do not continue to push forward now, it will be seen as a weakness," his father replied. But he didn't sound at all apologetic, and I was absolutely certain that he had also known what the reaction would be, and had done this on purpose.

"Why did you choose to start the education program in such a way?" I demanded.

"My people do not respond well to change," the emperor told me. "I cannot expect it of them. And the longer it takes to get everything started, the more time they will have to find ways to resist it."

The more I thought about that, the more chagrined and enlightened I felt. I had been spending so much time worrying about my situation and how I didn't seem to be able to do anything about it, that I hadn't spent any time at all thinking about what my father-in-law was facing. No wonder I hadn't been able to understand him. "You originally planned to introduce education to the peasant class in a much slower way," I deduced. "And then Dachahl returned with the news that there was a conspiracy of scholars terrified by what the changes you intended to make would mean for their class. Suddenly you realized you were facing the same problem I am facing. You needed the support of people who had every reason to not want to support you, and you had a time limit. You couldn't just wait and gradually allow people to become accustomed, not if some of them were already plotting against you. You had to settle the issue quickly. So instead, like a brave boy at a new school, you decided the quickest way to gain acceptance was to get in a fight."

The emperor bowed slightly in my direction. "If I force the scholars into a fast, ill-planned reaction, it will be followed by regret. That will do less harm to the nation than if fear and anxiety are allowed to build slowly and then consume them. If they are allowed time to plan out a revolution..." I remembered the long list of jobs that Dachahl said fell to the scholar class, and shuddered. They seemed to be the glue that held Changali society together. And Dachahl had also seemed certain that Changali's Tertar neighbors would be ready and eager to jump into the game at the slightest sign of a stumble. His father must have been afraid that the much more reasonable plan Dachahl had come up with would be too slow.

But Dachahl was not impressed with his father's reasoning. "How many people are you willing to kill to have things your way, father?" he demanded.

"As many as will listen so closely to their fear that reason has no hold on them. These I can afford to lose."

"This is not fair, father," Dachahl protested. "When you are hungry, when you are facing death, when someone you love is threatened, then reason doesn't seem so reasonable anymore!"

"You are a Cholipardo *hardoluno*, like your mother. You insist on trusting the untrustable, and believing in the unbelievable."

So the emperor considered his scholars a fire-hazard, and had been hoping to separate the residue, fire off the most volatile elements, and leave only the safer ones behind. If you didn't consider that this was people's lives he was talking about, it made a sort of sense. But I didn't like it much. I especially didn't appreciate the role I had apparently been assigned in all this. A program was a very diffuse sort of a target to attract the kind of quick fierce reaction the emperor was hoping for, so he set someone he felt he could afford to lose up as a target. Me. Although I'm sure he didn't hope for me to actually get killed—at least, not until after the baby was born.

But if I wasn't happy about it, Dachahl was furious—he'd gone all slit-eyed, and was clenching his hands into fists. And his father had to have known how he would feel about it. No wonder he had refused to tell Dachahl what he was doing.

"Will you oppose me then?" the emperor asked.

Dachahl's jaw tensed. "No, father. You know you have my loyalty. May my wife and I leave now?"

"I meant what I said about her attending planned events without you."

"Yes, father. I knew this would eventually be needed. I have already been preparing a solution for this problem. If you give me another two weeks, I think I will have things arranged." He hadn't told me about any preparations. And even after he told his father that he was making them, he still didn't tell me what they were—but he didn't seem any more tense than usual, so I didn't worry about it.

I discovered the answer a week later, when there was a chime at the curtain while I was working on the clock. I called come in, but it wasn't Langso or Falahni who entered, but Mama, and Papa, and Vanitri and Kasmir, and Naditte and Katrika and Mishok and Nikoli... and bringing up the rear and looking uncomfortable, Bos Kardos.

I almost, very almost, upset my tray of clock pieces, which would have been disastrous. Fortunately, Kasmir asked, "What's this, Batiya, a clock factory?" just in time for me to remember what I was doing.

"It's actually all one clock," I told him as I carefully put the piece I was working on back in its assigned spot. I stacked the trays where the boys wouldn't knock them over, and then I hugged Mama, and Papa, and everyone except Bos. Dachahl walked in right in the middle of it all, and I gave him the biggest hug of all, and told him that he was the most wonderful husband under heaven.

"Naturally."

He had actually come up with his plan to bring my family right after I had been shot at the marriage ceremony. Instead of sending my letter home with a Seafarers' Guild authorized quartermaster, he'd sent it by special courier, in the Volcanis. The Volcanis had docked in Makoviksi and began resupplying while the courier went on to deliver my letter and various gifts—including matching sword and *tirah-fa* sets for my brothers and for Bos Kardos—and an invitation for as many members of the family as desired to come.

I learned later—after the children had been put to bed, and Mama and Naditte had gone off with Chloys, Falahni, and a large collection of *lahnpran* to try on—that there had been a special private message to Vanitri and Kasmir, explaining that the accident mentioned in the letter was no accident, and asking if they would be willing, once again, to help protect their sister.

"You, I did not expect to see," Dachahl told Bos.

"You sent me a sword set, just as you did them." Bos jerked his head toward my brothers.

"This you earned. But Batiya's safety is not your concern."

"Nobody told me that it had anything to do with that. I just heard that her family was going to visit, and I told my uncle that if he failed to take advantage of my friendship with the Imperial House of Shanali to set up a branch of the business here, he was a fool. So I cancelled my temporary berth on the Queen Danyata, and begged for the position of engineer's assistant on the Volcanis."

Dachahl frowned. "This is all business?" Bos looked uncomfortable.

"I noticed that he was unusually interested in my younger sister when he came to our house," I told Dachahl in Hadahnchi, using scolding tones.

Dachahl's scowl eased. "Naturally, you are welcome as a friend of Batiya's family. No discourtesy was intended."

"What exactly do you need us for?" Vanitri asked.

So Dachahl explained, very reluctantly, about how the emperor had been pushing his social reforms through very fast, and how it was making me the target of hate attacks. And then he explained that my guards were expected to stand away from me and allow me to see and be seen, and to have them crowd around me before any fighting started would make me look cowardly and unapproachable, and in short would be politically unfortunate. "When I am with her, no one dares threaten her, but my duties do not permit me to be with her all the time. For the past two weeks she has had a guard sworn to her personal service, who can stand at her shoulder without causing the sorts of rumors that having the palace guards stand close around her would cause. Instead it causes a different sort of talk. Even with Batiya's secretary there also, it would be better if Batiya and her guard are not seen together so much."

"So you just need us to stand by her and watch for trouble?"

"Yes. Some of her ceremonial clothing can hardly be moved in. I need men who can stand beside her, not become distraught if there is suddenly fighting, and who won't hesitate to do whatever needs to be done to help her. Her guards can take care of the rest."

"Sounds like you don't expect us to even get our knuckles bloody," Vanitri said.

"I am deeply saddened to be able to offer you so little entertainment," Dachahl responded. I laughed, and so did Kasmir.

"I'm sure Van can survive for a few months," Kasmir told him. "But if things remain as tame as you say for much longer than that, he'll shoot his horse and jump the river."

"How long?" my father asked.

"I expect things to be worst just before and after the birth of our child."

"And that will be?"

"Two months," I told him. "You can stay for that long?"

Papa gave me a stern look. "We will stay for fifty years, if that's what you need."

Vanitri scowled, and Dachahl went blank-faced— which meant he was trying to hide just how horrible that thought was. I'm sure it wasn't my family staying that bothered him, but the thought that I would need this kind of protection for the rest of my life. I refused to believe it. "Don't be silly, Papa. I can't let Van stick around while my sons are growing up—unless he reforms."

"Oh, yes?" Van growled back. "Well you had better hope that you only have sons, because any daughter raised by you will end up with more turns than a corkscrew!"

Unfortunately Dachahl wasn't distracted by our squabbling. "My goal has been to have Batiya's sons accepted as imperial heirs," he declared. "Once this happens, she will be no more at risk than any member of the imperial family. If it proves impossible, there is no reason for her to continue to be exposed to danger. I can take her to my mother's lands in Cholipardo to live. My mother's people will accept her, and protect her."

There went all the sunshine of me seeing my family again. My family was annoyed with my husband for putting me in danger. My husband was in agony because he'd had to admit just how tenuous my position here was. And my baby decided that it was a good time to do some exercises. Tears began dripping down my cheeks, but I refused to acknowledge them.

My brothers, however, were horrified. "Batya! What's wrong?"

"I'm not crying," I explained. "It's the baby."

"Right, first go all soggy, and then blame the poor little beggar who can't speak for himself!" Kasmir told me.

I punched him in the shoulder. "It's true! Just ask Mama, you idiot. Anyway, I would really like to visit Cholipardo, but I don't intend to get exiled there. So don't you get your hopes up that my husband will let you leech off him forever."

"Hah! Hate to fool you, little sister, but we can live off him whether you want us to or not. We haven't eaten at home one night in twelve ever since the foreign minister himself dropped by to verify that you really were married to–" Kasmir stopped mid-sentence. "Could you wipe those tears off your cheeks, Batiya? I can't figure out if I'm supposed to be teasing you or consoling you!"

I laughed, and that seemed to convince everyone that everything was really all right.

"Would it be possible for me to share in the guarding duties also?" Bos asked. "I wouldn't want to make things look bad, but I'll feel like a coward, if..."

"I'm sure we can arrange for you to take a turn doing something dangerous," I told him. "It wouldn't be fair to let Forang prove his courage, and not you."

"Forang?"

"You'll meet him tomorrow."

I spent far too much of the next morning letting Mama and Naditte fuss over me, while Vanitri, Kasmir and Katrika amused themselves by examining the partially disassembled clock, and the boys annoyed everyone by running around the room and asking when they could see Chunru.

So I told Mama I'd take all the menfolk down to the practice yards to get them out of her hair, and summoned Chloys to take care of her while I was gone. I almost lost Vanitri's company before we even left. I guess he hadn't got a good look at Chloys the night before, or he'd been unusually tired or something. This time, she caught his gaze, and I think it was only the awareness that Mama and Naditte would be horribly in his way that made him decide to come with me.

Forang was there working on his sword skills with Dachahl's own sword master—an honor that I'm not sure he actually wanted. Master Goi Pen Pyung looked like he was about a hundred years old, and he liked to remind his students that when he learned the art, wooden swords were for children and cowards. He was always very careful not to hurt me, but when he was teaching the men, he whacked them with the flat of his blade every time they did anything wrong. But my arrival, as usual, interrupted everything, so that the officers could acknowledge my presence. Afterward, Master Goi Pen Pyung and Forang came over to greet us, rather than going back to lessons. Even Dachahl didn't merit *that* honor.

I started on the introductions, but as soon as I said "This is my father–" Forang dropped to his knees on the grass, and bowed his head low. Papa glared at me. "Stand up, Forang," I ordered. "You're making my father uncomfortable." Forang climbed back to his feet, clearly at a loss as to what he should be doing. "Hold your hand in front of you," I told him.

He did so, and watched in bewilderment as my father grabbed it, jerked it up and down and then dropped it and stepped back. "He is willing to touch me?"

"They're all going to touch you," I told him, grinning, as Vanitri stepped up for his turn. "This time you must squeeze as hard as you can, or my father's oldest son will think you are too weak to protect me."

"Who's the kid?" Vanitri asked as he stepped back and let Kasmir take his turn.

"This is my guard Forang. He's sworn to my personal service, not to the Imperial House."

"What's with the bad haircut?"

"His father tried to kill me."

Kasmir yelped and pulled his hand free of Forang's grasp.

"Swearing to protect me is his way of trying to pay me back for what his father did," I explained. "He's solid. Really. Chunru says he has potential."

"Right, sorry," Kasmir replied and buffeted the bewildered and uncertain Forang on the shoulder. "No offense taken, I hope."

Forang looked like he was about to drop to his knees again, and only remembered just in time that I had forbidden it. "My father's second son strikes you to show that he accepts you as a fellow warrior," I told him. "You should strike him back."

So Forang slammed the heel of his hand into Kasmir's shoulder hard enough to send him reeling across the grass. Vanitri laughed. "Don't hand it out, if you can't take it, little brother," he advised as he cuffed Forang's other shoulder. Valiantly Forang attempted to return that blow as well, but Vanitri grabbed his hand before it arrived. "Nice try, kid. Maybe next time."

Forang backed up a step, and bowed. "The oldest son is a mighty warrior."

"He leads the guards who protect my home district," I explained. "But we have no swords there. Chunru desires that they be taught the proper use of a blade. This is why I have brought them here." I went on to introduce Bos next, as 'the student of my uncle', and my younger brothers.

"You say they need to learn to fight with swords?" Master Goi Pen Pyung asked.

"Yes, Master Goi."

"Good. They will line up. You also. The beginners' drills you can still do, and this will be good for you."

I turned to my brothers and Bos. "Master Goi Pen Pyung is Chunru's sword instructor. He has offered to teach you. This is a very great honor."

"But?" Kasmir asked.

"He's an old-school disciplinarian," I admitted. "I apologize in advance, and please don't disgrace me?"

Vanitri glared at me. "If Haircut can take it, so can we."

They did take it. Even Mishok and Nikoli—when they discovered the offer included them as well. Only Papa stood back. And they made me proud. They weren't nearly as pleased with me as I was with them, though—a great many very evil looks were aimed in my direction, and when Dachahl finally showed up, it was while Nik was whining for the umpteenth time that it wasn't fair that Teacher never hit Batiya.

"My father gave my instructors permission to discipline me, and my colleagues permission to attack me with practice weapons so that I wouldn't grow up weak," Dachahl told him. "But I can't give any man permission to strike my wife."

"Batiya can take it, too! She's tough," Mish assured him.

"This I already know. This every man here already knows. But it would dishonor me to give permission. Instead, Batiya works just as hard as everyone else, without being disciplined."

"I don't suppose you can convince him that as Batiya's brothers, we are also able to work hard without being hit?" Kasmir asked.

"Stop whining, Kas," Van ordered.

"Who's whining?" Kas protested. "I was being curious."

"I can convince him that it is time to end the lesson," Dachahl offered.

Vanitri's eyebrow went up. "Looks like we've hardly started to me." He switched his practice sword into his left hand and flexed the fingers of his right, before running them through his sweat-dampened curls. "I'm good for another couple hours."

"This I am very glad to hear, because I was wondering if you might teach me."

Vanitri grinned. "Of course. Anything for a brother. Was there something in particular you wanted to learn?"

Dachahl drew his *tirah-fa* from his sheath, and the watchers gasped and stepped forward. "I wish to learn how you will stop me with your bare hands, when I attack you with this."

"Here now–!" Bos started to exclaim, but Kasmir grabbed him before he could get any further in his protest.

"It really is a lesson," Kas said, grinning. "Watch."

Vanitri laughed and handed Kas his practice sword. "Make sure the boys stay well back, that toy of his is dangerous."

Kas and I herded Mish and Nik backward with our practice swords while Bos followed, looking anxious and confused. When there was enough space, Dachahl dropped into his fighting stance, and then darted forward. The 'shortened' blade of the *tirah-fa* dove toward Vanitri and then missed—as Vanitri slipped past it, grabbed the hand that wielded it, and then slammed his other elbow into Dachahl's chest. Then Vanitri twisted away and out of range of the blade. "Want to try it again?"

"Naturally." Dachahl tried again, and again his hand was captured and the blade was held harmlessly away, while Vanitri gave him another couple bruises.

"You're making this easy for me," Vanitri told him.

"This, I believe," Dachahl admitted. "How?"

"Half an hour ago I wouldn't have been able to tell you. I would have just said that you have the strangest knife style I've ever seen."

Dachahl's eyes narrowed. "I've vanquished a number of other blades."

"And then there's poor little me with my bare hands," Vanitri countered.

"Yes," Dachahl admitted. "Explain this."

"You're moving like you've got three feet of steel to put between us, when you don't," Vanitri told him. "Your approach–"

I could see where this was heading. "Chunru!"

"Batiya?"

"I shouldn't abandon my mother and sisters for any longer. I will take Papa back with me. But can I leave my younger brothers?"

Dachahl looked over at Nik and Mish who were all eager-eyed and hopeful. "Yes. This can be done."

"Good," I told him. "Have fun!"

Papa and Katrika ended up helping me with the clock, while Chloys told Mama and Naditte all about the week-long celebration of my wedding. When the boys came back, sweaty, battered, and smiling, Bos and Kas came over to see how the clock was progressing, Mish and Nik proudly showed Naditte all the bruises they had got learning sword-fighting so that she could make faces and tell them how terrible they were, and Vanitri leaned against a wall and watched Chloys. I didn't like the look of that.

When Chloys got up to leave and saw Vanitri, she looked stunned, and stumbled a little as if her legs had gone all wobbly. I liked the look of that even less. Fortunately everyone was busy enough that, for the next few days, Van didn't really have time to do much more than stare. But a couple days later I found them standing far too close to each other. It looked like Vanitri was saying something to her. She looked more like a trapped rabbit than someone who was pleased about what she was hearing, but she didn't seem to be able to look away.

He saw me coming, smiled a twisted smile, and walked off—and I decided that it was time for me to say something to Chloys. "I don't think you want to be around Vanitri," I told her. "He is a lot like Chunru, so I don't think you'll like him, and..." I stopped, not sure where to go from there.

"He's... bigger," she said, sounding as if she didn't know if she should be more awed or dismayed.

"He's also a lot more dangerous. Especially when it comes to women."

She went pale. "Will he... hit me?"

"No, no, I didn't mean he hit women, he just..." To say he dishonored them seemed a bit too strong an accusation, but I didn't know a less awful way to say it. I was reminded of Dachahl telling me that his governess hadn't taught him the words. "... He makes them want to do things they shouldn't. So you should stay away from him." She looked even more terrified than she had when she thought he might hit her. And although I could sort of tell that she was trying to avoid him after that, it didn't seem to be working—every time she saw him looking at her, she froze.

Forang was the first one to notice besides me, I think. The day after, at sword-fighting practice, he asked a few hesitant questions, his face carefully blank, about the marital status and prospects of my father's oldest son. I told him, very frankly, that Vanitri wasn't looking for a wife—he'd rather have a different woman every season. Forang's face remained blank, but there seemed to be an extra bit of *moshisha* behind his strikes afterward.

That night Dachahl summoned all my protectors to discuss my schedule. In less than a week, construction would be completed on the ten schools that were being built in the capital city. Teachers had been found for them, and the emperor wanted to get them all running as quickly as possible. Naturally, he also wanted me to be involved in the opening ceremonies—ten opening ceremonies, one right after the other. If the school openings went smoothly, it would do a great deal to solidify both the validity of the emperor's program, and my own position. At least it would do a lot to solidify my position with everyone but the scholars. There didn't seem to be any way to make the scholars think me anything other than a very large nail stuck through their collective shoe.

Unfortunately Dachahl's own busy schedule meant that having him attend more than about half of the ceremonies would make it look like he was ignoring his duties as imperial heir in order to help me do my duties as princess. That would weaken my position.

"Batiya should have two of us with her always," Dachahl explained. "When I cannot be there, it should be

Forang and one of her brothers. Mister Kardos can come with me." And then he described the ceremonies. First there would be a little procession where the school's head teacher, accompanied by guards and various notables, would summon the children of the neighborhood from their homes, and lead them through the streets to the school. I would not be taking part in these or any other processions, Dachahl stated with such forcefulness that it was clear it had been suggested to him. Processions were a security hazard—there would be no more snipers.

"No *more* snipers?" Kasmir asked.

Dachahl very reluctantly admitted that I had already been shot, and then continued with the explanation of the ceremonies. I was to be waiting at the schoolhouse along with a few other important invited guests, and once the children had been led in and seated, and their mothers had entered behind them, I would give a very short speech, welcoming them to the school, as if I were a hostess welcoming them to their new home. "This must be very short," he explained, "because it is necessary that you say it in Stoi Kat also. Chloys will help you with this."

Forang interrupted at this point, to ask if it would be permissible if, when Chloys wasn't helping me, she might assist him in learning the Dostrovian language. Dachahl agreed, and then went on to describe the introduction of the teachers, the blessing of the school, and the distribution of writing slates and school books to the children.

"You're going to do all that in two different languages?" Vanitri asked. "Ouch. If I were one of those kids, I wouldn't want to sit through it even the first time."

Dachahl frowned. "It must be made clear that the school welcomes all children, and teaches in both languages. Having class struggles attached to this is bad enough, we cannot divide the kingdoms over it as well."

"Why don't you give them their slates and books before you do all the blessings?" Kasmir asked. "That way they'll have something to do with themselves."

"This would be a problem, since whatever they find to do will likely disturb the ceremony," Dachahl replied.

"Have them write a short prayer on the slates as part of the ceremony," I suggested. "Since they've never seen writing slates before, they'll be too busy trying to figure out how to make marks that look even vaguely like the prayer the priests are showing them to cause trouble."

My fellow Dostrovians stared at me in shock. "Write an entire prayer?" But Dachahl smiled at me.

"This is a good idea. I will see that it is added." Now they were staring at him.

I laughed. "Changali prayers are usually only two or three words long. The one Dachahl's aunt had me hang on a tree said 'healthy shining son', and it only took seven letters to write."

"And if any of the parents are unsure about the worth of an education to their children, seeing them able to write their own prayers rather than having to ask a priest to do it for them is certain to convince them," Dachahl concluded.

My father-in-law was keeping my husband much busier than he was keeping me, but Dachahl managed to make time to take the family to the imperial "power farm", located a short distance from the palace, and so won my sister Katrika's alliance for forever after. The power farms used water- and wind-powered turbines as sources of electricity, and the Empire's inventors worked at them, coming up with new toys and wonders— including a few flying machines. Dachahl even translated all Katrika's questions to the two men who were working on the flying machines, who spoke Stoi Kat, and then translated their answers back, while I did the same favor for Kas over in the electric workshop, where the emergency light Dachahl had given him had been made.

Everyone in my family enjoyed that trip except Mama and Naditte. I took them to the fabric market the next day to make up for it, while Dachahl took the menfolk to his favorite gun shop, so he could make sure that my guards were properly supplied with firepower.

A week later, Dachahl accompanied me to the first of the school ceremonies, and it almost went exactly as planned. Only two things went wrong. The first was that the procession was a little bit delayed. Apparently a street that didn't usually have horse-drawn carriages on it at all managed to have two crash into each other and everyone was quite certain it couldn't really be an accident. But the head teacher—personally appointed by the emperor, apparently—stayed calm, and simply turned onto a side-street and went around the site of the crash in a big circle. The children, excited at being the center of attention, didn't even seem to notice that there had been a change in plan. Their teacher led them into the simple two-room building with its tiled roof, corner columns of brick, a floor, and walls that were made of yellowish slats from the floor to my shoulder, and above that, panels of some cream-colored material I didn't recognize but which seemed to be slightly translucent, like panes of stained glass, and the adults present managed to settle them on the neat rows of mats that would be their seats.

The second thing that went wrong was that one of the invited guests didn't show up. It was the head teacher's own teacher, now a director at the national school. He came by the palace later to apologize to Dachahl for his absence. "My wife fell suddenly ill, Chunru," he explained, fingering his wisp of a beard. "I'm sure you understand."

"Naturally, I understand," Dachahl told the tall, austere-looking scholar. "And I am greatly saddened to hear of your wife's illness. I will have my imperial father's own doctor sent to her at once."

"This is a great kindness, but it is not necessary. My wife recovered quickly. I would not wish to take the emperor's doctor away from the palace for such a trifle. Especially when your own wife is so likely to be needing him."

"The Princess Pahtia ate well as a child, and is extremely healthy," Dachahl informed him. "But I am delighted to hear that your wife has recovered. This means that you will be able to attend one of the other school opening ceremonies that will be taking place this week. The one the day after tomorrow seems suitable. Your colleague, Master Geum Mev Dhou, has been invited. You can accompany him. I, unfortunately, will be unable to attend, but my wife will be there, with the oldest son of her house. I will introduce him to you, before you leave."

"Van's at the practice yards," I told him.

Dachahl looked over at me, and his eyebrows rose. And then he looked back over at the director. "If you would follow me."

"Oh, no Chunru," the scholar protested. "I wouldn't want you to go out of your way. I can meet your wife's brother wh–"

"This is not out of my way," Dachahl insisted. "I am usually at the practice yards myself at this hour."

Vanitri was engaged in a mock battle, bare-handed and bare-chested, with the commander of my guards. "As you see," Dachahl smiled, "my wife comes from a very healthy family." He summoned both combatants over, and did the introductions, and made a point of telling them both that the visiting scholar was expected at the school opening the day after tomorrow. I think the director hardly even heard him, he was too busy staring, horrified, at Van. I thought I heard him mutter something about hairy animals.

"The princess's brother is a warrior?" he managed to say, finally.

"He trains in the warrior arts when he isn't carrying out the duties of his office, as do I."

"The duties of his office?"

"What did you say your brother did?" Dachahl asked me.

"He designs..." I paused for a moment, unable to find a Hadahnchi word for motorcycle, or even a word for bicycle I could add the word for motor to. Perhaps they'd never heard of bicycles. "... motorcars with two wheels."

"Motorcars with... is this some kind of jest?"

"I traveled for several days on one while I was visiting my wife's country," Dachahl told him. "They are more maneuverable than a four-wheeled vehicle, much as a human is more maneuverable than a horse."

"And you say he *designs* these? He is an architect? A scholar?" He seemed to be trying to hide his horror, but he clearly wasn't succeeding.

"What set his boots on fire?" Van asked.

"We just told him what your job is, and he realized that you're a scholar—more or less," I explained.

"Mark it as less," Van advised. "His type doesn't like to get their hands dirty. I don't want to join his club any more than he wants to join mine."

Kasmir, Forang and Chloys came with me to the next schoolhouse the following morning. Before we even got there, it was obvious there was something wrong—people were running toward the schoolhouse instead of turning to stare at us, and there was shouting and the smell of smoke. I wasn't at all surprised to see flames running up one of the walls of the new school, just disappointed. "Where's the fire department?" Kasmir demanded. "Have they got everyone out of the neighboring buildings?"

"I'll find out," I vowed.

But apparently this was a Gar Mian district of the city, and the predominant language was Stoi Kat, and the guards that had been assigned to protect the site were missing. I ended up sending my guard commander off to find someone, anyone, who knew what was going on. And then I had Forang climb on top of our automobile and shout orders at the crowd. We seemed to be being successful in getting them to calm down and move away from the building, but when my guard commander got back he told me that the firefighters couldn't get through the press of people. "You need to take some of your men, and help them out," I told him.

"We can't leave you, Princess. Chunru would have our heads." If something happened to me while they were gone, that might even be true.

"Then I will have to come with you."

He protested. But what could he do? He wasn't allowed to touch me, Kasmir didn't know what was going on, and Forang was on the roof of the automobile. Telling Forang and Chloys to stay where they were and keep things here under control, I walked in the direction that he had said the firefighters were, and the commander and all his men had to scramble to push back the crowd and open up a way. Kasmir followed me, suspicious, but not confident enough that I was getting myself into trouble to stop me. Van would have grabbed me.

But it worked. My guards pushed the crowd out of the way, and I led the firefighters back to the school, and they managed to keep the fire from spreading, but by the time they had put it out, the wall was only half there and the other walls were a bit scorched and everything was filthy. "What do you think, Kasmir? Is the structure still sound?"

"I'll check it out."

He finished his inspection just as the procession of schoolchildren arrived with their teachers and the missing guards, who looked a little rumpled and very tense. I learned later that they had been lured away from the site by people throwing rocks.

"Is the building safe?" I asked.

"Yeah, it's solid. You want to know why?"

I didn't think I had time to hear his analysis; I was too busy leading the children inside the blackened and soot-covered wreckage. But that didn't stop Kas, of course, he just kept babbling to me about architectural designs where the walls did not support the roof, and so could make use of lightweight construction materials such as paper.

I started the ceremonies, cutting Kas off before he could tell me anything weirder, more incredible, and even more distracting than that Changali peasants built buildings with paper walls.

Dachahl arrived about halfway through. He must have heard about the fire, and left his other duties and come running. I smiled at him, and continued. Afterward he got caught in a discussion with the head teacher about repairs, and I had to wait for him at the automobiles. "You just walked all those children into a burnt building?" he asked when he finally caught up with me.

"Only after I had Kasmir do a safety check."

He laughed. "Batiya, I think my imperial father will like this."

I think he was right. That afternoon the emperor actually came to visit me in his chambers, and had me explain what had happened, and allowed me to introduce my family. And, just before he left, he told me that he had chosen craftsmen to work on the clock restoration. As soon as he had gone, my family, who had remained mercifully quiet while he was there, burst into a babble of speech. It started with Kasmir saying that now he knew where Chunru got the stick-like backbone from, and Mama saying, "Oh, Batya, poor dear, is he always like this?"

I didn't think I wanted to admit how much worse he usually was. Instead I just grinned and admitted that he could be scary.

"Is he going to chop your head off?" Mishok wanted to know.

"Oh, no, he can't do that. I'm his daughter-in-law." I was just painting the fence white. I didn't believe my being his daughter-in-law would stop him from ordering my execution. But I did think he was starting to believe that keeping me alive might actually be a good thing.

The next morning, the director who had missed the first opening showed up, just as Dachahl had insisted. He had another scholar with him—the one that had originally been invited to this ceremony, I assumed—and just barely before the ceremony was about to start about seven more scholars came trooping into the school. They were all young men, in matching outfits, and with an air of bravado about them that made my hackles rise. Beside me, Vanitri seemed to be reacting the same way. "Who invited them?" he asked in an undertone.

"I think they jumped the garden fence," I replied.

"So you don't know who they are?"

Not specifically, but they were too distinctive to be completely unknown... Scholar class. Young. Uniformed. "Students from the University?" I deduced.

"Frat boys," Vanitri growled. "Just what this circus needs."

Chapter Six

I Leave the Imperial Palace

A few of the officials were looking at the students uneasily, and shifting a bit as if trying to decide if they should do something about them, but then the head teacher arrived with the children, and the moment was lost as children trooped in and were shown their assigned seats. I said my little speech without incident, but when it was time to introduce the teachers, the seven students stepped forward and two of them began talking—in Stoi Kat. I looked over at Chloys.

"They are the current students of the head teacher's former tutor. They're saying they want to do a demonstration for their senior, showing their proper appreciation for his new office—but they're addressing him in the intimate register, I don't think–"

While Chloys was explaining, they had crowded around the head teacher, and ignoring his protest they had removed his hat. Suddenly Van launched himself toward them, and grabbed the arm of one, pulling him away from his friends. The student was holding a knife. A handful of the other students turned about to support their companion, throwing themselves at Vanitri. Meanwhile, the rest of them renewed their assault on the head teacher, one grabbing ahold of the long loose tail that fell down his back, and another pulling out a knife of his own. The children squealed, and leapt to their feet. The visitors and guests surged about, some racing forward, some drawing back, while a few of the more sensible ones tried to gather the children together, and there were shouts from the crowd gathered outside.

Forang leaped into the fray, sword drawn. There was a shriek, the knife spun off in the direction of the children who variously yelled and squealed and cowered, and people surged through the door. My guards were busy trying to separate Vanitri from the students; Forang, blood dripping from the blade of his sword, was guarding the head teacher; and still more people were pouring in, mostly men. Fathers wanting to know what was happening to their children? Some of the children had been picked up—by their mothers, I assumed, but most of them were retreating from the surging crowd, frightened and bewildered. I saw one little girl stagger and fall, and dashed forward and scooped her up before she could be stepped on. The bulk of my belly made holding her awkward, though—as soon as Chloys caught up with me, I pushed the girl into her arms.

Vanitri showed up next—apparently, my guards had managed to get him free, and he had remembered that I was supposed to be his priority. He pushed away a couple people who were about to stumble into me. "We need to get you somewhere safe," he hollered over the cacophony. "I don't know that the walls will hold."

Not being as tall as Van, I hadn't really noticed the walls—there were too many people in the way. Now that he mentioned them, I realized that they were shaking, as the crowd outside pressed against them. I still didn't see how they could possibly be made of paper, but Kas must have been right when he said that they were not built strong enough to hold up a roof. There was so many people inside the schoolhouse by then, I figured that three of the walls were as likely to fall outward as inward, if they ended up going anywhere. But against the fourth wall, there were frightened children huddling. "Van! What about the kids?"

"Aw, hell, Batya, I'm supposed to be protecting you!" But he turned and waded through the crowd, arriving just as a section of wall came loose and began pushing inward. He stepped over the children and slammed his shoulder against the wall, pushing it back as the children attempted to flee from the huge foreign man with ghost eyes and straw-colored curls.

"Forang! Forang!" I yelled. "Go help Vanitri!" I knew he could never hold the wall back against the force of the crowd outside all by himself. "Pick up the children!" I hollered. "Children to the center of the room! Guards! To the wall!" I think that at least some of them obeyed me, but now that I didn't have Vanitri's bulk to protect me, I got surrounded by the crowd, and was too busy being pushed and shoved about to see. It was especially awkward because people kept stepping on my *lahnpran*. I finally picked it up and looped it over my arm, which allowed me to move. Only I had barely taken two steps when one of the 'frat boys' bumped very painfully into my stomach, and grabbed me. I didn't know if he was just trying to steady himself or something else, and I didn't much care at that point. I stomped on his foot, gave him a bloody nose, and then when he staggered back away from me, I grabbed Chloys, still holding the crying little girl, and stepped into the space he used to be in.

"Chant with me," I ordered her. "Nobody move! Nobody move!" Chloys got the idea, and joined in, so I poked the crying girl. "You too," I told her. "Nobody move."

"Nobody move," she whimpered.

Then I got the attention of everyone around me, and ordered them to join. Eventually the crowd got the idea, and I heard the chant spreading across the room. Gradually the movement in the room stilled and the noise died down except for the chant and the crying of children and a moaning that was probably from whoever Forang had attacked.

Once the worst of the pushing and shoving had stopped I changed my chant. "Children move inward!" Gradually that one spread also, and dragging Chloys I followed the small ripples of movement until she and I and all the children along with some other children-toting women were in a knot at the middle of the room.

That chant gradually died down, and into the stunned and uneasy almost-silence I demanded in my clearest, most authoritative voice, "Forang, how is the wall?"

"The crowd outside has stopped pushing, Princess, and your father's eldest son is holding it in place without assistance."

"Good. You will return to your place at my side. My other guards will work their way over to the door, and clear a path through the crowd outside, so that those inside may leave. Anyone who is standing next to someone who is bleeding or incapable of standing without assistance, raise your hands into the air."

A few clumps of hands rose.

"The one who was in charge of the blessing ceremony will now assign people to attend to the injured," I announced. "Everyone else will remain silent so they can hear and follow his instructions."

An ancient priest began issuing instructions in a firm, if not particularly loud, voice, and I got to rest. It was nice to have someone else in charge for a while. I squatted down among the children, and let them touch my hair, and just waited for the press of people around us to gradually lessen as the people who shouldn't have been there were gently but firmly conducted back outside by my guards. And then, finally, there was only the mothers, and the invited guests, and the students that had started the trouble in the first place. And Vanitri, still leaning against the wall.

"Batiya, this is getting boring."

"Sorry, Van." I stood up and led the children over to the far side of the room, and then Vanitri stepped away from the loose section of wall and let it thump to the floor, sending dust billowing up everywhere. Through the hole, the watching crowd first gaped, and then turned away, as if worried that they would be held responsible for the damage.

Vanitri brushed off his hands, and turned to me. "I gotta say, little sister, you sure know how to throw a party." He strolled over to where the students were standing together watching as the priests bandaged up the arm of one of them, and examined them. "What happens to these string beans?"

"I have no idea. I don't think they meant to hurt anyone. I think they were just trying to give the school's head teacher a haircut."

"A haircut!" Vanitri exclaimed, turning around to look at me. Then his eyes narrowed as his gaze fell on Forang. "Right. A haircut." His hands sped toward one of the students, and a blade flashed. The student cried out in shock and outrage, as Vanitri backed out of the way, a knife that he must have taken from them in the scuffle earlier in his right hand and something long and dark dangling from the other. It was the student's tail of hair. Vanitri carried it over to the head teacher, and handed it to him. "Trophy," he announced.

All the students were protesting, and the two older invited scholars as well, but they had also, I noticed, backed away from their shorn comrade—not wanting to be associated with his shame. The director from the university took a couple steps toward Vanitri, thought better of it, and approached me instead. "This is an intolerable assault on the dignity of my school!" he complained.

"This was not what he intended to do to his own senior?" I asked.

The director shifted about uncomfortably. "This can't be proved."

"If the young man who lost his hair to my brother's sense of justice wishes to give my brother the same treatment in return, I promise that no one will make any move to stop him."

Everyone in the room turned to look at Vanitri's short curls. "But..."

"If he wishes some other form of recompense, he may take his case to Chunru. I'm sure my husband will be very just in his rulings."

None of the scholars present seemed eager to face my husband, either.

"If anyone here does not wish to present themselves before Chunru, then I suggest they leave immediately. I am sure that he has already been informed that there was a disturbance, and is on his way here. He is sure to demand explanations."

All seven of the young scholars, even the one Forang sliced, decided to take my advice. Six left with bows and polite if insincere phrases—the seventh in shamed silence.

"Good!" I said, and turned to my guards. "Please clear the floor so the children can return to their seats."

"You are continuing this travesty of a ceremony?" the director squawked.

"Of course. If ever a building needed a blessing, this one does. And the children must learn who their teachers will be, and receive their books and slates."

"Half of these slates you brought from your barbaric country were broken during the disturbance," I was told in tones that were far too cheerful for the delivery of bad news.

"The slates were made by craftsmen in the Wadz Kiar district. They will provide replacements. In the meantime, we will hand out the materials that we have—the children can practice writing characters on the floor, if no more suitable place can be found."

"On the floor! What sort of a school do you intend to make this?"

L. Shelby

"The sort that carries out the emperor's orders to educate these children, no matter what barriers lie across the path."

"Impossible. No school could do that! Everyone knows that most peasant children are far too simple to learn a scholar's skills."

"Are you telling me that Changali children are less able to learn than southerner children?" I demanded.

There were hisses from various parts of the room.

"I'm telling you it cannot be done!" he responded. "Look at these little ground-fowl. Dirty, noisy, ignorant, lacking any elegance. They don't have the soul for true understanding."

"I see nothing wrong with these children, other than that they have spent the past hour trying to avoid being walked on," I replied. "I assume they are just as capable of learning as the children in my home country, and although their souls may not ever understand all that yours does, they will probably understand a great many things yours does not. You must return to your place now, so that they may return to theirs."

"I am telling y–"

"Forang, this man is in my way. Remove him."

Forang stepped forward and lifted his blade. The director's eyes went wide. "I am–" Forang took another step forward, and the director stepped back. "This is intolerable!"

"If you do not feel able to tolerate it, you may leave. You can explain to Chunru why you were unable to tolerate it later today."

To my amazement, he drew himself up, spun about, and walked out of the schoolhouse. I didn't think he was

225

that stupid. The other invited scholar dithered for a bit, and then bowed and apologized before following him.

I looked over at the priests. "Does anyone else feel the need to leave before this ceremony is finished?"

None of the priests left, and we finished the introduction of the teachers, and the handing out of school materials—dealing with the shortage of slates by asking siblings to share—and were halfway through the blessing when Dachahl arrived.

"What took you so long?" I asked him afterward.

"This time, I finished what I was doing first," he told me. "I was certain you would keep everything moving forward without me."

"If I'm told to make a ceremony happen, I make the ceremony happen," I agreed. "But what about when I'm gone? Are these children going to be safe?" That was yet another thing I hadn't been considering it seemed. I had figured out that I would not be safe until the Changali people had accepted the emperor's new education program, but I hadn't realized that the schoolchildren themselves would be in danger. Dachahl was more right than I realized when he had said my safety had become all tangled together with the well-being of his empire.

Dachahl was frowning. "We very carefully chose the locations of the ten Pai Lan Chung schools, so that they would be in districts where the locals are particularly in favor of the new program. And we have arranged for imperial guards to be present for as long as we can spare them. But perhaps this is insufficient, and the school system will need to have its own special guard unit. I will speak to my father about this."

"And it seems that the school's teachers are particularly at risk?"

"This was already known. We have made what arrangements we could." His scowl deepened. "You are particularly at risk also."

"This was already known," I told him, teasing.

"As soon as all the schools have been opened, I want to send you to Cholipardo," he told me.

"Send? I thought you wanted to *take* me to Cholipardo," I protested.

"Yes. I would have taken you earlier if I could have, but now is a good time. It will look as if I wish to have my child born among my mother's people. This is very traditional. But with ninety more schools to be opened in the next two seasons, there are things here I should still be doing. With your family with you I can be sure you will be well guarded, and I can stay for a while without worrying, and join you later when my duties here are completed."

I didn't like it. But if having me in Cholipardo made Dachahl worry less, it was probably worth it. "You will hurry and finish as fast you can?"

"I will hurry and finish as fast as I can," he agreed.

"Good. Because if the baby comes before you do, I am going to be very distraught."

"This is something I do not wish to miss," he assured me.

He probably would have preferred to have missed the next meeting with his father, though. The director decided that he would make his explanations to the emperor, rather than to Chunru. His explanations included the claim that the traitor's son had gratuitously attacked one of his unarmed students and seriously injured him, and that Vanitri had demonstrated the most disgraceful conduct. So I had been summoned along with Chunru and Forang and Vanitri, and Chloys, to act as Vanitri's translator.

The director did not look happy to see Dachahl enter the room, although how he could have deluded himself into thinking Chunru would have missed this garden party, I couldn't imagine. He would have come even if his father hadn't ordered his presence. Dachahl seated me next to his father, and stood behind me, and then Vanitri and Forang were called forward to give their versions of the day's events. Neither of them had much to say. Vanitri said that he had attempted to take a knife away from some uninvited visitors and then had gone to 'help the kids', at my insistence. Forang said that he had remained beside me while my brother had dealt with the first weapon displayed, but when a second knife had made an appearance, he had felt it his duty to eliminate the threat.

"Threat?" the director protested. "The knife was very small."

Forang regretted that he had not brought a small knife himself, but had been armed only with a sword, and that he had yet to master my brother's art of vanquishing a knife blade with his bare hands, although he had been taking lessons.

"And the students were threatening my son's wife, with these knives?" the emperor asked.

Forang admitted that they had not directly threatened the princess, but that they were being waved around wildly, that Vanitri's attempt to take the first knife had been resisted, and that he had not been able to think of any acceptable reason for a knife to be bared in the middle of the ceremony at all.

The emperor turned back to the director. "And why were your students wielding knives?"

"This was mere youthful liverishness," the director proclaimed grandly. "A student's prank. The reaction of the princess's guards was completely disproportionate to the actual threat."

"The tendency toward youthful liverishness seen in the students at your school is precisely the reason I did not care to have my son attend," the emperor announced. "I do not consider youthful liverishness an adequate excuse for the disturbances caused by your students in areas other than the school district. If any more displays of youthful liverishness on the part of your students are brought to my attention, I will grant you the courtesy of allowing you to resign."

Looking as if he had swallowed about three frogs at once, the director bowed low. "I regret if my shortcomings as a director have caused you to hear unpleasant news," he said. But he still hadn't learned his lesson. "However, the foreigner cut the hair of one of my most promising students! Surely you will not permit such acts of barbarity to go unpunished?" So then the emperor had to ask Van why he had cut off someone's hair, and bit by bit the entire story came out. And in the end the emperor retracted the courtesy of allowing the director to resign. He was to be transferred to the national school in the Lahdungnar territories in the far north instead, and if the students there started suddenly to display youthful liverishness, *then* he would be allowed to resign. The school here would receive a new director—one who had the sense to discipline his students, starting with the ones who had such poor judgement that they attempt to play a liverish prank at a ceremony planned by the emperor and attended by a member of the imperial family and her guards.

But by the time the emperor made that announcement Dachahl had learned that I had been left at the mercy of the crowd for long enough to punch a student in the face, and he was very angry. Not so much with Vanitri and Forang as just with the state of the universe, but he invited Forang to accompany him to the practice yards anyway, and Forang knew as well as I did that by the time Dachahl finished sparring with him, he'd be wearing a skin-deep layer of black and blue. But he gulped, and agreed anyway.

Unfortunately, that left Vanitri free to chase Chloys. I did my best to protect her, by dragging her back to my rooms and making sure that she stayed in the middle of my family, while I explained about Dachahl's plan to send us all to Cholipardo in a couple of weeks—everyone seemed to think it was a lovely idea, except Katrika, who didn't want to be so far away from the power farm and its flying machines—but the presence of the family didn't make Van give up, it just made him change his tactics. He treated Chloys so gently, so politely, that even my mother couldn't find anything to complain about. That evening Kasmir approached Dachahl and asked what would happen if my secretary gave birth to a blue-eyed baby sometime in the next year.

"This is likely to happen?" Dachahl asked.

"I don't know that I'd say *likely*," Kasmir answered, "but everyone in West Borstev is careful not to mention that Mrs. Stapegaw's oldest girl looks more like our family than the Stapegaw's."

Dachahl turned to me, shocked. "Your brother doesn't support his own children?"

"*Mister* Stapegaw wouldn't thank him if he tried," Kasmir explained.

"This I forgot," Dachahl admitted. "The custom of a dishonored woman restoring her honor by marrying, I do not understand."

"Who told you that?" I asked.

"This was explained to me on the Majestique, when I wished to understand why you were being treated so poorly."

"Dotrossak told you that the only way to restore my honor was to marry me, didn't he?" I demanded.

"Yes. This was said."

"That isn't why you married me, is it?" I wailed.

"This was the reason I gave Captain Melius why we could not wait," he told me. "I knew it was unnecessary, because I knew you had never been dishonored. But I did not *wish* to wait."

Oh. I hadn't wanted to wait either. "That's fine then."

"But it doesn't answer my question," Kasmir pointed out. "If marriage doesn't make her respectable again, I guess you won't be bribing anyone to stand up in church with her, so what happens instead?"

Dachahl considered. "If an unmarried girl has a child, and she names a father and claims to have been forced, then he must pay her the child fee, and will be publicly beaten. She is then treated as if she was his widow, until she marries, if she ever does."

I knew Vanitri didn't force his girlfriends—he didn't need to. And I couldn't imagine Chloys saying that she had been forced when she hadn't been. "What if she doesn't claim to have been forced?"

"If no man steps forward to pay the child price, then they are usually drowned."

"What?" Kasmir didn't like that any more than I had.

"Nameless babies, not their mothers," Dachahl explained, as if that made everything fine. I didn't think it did, and from the look on his face, neither did Kasmir. But he only swallowed once, and then managed to ask what happened if the father paid, without saying anything unpleasant.

"The father may either raise the child himself, or the child price is given to a temple, and the child is placed in the orphanage there. The mother cannot marry, and so she often joins a temple also. Frequently the same one."

"Vanitri would pay," Kasmir said. "But by Belkov's toes, some women shouldn't become nuns!"

"Not you too!" I groaned.

"No, no. You know I'm the good one," he said. "But I no longer think you have coleslaw for brains for finding a foreigner attractive."

I grimaced. "Van's the one with coleslaw for brains."

"Maybe you could warn her away from him?" Kasmir suggested doubtfully.

"I tried," I admitted. "She doesn't seem to have enough *moshisha* to tell him to jump off."

"She might think that it is her duty to serve him," Dachahl admitted.

"What do you mean by 'serve'?"

"As a member of the palace staff, it is her duty to fulfill the emperor's requests first, and secondly to fulfill the requests of the royal family, and afterward the requests of any of the emperor's guests, and lastly the requests of any senior staff. Your brothers are guests."

"*Any* requests?" Kasmir demanded. "So if I asked one of the maids to spend the night with me, she would?"

"Yes," Dachahl admitted. "But this is not the action of an honorable guest, turning the Imperial Palace into a pleasure house. If you desire courtesans, they should be hired. I can direct you to a house with a good reputation."

"I can't believe you just admitted to knowing where to find a good whorehouse right in front of Batiya," Kasmir told him. "You're a braver man than I am! Unfortunately your courage isn't going to be much help. Van doesn't believe in paying for what he can so often get for free."

Kasmir wandered off, and Dachahl looked over at me with a crease between his eyebrows. "This makes you distraught, me knowing where a pleasure house can be found?"

I wasn't naive enough to believe it possible for him to have grown up without learning that much, and I was determined not to wonder if he had ever used their services. "What would happen to the maids, if my brothers requested their services?"

"If they have a child, it would be the same as if they had been forced. No loss of honor is suffered. They would keep the child if they desired, and your brothers would be required to pay the child price."

"With those rules, I would think that most women would claim to be forced, even if they weren't," I told him.

"This is so," he admitted. "He can attempt to establish his innocence, but any man who sleeps with a woman other than his own should expect to wear stripes."

"Stripes?"

"The marks where the bamboo rod strikes them."

"Does it ever happen the other way around? He says he forced her, even though he didn't really?"

"Naturally. If my father had continued to refuse to accept our marriage, I would have worn stripes for this child and for every child that followed."

I was glad I hadn't known that until after our marriage had been legalized. "Please don't tell my mother about any of this," I begged. "Not about how you would have worn stripes, and especially not about drowning nameless bab—" *Nameless* babies. *"This* is why they would drown my child if someone managed to... My baby wouldn't be allowed to have your name anymore. Why not?"

"An imperial heir must not have multiple fathers," Dachahl told me. "Some other man would be allowed to claim such a child if he desired, but I cannot."

"No child has multiple fathers," I protested.

"This is not true," he said, very seriously. "More than one father is possible. This is known. What is not known is how often it happens, and whether it can happen at any time while the child is inside the mother. The scholars who study births in animals seem to think that it happens very, very rarely, and only at the beginning. But the tradition in Nash Vaur and Gar Mian is that any man who is with the mother during the time the child is carried has an equal claim to fatherhood."

"That tradition is complete nonsense," I told him.

"Many Cholipardo and Holahchi men like supporting this tradition, because it means that a courtesan may never claim a child price from any of the men she serves."

"This is not a good reason to let your child be killed just because something bad happens to me," I told him fiercely. "You should have your scholars do a study, and show that it happens so rarely that it isn't worth worrying about, and that it can't possibly happen when the baby has been carried already for three seasons. And then you should change your law."

"That is a very good plan," he told me. "If I can find a scholar willing and able to do this study, I will have this done."

I contemplated the fact that his father was already sifting through the chaff, trying to find enough scholars willing to take on the task of teaching peasant children, and discovered that tears were pouring down my face.

"Batiya!" Dachahl exclaimed, horrified, "even with this law, our child is safe. I won't let anything bad happen to you!"

"I know that, silly man!" I told him. "I haven't flipped my wagon. This is just the baby, turning the taps on for me again." I wiped away the tears and gave him a hug, and then went off to tell Vanitri that Chloys would be running away from him as fast as she could, if it wasn't against the rules.

"As part of the palace staff, she's supposed to give you anything you ask for," I told him, once I had tracked him down at the practice yards. "And it's your job not to ask her for anything she shouldn't be giving you. That's how they work it here."

"What happens between me and Chloys is not your cart to haul," he growled at me, whacking his practice sword fretfully against his side.

"Oh, yes it is! I *need* her. She's the only woman in Changali that speaks and writes Dostrovian. I can't have her going off and becoming a nun. And I can't have her killing herself either."

"You don't know anything about it," he said, "so just keep your nose off my window!"

"I may be your little sister, Van, but I'm also a married woman with my own little 'interesting package' on the way. I already know what you are doing with your girlfriends, and I have a pretty good grasp of why they let you. But Chloys isn't from West Borstev. She grew up knowing it was her duty to do whatever Dachahl told her to do, no matter how much she hated it, and now she thinks she's supposed to do the same for you. Even if she likes what you're doing, I don't think she actually wants it to happen. So it's still the same thing as going to the Night District and buying some poor kid off one of the madams. It's unforgivable. It's *worse* than unforgivable. You don't touch anyone who works in this palace. I mean it!"

"Fine," he told me angrily, "I won't. But you have nothing to say about any girl and me after this. Grab that!"

I knew he meant it. If I tried to interfere, he might even do the opposite of what I asked just to spite me—but at least I had rescued Chloys from any possible disaster, and I could always hope that the next girl wouldn't be quite as helpless as Chloys was. It seemed likely—I had trouble imagining any girl more helpless than Chloys.

Dachahl came with me to the next school opening, and everything ran perfectly smoothly. That seemed to annoy him rather than please him. "Why don't they try anything when I'm *here*?" he demanded.

"Because you're fearsome," I replied. "I told you so before." But it seemed that the way the earlier incidents had turned out had discouraged people from trying anything else. Van caught someone painting words on the wall of one schoolhouse while the guard's back was turned, but he—even without speaking the same language—managed to convince them to paint them out again immediately, and other than that, the only notable incident from the rest of the ceremonies actually *did* happen while Dachahl was there.

We were standing together during the next-to-last school opening, listening to the blessings of the priests and watching the children struggle to write the assigned prayer on their slates, when we started hearing sounds of angry muttering in Stoi Kat. And then the government official next to Dachahl suddenly stumbled into him as if he'd been pushed. The mutters rose to shouts, and Dachahl stepped forward to get a better view of what was going on. The next thing I knew he had someone by the collar and was shaking him. Another man launched himself toward the two of them, and then stopped abruptly when he found the blade of Bos's sword blocking his way. The crowd murmured and shifted, but this time the guards knew what to do, and they moved to block the door so that the crowd outside couldn't try to join in.

I couldn't understand what Dachahl was saying to the two men, but he sounded pretty angry. I did hear voices shouting from outside, asking what was happening. One of the guards at the door answered, and there was a roar of laughter from the crowd outside. That seemed to get the two men's attention even better than having Chunru angry with them had, and they both seemed to cringe back. Dachahl said two more words, and they backed quietly into their places, looking like they'd just lost Kebvar Pass. Bos looked over at Dachahl, and then they both moved back to their places by my side. "I'd like to know what that was about," Bos muttered.

I wanted to know too, and as soon as we were back in the automobile heading for the palace, I asked. Dachahl grinned. "One was a minor government official, and the other was an assistant teacher. I don't think that anyone realized when the invitations were sent out, but they were also brothers by marriage, and had differing views on the value of educating peasants and just about everything else under heaven."

"And they somehow forgot where they were, and got into a fight right there, in front of all the children, and you and everything?" I asked, amazed.

"With insults said about each other's mothers, and references to bad behavior at weddings and everything." Dachahl laughed, and I laughed too, but when I'd had more time to think over what it meant, I realized that it wasn't very funny at all.

"The scholars are still really angry and scared, aren't they? The school openings going as well as they have doesn't really mean anything has improved. Things are still going just the way your father planned."

"Yes," Dachahl admitted. "The students at the national school are running wild, there are riots in the streets nearly every night, and the communication stations are seeing far too much activity. Because hardly anyone other than the scholars knows how to read the electronic codes, it's been impossible to find out what is being said, exactly. But a great many more messages are being sent from Pai Lan Chung out to various parts of the country than is usual. My father thinks that the scholars are planning to gather together and do something violent. He has everyone in the palace running about, trying to prepare for some kind of attack. I did not think I would ever say this, but I am very glad that you are leaving me the day after tomorrow."

Almost as soon as we arrived at the palace, Chloys came running out, and informed us, breathlessly, that Imperial Princess Lulahn had returned to the palace. "I was giving the princess's sworn guard a language lesson, and the emperor summoned me, and there she was. And then he took her to your family and introduced them," she added.

I couldn't imagine either Lulahn or my family enjoying that, but it sounded very hopeful for the emperor and myself. I looked at Dachahl to see what he thought, and discovered that he was frowning. "Why did she return to the palace?" he asked.

"This I do not know," Chloys admitted. "I regret–" But Dachahl was already striding off before she finished apologizing. I tried to keep up with him, but with only about a month to go before the baby came, I was showing a distinct tendency to waddle. By the time I caught up to him, he had managed to find one of his father's aides to interrogate.

"The Prince and Princess of Nash Vaur think that their daughter is not safe in the capital, and have decided to remove her to their own lands," he told me. "My sister does not like the climate there, and declined to accompany them."

I didn't think I cared much one way or another. Lulahn was sure not to like having my family about, but that was hers to worry about. I didn't think much about the effect Lulahn would have on my family, until Kasmir interrupted me as I was assembling the pieces of the Tilardu clock to tell me that he didn't think I needed to worry this time—he was pretty sure Vanitri was just amusing himself because he was bored.

I continued tightening the tiny bolt that held the mechanism for one of the dancing figures in place, and wondered if I was supposed to know what Kas was talking about.

"I mean, he couldn't really mean to do anything," he continued, "she's his sister-in-law! It was probably just the way she acted like we were covered in muck when her father introduced us. He figures she deserves to be taught a lesson."

I put down the wrench. "Kas, what is Van doing to the Princess Lulahn, exactly?"

"He's not doing anything to her," Kas responded. "He's reading a book."

Oh. Oh, dear. "Is it working?"

Kas looked over at where Dachahl was sprawled on a mat, the scroll he had been reading ignored as he looked up at me and Kas, a question in his eyes. Kas swallowed. "Yeah. It seems to be working even better than usual. But we're leaving the day after tomorrow, right? Even Van isn't going to get anywhere that fast."

"Yes," I agreed. "But thanks for the warning."

"What is reading a book supposed to do to my sister?" Dachahl asked once he had left.

"It gives your sister a chance to look at him," I responded.

"Why would she be looking at him?" he asked, puzzled. "Wouldn't she just ignore him?"

As a general rule, girls were about as successful at ignoring Van as I was at ignoring Dachahl. "It only works on girls who find him very..."

"This is the 'very' that you keep saying I am, and then not explaining afterward?"

"But they don't want to admit it to themselves. So they say, no, no, he's just a horse."

"He's a *horse*?"

"Strong enough to be useful when it comes to carrying things, and pretty enough to look at when running around in a field, but without much going on in the brain-box, and not something you want crashing about in your house."

"Yes, I can see my sister thinking this," Dachahl admitted. "But what does this have to do with being 'very'?"

"He uses it against them. Every time she looks at him, her heart beats louder and her knees feel weak, but she doesn't want to admit that–"

"Ah! So when you say I look 'very', you mean that I make your heart beat louder?"

"–so she says, 'he's just a horse, and I am far too important to feel like this toward a horse'–"

"And your knees feel weak?"

"–but then before she can turn away, he turns away from her—as if he's decided she's not worth it—and starts reading a book instead. Makes her feel–"

"And I can use this against you?"

"Yes, you should use it against me," I recommended at once.

He laughed, and tossed the scroll aside.

He didn't laugh when he actually saw Vanitri and his sister together, though. When I got back from the final school opening ceremony, he was out on the little island in the middle of the lake, scowling thoughtfully at the water. "Your brother is just amusing himself?" he asked me when I found him there.

"You mean Van? I haven't even seen him yet."

"She came to me. She said I had to punish him for insulting her."

"What did he do?"

"He *looked* at her."

I wanted to laugh, but it wasn't really funny. "I'm sure Kas is right. Van *can't* be serious—even if she wasn't his sister-in-law, he knows we're leaving tomorrow."

"My father wants to send her to Cholipardo with you."

I managed, just barely, to not groan. "This journey is how long?" Dachahl didn't answer. He knew that I already knew that it would be two very long days in the automobiles, and that I was just whining. "And how long will they be there together, afterward?"

"This is something you do not want to happen." His arms went around me, and he squeezed hard enough that the baby kicked him.

"This is something I don't want to stop from happening," I warned him. "Van may not be good to other women, but he makes me feel safer. If I can't have you with me, I want to have him. But it isn't right that your sister can't go to her own home just because my brother is there."

"I can't stop this from happening," he admitted. "Instead I'm going to go with you."

Yes! That sounded lovely. Yes, yes, yes! But... "You told me you couldn't."

"I will say that I had to assign all my work to someone else, because Lulahn demanded that I come."

I choked. It was supposed to be a laugh, but I was so startled it didn't come out right, and turned into a coughing fit. "You will blame it on *Lulahn*?"

"This I can do," he assured me. "She will not be harmed by this."

"But that's just not right, Dachahl! Why is it fine for your sister to demand you come, when I can't?"

"Because you are the mother of the next emperor, and she is not."

That made a strange sort of sense—although the thought that I was now a more important person than Dachahl's sister still seemed a little unnatural. It was also probably the reason she hated me. All her life she would have known that unless something terrible happened to her older brother, she would end up losing her place as the highest lady in all the land to his wife. She also knew Dachahl was likely to marry a nobody. She probably hoped for a sweet shy little thing she could patronize—instead he brought home a fierce strange-looking foreigner with oily fingers and a head full of gears.

It didn't make me like her any more, but I did feel a little sorry for her. And I was very willing to accept her company—anything so that I could have Dachahl with me.

Dachahl went off to tell his father his decision, and although I was pretty sure his father had argued with him about it, he returned looking so triumphant it was clear he had won. Packing was never a problem for Dachahl or me —Langso and Falahni did everything—so all we had to do was show up the next morning. Dachahl made sure that all my southerner guards had their guns and *tirah-fas* with them, and their swords stowed in the luggage compartments beneath the seats of the four imperial automobiles waiting for us, and then we seated ourselves in ours and waited. My family wasn't quite so comfortable leaving everything to the palace servants, and in all the confusion of them trying to get sorted and loaded, it took quite a while for anyone to notice that Katrika wasn't there.

While Papa prevented from Mama from panicking, and Kas kept Mish and Nik collared, Vanitri headed over to our automobile. Dachahl, who had heard the fuss, was out of the automobile before Van got there.

"Chloys!" Dachahl snapped.

Chloys jumped and hurried after him. I didn't even try. By the time I managed to maneuver myself through the door he'd be long gone, so Forang and I just stayed where we were, and I tried not to feel anxious. Vanitri and Bos trailed along. It didn't take them very long to return, but it did take a little longer for me to find out what had happened, because Dachahl went to Mama first. When he finally got back to me, he explained Katrika had somehow managed to sneak away from the palace and make her way back to the power farm all by herself, so she could say good-bye to the flying machines—and was still there.

"Your brothers will be coming with us to pick her up," he concluded, "and the rest of your family will go on ahead in the other two cars. I told Chloys to go with them, so that they will have an interpreter, in case they need to stop somewhere before we catch up to them."

"What about your sister?"

"She'll be with us."

The Princess Lulahn didn't say anything about having to go out of her way to pick up a wayward foreigner, because then she would have to acknowledge the existence of the foreigner. Instead, she settled herself across from Dachahl and me, and looked determinedly out the window—careful to stay as far away from Forang as was possible. When we got to the power farm, Forang remained with me again—although he got out of the car and stood beside it this time—and everyone else, even the princess, went off to fetch Katrika. I could only assume that Lulahn found that task slightly less horrible than being left alone in the company of me and a shame-shorn.

Katrika wasn't nearly as apologetic as she should have been for bringing us out of our way. She climbed into my car and started telling me about everything that had changed between this visit and the one almost a month ago. Bos, who had been close on her heels, leaned in the door she had left open after her and told her that she shouldn't have left without telling anyone where she was.

Katrika glared at him. "You are not my brother."

"Thank Belkov's bloody toes for that!" he retorted.

Kas, who was close enough behind the two of them to hear the exchange, said, "Well *I* am your brother, Katya, and I say you should be ashamed of yourself. Mama was frantic."

Katrika pouted. "I waited and waited for someone to take me!"

"I regret that I could not find the time to do so," Dachahl told her as he climbed in next to me. Then he looked at Bos and Forang. "Which one of you is going with us?"

Bos hesitated for about half a second before climbing in with us, and so Forang turned and headed for the other vehicle. Lulahn—the last to return—glared at Dachahl through the windows. "This car still has room for you if you don't mind getting close," Dachahl told her cheerfully. "Otherwise, you should probably try the other motorcar."

She made a face at Dachahl that said 'I never wanted to travel with you anyway,' and followed Forang.

"Now Van and Lulahn are together," I pointed out.

Dachahl didn't care. I decided I didn't care either. Maybe I should have cared. Lulahn insisted that her driver stop the automobile as they were traveling through the jewelers' district, and there was nobody there who had the authority to overrule her. Van might have succeeded in doing so through force of personality—or even just plain force—but he didn't speak the language, and didn't know what was happening. When we turned back to see what had delayed them, we discovered that she had spotted one of her friends out on a shopping trip, had told the driver that she wished to speak to her, and then had joined her, leaving the rest of the passengers and two of the four guards standing up behind—the other two had gone with her—to wait for her return.

Dachahl went slit-eyed, for a moment, and then his expression went carefully blank. He took two of the guards from our automobile, and strode off into the marketplace, returning half an hour later with his sister. He almost pushed her back inside her vehicle, and then spoke to the driver—from what I could catch of that conversation, it sounded like he was telling the driver to take orders from Forang only. But between Katrika's delay and Lulahn's delay, it was probably now too late to catch up with the rest of the family before lunch-time, so Dachahl made one more stop so that he could send a message ahead, telling my parents to continue on to Ghoo Shtow—the town where we had planned to stay the night —without us.

For the first day we traveled mostly through farming districts, the watery fields filled with thickly grown stalks ready for harvest. Some were already being harvested by farmers in white smocks and wide conical straw hats, their pants rolled up at the knee. We stopped for lunch at a place called Nen Koust. The tea-house where we ate was beside a picturesque hill that had these strange huge stone statues—with great big glaring tilted-eyed heads on squat little bodies, less than a quarter as tall—all around the base of it. Lulahn ordered a huge elaborate meal that must have put the hostess in a panic—although of course she only smiled at us and apologized for how long the preparations would take. Dachahl almost countered the order, but I told him that I was very, very, very glad to be out of the automobile, and wouldn't mind a chance to climb the hill and stretch my legs. By the time I had convinced him I really meant it—I did—everyone but the princess and the eight guards had said they'd also like to go. Although Kas spent nearly the entire walk begging Bos to change automobiles for the rest of the trip.

"I don't mind helping Haircut out with some language lessons, but Van slept all morning, and that means he'll be awake all afternoon, and having him and the princess in the same little space was bad enough when he was sleeping."

"Why?" Dachahl demanded. "Did my sister misbehave?"

"No, no!" Kas hurried to explain. "Van was the one that was behaving badly."

"While he was sleeping?"

"He started out sitting beside her, and he was using way more than his fair share of the space, so your sister told Hair–, told Forang to switch places with her. I guess she thought that would get her out of Van's way, since it put them in opposite corners. But Van leaned back into his corner, put his feet up on the seat between her and me, and then fell asleep. As we went over bumps and things, he would slip a little lower, and his feet would slide a little closer to her, and she would slide a little closer to the door and look a little more sour. If she goes with you–"

"–then I can put my feet up on the seat and squish her into a corner instead!" I suggested brightly.

Dachahl laughed, and agreed to rearrange seats so that Lulahn was with him. But even with the promise that she would not be with Vanitri this time, by the time we managed to get Lulahn back inside a vehicle it was looking like we'd be arriving at Ghoo Shtow very late indeed. But Dachahl didn't want to try to push the procession any faster than it was already going—the countryside was getting hillier, and the roads were getting worse, and I was finding the jolting more and more uncomfortable, although I tried not to show it. When we stopped for supper, Dachahl went off to call the others and tell them how far we'd fallen behind, and when he got back he was looking worried.

"The guards said someone was asking about Batiya," he announced. "They asked the staff at the inn about him, and the staff all said they'd never seen the man asking the questions before."

"That's bad?" Bos asked.

"If he didn't know anyone at the inn, how did he find out Batiya was supposed to be staying the night there?"

"News spreads?" Kasmir suggested. Vanitri just frowned.

"I told them we probably wouldn't make it that far tonight. I think we should find somewhere else to sleep."

"No problem at all!" Kasmir told him. "I'm sure every village around here has a nice big barn that'll sleep five foreigners, eight guards, two drivers, and an imperial prince and princess."

Lulahn wasn't nearly as cheerful when she was told the news. "You must get me to Ghoo Shtow," she told Dachahl. "This is where my luggage and my maid are! We should be there already!"

Dachahl paid more attention to Kasmir's objection. He and his driver poured over the maps of the area, trying to find an inn that was likely to be able to handle the sudden influx of important guests. They finally decided to leave the planned route and travel a little way further north, to a town famous for its healing spring. In the middle of the harvest, they shouldn't have nearly as many visitors as they did during the heat of summer—so even if our party ended up displacing some less important travelers, it shouldn't leave them with nowhere else to go.

The staff at the inn Dachahl chose set up four sleeping spaces in their biggest room. One for Dachahl and I, one for Lulahn, one for Katrika, and one for my brothers, Bos and Forang. Katrika looked at her space and asked, "Can I sleep with Kas?"

"You are way too old to sleep with your brothers," Vanitri told her.

She looked down at her toes.

"I'll just be on the other side of the screen from you," Kas told her cheerfully. "If you wake up in the middle of the night and are feeling lonely—or maybe just a little bored—I recommend yelling loudly enough to wake me —and the princess. That ought to liven things up. If you yell loudly enough, you might be able to bring all the guards running, even!"

"Yes, that will be cartloads of fun–" Vanitri agreed, "– a midnight panic."

I don't know how well Katrika slept, I only know that I didn't sleep very well at all. My back and belly ached, and I felt uncomfortable and restless. I was very glad to get moving the next morning, even though I had to listen to Lulahn complain. Dachahl was less willing. Especially after he discovered that a missing bridge was going to prevent him from getting back to the main road by the way he had already planned, and a new route would have to be decided. He finally rearranged the cars so that Lulahn was with my brothers and Bos, and Forang and Katrika were with us.

We ended up on a road that was little more than a dirt track, winding its way through some of the prettiest country I had seen yet, rolling hills covered with trees, all turning colors with the coming of fall. We reached a long bridge over a distant river, and I got out of the car while the guards investigated the bridge very thoroughly to make sure it was safe. Dachahl was glaring at his map, so I tapped him on the shoulder. "It's very pretty," I told him, indicating the hills, and the river tumbling its way between them, down below us.

He looked up at me, and then looked around in surprise, and then smiled. "We are almost to the border of Cholipardo," he said. "Here the villages are mixed. Some cling to the ancient Cholipardo customs far more fiercely than any of the villages that are actually in Cholipardo. Others are just as determinedly Gar Mian."

"And looking about is wonderful!"

"No." He grinned. "This is still a few hills away."

I couldn't make that make sense. "What is still a few hills away?"

He wouldn't tell me. He just looked happy.

Map of Changali

Chapter Seven

I Find Running Difficult

The guards declared the bridge safe and everyone got back in the car, but halfway up the hill on the other side the second car stopped following us, and by the time we realized it was not just Lulahn causing trouble again, Van and Kas had managed to get in such a heated argument with their driver—although argument couldn't exactly be the right word, since they couldn't actually talk to each other—that Vanitri had the driver in a headlock and the guards were standing around in threatening attitudes that couldn't quite manage to cover up their air of bewilderment.

"What is happening?" Dachahl demanded.

"The southerners were trying to take the motorcar apart," one of the guards replied. "Chungdu tried to stop them."

"My wife's brothers build and repair motorcars," Dachahl told them. "That is their craft."

"I thought they were warriors!" someone protested, but they stopped attempting to look threatening.

"You can let go of him now," I told Van. "He'll stop trying to get in the way."

Kas worked his fingers around the bonnet of the automobile, found the catch and lifted it.

"It sounded like the transmission to me," Van told him, lying on the ground and wiggling his way under the automobile.

"Of course it was the transmission," Kas replied. "I'm just being curious. Oh, blessed saints, what is this? An electric starter? Sweet!"

"What?!?" There was a thump from under the automobile. "Ouch. That better have been for real, Kas, or I'm tying your tongue in knots later."

"It's really real. Here's the battery. Other than that, we're looking at six cylinders and–"

"The *gear box*, Kas! See if there's any kind of access from the driver's compartment."

"Fine, fine! But why did I never think to poke around in one of these things earlier?" Kas asked as he climbed into the driver's compartment.

"You were too busy panting after the exotic local beauties," Van told him.

"*I* was too... Coming from you that's a bit sassy!" I couldn't see what he was doing, but I heard him moving about. "I think these might be screws, but Belkov's toes, you should see the head pattern!"

"I need a wrench. There's got to be a toolbox somewhere."

I asked our driver about a toolbox, and he showed me how there was one built into the side of the driver's compartment of our automobile. "On the right, behind the little brass tortoise," I told Kas. "Push his head down."

"No tortoise here," Kas replied from inside the other vehicle. "I'll give this cow a try, shall I?"

"What size of wrench do you need, Van?" I asked.

"About a seven-eighths?"

I found a wrench that looked about right and handed it to Katrika, who crouched down so she could pass it to Van. "Will they be able to fix it?" Dachahl asked me.

"If it's really the transmission—probably not," I admitted. "How far are we from the nearest town?"

"Up and over the hill, and all the way down the other side," he told me. "That's where we join the main road again."

"Does it have some kind of metal workshop?"

"Yes. But I don't know that it will do what you need it to. We'll find a communications station there, though. We can ask the Royal Palace at Rafahdo to send us another motorcar."

"I'm tired of looking around, and I am eager to rejoin my luggage," Lulahn announced. "We will move on now."

"You want to share space with seven other people?" Dachahl asked her.

"The remainder of the procession will join us later," she told him.

"I need the next size smaller now," Vanitri yelled. "Hie! Batya?"

I grabbed the next smaller wrench and handed it to Katrika. "Maybe that would be best—sending one car ahead," I suggested to Dachahl.

"We wait to hear what your brothers have seen," Dachahl told me.

Kasmir made the report. "The gear shift blew," he said. "You've completely lost your high gear and reverse—that's not so bad in hills like this, you wouldn't be using high gear anyway, the problem is that when the harness for those gears went, it damaged the shifting rod for low and medium—pulled this whale of yours out of gear completely, and stuck it there—so right now it's got nothing."

"Can this be fixed?"

"Not with the tools we have here. But we might be able to force it into one of the two gears you've got left—and hope that it stays there until we arrive somewhere."

"Can it get us to the top of the hill?" I asked him.

"Why not? Even if low gear goes too, we've got a backup system with twelve-manpower output, that ought to be able to get even this beast up and over."

"Don't sound so cheerful about that," Vanitri advised him. "For once in your life, you won't be chosen as the guy who does the steering."

"Do this," Dachahl ordered.

"Right." He saluted. "One tin turtle special ready shortly."

"Batiya, if you don't have a hammer, then get me the heaviest wrench in the box," Van called.

It didn't take them very long to get the automobile stuck in first, instead of stuck in neutral, and then put everything else back together. Kas finished first and came over, wiping his hands on a cleaning cloth that had been very helpfully tucked into the toolbox by the palace mechanics. "The gears have a very interesting feature," he told me. "It's a friction pad. I couldn't figure out what the heck it was for at first, but when we started her running, I finally caught it. It's so the gears will match speeds all on their own, and you only need to clutch it half as often. Very clever."

Van finally crawled out from under the car, absolutely filthy, and covered in grease. Lulahn looked at him, horrified, and then promptly began climbing into the other automobile. "Oh, no you don't, pumpkin!" Van said, and grabbed her by the arm and pulled her back out again.

She screamed—which Van hardly seemed to notice—and then lifted her hand as if she would have hit him if she hadn't realized that she would have to actually touch him if she did, and then stood there frozen, staring at him. "Ch-chunru!" she finally managed to say.

"Kas and I better stay with the turtle, but we should try to keep the load light," Van told Dachahl. "That means she and Katya should be the other two passengers." He looked over at the lounging guards. "And we can shift some of them over too?"

Dachahl gave the order, and then told his sister to go with Vanitri. Her eyes widened. "With *this*? You can't!"

"With *him*," Dachahl corrected. "If you get in the motorcar by yourself, he won't touch you." And then he told Van, "I told her."

"Good." Van let go of her, and accepted a cleaning cloth from me. He wiped his face first, and then looked over at Lulahn as he wiped his hands. "Well?" he asked her.

She looked from Van to Dachahl, and then held out her arm. "Look what he did to me!" There were greasy black smudges showing on it. Van held the cloth he had been using out to her, and she jumped backward, squeaking, and almost dived into the automobile.

Katrika climbed in, and Dachahl helped me get settled, and the guards jumped back on their perches, six clinging to our automobile and two clinging to the other one. And then we were on our way again, finally. We reached the crest of the hill, and coasted down the other side into a deep valley with a bright blue lake, tumbling streams going in and out of either end. On the far side was a huddle of buildings that must be the town Dachahl had spoken of.

The thin line of the main road could be seen sensibly entering the valley along the edge of the hill instead of climbing over it, and then dipping toward the little town. Down below us, our road divided, each branch curving along one side of the lake. One met the other road just before it crossed over the stream on a bridge of some sort, and the other looked like it went all the way around the other end of the lake—although I couldn't actually see it because the slope of the hill was in the way—and through the town and then apparently joined the main road on the far side of the valley.

There seemed to be something going on by the bridge. There were a lot of tiny specks that must be people over there. But I could only see them when there were gaps in the trees, and I couldn't make out what they were doing. I wasn't the only one who had noticed them, though, and as we approached the fork in the road our driver opened the window and told us that it looked like maybe the bridge was down. "A big crowd and stopped carts are there, Chunru," he said. "Should we go around the other way?"

"We'd better check to make sure the other car can still go anywhere first," Dachahl told him. "We can roll from here to the main bridge, but we can't roll all the way around the lake."

So the driver stopped the car right before the turn and ran back to talk to the driver of the other car. Dachahl climbed out too, and followed him. I shifted about, wondering if sitting had always been this uncomfortable and I just hadn't spent enough time sitting to realize it before, or if this was something new. Bos tapped me on the shoulder, and pointed out the window.

There were people walking up the road who had just come into view through the trees. One carried some kind of flag or banner, with words on it, and the rest carried rifles. The guards must have seen them too, for one of them shouted, and they jumped off their perch to take up positions around the automobile, their rifles ready. I checked my own little hand gun, and beside me Bos was doing the same, while Forang was getting into the under-seat compartment and pulling out the swords and the spare rifle that had been stowed there.

I heard the rumble and bounce of the other vehicle pulling to a stop beside us, and then Forang was passing Dachahl his sword through the window. "Children of the Stork," Dachahl said. I assumed he had succeeded in reading the banner.

"Can we just drive away?" Bos asked.

"Only if we can fit everyone in this motorcar."

Vanitri emerged from the other automobile, holding his sword in one hand and the arm of a terrified Lulahn in the other. "Get the girls out of here," he ordered, and started pulling Lulahn toward our automobile. But the Children of the Stork had already readied their rifles, and a scattering of shots thumped into my automobile, and I was too busy ducking to see what was happening.

I could hear a lot of noise. Shots fired and shots landing, and the glass window above my head shattering. And lots of yelling and screaming. Dachahl's hand reached out and grabbed me, pulling me out of the automobile. "More are coming the other way. Run for the woods." He pointed, and I grabbed my belly and ran. Once out of the corner of my eye I saw Vanitri with someone's legs kicking wildly just past his face. And when I stumbled just inside the line of trees, Katrika, her skirts hiked up past her knees, sprinted past me. "Forang, take the lead!" I heard Dachahl ordering in Hadahnchi. "Head uphill, northeast toward the lake headwaters, and then turn north."

"Everyone follow Forang!" I yelled in Dostrovian.

We crashed through the woods, branches pulling at us and underbrush tangling our feet, but in spite of my belly, Katrika's shorter legs, and Vanitri being burdened by a still-screaming Lulahn, we seemed to be gaining ground—I think because our people were much better shots, which forced our pursuers to keep their distance. But we ran out of breath first—at least, I did—and our party stumbled to a halt while we could still hear them crashing about below.

Vanitri put Lulahn down so roughly it was almost fair to say he dropped her. "Useless sow," he snarled. "We might be able to do some sneaking if she just pinned her jaw shut."

Kasmir considered the sobbing princess. "I could gag her with this." He pulled the cleaning cloth he had used earlier out of his pocket. "It's a little dirty though. Do we care?"

Dachahl crouched down beside his sister. "You will stop that noise." Her sobs continued just as noisy as before.

"Hit her," Vanitri advised in a growl.

Dachahl's eyes went wide. "I can't..."

Kasmir stepped around him and crouched down and put his hand over her mouth. "You can hit her, I can gag her, or Vanitri can kiss her. Lots of options—let's just make up our minds, shall we?"

Dachahl looked grimly at his sister. "You will be silent, or I will give you to Batiya's brothers and they will make you silent. This is understood?"

The stifled noises from behind Kasmir's hand gradually stopped and he cautiously released his hold. When the noises didn't start up again, he wiped his hand off on his pants, and told Vanitri, "You had a lucky escape. I wouldn't want to kiss her."

"We've got to keep moving," Dachahl said. He looked over at Katrika, who was clinging to a tree gasping, with Bos hovering over her anxiously. "You can keep up?"

She nodded, and a look passed between Dachahl and Bos. Then Dachahl turned back to the rest of us. "A watch tower is on the top of the ridge over that way," he said. "We're going to try to get there. It can't be seen from here, so hopefully it will take a while for them to figure out where we're going."

"Could they take an automobile around by road, and get there first?" Kasmir asked.

"We don't know that they have an automobile."

"Yes, they do," I told him. "They have ours."

Dachahl looked back in the direction that the tower was supposed to be, and growled. "Forang!"

"Chunru."

"I need you to secure the tower. You'll take three men." He looked around at the guards. "The three of you best at running long distances. Someone should be there already. Tell them what is happening. If they don't accept your uniforms and your story, don't try to force your way in. Just conceal yourselves where you can assist should these Children of the Stork decide to attack."

"Yes, Chunru."

Forang turned and trotted off into the trees, and three of the guards followed him. Dachahl turned to my brothers. "I am sad to have to ask this, but will you two handle my sister?"

Vanitri jerked his head toward the remaining guards. "What about them?"

"She is an imperial princess. They're supposed to obey her."

"A fate no man deserves," Kasmir admitted. He looked at Van. "I'll poke her with a stick if she stops moving. And if she screams, you can kiss her quiet."

"Why do you get all the fun jobs?" But Vanitri looked over at Dachahl, and nodded.

Dachahl pulled his sister to her feet. "You stay with the rest of us, or Batiya's brothers will carry you. You will keep silent, or Batiya's brothers will silence you. Do you understand this?"

"Yes, Chunru." She gave Dachahl a look that could curdle milk and kill moths.

We moved on at a half-walking, half-jogging pace. Two of our five remaining guards trotted ahead, and the rest spread out behind. The drivers just kept as close as they dared, looking nervous. I saw Bos hand one a rifle— it must have been the one Forang had taken from under the seat. Moving as quickly and as silently as we could this way, we reached the stream that fed the lake without incident, and our scouts crossed successfully. But my ungainly belly made me clumsy. I set a foot down awkwardly, and unable to regain my balance, fell with a splash.

Dachahl immediately seized my shoulder, and clinging to his arm, I managed to get myself upright, but we heard cries from a short distance downstream and as soon as I was steady, Dachahl left me—running barefoot in the direction of the call. Kasmir waded out and offered an arm, and Vanitri just picked Lulahn up and tossed her over his shoulder again. Bos, looking at the fast-running water, did the same for Katrika. We were all on the other side when Dachahl returned—his boots back on his feet.

"They're coming this way," he announced. "We're going to have to run."

I gave Dachahl my gun to hold as we ran. My *lahnpran* was only calf-length, but the soaked skirts tangled with my soaked pants, so I pulled them up and out from under my sash, took the *lahnpran* off completely and tucked it under my arm. Dachahl handed the gun back, and I tucked it back into my sash. Behind me I heard Lulahn falling down twice, and the next time we all paused to catch our breath, Vanitri grabbed her, while Kasmir undid her sash and pulled her ankle-length *lahnpran* off of her. She fought them with futile cuffs and terrified little mews, but they ignored her protests—setting her back on her feet when they were done. She ran faster after that, but I'm not sure if it was because the *lahnpran* had been slowing her down, or just because she was even more desperate to keep ahead of my brothers. Katrika already had her skirts pulled through between her legs and tucked into her waistband.

And we kept on running, past the grey trunks of the towering trees, skirting the drifts of golden leaves. My belly ached, my breath was short, my balance was off, and there seemed to be something wrong with my hips. If Dachahl wasn't constantly at my side with a strong arm, I think I would have fallen again—as it was, I completely lost track of time and space. Each stumbling step was a nightmare, and each rest far too short. Finally Dachahl held up his hands, and said, "Batiya needs to stop."

"They're still looking for us," Van said, but Lulahn collapsed in a heap on the ground and began sobbing silently.

To my horror I realized that I had tears trickling down my face as well, and I hurriedly wiped them away. "I'm fine," I told Dachahl. I don't think he believed me.

Dachahl indicated the heavy ground cover. We were in an area mostly clear of trees and filled with stalky plants with big wide leaves spreading out on top. "We will lie down under these. The leaves will conceal us. If any searchers get too close, we will try to deal with them silently."

Vanitri jerked a thumb at Lulahn. "I don't think she's ready to lie quiet."

"Can you keep her still?"

"You are her brother. You won't like my methods."

"I am not so fortunate in my sister as you are in yours," Dachahl replied grimly.

"I'll try," I managed to gasp. I dropped to my knees next to her. "You must hide under those plants," I told her. "If you stay in the open, our enemy will shoot you."

"I cannot move," she told me, tears streaming down her face.

"You will move," I said very firmly. "You will move, because you are an imperial princess of Changali, and you are too proud to be picked up and dropped by my brothers like unwanted luggage."

"He wants me," she said. "He thinks I am beautiful, but he does not know how to treat me, because he is a beast. But he wants me."

"This is so? *Look* at him."

She pushed herself up to her knees so that she could turn to look at Vanitri, and discovered that he was looking back along the trail, checking for pursuers. Lulahn let out a little shriek of frustration and fury, but Vanitri didn't even turn to look. Kasmir just dropped her sash and *lahnpran* over her, and then went down on his belly and slithered under the leaves.

Lulahn beat an angry fist against the ground. "Over there," I told her, pointing. She crawled forward, but she was making sounds that were half sobs and half angry grunts. I grabbed her *lahnpran* and shoved it through the leaves at her. "Lie on it," I advised. Then I crawled in close by. Lulahn's sobs were getting louder, and Vanitri said, "Batiya!" in an irritated way.

"You are making noise because you want my brother to come and hold you?" I asked Lulahn sharply. There were a series of gasps and then silence.

I settled myself as comfortably as I could, which wasn't very, and put my head on my arm, and closed my eyes. My wet clothes were making me feel clammy and achy, but resting was good. Resting was necessary. The baby didn't agree with me, and my belly bulged and twisted as the child inside made its opinion of the day's activities known. I tried a soothing hand, but there was nothing to touch—a bulge, a lump... knees here or heels there, I couldn't tell. I just tried to relax as best I could.

A while later, just as the baby finally stopped squirming, there was the sound of voices approaching. The leaves over by Lulahn shook, and I snaked an arm over so I could grip her by the shoulder, and squeeze. The voices kept coming nearer and nearer and I fought an urge to move—to pull my feet up and under me, and to get up on my hands so that if something happened, I could run.

But running wouldn't do me any good. I was the slowest member of the group. I had to stay still, stay still, stay still. I could hear actual footsteps now—there seemed to be two men, some distance apart. Maybe if we were lucky, they would walk right past us. The footsteps got closer and closer, and then there was a soft thud, and a confused exclamation. Then a sharp grunt, and the sound of a body falling to the ground.

I heard the man who was further away call, and call again. His steps turned, heading in the direction of where his companion had last been seen. And then there was a cry that was cut off abruptly, and another thud. Then silence.

I strained my ears, wondering how soon the two men would be missed. I could hear the wind in the leaves, and the calls of birds and insects, and occasionally what I thought must be a voice—but a long way off.

And then a thrashing and screaming erupted right by my ear. By the time I had managed to climb to my feet, Vanitri was holding Lulahn tight, a hand clamped over her mouth. "I thought you said you'd keep her quiet," he hissed though clenched teeth.

"How was I supposed to know she'd suddenly start screaming?" I asked, as I squatted down to scoop up her *lahnpran* and mine. And then Dachahl was beside me, his hand on my elbow, urging me forward again. We didn't get far enough away that we couldn't hear the cries when the bodies we had left behind were discovered, and the sounds of anger and outrage followed us as we went up and up, past rocky outcroppings and stands of stately pines.

I was getting cramps in my sides and across my belly that made me stumble and wheeze and clutch at Dachahl. When he finally let us rest again, I fell to my knees and stayed there fighting for breath.

Katrika came over and knelt beside me, clutching my arm and holding tight, and it wasn't until I became aware that she was quietly crying and that I hadn't noticed, that I realized that it was starting to get dark. Not so dark that I couldn't look questioningly at Bos—who had been watching out for Katrika and so seemed most likely to know what was wrong—and have him jerk his head at Dachahl and draw his finger across his throat in reply. Katrika must have seen Dachahl cut the throat of one of those two men earlier. I put an arm around her, trying to comfort her, and instead found myself gasping as I was seized by another cramp.

"Batya?" she asked in a whisper. "What's wrong?"

"I'm just getting tired," I told her when the pain faded. I held her, and stroked her hair, and warned Dachahl away with a look when he came over to see how we were doing.

Lulahn was leaning against a tree, but there was a crack of a gunshot, and Vanitri grabbed her, throwing her to the ground, and himself on top of her, wrapping himself around her so that she couldn't even wiggle. They might have looked like lovers except for the hand clamped over her mouth. Katrika and I, already crouched down, just huddled a little closer to the ground, and Bos dropped to a crouch in front of us. I couldn't see anyone else, but I could hear people moving—Dachahl, I thought, and one of the guards.

Finally Dachahl said, "I don't think they saw us. Maybe it was some kind of signal."

He came to offer me his hand, and Katrika offered me her shoulder, but halfway up another wave of pain ran across my middle, and there was a warm trickle of water between my legs.

"If you needed to stop behind a tree, you should have said, Batya," Kasmir told me in a half-amused, half-worried tone.

Vanitri looked over me and frowned. "Did you think we couldn't stop that long?"

"But I..." I had needed to call a halt, actually, and had been putting it off. But I was now standing in a very embarrassing puddle, and yet, I still felt like I needed to call a halt soon.

"This we do not have time for," Dachahl said, taking my hand and pulling me forward. I took one step, and found myself whimpering because of the strange pain where my legs joined the rest of me.

Dachahl stopped and turned to face me. "Something is wrong. Tell me."

"I don't know. It just feels like the baby is sitting lower down, or something, and it's just... harder to move somehow."

"Pains," Vanitri said abruptly. "In your belly."

"I've been bouncing the baby around all day," I told him crossly. "Of course I'm uncomfortable."

Vanitri shook his head. "It hurts, and then it doesn't. And several minutes later it hurts again. Repeating regularly?"

Everyone was staring at him, especially me. "What if it is?" I asked him.

"You're having the baby," he told me.

"Of course I'm not having the baby," I replied. "Not for another month." I took two waddling steps forward, my freshly-soaked-all-over-again pants clinging and rubbing very uncomfortably, and then another cramp hit, and I stopped, hissing in pain.

Dachahl grabbed me, which was nice. With him holding me upright, I could just concentrate on hurting. "She can't be having the baby yet!"

"I'm the oldest of seven," Vanitri growled. "I've seen this before."

There was a long silence and then Dachahl asked, "What happens next?"

"They don't let me see the rest. Mama goes off into her bedroom, I'm sent running for the midwife, and sometime after midnight there's a bit of a racket and then the midwife comes out and tells Papa, 'Congratulations, it's a...'"

"Bedroom?" Dachahl asked hoarsely. "She's supposed to lie down?"

"I can't lie down here," I told him very firmly. "We have a good long time to go before midnight. So we should look for a better stopping place." Walking wasn't that bad, really. It had just been that abrupt and too big step forward that had hurt so much. If I walked a little more carefully there was no problem.

Dachahl walked along next to me, clutching me, and muttering, "But you can't have the baby now, it's too *soon*."

"Unless you got started early," Kasmir noted. "Nine months back from now, that gets us..."

"Alone on a boat in the middle of the ocean," Vanitri bit out. He was following close on my heels, pulling an exhausted, bewildered and overwrought Lulahn along behind him. "I ought to pound you good," he told Dachahl.

"You can't. It's not true," I protested.

"Of course you'd say that," Vanitri responded grimly.

"He didn't even kiss me until after we were married, and he didn't do anything else for a whole week!"

"Oh, now there's a likely story!" Van sounded even crosser than before.

"We had to wait until his stitches were out, Vanitri Latikov," I barked. "And it's no cart of yours anyway!"

"She's telling the truth Van," Kasmir said. "Leave them alone."

"I *know* she's telling the truth," Van snarled, "I just wish she wasn't!"

Everyone got quiet after that, leaving me free to think about what Vanitri had said. Could I really be having the baby now? Babies could come early, I knew. Seven-month babies were a bit of a joke, though. 'Seven months, and nine pounds, my my my!' But that meant that seven months by itself couldn't be impossible. And nobody laughed about eight-month babies.

"This can be managed," I told Dachahl. "This is early, but not scary early. The baby will be fine." And then another pain hit, and I stopped walking, and my hold on Dachahl tightened.

Dachahl called out to the guards, and then asked them and the drivers if they'd ever seen anyone—or even any animal, give birth. The no's came back snappy and disciplined, and then the realization of why Chunru would ask that particular question hit, and they all stared at me with anxious faces. "Chunru...?" one asked. He didn't finish the question—he didn't need to.

"We need to find someone who knows something about birthing children," Dachahl announced.

"In the village?" one suggested.

"Where the Children of the Stork are probably staying?" another countered.

"I think you should take me to that tower, just as you planned," I told Dachahl when I wasn't too busy hurting to speak anymore. "If there are people there, they will probably know where we could look for someone."

Nobody had a better idea to suggest, so we started walking again, only to stop a moment later at the sound of distant voices. Dachahl summoned the guards. "Defensive position," he said quietly. "Find one."

They nodded and fanned out, and I started walking again. I wasn't going to get anywhere standing in place. But we must have been moving too slow, or sounding too loud, or something, because the sound of pursuit kept getting louder, and finally Vanitri pushed Lulahn at Kasmir and came and scooped me up in his arms. Dachahl didn't even protest, he just bobbed his head at Vanitri, and then moved ahead. I couldn't complain either, because even carrying me, Vanitri was going faster than I had been. That couldn't last for long. Strong as Vanitri was, carrying someone in your arms is horribly awkward. I should have been on his back, or even up over his shoulder—but neither of those seemed possible in my current state.

Dachahl reappeared, and motioned for Vanitri to follow him. He led the way to a small cliff-space that leaned slightly inward. A few tumbled rocks lying in front of it provided cover. Two of the guards were already there —this must be the defensive position Dachahl had told them to find.

Vanitri set me down with a relieved grunt and Dachahl led me over next to the rock face, and told me to get down. I got down on my hands and knees and panted, while Dachahl motioned for Katrika and Lulahn to join me. Katrika hurried over, but Lulahn didn't move until Kasmir shoved her in my direction, and then she staggered over and dropped down on my other side.

The men gathered around us, drawing swords and checking their guns. "Batiya, what happens now?" Katrika asked.

"Try to make your sister comfortable," Dachahl answered for me. "We might be here for a while."

"Here?" she asked, and I thought she was frowning but everyone's face was just a blur in the darkness by then. "Can we have a fire, or something?" she whispered.

"No," Vanitri told her.

"But Batiya's all over wet, and really cold."

"What about that robe thing she was wearing?" Kasmir whispered. I was still holding it. And Lulahn's too. I had been carrying them so long, I had forgotten I had them, but they had been tucked under my arm the whole time. I started to pull them out, and Katrika snatched them from my hands, discarding mine because it was still damp, and tenderly placing Lulahn's around my shoulders. As soon as Lulahn saw it, she grabbed it and started putting it back on.

Katrika let out an angry yelp and grabbed a lock of Lulahn's long flowing hair, and pulled it. Lulahn squealed with outrage and pain.

"Silence!" Dachahl commanded in a fierce whisper.

The privilege of wearing Lulahn's dry *lahnpran* didn't seem worth dying for, so I just quietly spread my own *lahnpran* across my shoulders—the top part was mostly dry. Katrika didn't think that was good enough. She reached forward and tugged on Dachahl's *choliang*. It only took him one glance to figure out what she wanted, and he put down his weapons for long enough to take off the *choliang*. Katrika snatched off my *lahnpran*, and replaced it with Dachahl's *choliang*. I clutched it gratefully. "Katya, I own you six cartloads of sunshine," I whispered.

"You need to change your... pants," she whispered back.

Even if I had something to change into, there was no point. Each of my pains brought with it a small trickle of wetness. "Maybe I should just take them off?"

"In front of..."

I wasn't in front, I was behind. And it was getting dark. "Hold up my robe," I told her, although I was sure everyone was far more interested in watching for attackers than looking at me.

I set my sash and my gun to one side, and made the attempt. Wiggling out of the pants while crouched down in close quarters was not easy, but no longer having the wet cloth between my legs was such a relief, I couldn't quite manage to feel as uncomfortable about being half-dressed as Mama would have liked. Especially since the Children of the Stork had arrived.

In the near-darkness it was hard to tell how many of them there were. It depended on how many of them were carrying the ingenious Chang electric torches.

"We'll never be able to hide from them if they're carrying those," Kasmir whispered.

"We shoot them before they get close enough to see us," Dachahl explained.

"That's not going to stop them from finding us."

"Shoot the ones with the lights, and they'll never see us at all."

Another wave of pain swept through me, and my breath hissed loudly in my ears. When it was over and I had attention to spare, it seemed that the lights had got much closer. How long had the pain lasted? I was sure that they came closer together and lasted longer now, and I was a little afraid of what that meant. After midnight, Vanitri had said. I tried to remember the stories I had heard, and I didn't think the timing was so certain. Most of the stories I could remember, that was what they were about—babies coming at the wrong time, in the wrong place. I tried to find some strength in that. If Datrissa Bastok could have a baby in Sawvi's Drugstore on Thirty-Second Street, I could have one on a hillside in Cholipardo.

The bright circles that marked the flashlight beams slid back and forth across the rough ground, and I could hear the people hunting for us talking, although I didn't understand much of what they said. Either most of it was in Stoi Kat, or I was too tired to deal with a language that wasn't my own. Probably both.

I could hear everyone breathing. It seemed so loud, I wondered how anyone could have failed to notice us. But the closest of the lights swept toward us, and then away.

That wasn't a random pattern, I realized, it was a coordinated search, with men in a line, covering every inch of the ground. They weren't taking any chance of missing us, but they also weren't moving very fast. If only I had been able to run, we could have left them to watch our footprints blow away.

Two more passes of the lights. Three. One of the rocks at the edge of our hiding place slid into view, and Dachahl gave the word. The air filled with thunder, and there were cries out in the darkness. The lights stopped their steady searching; some jiggled wildly, and others lay still, but further away there were more turning in our direction. Lulahn started screaming and I threw myself on top of her, my hands seeking her mouth. I finally got one across her face, muffling the noise, but not before she elbowed me in the stomach. I fought away the will to smother her. She was too much—I didn't want to have to deal with her. But was she Dachahl's sister. And she was frightened.

I was still hanging on to her when the next wave of pain came. My grip tightened, and then tightened some more. Lulahn whimpered. Bullets ripped past us, two or three at a time—mostly not very close. "Don't shoot if you don't have to," Dachahl warned in a whisper. "They'll aim at the sparks." He repeated the instructions in Hadahnchi. But not long after the pain faded and my hold on Lulahn loosened, the command to shoot was repeated and this time the return fire was more accurate.

There was a hastily stifled sound from one of the guards, and letting go of Lulahn I felt around until I found my sash, and pressed it into Katrika's hand. "Bandages," I told her, and pushed her in the direction of the sound I'd heard. We were so crowded together that she couldn't have had far to go, but I still completely lost track of her in the darkness.

The Children of the Stork had figured out that their hand torches were hurting more than they were helping, and they'd all been shut off. With nothing to shoot at, our own guns had fallen silent. But the other side kept up a fairly steady stream of bullets. "They will charge us soon," Dachahl announced. "When I say, empty your guns. Then swords."

I wondered how well Vanitri, Kasmir and Bos would do with their swords, but I didn't have long to think about it because I was starting to hurt again, and although I noticed the thunder of shots it was hard to do more than just wince and hiss.

"Batiya?" Katrika was back with me. She pushed me back against the cliff and pressed herself to me. The wave of pain retreated, and I peered into the darkness. Everything was in confusion. I could tell that people were fighting all around me, but not who was fighting with who.

Someone staggered back, stepping on Lulahn—who screamed—and falling to the ground. My hands met a southern coat sleeve. "Bos?" He groaned. It really was Bos. I felt about him for blood, and found some on his left arm. Pulling his tie loose, amazed that he was still even wearing it, I wrapped it around the cut and pulled it tight.

Bos got back on his feet and held his sword up, but was clearly just as confused as I was. He paused, hesitating, and then someone else stepped on Lulahn, and she screamed again. The astonished and delighted exclamation of the stepper couldn't possibly be from anyone who had been traveling with the princess. Bos launched himself in that direction.

"Was he...?" Katrika asked.

"He's fine," I told her. That didn't mean that he'd stay fine. But I did think they were doing more damage to each other in the darkness than they were to us—and I must not have been the only one to think it, for I heard an order in Stoi Kat, and the sounds of battle seemed to fall back a little, and Dachahl said "Stand!" in Dostrovian and Hadahnchi.

"We need to see who's hurt," I told Katrika in an urgent whisper. "I'll check the guards and drivers. You check the others."

I crawled past one of the drivers to where three of the guards were positioned on the one side, and found one nursing a bad leg wound, and the second tying a sash around the arm of the third.

Crawling back to Dachahl, I had just started my report when I was hit by another wave of pain. I tried to speak normally, but Dachahl could tell something was wrong, and I felt his hand on my shoulder. "Don't worry," I panted. "It's still a long way before midnight."

Katrika arrived and reported in a whisper that Bos had an arm wound that was not serious, and that Vanitri had a head wound that was bleeding all over, but he said he was okay. Dachahl started removing his sash, and as soon as I could move again, I crawled off to check on the last two guards and the other driver.

One guard had a slice across his ribs, and the other was lying on the ground, his arms wrapped about his middle, while the driver hovered over him uncertainly. His arms were soaked in blood, but there didn't seem to be anything I could do for him. So I crawled away and had almost reached Dachahl again when the next pain hit me. Dachahl was reloading his gun—I could tell from the small scrape of metal on metal in the dark. "Batiya?"

"Yes," I panted.

"I think they'll try one more attack. If that doesn't succeed, they'll pin us down until morning."

I wasn't sure how another attack could fail to succeed. A bullet whizzed past overhead, pinging against the rock above and behind us.

"Batiya, I regr–"

"No." The pain was fading and my hand found his mouth in the darkness. "It is still a long way until midnight. It is not time for regrets yet." I brushed my fingertips down his arm, squeezed his hand, and then crawled back to Lulahn. Katrika was already there, and we crouched down together, waiting for that final rush from the Children of the Stork.

We didn't wait very long. There were more shots, some yells, and the sound of approaching feet. Once again our little group waited for Dachahl's signal and then shot together. I heard a cry of pain that sounded like Kasmir, and then the first of the attackers arrived, and once again things became too confused to make out.

This was as twisted as a cat's toy string. Why were they attacking at all if they could wait until morning? Why didn't they just let me have my baby in peace and then kill us all when it was light enough to see what they were doing? Why didn't Lulahn just shut her yammer already? And why was there the sound of gunfire way off in the distance?

The answer to the first and last question was the same, I realized. "Dachahl, Dachahl! Help's coming!" I repeated the last part in Hadahnchi, hoping the guards and drivers would recognize my voice.

And then someone crashed into me waving a sword, and I was too busy trying to keep him from actually hitting anyone with it to pay attention to what was happening elsewhere. I couldn't stand, but my little gun was still somewhere on the ground. I felt for it. My hand met Katrika. And then there was the click of the trigger, and an oddly muffled bang, and the attacker fell down on top of us, twisting and screaming. I curled around my belly, trying to protect it and my head from what I was sure was random thrashing. There was another explosion, and the man jerked a couple times and was still. "Katrika —thank you!" I said, and that was all I could say because I hurt so much.

But even as I fought to relax into the pain and stay silent I could hear a voice calling "Chunru! Chunru!" It was Forang.

Chapter Eight

I Can No Longer Sleep at Night

It took Forang a while to get to us, but when he did he brought what sounded like an entire army, complete with horses. The few Children of the Stork who hadn't fled by then were being pulled off the ground and hustled away. I could see a glare of lights, and turned away from them, huddling in Dachahl's *choliang*.

Dachahl was talking to Forang, Katrika was crying, Lulahn was demanding totally unreasonable comforts and luxuries. Another wave of pain hit me. And then Dachahl was at my side. "Forang brought some of the Cholipardo Royal Horse Guards," he told me. "They were stationed at Dofahsu Tower. We can take you there, but there's no midwife. Just a horse doctor."

"A horse doctor is probably better than nothing."

"Or, now that we've reinforcements, we can attempt the village."

I didn't know enough to decide. "Ask the horse doctor."

He disappeared again, and Katrika and Vanitri helped me to my feet. Lulahn was also on her feet by then, practically screeching her demands.

"What's she hawking toothbrushes for?" Vanitri growled.

"She wants a motorcar, a change of clothing and a bath," I explained. "And a bunch of other things too. Food. A foot rub."

Vanitri growled. He left me, headed in her direction. "If you don't cut that yammer I'll give you a bath, honey-cakes!" Miraculously her shrill demands did stop. But then someone turned a light in their direction. Lulahn was standing frozen, her face aimed at Vanitri, and when she saw his blood-streaked face she screamed and screamed and screamed.

"Please assign some of the walking wounded to escort my sister to the tower," Dachahl said. Then he walked over to her. Vanitri pushed her at him, and Dachahl shook her until she stopped screaming. "Lulahn, you will accompany these men, and you will make no demands. If I hear that you have given any orders, any at all, I swear I will lock you in a room with Batiya's brother and walk away."

"How can you say that? He's an animal! A wild boar!"

The light had moved off her by then, so I couldn't see Dachahl's response, I could only hear his words. "He's a tiger," Dachahl corrected. "But I don't think he'll eat you, Lulahn, he doesn't like how you taste."

He found me in the darkness, I'm not sure how, but I felt his hand on my shoulder before he spoke. "The horse doctor begs that we not leave this in his hands. An experienced midwife can be found in the village, and the village is as close as the tower and downhill. If anyone dares get in our way, I will remove them."

"Yes." I approved.

"You will have to walk."

"This is nothing," I lied.

"Katrika?" he asked, switching to Dostrovian. "My sister is going somewhere safe. Do you wish to do this also?"

"But not Batiya?"

"The rest of us go to try to find someone to help Batiya."

"I'm staying with Batiya," Katrika said. "I won't slow you down."

"This I already know," he said. "Thank you."

I tried to walk, but the pains were coming each on the heels of the last, and when they hit me, I could hardly move.

"Why don't you put her on a horse?" Bos asked.

"No," Dachahl said. "If she falls..."

"I didn't mean by herself. She probably can't sit a horse anyway. Someone could hold her."

Dachahl shouted for a horse. "The steadiest and slowest you've got!" There was some moving around in the darkness, and then Vanitri and Forang lifted me into the arms of my husband.

"Is this good?"

"This is *very* good," I told him. "Are we going to gallop together into battle?"

"In the dark?"

"I knew there was something wrong with those books."

"The ones Naditte reads?"

"Everyone is always galloping from here to there in... the middle... of..." Another pain had caught up to me and my grip on Dachahl tightened.

"Yomhapo, another one," Dachahl reported. Apparently the horse doctor was trying to track when I started and stopped hurting.

"You need to hurry," an unfamiliar voice said in the darkness.

"We can go no faster than this until we find a road."

"Yes, Chunru."

"I want Katrika on a horse also," Dachahl declared in Dostrovian. "Katrika, have you ever ridden a horse?"

"No," I told him. Katrika just gasped.

"I have," Bos announced. "I could go double with her."

"Yes. Do this. Vanitri, Kasmir, do you want horses?"

"Not unless you've brought a pretty horse-women to help me ride it," Vanitri told him.

"If you go slow, we can keep up, and if you go fast, we'd fall off anyway," Kasmir agreed.

Everything after that was a confused muddle. I remember being very glad that I could hang on to Dachahl, and I remember that the ride went on too long, and hurt too much. And then we weren't in the woods anymore, and the moon came up, and I could see fields, and someone in the fields could see us, and we were being shot at again.

I think Dachahl pulled out his gun, but everything was going grey and sideways on me. The pains were piling up on top of each other, my belly was convulsing and I felt like there was something I was supposed to be doing to help it. "Dachahl, the baby needs to come out."

"Not yet, Batiya. We're almost there."

"It needs to come out now," I insisted.

Dachahl started yelling, but he wasn't yelling at me, and I couldn't seem to understand anything except that the baby couldn't come out on a horse, and my growing conviction that it was trying to do just that.

And then the horse heaved beneath me, and I was carried forward in a series of jarring thuds. I couldn't scream, I couldn't even breathe, I could only do my best to hang on. I caught glimpses of other horses, beside and behind us, and then buildings, and then the horse's hooves clunked oddly and Dachahl was dragging me off the horse. We passed into deeper darkness, and then, light. We were inside.

"I am Chunru," Dachahl announced. "You will bring a midwife, now."

There were people in the room, cowering, there were people coming in the door behind me, and I didn't care. I pulled myself out of Dachahl's arms so that I could collapse onto my hands and knees. My belly was trying to turn itself inside out and the pressure between my legs was both an agony and a relief. I made a sound that was half grunt and half scream. And someone ran past me out into the night.

I could hear Dachahl saying something about a baby, and suddenly there was a Chang woman at my side. "The child comes now?" she asked, but I couldn't answer because it was time for my belly to turn itself inside out again. I felt her hand on my belly and snarled, and then she was saying, "No, not now, my husband fetches a midwife. Wait!"

"I cannot!" I managed to gasp.

"What must be done?" Dachahl was demanding.

"Out!" the woman said. "Everyone out!"

"Outside are men with guns," Dachahl told her. "I will not leave her unprotected."

And then Katrika arrived at my side, and spread out my *lahnpran* to screen me from the rest of the room, and the stretchy pain between my legs intensified again, and then there was a new voice telling me to squeeze down.

Squeeze downward. Yes. That was what I had been needing to do—and people had kept telling me I could not. But now, finally I was being told that I could squeeze, and I did. I squeezed my belly until I ran out of breath, and the pain down below stretched and pushed.

"Good!" the voice told me as I gasped, trying to get my breath back. "Again."

I gulped in some more air, and squeezed again and something tore and passed through, and there were pleased cries from behind me.

I panted, trying to get my breath back, and listening to the exchange of shots through the window. I was still in the middle of a battle—but I was also on the floor, I couldn't move, and I could feel the urge to squeeze building up again. I groaned.

"Yes," I was told. "Squeeze again." I squeezed downward, and this time it seemed almost easy. There was the feel of something passing between my legs, and more pleased cries. "Enough," I was told. "Rest."

My shaking elbows gave way, and I let my cheek press into the dirty wooden floor. Something tugged between my legs. And then a baby cried.

There was a sudden silence in the room.

It was broken by cheers, and another rattle of gunfire. And another wail from the baby. "A son, Excellency. You have a son."

"My wife?"

"A quiet one, but strong. She must still pass the..." I didn't understand the next word. But I understood that it wasn't quite over. The hard part, though—the hard part was done.

Another pain came, but it was a pea to the pumpkin of what had gone before. Whatever it was that had still been between my legs slipped out with an unpleasant-sounding splat.

"Good," I was told. "This is done. Lie down and we'll clean you."

"Baby," I said, as I rolled awkwardly onto my side.

"Yes. Right here." A strange woman crouched down beside me, holding out a bundle of cloth, and then she shrieked and snatched it back.

"No!" I sat up, heedless of the pain, and reached for the bundle, but the woman was backing away, past the fabric to where I couldn't see it.

"Dachahl!" I cried.

"What is happening?" he demanded.

"She's taking my baby!"

I could hear her babbling something about demons or ghosts or something like that, and I started crying.

"Batiya, I have him. I have our son, I am bringing him to you."

"No!" Katrika protested. "She's all over blood and everything."

"I have seen her 'all over blood' before." I heard his boots on the floor, and then he was beside me, the bundle held awkwardly in his arms, and I reached over and took it from him. There peeping out of the blankets was a tiny red scrunched-up face. A rattle of bullets crashed into the side of the house, and the face screwed itself up and let out a wail.

"This should be familiar to him, by now," Dachahl said, and I almost managed to laugh, but somehow cradling my son in a comforting clasp seemed more important.

The midwife peeked anxiously around the curtain at us. "Excellency?"

"This is my southerner wife," Dachahl told her. "Her eyes are supposed to be pale. Look at her sister!" He pointed at Katrika's nose, and I guess that was the first time the midwife had got a good look at Katrika, because she shrieked again. Then she frowned, and looked from Katrika to me and back again.

"The child was well formed, Excellency," she said at last, slowly and carefully. "He was early?"

"Yes, a full moon."

"For an early birth, he looked... normal."

"Naturally," Dachahl told her. "See that my wife is cleaned up and made comfortable, and then move her into another room. Her sister's arms must be getting tired."

The two women hurried about, washing me and the floor and everything else. I felt like apologizing to them, but I didn't think Dachahl would like it. Finally they helped me to my feet and, holding both me and the baby so that I couldn't possibly drop my precious bundle, they walked me into another room, with Katrika following closely behind. Then they placed cloths on the matting, and helped me lie down on them. I was still bleeding and had left a trail of blood across the floor where I'd walked, but it didn't seem to bother them, so I assumed it was normal.

Katrika sat down next to me. "May I hold the baby?"

I nodded and held him out to her. "I thought maybe I was supposed to feed him, but he seems to have fallen asleep."

"I'll give him back if he wakes up," she promised. But somehow, in spite of the occasional sounds of conflict outside, I fell asleep too.

When I woke up it wasn't Katrika who was sitting beside me, holding the baby, it was Vanitri.

"Chunru says that the midwife said that you are to feed this fellow as soon as you wake up," he told me. "But Chunru also says you are to have a guard at all times, so I'm not going anywhere."

I took my son from Vanitri, and slipped a finger in his mouth. He seemed willing enough to suck. I thought I could figure out the rest. "Turn around," I ordered.

Vanitri swung around so that his back was to me, and I did my best to arrange my son comfortably in the crook of my arm. "He's so small!"

"Seems Chunru did a full interrogation of the midwife while you were sleeping. He's a bit undersized, but not enough to worry about. And he's breathing well and can scream up a storm, which is a very good sign in a baby that's early."

He also—once I managed to get his mouth in the right place—appeared to be eating well. "I did good."

"You showed what you were made of, and it wasn't princess," he agreed.

"I haven't seen Kasmir?"

"He got more banged up than I did this time, but nothing serious."

"Dachahl... is busy?"

Vanitri barked a laugh that wasn't about funny. "It's a mess, Batiya. Apparently these Children of the Stork people meant to take you prisoner, so that they could use you as a negotiating point about that whole school thing. They didn't expect Chunru to be with you—they didn't know about his sister and the change in plans. Then you arrived from the wrong direction, and instead of immobilizing you at the roadblock by the bridge and surprising you with a show of arms before you could react, we surprised them. When they saw your guards readying their rifles, they panicked and fired. And shooting at Chunru is treason. So now everyone is running around, denying, and pointing fingers. A coop full of headless chickens would be nothing to this. If he takes the testimony of two witnesses as guilty, there won't be a person in this valley over the age of twelve who escapes hanging."

They didn't hang people here. But I didn't want to think about that. Instead I thought about how the baby's sucking was making me a bit sore, and I hoped that didn't mean that I was doing something wrong. Changing sides might be worth a try, if I could just figure out how to get him to stop long enough. Pulling him away just made him suck harder. I tried stroking his cheek, and finally slipped a finger in his mouth. That did it. He blinked at me—his eyes were a darker, browner grey than I seemed to be expecting, and when his face scrunched up to complain, I could see that they had a definite tilt. "Have you seen him without the blankets?" I asked. "The midwife said he looked normal?"

"Batiya, you *know* they always look a horrible mess at first. Yours is worse than usual because he's a bit early, but he seems healthy and he's got all the right pieces... uh, and apparently that blue mark a little below the belt-line in the back is perfectly normal in Chang babies, and it'll gradually fade away."

"Blue? Thanks for warning me." I switched him over to the other side. He clamped onto me, and I stopped worrying that I had got it wrong before, because this time it was obviously wrong—it hurt! I slipped my finger in his mouth and tried again.

"How is feeding going?"

"He's very determined about getting what he wants," I answered. "He reminds me of his father."

I heard the rustle of a curtain falling into place, and I turned to see Dachahl, all cleaned up and looking most unfairly magnificent—except for the bruise decorating his right cheek.

"I'll be going then," Vanitri said, standing up.

"You should get some sleep," Dachahl told him.

Vanitri pushed out a scornful grunt. "You first." He walked out, careful not to look in my direction.

Dachahl came over and knelt beside me, and now that he was so close his bloodshot eyes made it obvious that he hadn't slept at all yet.

"Batiya–"

"You need to sleep."

"I can't. Everyone is supposed to be celebrating the birth of my son, and instead it's lies and hate and blood."

"Did any of our people die?" I asked.

"Yes."

I stroked my son's tiny red face with a finger. "It isn't a nice way to start his life story, is it?"

"Bold father, strong uncles, brave aunt... *wonderful* mother. This is not a good start?"

"Happy village?"

He frowned. "I can't be gentle about this. An attack on my wife or heir must never be seen as a possible way to deal with political disagreements."

"You would have liked it better if they had planned to attack you," I concluded. "Vanitri said they weren't expecting you, but why weren't they? They seemed to know everything else about our expedition."

"Far too much, and yet too little." His eyes narrowed. "As if one of the palace staff betrayed you, but not me."

"That would be a bit silly of him, wouldn't it?" I asked. "Not realizing who you were until too late was what made everyone panic." I considered what I had just said. "Maybe it's like the restaurant attack back in Xercalis. He didn't warn them because he couldn't, not because he didn't want to?"

"It doesn't matter why I was not betrayed, that you were betrayed is enough. The Children of the Stork must die."

"But not the villagers. They were invaded by these people."

"Some of them must have been assisting willingly. I can find no other explanation for what happened here."

"But you are having difficulty figuring out who, exactly."

"Yes."

"Then let them all live. Let everyone think you are so happy that your son is safe that you are ready to believe all sorts of unbelievable things. When you arrived with me at the village, the villagers helped you—clearly they are innocent." I studied his face to see how he felt about the idea, but all I could see was the carefully calm mask that hid his exhaustion. "Does that work?"

"I think it will work. Yes." He sounded too tired to even be pleased.

"So now you can get some sleep?"

"The Children of the Stork must still be–"

"Tried and executed? What about their families?"

"Always you must worry about their families!" Dachahl protested. "What about my family?"

"We are doing fine," I told him. "And I don't think that killing other people's sons is a very good way to celebrate the birth of my own."

"Fine," he told me. "I will allow them to kill themselves. Then there will be no need to try them, and so I will not have to condemn their families. They will live only long enough to know the shame of owing you the lives of..." He stopped. He barked a short rasping laugh. "They'll owe you their families' lives, Batiya."

"I don't believe in killing people who aren't even guilty," I replied.

"They attacked you, and you respond by giving them their families' lives."

I wasn't sure why he was having so much trouble grabbing that. He must know what I was like. How could it even surprise him? But it wasn't my suggestion that had startled him, it was what it would mean to the rest of the country.

"Batiya, everyone that shares their blood will owe you. All their cousins and second cousins and distant kin will feel the weight of that debt. And supporting a proposal they would not otherwise agree with is one of the seven standard forms of recompense. They will have to support my father's schools after this, or they will have no honor left."

"So your father's plan worked, at least a little?" I asked, feeling as suddenly bewildered as he must have felt a moment ago. I had won?

"My father's plan very nearly..." He choked the rest of that reply into silence. "This is your victory," he said instead. "Not his."

"Your victory too," I assured him, wishing that we had found a less bloody way to succeed. I looked down at my son. Poor baby. Why did I have to go and make him a prince? But if he wasn't, his father wouldn't be Dachahl. And I wouldn't have wanted his father to be anyone else. "He needs a name."

"This is your office," I was told. "Each prince is named in the tradition of his mother's house."

"So if I say Vanyl is a good solid Dostrovian name, that won't bother anyone?"

"Fanahl?" Dachahl sounded worried. "Batiya, that means short and round."

"Very fitting for the first two years, but not once he grows to look like his father," I agreed. "Moskov?"

"Nahchahf?" He sounded horrified. I must have been very lucky that Pahtia meant nothing at all.

"Gostvan? Borkov? Yavani?"

"Hafahni? This is good."

"Yavani," I agreed. "Only one name?"

Dachahl stared at me. "How many names do you want?"

"Our royals usually have six or seven."

"So you can choose the one with the most favorable aspect when they ascend to the throne?"

"I don't think so. I think it's a family thing. If everyone has six names then everyone has at least one name that matches everyone they might get named for."

"Named... for?"

"Giving the baby the same name as someone else you wish to honor. Usually a relative."

"But this is very dangerous!" Dachahl protested. "What if their fortunes got crossed?" I laughed. "Who is this Yavani that you name for?" he demanded.

"It's just a name," I told him. "The Latikovs are farmstock. We only give one name, and we just try to pick one that doesn't match any of the cousins, so nobody gets confused at family drop-ins."

"This is the better way to do it," Dachahl assured me. "This way all his ancestors will be watching out for him, and not just one."

"But I might have an ancestor named Yavani. I can only remember the name of one great-grandfather, and nobody even knows who one of the others was, even."

"What do you mean, nobody knows?"

"I mean, my great-grandmother never said who my grandmother's father was."

Dachahl's breath hissed. "This..."

"Yes?"

"Don't tell my father."

Yavani had finished eating—at least, he ought to have finished, he had fallen asleep. I detached him, and then—unable to resist—I freed one of his fists from the blankets, and put my finger to his palm so that he grabbed it.

"Even sleeping, he holds you?" Dachahl noted.

"He'll grab anything you put in his hand," I told him. "All babies do." So then Dachahl had to try it too.

"If you're done feeding him, Batya," Vanitri said from the other side of the curtain, "you need to burp him."

"Burp?" Dachahl didn't even know the word. I remembered vaguely something about patting babies on the back, and tilted Yavani up against my stomach so I could do so.

"How do I know if it's working?"

"I'll do it," he responded, exasperated. "Are you decent?" He came in, found a cloth to put against his chest, and then took Yavani and expertly jiggled and patted him until he made a small sound and spit up some milk.

"You have annoyed his stomach," Dachahl protested.

"No, he's supposed to do that," Vanitri replied. "I can't believe I'm being a baby expert."

"Why not?" I asked him pertly. "You're a father, aren't you?"

"That is not your cart to haul, Batiya!"

"Where's Katrika? She likes looking after babies."

"She's asleep." Vanitri assessed Dachahl with a narrow-eyed gaze. "You make your announcements, and then it's your turn. I'll trade places with Kas and Bos as soon as they wake up."

Dachahl slid his hand along my arm. "I will get you somewhere more comfortable soon."

"This is fine. You go do what you need to do."

"Yes." He slowly pushed himself up onto his feet, and walked out of the room.

"I guess he's mostly pretty solid," Vanitri told me after Dachahl had left, "but some of the ways they do things here..."

"I know. But some of the ways we do things aren't so wonderful either."

"I guess." He settled himself on the floor, still holding Yavani. "You get what rest you can too, Batya. There's no such thing as a good night's sleep with a new baby."

For the next two days my world was one small room, and sometimes I felt guilty for taking up that much of a house that I soon realized only had two rooms. Everyone seemed to think I should stay lying down in bed, but once I had ten good hours of sleep behind me—even interrupted by feeding sessions—I didn't feel much like lying down. But keeping Yavani and me safe was Dachahl's first priority. If staying where he put me made things easier for him—it wasn't as if there was much to do, or anywhere to go.

The village had celebrated the birth of Chunru's heir —whether they wanted to or not—and all the most important people in town were brought to view the baby, and then meet me. It always happened in that order, and meeting me always seemed to be a terrible shock—even though Katrika, my brothers, and Bos were a very visible reminder of the southern connection. But Yavani looked so normal to them that I guess they somehow expected that I would look normal too. Dachahl made very sure that they all knew that they owed the fact that they were still alive to celebrate to me.

On the third day Dachahl announced proudly that we could leave that very morning, if we wanted to, and then asked me, unusually hesitantly, if I would be willing to go somewhere with him first. "This will involve walking," he admitted.

That sounded wonderful, and I agreed with an enthusiasm that made him smile. Everyone crowded into our one remaining imperial automobile except for Bos, who was riding up with the Cholipardo Royal Horse Guards. I was tempted to tell Dachahl to ride a horse too, but it was clear he wanted to be with me, and I didn't want to argue with that. We headed up and over the base of the ridge we had been climbing all over that day, and then up the other side. It seemed like a very short ride. And then there, looming above us, was a huge tower, with a domed roof that reversed its curve and then soared up to a high point. It was so huge that I couldn't imagine how I had failed to see it from the other side.

"Ancient Cholipardo lay between fierce Mountain Tertar clans to the west and even fiercer Tertar horse clans to the north, and land-hungry peoples speaking Stoi Kat to the south and east," Dachahl told me. "It is famous for its towers and this is one of the largest and most famous. When you were so happy with the view from your water-tower, I wanted to bring you here."

"Had to prove you could do it bigger and better?" Kasmir asked.

Dachahl ignored him. "I meant to come for a short visit, after we settled at Tohung Fortress," he told me sadly. "Not like this."

Princess Lulahn greeted us upon our arrival like a grand hostess inviting us into her home. Her luggage had obviously been brought to her at some point, and she looked lovely, and precise, and elegant in her floor-length *lahnpran*.

"She does it all up nice when she does it at all," Kasmir told Vanitri. "But the question must be asked—is there enough rose there to make up for all the thorns?"

"Shut up, Kas!" Vanitri said, but he really didn't seem to me to be showing much of an interest. And since absolutely everyone agreed that I should not attempt the tower stairs while carrying Yavani, he volunteered to carry him up for me. "That way Chunru's free to help Batiya."

Katrika darted for the spiraling stairs, Bos and Kas on her heels, and I heard their voices floating down as I climbed much more slowly, and painfully, toward the top. By the time I got to the round, open-to-the-wind observer room, just under the roof, I was really hurting. I guess what they had said about my underparts needing time to heal was true.

But when I went to lean over the railing, I was sure it was worth it. The view from the top was amazing. I could see rolling hills covered with the bright color of tiny autumn trees stretching off in all directions in reds and golds until everything disappeared into a misty purplish haze. When I looked downward, I saw the dramatic rocky outcrop the tower was built on, and then past it the slopes of the valley, and several blue glitters as parts of the lake emerged from the rocks and hills and trees.

But I didn't see the village, and although I could see most of the main road, and bits and pieces of the road that went around the lake, I didn't see the road we had entered the valley on at all. I puzzled over that, and then I began to laugh. "Cholipardo built the tower first," I concluded, "and then the Gar Mian built the village afterward."

"Yes," Dachahl agreed. "This tower was a military mistake. It was built by a very great builder, but he was not a warrior. From here you can see very far... but the rocks of the ridge block off the view of much of what is close. The Gar Mian found that it was possible to sneak an army into the valley and right up almost to the base of the tower without being seen. The village started as an army camp. One that the Cholipardo warriors could not watch without leaving their mighty watch tower. This I learned in my history lessons, and this was how I knew it was possible to reach the tower without going around the village to the Cholipardo side of the ridge." His explanation fell silent for a while, and then he said, "You need to look out the other side."

I turned around, and got a dizzying view of Cholipardo. This ridge was the tallest of a series of steep folded hills that dropped down into a gently rolling country before building back up again to row after row of soaring snow-topped peaks. I gasped.

"I wanted to spend the night with you here," Dachahl told me quietly.

"What? *Now?*"

"No, when I was on the water tower, and I thought of bringing you here. I wanted–"

"You can bring me back here later," I told him. "You can bring me back as often as you like. I think at least twice a year would be good—once to celebrate Yavani's birthday, and maybe once in the spring. Is it nice in the spring?"

"Yes. I will bring you."

"And can we go visit those mountains too?"

He didn't look too certain about that. "Tertar live in those mountains."

I still wanted to visit them, but I thought maybe I shouldn't tell Dachahl that yet. He'd had a year's worth of scares in the past week alone.

"Batiya, when the Children of the Stork attacked us here, there were several other groups of scholars who found weapons and started protests of various kinds at the same time. The scholars are good at communicating with each other, and these different groups hoped that by acting together they would be more likely to succeed. My father wants me to visit all these places, take care of any problems that remain, show my support of his new education programs, and spread the news about what happened here."

"You're telling me you have to leave."

"I will get you comfortably settled with my Aunt Prahnani first," he assured me.

"How long will you be gone?"

"Three weeks?" He reached out and clasped my hand. "I do not want to leave you or Yavani. But this should be done, it should be done quickly, and I do not think you should come. But this is a good thing, Batiya. It will give many people a chance to find out how wonderful you are."

"If three weeks without you is the price for having you with me three days ago, I am very willing to pay," I told him.

"Yes," he agreed, his hold on my hand tightening. "But after you have rested, they will expect you to return to Pai Lan Chung for the celebrations and ceremonies surrounding the birth of a member of the Imperial House."

"They won't wait for you to be there?"

"The first half of the celebration is for the mother," he told me, smiling. "I'm not even wanted until the second half."

"How long does this celebration last?" I asked.

"A week and a half?"

"But that's even longer than our marriage celebration!" I protested. "You Chang spend so much time celebrating everything, it's a wonder you ever get any work done!"

He laughed. "This is really two celebrations together. The first is the birth celebration. This will last six or seven days, and does not involve me until the last day. The second is the celebration of my declaration of an heir in the imperial line. This will last another four or five days. Usually there is only the first celebration."

"Six or seven days is still way too long for a birthday party," I told him. "But I'll take it—big party, drums and trumpets, gifts and crowds and everything, if it means that the father absolutely must make his appearance on that final day and nobody can come up with an excuse to keep you away for longer."

"I absolutely must be there that day," he assured me, smiling. "No one will keep me away. Even if there is a war, it will have to start without me."

There were only a few drums, and no trumpets, but there were lots and lots of gifts. They started with the commoners, bringing food to the back door, and then it was everyone of rank that lived in Cholipardo bringing household goods, it seemed like. Fortunately I wasn't expected to write thank-you notes to all of them. Instead, I was supposed to provide a feast and some entertainment. And sit around and be complimented. And have Yavani there to be seen and complimented also.

I wasn't supposed to be the one holding Yavani, though, and after a long discussion with Aunt Prahnani, I agreed that she should ask Lulahn to do it. Katrika was furious, and my older brothers insisted they stand near her to guard him. "Otherwise she might drop him on his head!" But I assigned that job to Forang instead, and let the rest of them take turns guarding me. I worried that Lulahn would resent holding my son, and maybe she did, a little, but she also enjoyed the attention. Especially since every time Yavani cried, she could hand him back to me, and I would leave to take care of him and then she became the most important person in the room again.

That happened a lot. I guess Yavani, because he was early, had a small stomach. He needed to be fed often. Even after we returned to Pai Lan Chung and they started the official blessing ceremonies, we hardly got through a single one without him deciding it was time to eat. And everyone would just stop what they were doing, and Chloys and Aunt Prahnani would take him and me off to some prearranged spot, and then everyone would wait for me to bring him back, peacefully sleeping, and then they'd go on with their speeches, and their incense burning and whatever else they had been doing. And they all seemed much happier than I expected them to be. I had messed up, and had the baby early, but for once they didn't seem to be in much of a mood to blame me. It seems they were too impressed that I'd managed to have the baby at all—as if having a baby was something you could stop halfway through.

After the blessing ceremonies, it was the gift giving all over again. I don't remember anything I was given—I was getting up three and four times a night to feed Yavani, so I spent the whole week I was in Pai Lan Chung tired enough to trip over the night lantern. All the receptions—from the first garden parties, to the later formal receptions inside the palace—were just a series of strange faces. I accepted gifts, and I smiled, and counted the days until Dachahl would return.

And then finally it was that morning. The morning of the day that Dachahl had to be here, no matter what. Yavani woke me early, as always, and I was still feeding him when an escort of imperial guards entered my room unannounced. With blank expressions they carefully looked anywhere other than at me, as their leader informed me that the emperor wished to speak with me.

"Is it an urgent matter?"

"His Magnificence did not say."

I weighted the disadvantages of a cranky baby against those of an angry emperor, and for the first time in his life, Yavani found himself on the losing end. "If you will give me three minutes to dress?"

They did not leave the room, but neither did they follow me into the other chamber. When I came out, properly dressed and carrying Yavani, they closed around me as I followed their leader. I could tell that something was very, very wrong—and it seemed to be me. I'd done something I shouldn't have. Or maybe they just thought

I'd done something I shouldn't have—I couldn't think of anything I might have done. But Yavani was already fussy enough without having me upset him more, so I jiggled him a bit, and patted his back, and tried to remain calm.

When I arrived, the emperor dismissed everyone— even the guards. Dachahl said it was an honor, but I thought it smelled of trouble. And I was right. When everyone was gone, the emperor's calm face twisted into a glare. "I have had a report that you were seen embracing men other than my son."

People would say anything—why believe them? "No. This I did not do."

"You cannot know what you say," he said fiercely. "I asked. I asked more than one person. And this was seen by all of them."

I was confused. Between formal receptions and feeding Yavani, when was I supposed to have found time to cuddle with some man? No, not even a man—*men*. "This I do not understand," I admitted. "What I thought you said is something I could not have done. Where did they say I was when I did this?"

"At the palace. These past two nights."

"I was accepting gifts these past two nights. The only times I left the reception was when I had to feed Hafahni. As soon as the receptions were over, I went straight to bed and slept."

"Then you still deny this?"

I stared at him bewildered. Deny what? Embracing men? It was just impossible—unless I had been walking in my sleep? I certainly dreamed often enough of being held and of holding. But if I had been walking in my sleep, then why was I always where I should have been when Yavani cried for me?

But he said he had asked more than one person. Dachahl's father was no idiot—he had woken up long before the milk came—he would have asked reliable people. This made no sense. But there was one thing I was sure of.

"I have not done anything that would dishonor me or my husband," I declared.

His eyes widened and his eyebrows jumped. My answer must have surprised him. He looked away from me, staring at the wall. Thinking. "Chunru returns today."

And he would return to this. I felt like crying. I thought I had been doing well. Everyone seemed to be pleased with Yavani—or at the very least, unable to find anything wrong with him, no matter how much that fact surprised them. Aunt Prahnani and Chloys hadn't told me I was doing anything wrong, my family had stayed out of trouble, and Lulahn had almost stopped sneering. "This I know," I managed to say.

"I will speak to him. You will stay in your chambers."

"You are kind," I told him as if he had done me a great favor, and that surprised him again. But staying in my rooms and doing nothing sounded wonderful.

Although I didn't quite manage to do nothing. I should have been sleeping, but I was too nervous. The last of the cosmetic work on the Tilardu clock had been finished and everything was just waiting for me to finish assembly—but I had been too tired and too busy to work on it. It seemed the perfect task to distract me from things I did not know how to fix. So after finishing feeding Yavani, I left him asleep on my bed, and knelt in front of the trays and carefully put pieces into place. This gear here and that gear there, the teeth intermeshed—I hadn't broken anything, and I hadn't lost anything—eventually I would have all the pieces back where they belonged.

Everything had to fit together somehow. I just had to keep believing that.

Changali Ceremonial Flower Fold

Conclusion

Honor Duels Custom, and the Price for a Stranger's Child is Greater Than Jade

My father had been right, at least in some ways. I saw much less quiet resistance in the scholars I met after the uprisings than I had before. Instead they showed regret, and an eagerness to prove themselves still loyal. But there was also a great deal of fear and blood. I could not like this. I would have preferred to take some other path.

I had brought as many of the guards who had been with Batiya and I on that day as remained able to travel, so they could tell people her story. That choice seemed justified. Hearing how she brought my son into this realm while herself facing violent death impressed noble, warrior, and commoner alike. And the story of how she had begged that the families of those who attacked us be spared brought hope to penitent scholars, and guilt to the defiant. And I did spare as many as I could, always naming my wife as the one who had asked me to show a soft face.

But even so I was wearied of executions, and of watching the survivors drink the bitter tea of shame that my father had brewed for them, and that they had been unwise enough to take from his hands. I wanted to see Batiya again. More than anything else under heaven I wanted my wife.

So I had woken up before the first hour of the morning, and I had forced my escorts to leave early so that I could see her sooner. And this was a good thing, because I was surrounded by excited screaming crowds from the moment I entered the city. If I had left at a reasonable hour, I would have arrived late. Instead I was on time, and the palace must have learned of my arrival well in advance. I hoped Batiya would be standing by the drive when I arrived—holding Yavani. Smiling. Instead, a pouting Lulahn stood next to the drive. And behind her and to one side was Forang, looking as blank as a windless lake under a clear sky. That was bad—there was no need to create a calm surface if there was nothing to hide.

"Why did you do this to me?" Lulahn demanded the moment I climbed out of the motorcar.

"What is this?"

"Why did you bring that thing into the palace? How could you have a child on her? Why did you have to ruin everything by claiming your pale-eyed courtesan as a wife? Now I'll have to produce the next Chunru! This isn't fair! I was supposed to be able to depend on you. I can't believe I almost thought this might work. That nameless brat she produced looked normal en–"

"Nameless?" My hackles rose. "Hafahni is Dachahlru."

"You're Chunru, you can't claim the child of a courtesan as your son!" Lulahn told me.

"She was never a courtesan. Her honor is unquestioned. Hafahni is my son and only my son."

"Her honor might have remained unquestioned while you were watching her, but look what happens as soon as you're gone!"

Heart pounding, I turned to Forang. "What has happened?"

"Your wife is in her rooms, with guards outside the door. Neither I nor her secretary have been allowed to enter, by order of the emperor," Forang told me. "His Magnificence wishes to see you the moment you return."

"Where is he?"

"He is in his rooms."

I didn't run. Running was undignified, and also made you look panicked. Even if I was panicked I didn't want anyone to know this. The guards didn't stop me, and the curtain was lifted before I needed to slow down. My father was seated at his writing desk looking grim and tired. "What is happening?" I demanded.

"Nothing is happening," he told me. "I have been waiting for you before deciding what should be done."

"Done about what?"

"This morning I received an unsigned letter. It was sealed with Lord Ranglo's seal, but he says he did not send it, and that he had a great many visitors last night, any of whom might have slipped into his document room and made use of his seal."

"What did it *say*?" I didn't want to know all about who had or had not sent a letter, I wanted to know what had happened to Batiya.

"It said that your wife embraced several men last night."

I corrected myself. I *did* want to know who had sent the letter. "Did you have him give you a list of his guests?"

"This is not what is important now, Dachahl," he told me, sighing.

"I need to know who said this, so I can rip out his lying tongue," I explained.

"Dachahl, it may not be a lie."

He must have lied. Batiya would never do anything to dishonor me.

My father must have known what I was thinking. "The letter listed lords who could verify this truth. Lord Narsh Dah Shu, Lord Choosh Ti Geum, Lord Hungahn., and so I sent to them, asking if it was so. These are men whose words cannot be doubted."

"Batiya's words are not to be doubted!" I countered.

My father sighed again. "Dachahl, she did not deny this... exactly."

What? "What do you mean, not exactly?"

"At first she denied this." At first? I prayed that didn't mean what I feared must be meant. "Then when I said there were many witnesses, she changed her words."

No, no, no! This couldn't be happening! Even if she had accidentally done something that looked bad, Batiya would never have lied to my father. She had even told him how she had spent a night with the Dostrovian ambassador! "She admitted that she had lied?"

I saw my father hesitate. "I asked her to deny this again, and she did not."

"What did she say, exactly?"

"She said she had done nothing to dishonor herself or her husband."

Yes, just as I thought. "Father, this is a misunderstanding. Somewhere there is a mistake. You must summon her here and we will figure out what really happened."

"No. All the city claims that the southern woman beguiles you, Dachahl. That your faith in her is beyond reason, and that she works your levers like a puppet. You must not see her in private until this is settled."

"To have faith in Batiya is very reasonable!" I roared back. But this was not the way to convince anyone of anything. "If I cannot get my explanation from Batiya, then summon these men whose words cannot be doubted. We will have a fuller truth from them, and then you and everyone else will see that I am right."

"And what if you are wrong?"

"Then I will regret a great many things," I admitted. "But I am not wrong."

Summoning one of the men who had testified against Batiya was much easier than I expected. Lord Choosh Ti Geum was already in the palace. He had arrived a little early for the naming ceremony. Lord Choosh always arrived everywhere early, because he knew he moved like a tortoise and feared he would not arrive at all if he tried to be on time. He was kind, honest, careful and exact in doing his duty, and one of his grandsons was a friend of mine. We waited for him to arrive, and for an aide to seat him.

"Your Magnificence?" he said, bowing over his knees. "Chunru?"

"My imperial father sent you a message this morning, asking if you could verify that Princess Pahtia had embraced a man last night, and you said that this was truth. This was something you saw happening?"

"This was something I could not have failed to see, Chunru," he said. My blood began boiling, even though I was sure this could not be how it sounded.

"Whom did she embrace?" I demanded, desperately thinking of still mountain lakes, and trying to remain calm.

"She embraced me, Chunru," Lord Choosh responded.

"She embraced *you*?" my father exclaimed.

"Is there some sort of problem, Magnificence?" Lord Choosh asked, concerned.

"My father did not attend my wife's reception last night," I answered, "and he found some of the reports he received puzzling. When did my wife embrace you?"

"I gave her a gift, to celebrate the birth of her son, and she thanked me and put her arms around me. Is this a southerner custom?"

"Yes," I said, remembering the day all her cousins and aunts and uncles had come to her house, and she had put her arms around a great many people that weren't me. I hadn't liked this then, either. But I had been unhappy because I wanted to be the one standing next to her, and because I wanted to have her arms around me. I did not fear for my honor, and there was nothing inappropriate in what she did. This southern custom seemed a bit childlike, but Lulahn behaved like a child for worse reasons and was a great deal less charming. "What did you think of the Princess Pahtia, Lord Choosh?" I asked.

"I cannot in honor deny that her appearance is unusual. But the son she produced looked well enough. A little early, I hear?"

"Just a little."

"But healthy," Lord Choosh stated. That wasn't a question, he really didn't seem to think there was any doubt. "Princess Prahnani says he has a bluemark in the shape of a hawk. A very favorable omen!"

My father choked.

"Your wife reminded me of my granddaughter Choosh Pian Tik," he concluded. "Perhaps a dignified distance would be more suitable in the wife of Chunru, but you are Cholipardo—she was not raised to this office?"

"No."

"She behaves very well. A little more distance, and there will be nothing to complain about. You tell her this."

"Thank you, I will."

My father was very, very quiet after Lord Choosh left. I finally interrupted his contemplations. "My wife must be very confused and worried."

"She reminded him of his granddaughter?"

"Why not?"

"While she was putting her arms around him!"

"In exactly the same way that she would have done with her own grandfather. I saw her do this, in her own country, for all her uncles. This was not what you thought, and the person who wrote the letter was deliberately trying to deceive you."

"I can believe this," he admitted. "For as long as I have known her, your wife's behavior has been good.

What troubles me now, is that she lied and said that she had not."

"I don't know what happened, father, I was on my way back from Zdazh Soog where I had to order the execution of three very foolish scholars and where I will never again be truly welcome because of that. If you want an answer, ask my wife!"

My father eyed me steadily. "How certain are you that she will have an answer?"

"I have never known her to be dishonest. I cannot believe it of her."

"And you are certain that no substantial accusation can be brought against her. Nothing concerning the parentage of her son, perhaps?"

"Yes, I am certain. How often must this be said? He was early, not late, and I know my wife had never been with any man before me. He is Chang. His eyes look like ours. That bluemark Lord Choosh mentioned is something that is never seen in the babies of the southerners. Batiya and her brothers had never heard of such a thing."

"And it was shaped like a hawk."

"I thought you didn't believe in omens, father."

"You also had a bluemark shaped like a hawk."

"This is truth?" I was staring at my father in astonishment when an aide interrupted us to say that the guests had started arriving for the naming ceremony.

My father started and looked at the clock. "Already?"

"They probably heard rumors that something was amiss, and came early in the hopes of catching us off guard," I told him. "If I discover that Lulahn has said to them any of the things she said to me, I swear I will strangle her."

"We will summon your wife to the main reception room, and we will question her before our guests," my father announced.

I stiffened. "Why would we do that?"

"Because, Dachahl, if this thing that you have demanded of my empire is difficult for me, how much more difficult must it be for the rest of my people? We must teach them to know her as well as you know her, and give them no room to doubt her when malicious nothings like this one are aimed against her."

What? I stared at him, startled into stone. I could not believe that I heard him say what I had just heard him say. He wanted her to confront the accusations made against her in front of everyone, because he believed me, and he thought it would be the best way to clear her of suspicion? "Thank you father," I managed to say. "I know that to accept my southern wife is a difficult thing–" A very difficult thing. I knew this better than most. I had seen the distrust in the eyes of my people when they looked at Batiya, and I had also seen it in her people when they looked at me. There was something deeply human that made us want the safety of our own people and our own ways. "–But this is still a good thing to see done. This is the path to true harmony, and my duty and office as a man who would not just rule, but lead. I cannot regret having placed this burden upon you all. The empire will stand, and will become stronger for having learned this new kind of courage," I vowed. "Batiya and I can make this happen. All we need is to have your true support."

He snorted. "You are bred to be *hardoluno*. You may not like the form my true support takes."

Having seen the means by which he supported the path of progress, this was something I already knew. I knelt before my father and bowed my head. I needed the support he could give, whether I liked the form of it or not.

"We will reveal those who oppose your wife as the fools they are," he decreed. "You will not approach her in the meantime. No one can be allowed to say that you told her which answers to give. You will be very visibly somewhere else."

"Agreed," I said, though my blood was cold. I could not even explain to her that I had never doubted her, and warn her what was coming?

"You should go now and show yourself to those guests who arrived early."

I took my leave of him, but I had something I wanted to do besides entertain guests who had not arrived in their proper time. There had been one too many hints suggesting that there might still be a traitor at the palace. First there had been those many attacks on Batiya while she was following my father's schedule that had ceased when my father no longer knew what her schedule would be. If my father wasn't to blame, that strongly suggested someone else was. Someone willing to trick peasants into sacrificing themselves for the wrong cause.

Then there were the Children of the Stork, who not only knew too much of my wife's plans, but who also seemed to know far more than they should of my own nightmares. According to the leaders I had questioned, the threat the Children of the Stork had planned to send me was not that they would kill my wife, but that they would rape her—forcing me to order my own son to be drowned.

And now here was a similarly poisonous and potentially deadly scheme designed to work on my father's distaste for wayward passions. A distaste that he always tried to hide, because it grew from his horror of his own tainted past. Somewhere close to him, somewhere in this palace lurked a small but poisonous snake who used others to achieve his venomous goals. I needed to find him before he could cast another shadow across the victory my wife had won for herself. And Batiya herself had probably given me the key to doing so.

Forang was waiting for me outside still looking carefully blank, and I explained to him that someone had been spreading lies about Batiya, and my father would shortly hold her up to the sun, so that everyone could see that she was stainless, but that we could start hunting for traitors even before that. "You will tell Chloys to discover which of my father's staff was out of the palace between the time I had changed my plans to visit Cholipardo and the time the attack was made. Then you will go to the palace communication station to fetch the lists of messages sent." If Batiya's guess that the traitor would have warned his friends that I was coming if he could was correct, one of those two paths of investigation should reveal him.

My decrees made, I wandered through the audience chamber, greeting the scattering of early guests, and trying very hard not to look as angry as I felt. Forang, given the easier task, returned first, and I withdrew to a corner of the room and scrolled through the log. There were no suspicious messages sent directly to Ghoo Shtow, or Dofahsu, or any other communications station along that line. But of course there wouldn't be. If our traitor was so careless, he would have been caught a long time ago.

I handed the scroll back to Forang. "I need a chart made that lists the people who have used our equipment for personal messages along one side, and all days around the attack of the Children of the Stork and for some time before across the other, so I can see who has been sending messages when."

"I should tell your secretaries to do this?" he asked, sounding puzzled.

"I don't trust my secretaries. I trust you."

"Yes, Chunru." He withdrew, and I spoke with more guests until Chloys arrived with her list, and then I retreated once more to the corner. The information here was much easier to visualize, and I carefully considered each name on the list, trying to imagine how they might have come by the means to carry out treason. Two names seemed particularly promising. They were members of my father's staff, who would have had many opportunities to start rumors and discover close-held secrets. One was one of my father's many secretaries, and the other was one of his personal attendants. At first glance the secretary seemed the far likelier—what reason did one of my father's attendants have to turn traitor? But I was wary of the obvious answer, because of its obviousness. Besides, General Duprang and I had investigated all of my father's secretaries very, very thoroughly. I told Chloys to learn all she could about the attendant, and she hurried away. And then I needed to be sociable again, and I did not want to be. Lord Lichorta, whom I had learned not to like during what he had called a hunting expedition, but where he had provided only courtesans to be chased, sidled up to me and asked me if I had discovered who had been spreading the rumors that my wife had been caught behaving inappropriately.

"What rumors are these?" I demanded. "Will I have to deal with more fools the way I dealt with the traitor Rodahn?" Lord Lichorta shuddered, and assured me that all the rumors he had heard had been far too vague to be worth killing anyone over. "This is good," I told him. "I weary of my countrymen shaming themselves before my wife and her family." And by then the room was full, and my father was due to arrive. I took my place on the dais beside his seat.

My Aunt Prahnani arrived first, looking so blank that I knew she was anxious, and then my father, who looked grim, and then, finally, Batiya came. She was dressed in a formal *lahnpran* and carried a bundle that I knew was Yavani, and she looked so lifeless that for a moment I was afraid I had made a mistake somehow. But then she saw me, and she smiled, and I could see that she was not burdened with guilt, but with weariness.

"Before we continue this ceremony, there is an important matter that must be attended to," my father stated. "Princess Pahtia, you will give your son to the Princess Prahnani to hold."

She looked almost frightened for a moment, but then she looked at me, and that seemed to calm her, and she smiled at my aunt when she handed Yavani away. And then she approached my father's dais, and bowed. "What may I do for you, Magnificence?"

"I have been informed that you embraced men other than your husband. I believe that all justice should be carried out before the world. Therefore my will is that you explain your actions, now."

She lifted her chin. "I have done nothing I thought would dishonor myself, or my husband." Then she looked at me, and grinned. "I didn't even do anything I thought you would dislike, Chunru."

"This is your answer?" my father asked her.

"Yes, this is my answer."

"Why do you not either explain why you did this thing, or say that you did not?"

"I regret, but I have been speaking Hadahnchi for less than one year. I think I might not understand the meaning of this word 'embrace'. I am sure your people would not lie to you about such a matter, but I did not think I had done this."

"You have heard the word before?"

"Yes..." She grew a little redder under her fair skin. "My husband taught me this word."

"But you don't know what it means?"

She hesitated. "I... can show you what I think it means."

I didn't think she could possibly have meant what I thought she meant. I was wrong. She walked over to me, slipped her arms under my *choliang* and tightened them around me, laying her head on my shoulder, so that her curls tickled my chin. This felt wonderful. Preventing my arms from going around her in response was difficult, but I had no excuse to do so in such a place.

"This is most certainly an embrace," my father said at his most understated.

Batiya slipped away, and I felt bereft. But this was for the best, and I would just have to wait until we were alone before ordering her to do it again. "This is the only thing that is meant by embrace?" she asked my father, her face delightfully pink.

"No," my father told her. "But this is what I assumed was meant by your accuser. If this was not what you were seen doing, why would this be a matter that needed my attention? This, you deny doing with any other man?"

"I have never done this with any other man."

As my father looked out over the assembled guests, I saw Forang slip in through the curtains, a roll of paper in his hand. "If anyone has seen the Princess Pahtia doing this with a man other than Chunru," my father declared, "my will is that you say so immediately."

Everyone stayed silent. My father scowled. "Then why was I troubled with this matter?"

"Perhaps whatever she was doing was inappropriate for some other reason than the one you assumed?" someone said from the back of the room.

I felt the flame of anger rising, and glared over toward the speaker, only to realize that General Duprang was the one who had spoken. I stared at him in shock. I wasn't pleased that he hadn't found our traitor, but I was guilty of the same lack. And I could not believe he opposed me, or my father, or even my wife. He, like most of the palace warriors, had been a strong supporter of Batiya since she had been hit in the chest with a bullet, and then had stood up and calmly completed her ceremonial duties. "I fear this will be said of the matter, if an answer is not given," he added apologetically. "Was the Princess Pahtia embracing men, and if so, why?"

Everyone was staring at Batiya, who stared back, bewildered.

"I do not understand what I am supposed to have done," she said. "Will someone please explain?"

"I think you should just do this again," I told her. I handed the *tirah-fa* I was carrying to my father. "Would you please present this to my wife as a gift, father?"

He held the weapon out toward Batiya. "My daughter, allow me to present you with this most unusual gift."

She stepped forward, and her hands reached around to the back of his arms, and then her head and shoulders leaned toward him a bit, as if she was pulling them inward, and she said, "Thank you, father, I will treasure it." If I had been able to give her the *tirah-fa* in our rooms later, as I had planned, she would have thrown herself at me, and flung her arms all the way around me and squeezed me as tight as if she was a panda, and I was the tree she was trying to climb. And she would have done the same if her own father or one of her brothers had given her something. I felt a bit sad for my father; he was losing much for having set her at a distance.

Batiya's thanks spoken, she moved back, took the gift from the emperor's hands, and then she looked at me. "This was 'embrace'?"

"This could be described that way," I admitted. "In Dostrovia, what would they say you had done?"

"We call this a little bear..." She hesitated, as if only then realizing she didn't know of a Hadahnchi word other than embrace to use in place of the Dostrovian word 'hug'. I couldn't think of one either. "...Squeeze," she finally concluded.

I turned to General Duprang. "As you have seen, she gave this 'little bear squeeze' to some men, including my imperial father, because in Dostrovia this is the proper way to receive gifts. Are all questions answered?" To my dismay General Duprang looked... disturbed, rather than satisfied. "I see that they are not. Please ask your next question."

General Duprang hesitated for a little while longer, and then asked, "If this is the proper way to receive gifts, then why did she not receive all her gifts in this manner?"

"Because there are a great many rules for such things in Dostrovia," I responded. "More, I think, than there are here. I have seen her use at least four different gesture forms for receiving gifts, depending on who gives the gift, and where the gift was received–" At the back of the room Chloys entered, leading a scholar I could not recall having seen before, and sent me an agonized look. "And so I will have her explain these forms to you now," I concluded.

"Chunru," the emperor objected wearily, "we are trying to hold a naming ceremony."

I bowed at him, and politely pointed out that we could not hold the ceremony yet, because my wife's family were not present. Everyone who should have seen that they came to the ceremony looked guilty. "I will see what the delay is, while my wife explains Dostrovian gift-receiving customs," I said. "To have people continually misunderstanding and misinterpreting everything that my wife does simply because she comes from further away than Abiniach is unacceptable."

I left the dais and strode boldly toward the door, motioning for Chloys, Forang and the strange scholar to follow me out of the room.

"Who is this?" I demanded when we had got through the curtain and far enough down the hall that the watchers in the alcoves could not overhear us. The scholar gulped, and managed to greet me with my title and say his name, and I realized why he was here—he had the same father as the suspected attendant. "I am Lord Ranglo's secretary," he added.

"Your brother works as an attendant to my imperial father?" I asked, just to be sure.

"Yes, Chunru." He looked anxious. He should have looked terrified. I held out a hand to Forang, who placed the chart I had demanded in it. The attendant had made several personal telegraph messages before the attack, none, of course, during the days Chloys had reported him gone from the palace, and one urgent telephone call early on the day he had returned. It would have arrived too late. Shots would already have been fired at me by then.

I turned to Chloys. "How did you get his brother here so soon?"

"He was already here, Chunru. Half the city is here for the celebration. As soon as I started asking questions, he was pointed out to me."

She probably wouldn't know much else then. I told her to please fetch Batiya's family, and looking very relieved she turned and hurried away. Then I turned to the scholar. "You said you are on Lord Ranglo's staff? Did your brother visit you last night?"

"Yes. Was he... was he supposed to be on duty?"

"Why did he visit you?"

"I am not entirely clear about that. He said he just wanted to come and see my face." He looked down at the floor. "Might I know what is happening, Chunru?"

What was happening was that he, all unknowing, was helping sentence himself to death for his brother's crime. That made me uneasy. "How many are there in your family?"

"My family?" He was even more bewildered than before. "I've three brothers, two sisters, a son..." A son. A child—he wasn't old enough to have a grown son. And what of the other two brothers, what if they also had young families? This was not the triumph I had hoped to feel. And if I was finding this a bitter victory, how would Batiya feel? I looked back down the corridor to the curtain leading to the audience chamber, where my very bewildered wife was explaining Dostrovian manners. "Chunru?" I could not believe that he had even the slightest idea what his brother had done, and Batiya did not believe in executing people for someone else's crime.

"Right now I am celebrating the birth of my son and heir," I told him. "When I am finished celebrating, I am certain I will find the time to tell my imperial father that I think one of his attendants was involved in a plot to destroy my family. A plot that also came very near to killing me. The emperor will demand an investigation, and if I am proved mistaken, nothing more will be done. But if I am correct, the traditional punishment will be no doubt be carried out. My wife always wishes to save anyone that can be saved, no matter the cost to her, but the emperor is not so gentle in his justice." I pulled my pistol out of my boot, and thumbing open the handle, emptied the bullets out into my palm. There would still be a bullet in the chamber. "If the traitor dies before the celebration is over, there will be no need for me to tell my father anything," I concluded, and held the pistol out to the scholar. He stared at it, distraught. "Give this to your brother, and tell him what I told you. Forang will accompany you."

"No! This can't be true! He wouldn't... I knew he was unhappy in his office... but what else could we do for him when he could hardly read? He was as clever as any, but he said the characters kept wiggling away from him. That's why we found him this... an imperial appointment is always an honor, even if... but he wouldn't..."

A scholar who held an office normally filled by a peasant, and who could hardly read? No wonder I had failed to find him the first time. "I am not, yet, entirely certain he is a traitor. But by the time I am certain, avoiding what comes afterward will no longer be possible," I explained. I placed the pistol in his hand. Forang had taken his own revolver out of his boot also by then, and held it ready, just in case someone decided to use my single bullet for something other than its intended purpose. But I thought my pistol would more likely be dropped than turned against me. "Right now," I explained, "your brother is the only one who knows whether or not he could become the deaths of you, and your son, and your brothers, and father, and uncles..." I heard a sob, and I stopped the recital. "Your brother knows. He must decide whether or not to make use of this opportunity. I have done everything I can." Batiya's family was approaching down the corridor. "You should take her eldest brother with you," I told Forang. "I will explain to him."

Vanitri was already striding ahead of Chloys, and I was glad to see he'd come prepared for a formal Changali occasion and so was wearing his sword. "Hie, Chunru!

What's going on?" he demanded. "Why haven't we been allowed to see Batiya all morning? Chloys doesn't want to explain."

"A little misunderstanding. There was a bit of trouble with the celebration arrangements, and we haven't been able to spare anyone who speaks Dostrovian to come explain to you. The naming ceremony should be starting very soon now. Please, go in." I spoke to them all, rather than just Vanitri, and when he moved to step past me, I held his arm. "I still have one urgent errand I want your help with," I told him. As soon as the rest had gone in, I explained about my search for a traitorous informer, and the unfortunate result of his being formally charged. "This should be kept very quiet, but I don't want to give the brothers a chance to team up against Forang and run," I concluded. He looked over at the terrified scholar and the determined Forang and nodded grimly. "I'll go. But you owe me a cartload."

I walked back into the audience chamber, knowing that everyone must be waiting for me and trying to look unhurried and calm.

"There are a few other rules as well," Batiya was saying as I entered, "but my family has arrived now, and we can continue with the ceremony. Everyone has been very kind to listen to me explain the customs of my people."

"I want everyone to see that you were behaving very properly in the manner of your own people," I announced, striding toward her.

"Naturally you would wish this, Chunru," she answered, "but I see now that I should have been receiving gifts in the Changali manner while I was in

Changali. I regret that I did not realize that anyone would be troubled to see me do this in the manner of my home country."

"This was my error, not yours," Aunt Prahnani told her. "My office was to advise you in such matters, but I knew that feeding Hafahni every three hours had wearied you, and I thought your Dostrovian manners were charming. I saw no reason to ask you to change."

"Every three hours!" I spluttered. "You feed him every three hours? All through the night?" No wonder she looked half dead. Except that she brightened up when she saw how horrified I was, because she was laughing at me.

"This is the duty and office of a mother," she informed me. "But you should be very proud of me, Chunru. He is growing very fast, and everyone says he looks just like you."

Yes, I was sure she was a wonderful mother. "But when do you sleep?" She *hadn't* been sleeping, that was obvious. Which explained why she had reverted to accepting gifts in the Dostrovian manner... all the clarity she had left must have been used to continue to speak in Hadahnchi. I remembered how difficult hanging on to Dostrovian words had been when I was in a similar state. "You must go rest," I ordered.

"The ceremony," my father reminded me.

Batiya grinned, held my son out to me, and in the age-old words of the naming ritual declared him a son of my flesh.

I took the long string of gold pieces that was the child-price for an imperial heir out from where it was looped around my waist, and placed it around her neck.

And then I took my son and held him out for everyone to see. "Hafahni Dachahlru!" I said, and everyone cheered except for Yavani. He woke up, and complained.

Batiya took him back, expertly jiggling him into silence, so that the six priests who had been standing by could troop in and recite blessings for the six seasons of Yavani's life. Vanitri and Forang returned in the middle of the autumn blessing, and Vanitri nodded at me as his right hand formed the shape of a gun and tapped his heart. Somewhere in the palace a traitor had just died, and my prayers to my ancestors had been answered. The celebration of my son's birth would not be followed by the execution of anyone else's child.

And then, finally, the boring parts of the ceremony were over, and we could get to the fun parts. "Mother of my Heir," I addressed Batiya, "Wife of my Liver, Treasure of my House... I have a small trifle I wish to give you." I had worn Batiya's gift around my neck, for fear that it might catch in the long string of coins that made up Yavani's child-price, so I now pulled the cord over my head, and presented her with a jade insignia carved with the rearing horse of the House of Cholipardo.

"This is a trifle?" she asked me, her eyes admiring, and for a moment I thought the guests might get a demonstration of one half of the 'big bear squeeze'. Only half, because she was still holding Yavani. But instead she took the gift from my hands, and said, "You show me much kindness," and bowed in the proper Changali manner. I was sad that I had already let my father give her the tirah-fa, and so had nothing else to give her privately. Yavani didn't seem to like the Changali custom much either; he made annoyed sounds and his blanket bulged and squirmed. He seemed to be trying to kick his way out of it.

"Compared to the weight of my heir's child-price, this is a mere nothing," I assured her.

Batiya turned to my father and asked, "I would like to present a gift now, Magnificence, if I may?"

"The mother present a gift? This is not traditional."

"It is a gift to your entire empire," she explained. "And with so many people already gathered, it seemed efficient to do my presenting now. My training has made me value efficiency very highly. But naturally I will wait for another time, if you feel that is more appropriate."

I saw my father's eyebrows jump, as he realized what the 'present' was. Batiya must have finished assembling the Tilardu clock. I was delighted at her wonderful timing, and at the same time almost angry with her, because I was very certain that she should have been sleeping instead of fixing clocks. But I needed to stop telling her to go to rest, no matter how much she needed to do so. My concerns were shadowing her moment of triumph. So instead I took Yavani from her, and when Forang signaled that he needed to talk to me, I stepped away from the dais, letting my father hold the eyes of the guests as he proclaimed that of course he would be delighted to have his daughter-in-law make a special presentation on this most auspicious occasion, and moved all the way to the side of the room where Forang and I could whisper without distracting the guests.

"Did all go as intended?" I asked Forang. "He killed himself? The matter will not intrude upon the celebration?"

"He did not kill himself Chunru," Forang replied. "The brother shot him."

"The brother? Did he admit his guilt first?" Could we have chosen the wrong man?

Forang looked apologetic. "I could not follow all that was said. He denied at first, only the brother seemed not sure if he could believe him, and then suddenly he started talking about how you never should have been on a ship named the Pei Tan Kom, so how could he have known that you would be, and that nothing that happened could really be his fault. And his brother stopped trying to get him to take your pistol, and instead he... shot him. His own brother."

Perhaps the tragedy of which hand had pulled the trigger would be enough to keep the warriors who had fallen defending me on the Pei Tan Kom from crying out against me from the ghostly realms for allowing their betrayer such an easy death. "My father's attendant killed himself," I stated firmly.

"But... What do I do with the brother?"

"He was there when this happened, and is understandably distraught. He should be allowed to go home and compose himself."

"But he..."

Spilling the blood of a brother is a crime against one's ancestors. "He had to choose, Forang. One brother against two brothers, himself, his father, his son..." his grandfather if he was still alive, and any uncles, cousins, and nephews there might have been. "He has seen justice done, and I have nothing I wish to accuse him of. Send him home."

Forang bowed. "Yes, Chunru."

His departure coincided with the arrival of the clock, carried high on the shoulders of four of the palace servants. Two more carried the trestles that would support the clock until some more appropriate place could be found for it. And having already seen more than I wished to of that clock, I took advantage of the fact that nobody was paying me any attention at all to get a better look at my son. I was pleased to discover that although he had gone from a strange-looking reddish color to an even stranger-looking apricot, he didn't seem quite as terrifyingly small as he had when he was born, and his face looked less bruised and not as squashed-looking. I measured him out along my arm, and then not believing the results I measured again.

I heard Vanitri laugh. "Yes, he really is that much bigger than when he was born."

If Yavani was growing this fast, no wonder Batiya needed to feed him so often. With the touch of a finger, I brushed at the feathery fluff that grew from my son's head. "This looks like two different types of hair."

"That's just his real hair coming in under his baby fluff. It's normal," Vanitri said.

Up on the dais Batiya said something about how honored she was to be allowed to work with the famous Changali clockwork, especially so great a treasure as this one, and named the other craftsmen who had contributed to its restoration. Then my father declared that he had granted her the honor of repairing the clockwork because, like Tilardu himself, she was both a craftsman and a scholar. He explained that he wished to introduce the southern practice of educating peasants, not because he wished to make Changali just like the south, but because he wished to revive some of the strengths that Changali had known formerly, and to allow his empire to blossom unshadowed by the achievements of the rest of the world. And then the hour struck and the figures on the clock began their dance, and all the guests forgot that they were dignified Changali nobles, and crowded forward to see.

"While everyone's busy," Vanitri drawled. "Maybe I should collect on what you owe me."

"You want the best jewels in all my empire?" I suggested lightly.

"I'm interested in a different kind of beauty. Batiya has put quarantine signs around every girl in your palace. I think she'd almost rather I took your sister for a ride— but I don't believe in keeping things in the family. I wouldn't have touched her even if she wasn't–"

I was glad he didn't finish that sentence. I didn't want to defend my sister from insults I probably agreed with. "You are looking for a courtesan."

"Or six," he agreed. "I don't want to make trouble for Batiya, but there are limits. So point me somewhere trouble isn't likely to go hunting, and we'll all be happy."

"And if they demand more payment than you carry?"

He smiled a very wolfish smile. "They won't."

The girls might not, but the hostesses of their houses would probably try to approach the palace later. I would warn the staff to make sure any messages went to me, and not my father. "When Batiya finishes impressing all my father's court with her restoration of the Tilardu mechanism, I will take Yavani, and lead a procession that winds its way through the palace and out into the gardens, where half the city is waiting to hear me acknowledge him my heir. Then there will be music and dancing and acrobats and, when darkness comes, fireworks. Over by the lake there will be two pavilions with dancing girls. My sister should be near one of them. This is the one you don't want. At the other pavilion they will be serving *dadung*. Even if you don't see my sister, you will be able to tell the difference?"

"I got up a real long time before the milk was delivered," he told me.

"I hope you enjoy the celebration," I answered absently, and brushed my finger along Yavani's head again, separating as best I could the 'baby fluff' from the 'real hair'. I saw again what I thought I had seen before, but I didn't get a chance to show Batiya what I had discovered until much later, when we were seated next to my father watching the acrobats. "Look, Batiya, you must see this," I insisted. "When they told you that he looked exactly like me, they were mistaken. See! His new hair, it's curling!"

Batiya bent down to examine Yavani's head. Then straightened up and sighed. "Well, if that's the only thing I did wrong, I think they'll forgive me."

"His hair... curls?" my father asked, his eyes wide with amazement.

Batiya took Yavani and held him out to my father so he could see for himself. To my astonishment, but complete delight, my father took him from her, and after examining his head, unobtrusively peeked at his backside, trying, no doubt, to see if Yavani's hawk-shaped bluemark really did match the one I had as a baby.

"Do you think they will forgive me, Magnificence?" Batiya asked.

"This is not something that needs to be forgiven," my father told her. "It is a sign that my grandson takes in some part of his mother's character, and so brings her strengths into the imperial line. Just as my son brought the strengths of his mother, and I brought the strengths of mine."

"Exactly," I responded, in complete agreement with my father for possibly the first time since I had returned to Changali with my southerner wife. "Yavani's curls are wonderful," I assured Batiya. "My son is wonderful. He is as wonderful as you are, and someday he will make me just as proud."

"You say that now," she told me, taking Yavani away from my father, and smiling at the enthusiastic crowd. "But tonight you are going to wish we slept in separate rooms."

She was wrong. That night I was so happy to have her with me again that I did not mind waking up three times, and knowing she was there. The night that followed was when I began praying for the time when my son would sleep an entire night through.

But even then, I had no regrets.

Glossary

Abiniach

Pronounced 'Apiniach' by most Chang, Abiniach is a group of islands found off the eastern coast of the Larsian continent. It is believed that they were settled by seafarers from the Yargin Archipelago, who then interbred with the Tertar living on the nearby mainland. Expert seamen, the Abiniach people are as fond of politicking as they are of fishing, and have formed and broken alliances with all major political entities of the Larsian region, except for land-locked Cholipardo.

Saint Belkov

Belkov is a legendary religious figure from Dostrovia's early history, usually depicted as a thin middle-aged man with a black ankle-length beard. He is said to have climbed an icy mountain trail in bare feet in order to prevent an attack on a monastery that was guarded only by a few men and filled with panicked refugees, mostly children.

Chang

An adjective meaning "of Changali", or a noun meaning "a person from Changali". The Chang and their close neighbors are easily differentiated from all other peoples of Verdaia by their 'tilted' eyes, which are significantly higher at the outer corners than the inner corners. (This is *not* the same trait as our world's epicanthic/asiatic fold.) Due to their isolated geographic location the Chang people have limited contact with the rest of the world.

Changali

The Changali Empire takes up almost half of the continent Larsia, which is roughly the size of our world's Australia, but lies closer to the pole, and is found in the northern, not the southern, hemisphere. Changali was created when the four principalities of Holahchi, Gar Mian, Nash Vaur and Cholipardo decided that mere alliances were insufficient and that they should combine forces in a more substantial way. (A decision prompted in part because a recent marriage alliance between Gar Mian and Holahchi was making it look likely that the two countries would find themselves ruled by the same prince anyway, giving them far more leverage in international diplomacy than seemed fair, and in part because Cholipardo and Nash Vaur were engaged in conflicts with the Tertar at the time, and were badly in need of military assistance.) The first emperor was of the enlightened variety and fiercely determined that his empire would treat all of the member nations equally. He was also a canny propagandist, and by providing five free "national schools", one for each principality and one for his new capital, he ensured that the next generation of the scholar class would be well trained in the art of encouraging imperial fervor in every corner of his realm. Additional territories were added to the empire generations later by the treaty of Lahdungnar, in which nine of the greatest chiefs of the Tertar horselords to the northeast of Changali made the unprecedented decision to join with Changali instead of fighting with them, and then subsequently proved the benefits of this change by using Changali resources and military assistance to completely and totally subjugate all the other tribes in the area and force them to join Changali also.

choliang

A robe without fastenings that Chang men of high rank wear over their other clothing. Currently they are made out of elaborate multicolored silk brocades and are worn loose, but in previous eras they were more usually made of finely woven and heavily embroidered wool, and were belted or sashed so that they could more easily be worn with a sword.

Cholipardo

One of the four Kingdoms of the Changali Empire, Cholipardo is situated in a large valley between two chains of mountains of the Forahdani mountain range, which runs from the southwest corner to the center of the Larsian continent. The eastern end of the Cholipardo valley opens onto the Lahdungnar plains, and genetic and cultural ties between the two peoples are evident in the greater height of the Cholipardo people as compared to other Chang, and in the similarities between the native Hadahnchi language and the Tertar dialects spoken in Lahdungnar. The Cholipardo peoples also share the Lahdungnar's love of horses.

dadung

A hard liquor derived from sweet potatoes.

Dostrovia

A country in the southwestern (Tycherian) portion of Verdaia's largest continent. Consisting mostly of fertile lands between the Osmark and Chadach mountain ranges, it is famous for its agricultural produce and its apparently limitless supply of farmers. The Dostrovian people are noted for being 'handy' and practical, and Dostrovia is one of the most industrialized nations in Verdaia. Its largest neighbors are Rachine in the northeast, Xercalis in the west, and Tsan in the southeast.

Dostrovian

The adjective form of Dostrovia. Also used as a noun to refer to either a person from Dostrovia, or the native language of Dostrovia.

Empress Katronika

The Empress Katronika is Verdaia's first diesel-powered passenger liner. It was built in Dostrovia, and named after a historical Dostrovian queen.

The Empress's Tomb

The latest empress died during a miscarriage brought on by a fall from her horse, and was buried in a parkland area that is technically the property of the imperial family, but which is left open to the public. The relatively small but costly monument placed over her burial place is a popular destination for the park's visitors, due partially to its artistry, but mostly because of the extremely picturesque location, atop a small hill, with a cherry-tree arcing over it. At least six major works of art feature depictions of the site, including a painting entitled "Cherry Tears" showing the widowed emperor standing beside the monument with cherry blossoms swirling down around him, which hangs on the wall in the emperor's private study. The cherry tree is symbolic of beginnings, love, and renewal, and is a very unusual choice for a grave marker.

fiahn

A long linen or cotton under-robe worn beneath Changali ladies' expensive formal lahnpran gowns, to protect them from road dust and body oils.

First Revisionist

In many ways a very pragmatic church, the First Revisionists are a branch of the Church of All Saints that decided that the word "All" was being taken a little too literally when two dogs, a rooster, and a donkey were added to the roll of saints. They broke off from the main church and 'revised' the rolls to remove the animal life. Unfortunately this notion of revising the roll of saints to suit oneself got to be a little too popular and a short while after the Revisionists first made the break, they started splintering into a plethora of smaller churches, each of whom had found some reason to remove certain saints from the lists, and who did not, of course, agree with any of the other splinter churches' revisions. Eventually the fragmentation got so bad that no two revisionist congregations were worshipping the same set of saints, and a counter-movement was started aimed at recombining the groups under the terms of the first revision: no animals. The First Revisionists are currently the second-largest religious body in Dostrovia, outnumbering the Church of All Saints by nearly double, but falling short of the extremely popular Church of the Ascension. Other than their ban on animal saints, they are mostly noted for not putting too much value on textural artifacts: what can be written can be rewritten—true devotion lives in the heart.

L. Shelby

Gar Mian

Gar Mian is the largest of the four 'kingdoms', or principalities, that make up the Changali Empire. It consists mostly of an interior flatlands fed by several large rivers, and has the largest agricultural production in the empire. It also has the second-longest coastline. A disaster to the royal line of Gar Mian was what brought about the creation of the empire. Both of the Gar Mian heirs died in childhood, and their grieving father's attempts to sire new heirs were unsuccessful. He desired to leave his country to his only grandson, the son of his daughter... but she had been married to the Holahchi Prince, and his grandson was the heir to Holahchi. The Gar Mian people feared that Holahchi's heir would be more sympathetic to Holahchi interests than to Gar Mian interests, and asked their prince to name some other heir. The grandson pointed out that considering the troubled and dangerous nature of the times, joining together might be the best idea, but agreed that each country could use a ruler of its own. He suggested that if he could produce three heirs of his own, then one could inherit the combined rule, one could inherit Holahchi and one inherit Gar Mian. As he was, at the time, not yet married, his suggestion wasn't taken too seriously—even if he should be lucky enough to raise three heirs, it was pointed out, neither Gar Mian nor Holahchi would be happy about being assigned to the rule of a younger son than the other. So no official proclamation was made as to who would be the Gar Mian heir until after the grandson married a princess from Nash Vaur, and had first a boy baby, and then twin girls. The aged Gar Mian prince declared that the twin princesses were clearly a sign from heaven that his grandson was destined to rule two principalities, and

343

officially proclaimed him his heir. Perhaps the old prince would have predicted a little more accurately if he had lived to see the next royal birth: another set of twins.

Geshik

An equatorial city on the west side of Verdaia's largest continent. Because of its central position and lack of clear national bias it was chosen as the location for the summit meeting that established the Seafarer's Guild as the international organization in charge of naval regulation and law.

Ghaz Mien bonnet

A type of hat that looks like a basket turned upside down over one's head. It is named after a Gar Mian village where the style presumably originated. Legend has it that the ladies of Ghaz Mien adopted the headgear in order to foil the attempts of a neighboring lord to seduce a particularly lovely and respectable lady whose family had fallen on hard times. Insufficiently familiar with the village to tell the women apart when their heads were so covered, he constantly found himself making advances to the wrong one, until finally he gave up in disgust and turned his attentions elsewhere. He was eventually beheaded by the enraged father of one of his more successful conquests.

Ghoo Shtow

A reasonably large town roughly halfway between the Imperial City and the capital of Cholipardo, Ghoo Shtow is famous among the Chang nobility for its poor hospitality and horrible hotels. What the unsatisfied lords fail to realize is that Ghoo Shtow is a crossroads, not an end destination. Faced with a huge influx of one-night-only guests, most of them members of the merchant class, Ghoo Shtow hoteliers concentrate on efficiently getting their customers inside, getting them the necessities of food, baths and bed, and then removing them from the premises the following morning. This practical approach is not much valued by a class used to the more relaxing atmosphere and personal service provided by luxury establishments in resort towns and large cities, but many less self-indulgent travelers admire the no-nonsense efficiency of Ghoo Shtow hoteliers.

Hadahnchi

One of the two official languages of the Changali Empire, Hadahnchi is the native language of the Cholipardo and Holahchi regions. It is more closely related to the Tertar dialects than it is to Changali's other official language, Stoi Kat. Hadahnchi was the first language on the Larsian continent to acquire a written form, and uses a syllabic writing system of 100 characters and a few punctuations marks. When Hadahnchi scholars wished to also transcribe Stoi Kat, they used these same hundred characters, choosing the ones that sounded most like the Stoi Kat words they were attempting to write down. But the much greater variety of sounds in the Stoi Kat language led to the exact same characters being used for several different words, and confusions arose. The Hadahnchi scholars solved this problem with the addition of 'flags': simplified symbols that could represent numbers or sounds that were added to the end of Stoi Kat words as an aid to determining which word was which.

Unfortunately, as a system designed by non-native speakers, the choice of flag usually hinted at a Hadahnchi word that meant the same thing. When non-Hadahnchi-speaking people tried to learn to use this system to write Stoi Kat, they found the flag system arbitrary and difficult to remember. Perhaps a more practical alphabetical system of writing might have been developed had the Tertar not had the idea first. Stealing and altering—not the actual Hadahnchi characters themselves, but the simplified flags, they created an efficient and flexible writing system for themselves, but also provided a negative association which soured Chang people, perhaps forever, on the entire concept of alphabetical writing systems.

hahlu

The Hadahnchi word for a bathing pool or bathtub. The Hadahnchi-speaking peoples have long had an obsession with bathing, perhaps due to the abundance of mineral and hot springs that could be found in the mountainous territories that were their home. When they allied themselves with the rest of Changali, they passed on the taste for soaking in hot water, but could not, unfortunately, pass along the actual springs. Gar Mian craftsmen began to experiment with the construction of artificial springs, finding a number of ingenious—but not always safe—ways to heat the water. The eventual conclusion, however, was that the bigger the pool, the less efficient it was to heat, and the harder it was to justify the expense. Most large bathing pools in Gar Mian territories are part of shrines or temple complexes and are heated only for special occasions. The rest of the time the Gar

Mian people make do with portable tubs, some buckets, and a kettle of hot water.

Hintangee

Hintangee is a tropical port city in Aurastia famed for its primitive infrastructure and the lack of sophistication of its native inhabitants. This reputation is overstated, if not entirely unearned. It's true that the locals have been remarkably resistant to adopting foreign customs and technologies that they can't reproduce themselves, but a recently discovered native gunshop in a nearby village demonstrates that the list of "technologies they cannot produce themselves" has been shrinking at a very rapid rate.

Holahchi

Holahchi is one of the four Kingdoms of the Changali Empire. It is the most central of Changali's main divisions, and has the most varied terrain, including mountains, highland plains, swampy lowlands, and fertile coasts. In general the Holahchi people are reputed to be practical, hard-headed, and maybe a little cynical, but the love they and the Gar Mian peoples share for order and regulation has been the glue that holds the empire together. Most of Changali's greatest architects and engineers have been from Holahchi.

Holy Grove at Chazd Ngar

A stand of trees near Pai Lan Chung that the Changali people believe hosts beneficial spirits. Since the area has been nearly completely deforested due to population pressures on shipbuilding and fuel, this is one of the few examples of mature mixed-species woodlands in the area.

Indigo Islands

One of Verdaia's two 'sunken continents', the Indigo Islands are a large archipelago located in tropical waters. They lie almost exactly halfway between Changali and the southern countries of Xercalis and Dostrovia.

Lahdungnar

The northeastern region of the Changali Empire, the plains of Lahdungnar are formed into a handful of territories subject to and administered by the Changali throne. The peoples of Lahdungnar are primarily nomadic horsemen of Tertar descent, and are proudly independent with a strong warrior tradition.

lahnpran

A gown worn by Chang women, constructed with a cross-over front that buttons under the arm. Casual lahnpran are typically knee-length, cut high at the neck with shoulder buttons, made of cotton or wool, and worn over a shirt and baggy pants. Formal lahnpran are typically made out of lightweight silk brocades with subtle patterns, and are occasionally longer than floor length. They also often feature plunging necklines that reveal an intricately-embroidered undergown.

Laochar District

A poverty-stricken area in the Changali capital of Pai Lan Chung, the Laochar district is primarily inhabited by people of Holahchi descent. Every time there is a drought, thousands of farmers make the long journey to the capital city hoping to find a future there, and although some do, even more end up starving in one of the city's many slums.

Makoviksi

The Dostrovian capital, Makoviksi is a huge sprawling metropolis situated at the mouth of the Karda River (the largest river in the Tycherian region). It is a major shipping and manufacturing center.

Nash Vaur

One of the four Kingdoms in the Changali Empire, Nash Vaur is situated on a large island just off the southern coast of the Larsian continent. Although Nash Vaur is primarily famous for its sailors, the lush rainforest covering the island is also home to an extraordinary variety of poisonous animals and plants, the toxins from which were frequently employed in the myriad succession squabbles that occupied the Nash Vaur nobility before they elected to join the Empire.

Nen Koust

The location of one of the more notable prehistoric artifacts in Changali, the Neni statues. These bizarre-looking stone carvings are placed in a circle around the base of a hill, their huge heads balanced atop short stumpy bodies, all staring outward as if guarding the mound of earth behind them. What they are guarding it from and why it is worth guarding has been hotly debated by Chang scholars, with all the usual theories about it being the burial place of some ancient ruler or a religious center. They completely discount, and possibly rightly so, the local legend which states that a giant heron flew down, lay an egg, built the hill over top of it and then coughed the statues out of its croup, before setting them in place and flying away. Although it is true that the stone the statues are carved from is not local, and the closest likely source is over a hundred miles away, the material could have been shipped on barges down the river, so no intervention of a mystical flying bird was necessary to bring the statues to Nen Koust.

Osmark mountains

A mountain range that runs down the western side of Dostrovia and forms the eastern shore of the Gulf of Kastonik, which separates Dostrovia from Xercalis.

Pai Lan Chung

Pai Lan Chung was originally a small port city on a peninsula that was part of Gar Mian. When the empire was created, the peninsula was designated a direct imperial holding (rather than being held in fief by the Gar Mian prince), and Pai Lan Chung was chosen as the new imperial capital. This choice was a bit unusual in that there are no major rivers leading to it. Instead the city's water supply is provided by five artesian springs, which were considered holy by the locals. Drinking the water is supposed to cure a variety of ills, and send good dreams. When fortifications were added to the city in the following years, walls were also built all around the spring heads and their associated shrines. Stretches of parklands were also protected, and these areas, generally used for burial grounds and recreation, could be cultivated in times of trouble. In spite of bounteous evidence to the contrary, Pai Lan Chung retained the reputation of being a place of pleasant dreams. The reputation for being an extremely healthy city, however, is justified. The water from the five springs and the other artesian wells in the area is a great deal cleaner than that found in the average Gar Mian river.

parsahi cloak

A loose cape-like overgarment, made of heavy fabric separated into two or four sections by deep gores that allow for the free movement of the arms. Commonly worn by Chang peasants, it is also popular as a part of outside uniforms or liveries, as the wide panels are an ideal place to display house symbols.

Pek Char

A statue of a crab, twenty feet high, built as a monumental display of the metalworking techniques of a Pai Lan Chung artisan house, roughly 60 years ago. It was the subject of such an intense debate over which of two rival neighborhoods should have the honor of displaying the massive statue that the current emperor's father, sick and tired of having the matter brought to his attention, declared that it should be put directly between the two. This placed it right in the middle of the road. The rest of the city, almost as tired of the bickering as their emperor, thought that this was an ideal solution—the road in question, although fairly busy, was not a major through-way, so mostly only the residents of those two communities would be inconvenienced. They were inconvenienced even further when the statue became a tourist attraction, and gawking (and laughing) spectators added to the traffic congestion. Under the Pek Char is, however, considered one of the best locations in the city by street food vendors, being surpassed only by High Gate, and outside the City Administration building.

Rachian

The adjective form of Rachine. Also used as a noun to refer to either a person from Rachine, or the principal language of Rachine. Rachian words should be pronounced as if they were French.

Rachine

A country with a fertile climate and varied terrain, Rachine specializes in being eclectic, artistic, and elitist. Besides a wide variety of agricultural products, its many manufactories and workshops produce glass, fine metalwork and jewelry, and high-quality fabric and leatherwork. It shares a very long border with Dostrovia, and each country has played a major role in the history of the other.

Seafarers' Guild

An international organization that inspects and registers ships and crew, tracks sea-travel, legislates, judges and enforces marine law, and otherwise governs the oceans. Established by the Geshik Pact, it is supported by most of Verdaia's coastal nations (and even a few land-locked ones), and because of the vast range and economic importance of its jurisdiction it has become the single most powerful governing body in Verdaia. One of the many functions it carries out is the orderly and reliable delivery of cross-oceanic correspondence.

Sea House

One of several imperial residences, it was built by the current emperor's mother to house her insane aunt, and so prevent the embarrassment of having her entertain any more imperial guests with seagull impersonations. The aunt only lived there for two years before attempting to fly off the cliff, after which the sea house was assigned to the emperor's younger brother, whose behavior as a teen was so restrained it was embarrassing his father. The prince decided that loosening up was a better option than exile, managed to find a few bad habits he didn't mind acquiring, and so won his way back into his father's good graces. Later, he allowed the house to be used as temporary housing for those of his father's bastards who had not yet been found suitable positions. After his death, his widow lived there for a while with her handicapped son, but it was decided that the location was too dangerous for the young prince, and currently the house has no permanent residents other than staff.

Shan

The way Dostrovians (and most other southerners) say "Chang". It has been theorized that the word must have arrived in the south through the offices of a Rachian or perhaps a Besietenalan traveller, since the family of languages native to those regions lacks a 'ch' sound. (Rachine is pronounced with a 'sh'.) The traveller would have landed in Xercalis on his return, and there, the word would have lost the 'ng' sound, which doesn't exist in Xercali, before moving eastward to Dostrovia.

Shanali

The way Dostrovians (and most other southerners) say "Changali".

The Spring Gardens

One of three public parks that were a gift to the people of Pai Lan Chung by the imperial family. The Spring gardens are supposed to be most beautiful in the Spring, the Summer gardens most beautiful during the Summer and the Fall gardens most beautiful during Autumn. The truth is that all three are spectacular in every season of the year.

Stoi Kat

One of the two official languages of the Changali Empire, the Stoi Kat language is native to the kingdoms of Gar Mian and Nash Vaur. A complex and highly socially inflected language, it appears to be unrelated to Hadahnchi, the other official language of Changali. It has been theorized that it is a distant cousin of the Abiniach language, and so an offshoot of the Yargin family of languages, but many scholars deride this suggestion, pointing out that the rare duplications between Stoi Kat and Abiniach are more easily explained as a simple case of borrowing. A more believable explanation is that Stoi Kat was spoken by the original inhabitants of Larsia, who were pushed into the southeastern corner of the continent by Tertar invaders long before the dawn of recorded history.

Syrcan

The capital city of Xercalis, and location of the Changali Embassy to Xercalis.

Temple of the Singing Wind

One of the many temples and holy places scattered around Pai Lan Chung, the Temple of the Singing Winds is supposed to be the home of a beautiful and particularly beneficial wind spirit, and the temple incorporates an amazing number of wind-organs, harps, and chimes, which make it 'sing' at the slightest breeze. When the temple falls silent, it is said to be a sign that a particularly fierce storm is on its way.

Tertan

The collective name for the lands controlled by the Tertar people.

Tertar

A tribe-based society that controls just over half of the Larsian continent. The Tertar are the traditional enemies of the Chang peoples. They are known principally for their fierceness and their lack of political cohesion.

Tilardu Doduchru

A famous clockmaker from the city of Prosuang, in Holahchi, Tilardu was famous for incorporating intricate mechanical figures into his designs. The genius of his clockwork marvels soon made him famous across the empire, and upon his death his creations were declared imperial treasures, and the imperial house began a concerted effort to acquire them all. Everyone knew that the gift of a Tilardu mechanism was an instant ticket into the emperor's favor, and few could resist the temptation to cash in, so by the time a hundred years had passed, other than a few minor mechanisms that seemed to have been damaged or lost, only one mechanism remained that had not at some point been carted off to the imperial palace. The great clock in the town center at Prosuang, a fifteen-foot high edifice with ten sets of three to six four-foot-tall animated figures, proved to be a little too unwieldy to succumb to the acquisitiveness of the Imperial House, and remains in the possession of the locals.

tirah-fa

A Chang term combining the word tirah, which means 'sword', with the suffix -fa, which means 'cut off'.

Tohung Fortress

One of the residences of the royal family of Cholipardo, Tohung was at one time a genuine military stronghold. When Cholipardo joined the Empire, however, it was deemed unsuitable to posts guard units on the border with Gar Mian, so the military part of the fortress was designated a 'training center' and the royal residence portion soon became a favorite habitation for young Cholipardo princelings who were too relieved to have temporarily escaped the stifling ceremony of the imperial court to want to plunge back into the slightly less stifling Cholipardian version of the same thing.

Tomb of the First Emperor

The tomb of the first emperor is unique in two ways. The first is that it is found in the city proper, when all the other emperors' tombs are found in the "Imperial City of the Dead", a park-like Changali burying ground where only members of the imperial family are allowed entry (except for funerary construction workers, and a couple caretakers who get special dispensation). The second is that it's empty. The first emperor died at sea, and his body was never recovered. The place that was originally designated for his tomb was used for his son instead. But the empire wished to honor him, and created a monument that looked a great deal like what his tomb might have looked like in regards to architecture and decorative elements, except that it contained neither the funerary bed, nor any of his personal belongings (these were dropped into the sea, instead). As it contains no holy relicts, it was considered suitable to put it in a public place, so that it could be admired by all. The people of Pai Lan Chung burn incense and pray there when they wish to honor the first emperor or beg his assistance in some matter. Members of the imperial family do their public devotions to their most honored ancestor in a less practical location—on a boat.

Verdaia

The world in which this story takes place. Its largest continent is roughly the size of our Eurasia, but spreads north to south rather than east to west. Ancient geographers divided it into four regions: Valachia, Tycheria, Saradia, and Mabinia. The four regions together were Verdaia: 'all lands' or 'everywhere'. Later they discovered that two additional continents lay out past the western islands, and these were named Larsia and Aurastia. In addition to these three major land masses, Verdaia has two 'sunken continents': the archipelago of Yargin in the north, and the Indigo Islands in the tropics.

vlai flower

The vlai tree is an unusual member of the magnolia family of trees, in that it prefers rocky highland slopes. Native to the interior of the tropical island nation of Nash Vaur, they blossom all year round, dropping a seemingly endless supply of waxy concave scarlet petals into the streams of the Nash Vaur highlands. These make excellent boats, and occasionally manage to float all the way to the shoreline. Since not much economic development has been accomplished in the interior of Nash Vaur, and many of the young people of the interior end up moving to the coast, the brightly-colored petals invoke memories of childhood and home, and finding one is considered lucky.

Wadz Kiar

Wadz Kiar is a primarily Nash Vaur district, lying outside the city walls toward the harbor. It is generally fairly poor, but the inhabitants, whose principal occupation is usually shipbuilding and repair, are reputed to have 'clever fingers'. When someone in Pai Lan Chung needs something unusual built or a particularly difficult repair done, Wadz Kiar is the first place they will think to go. But there is a darker side to the neighborhood reputation: it is estimated that at least two-thirds of the city's pickpockets were either born in Wadz Kiar, or learned their trade from someone who was.

West Borstev

One of the boroughs in Makoviksi, inhabited mostly by factory workers.

West Gate market

Pai Lan Chung's West Gate is on the hilly side of the city away from the harbor, and is much less busy than the North or East gates. Although a number of merchants who regularly follow the north road down from Gar Mian choose to go around to the west side of the city to avoid the worst of the traffic, the West Gate is mostly used by local farmers. Thus, it is considered the best place in Pai Lan Chung to go for fresh produce—unless, of course, you are looking for fish.

Xercali

The adjective form of Xercalis. Also used as a noun to refer to either a person from Xercalis, or the principal language of Xercalis. In Xercali words 'c' should always be pronounced as if it were a 'k' even in combination with h, every 'g' is hard, ph is 'f' , and there are no silent letters.

Xercalis

A mountainous country in the southwestern (Tycherian) portion of Verdaia's largest continent. It is famed for its goat cheese, its bandits, and its inhospitable shoreline.

Air Castle Media
www.aircastle.org

Made in the USA
Middletown, DE
16 July 2021